virology

also by ren warom
and available from titan books

Escapology

TITAN BOOKS

virology

Print edition ISBN: 9781785650949
E-book edition ISBN: 9781785650956

Published by Titan Books
A division of Titan Publishing Group Ltd
144 Southwark Street, London SE1 0UP

First edition: June 2017
1 3 5 7 9 10 8 6 4 2

A CIP catalogue record for this title is available from the British Library.

Printed and bound in the United States

For my three stooges AKA the spawn.
If I could have kids all over again, I'd choose you every damn time, no matter what I might say about swapping you for hamsters…

part one

zen awakening

Zen strides the city of Foon Gung with her Queens, laughing. Her Queens are finally free, permanently unleashed from their virtual prison, the Slip. They will have their fun and then come for her, bring her down to them. Until then, she rides within them, dreaming all they see. Being all they are. Immense. Goddess-like. The ground so far below it's nothing more than a game of the world in miniature.

Clouds brush past. Drones buzz in her ears. Screams drift up as laser fire lays waste to the inner city; all those 'scrapers in too-close proximity, helpless to defend themselves or the thousands caged within them. All those fragile lives. For a moment, she's the very sky falling upon them. And then it all goes wrong.

The Haunt and his Hornet swarm. His pirates.

They ruin everything.

Somehow the Haunt pulls a Kraken from the depths of Slip. Some lost or abandoned avatar, a thing of hungry coils. This thing, this hideous id best left in Slip to rot, is set loose on the nodal-Queen. High-pitched, her cries echo across the Gung, calling the others, who come running, and Zen comes with them.

She revels in the destruction of the Kraken, urges them after the Haunt, to tear him to shreds in the same fashion. To stop him.

They get to his second avatar first. His Shark. Desperately trying to get back to him. She screams at them to destroy it. Destroy him. Claps her hands as they snap that connection, injuring him as she was injured. And she's laughing again as she urges them to rend into his mind, dig a hole deep enough for all six Queens to cocoon within. Use him as he used the Kraken.

As his mind begins to cave, she longs to be there, to take part. To feel him break apart in her hands. Unexpected then, the sudden snap. Pain unimaginable. Enough to wake her. Wide-eyed and gasping.

Awake for the first time in… how long?

She didn't know she could wake.

But the Queens are gone. Her connection to them, though minimal since Josef's accomplice, the J-Hack, Breaker, replaced her proper link to her Queen with the link to Polar Bear —the intruder-avi, her jailer—is gone. Nothing but silence where once the talk of the Queens lulled her in her dreams.

Cut off and denied, awake, she stares out into endless white, desperate to close her eyes.

She wants to sleep again.

Anything but being back in this two-fold prison—her

sphere and within in the warm sleeping womb of Polar Bear, who was never hers, never meant to be hers, whose presence is punishment. Cruelty. Bear is still sleeping, of course she is. Bear will always sleep. Once that meant that Zen would always sleep too. Now she has no idea what it means.

Zen will never escape her though. Not without help.

And Bear is not all there is. There is the orb, the glass that contains them both, floating in this sea of white. Glass should be breakable but she imagines this glass is far from it, and she has no idea where this white space is, only that is it formless and so warm it crackles with static. How long has she been here? It might be over a decade. Longer. She should be in pain, should be starving. Broken inside. But Josef couldn't see her hurt no matter how much she hurt him. And she did, didn't she? She enjoyed it too.

She's a little disappointed in him. Punishments *should* hurt. His did.

Zen and the Queens made sure of that.

Josef. Thinking of him, she remembers what happened in the tower before her Queens walked the Gung. Did he die when her Queens stepped through his eyes? Oh she hopes he died, long and slow. He betrayed her. Betrayed her Queens. Helped Breaker diminish her… Zenada screams as if some dam has broken, surprised to hear her voice. She remembers. Her Queens. The *Haunt*. He stole her Queens. He stole her *key*.

She stares with burning eyes through the golden

shape of Polar Bear and the glass of the sphere. Smooth. Impenetrable. Inescapable.

She's helpless and not helpless. The Haunt isn't the only one with bio-ware in his head. Though hers, admittedly, is far from the sophistication of Emblem, which once kept the Queens locked in Slip, she's had longer to learn it, to make it work with her. For a long time, it was all she had left of real awareness, her only connection to life.

She's been experimenting with it in her dreams. Using it to travel Slip, attaching new protocols to scraps of code, forcing them to erupt to change. To evolve. Reaching out to put her mark on the real world through the medium of the virtual, the Slip, *her* Slip, and the results are already out there, written on the flesh of Zeros. Trapping them within their bodies as she's been trapped. Soon they'll be more code than person. Drivable.

There's a game here. A way to have them bring something to her. Someone. Someone who can unlock her prison. A key in human form. A Haunt remade to a key.

Long used to patience, to dreaming, Zenada dreams of all that might be possible when she has what he has. Of ways to make the world pay for all she's had taken from her.

Of punishment. Richly deserved, and dealt with absolute pleasure.

I am a mountain

At the rear of Foon Gung's seven-hundred-mile sprawl, Shandong's mountain ranges rise from the mist, crooked and vast. Around them, abrupt and impatient, juts an array of interlocked high-rises, reflecting mountains, mist and sparse greenery back at itself from every window, turning mountains into a maze, a confusion. These ranges span miles, interweaving concrete and stone right out to the sea where occupied bridges—intricate as cobwebs—connect the mountain habitations to broken spars and ranges too treacherous to live on, all surrounded by furious ocean.

On clear days the sight of spars retreating into the sea, a terracotta army shrunken with age, is both beautiful and sad. A reminder of what the world lost.

On an outcrop above a rolling expanse of restless mist sits a lone figure built from golden code bright as fireflies and scintillating in the rise of sunlight: Shock Pao.

Once a Haunt, a hacker able to pass unseen, signal-less in Slip and IRL, he's now fugitive and stranger than human.

Around him a temple forms, built in gradual increments from a delicate swirl of gold, chain-like filaments. A perfect facsimile from its tiered and sway-backed roof to the rows of prayer lanterns jostling in the breeze. Inside, thick banks of incense give off sickled drifts of golden smoke, floating away to particulate embers of code. Before them the restless ghosts of monks stand bowed and chanting, their voices a murmur on the breeze, low enough to enter the skin like warmth, in tingling vibrations.

Across the floors, around the pillars, avatars bloom into being, roving in curious bursts about the walls. After he freed them from Slip so his friends could trap the Queens in Core, the dark centre of their Hive, the avatars have grown bold, exerting their independence. Why would they not? The lock is gone; the gates open. They have a choice now, and they choose, in general, to leave. To play. To make up for a lifetime of being locked in. There are people who can't understand that. After all, the Slip is an ocean so vast it defies measurement. But is anywhere really big enough when you know you can't leave?

A shoal of fish darts between lanterns, briefly flaring bright and shade under golden flames. Shock touches them and feels somewhere far away the shape of the mind attached. Masculine. Reclined in a leather chair. Faint scents of whiskey and musky aftershave. Eyelids twitching. By the lazy swirl of his thoughts he imagines himself dreaming. Dreaming in Slip. Cute. Also impossible, considering Slip is pretty much already a dream. Real but not at all real. Shock smiles to himself, wondering what this man would do if he knew this temple was just an illusion of an illusion. A dream about dreaming.

This is where Shock hides. In this place. In moments like this. To escape from everything, even when he shouldn't be, because there are days that imprint into your psyche, that make or break you, but always change you and, until four weeks ago, Shock thought that was the worst a day could do. He'd give a lot to still be that fucking ignorant. Four weeks ago he went through twenty-four hours that dismantled him. Tore him apart cell by cell and remade him. Literally. What he is now is not quite human, not quite together, a mishmash of aching scars, bio-ware and brokenness walking around in a human skin trying to look normal and feeling whole fucking universes away from it.

Long-ass story of that twenty-four hours in short form? He kind of broke the world.

Short story long? Where to begin? Foon Gung, the last land left on earth not leering out of the sea at an awkward angle, the only bit that survived when they physically broke the world a few hundred years back—on purpose as it happens—used to be run by the Corporation known as Fulcrum, created and run by the Lakatos family. Why did Fulcrum run the Gung? Simple influential and financial weight. They owned the Slip, the virtual world that everyone everywhere uses—jacking in to ride inside golden avatars in the shape of ocean creatures that until four weeks ago he thought were more thing than person. Turns out he was wrong there too. Avatars are made *from* you. They're alive. Real. *Beings*.

Which is kinda why he had that twenty-four hours to begin with.

Slip was run by the Hive Queens, giant AI avatars created by Fulcrum to manage the vast amounts of data created by billions of service users. The Queens were ants. Giant. Fucking. Ants. Why ants in a Hive? Why a Hive at all when Slip is a virtual ocean? Who the hell knows? Fact is, not only were these Queens ants, they were fucking lunatic. Wanted to bust out IRL and take shit over, Old Testament style—that whole giants walking the earth shit. Only thing keeping them in? Emblem, a tiny shred of bio-ware, the lock and key between Slip and RL, hidden away in Core at the centre of the Queens' Hive, the only place they couldn't go.

Now Emblem's in his head, so meshed with his brain he can't tell where it ends and he begins. Yeah, long-ass story.

Suffice it to say that in twenty-four short hours, he pulled off the most extraordinary heist in hacking history—because, yeah, no fucker's ever got far enough to jack Hive, let alone Core—got hijacked by said bio-ware, chased by gangsters, caught and tortured, rescued, chased again, electrocuted by a psychopath, killed her and her crazy brother, jacked every avatar out of Slip, got head-jacked by the Queens and had his second avatar, Shark, torn away from him. That's like losing a piece of yourself and FYI Shock knows that shit inside out too, having lost several fingertips when he was tortured.

His fingers tingle at the memory and he lifts his hand,

staring at biotech tips, functional instead of familiar. Gold at the moment, they're silver against the soft tan shade of the flesh they cap IRL. As it happens, you can replace fingertips and teeth, but you can't kill the memory of loss. You can't mend invisible damage.

The only reason he's still here wasting air is because, in all the chaos and cruelty of that day, life chose to send him a break or two. His friends. Amiga, a Cleaner sent to kill him who instead decided to save his stupid wreck of a life; the Hornets, a J-Hack crew of super-smart and sassy drop-outs; and the people of the *Resurrection*, a floating city of pirates, scientists, lunatics and damn good folk, who put their lives on the line to help save his so he could save the Gung. He's not sure he did that. In fact he's certain he didn't.

By the end of that twenty-four hours everything he knew about the world and his place in it was re-written. But it didn't end there. If fucking only.

Without Fulcrum, the Gung, too big, too messy, too full of people and now too scarred, littered with the fallout of one day of unmitigated disaster, is vulnerable to Corp takeover. Right this moment the big names are slugging it out for control, like Kaiju smashing each other senseless with whole buildings ripped from their foundations. And the people of the Gung, forced to see the lie their lives have been, are slowly boiling to agitation. They won't stand by and watch the power struggle for long. They're itching to join in, and fuck knows what happens then.

The only thing he knows for sure is what happened to

everyone who fought with him that day.

Captained by Cassius Angel, a scar-patterned sprawl of a man with few foibles and a hot temperament, and carrying Volk, the Pharm whose drug locked the Queens in Core, and Petrie, the man-mountain bosun who led a rabble of well-armed pirates to save Shock's ass, the land ship *Resurrection City* took her people back out to sea, to the ruins and remains of North America—tilted land masses forming vast valleys around white water estuaries. They've dropped anchor by the remains of Louisiana, a vertical swampland of vast twisted oak, cyprus, banyan and water tupelo crawling with fifty-foot long alligators, to fix their ship, half destroyed by battle on the way to aid his sorry ass. He pops in to check on them every now and then, trying and failing not to freak them out with this new avi-form of his, but mostly he just misses them.

As for himself and the Hornets, he kind of (totally did) fuck things badly. Call it grief, call it stupidity, whatever you fucking want, but he forgot to shield them from the outcome of what they'd all done that day. Apparently shit like removing crime lord threats and freeing the Gung's citizens from Fulcrum's control is illegal even when it saves people's fucking *lives*. And apparently, even with Emblem being unpredictable as hell, he's still considered a primary asset by... oh... just about everyone anywhere who equates controlling Slip with power, which is kinda *everyone*.

Not long after the dust settled, all eyes turned on them. No matter that Shock scrambled at that point to scrub them from the Slip, from any memory anywhere, he was still too slow.

Which is why they're hiding. And hunting.

He should be in Slip helping them right now, trawling the messy, cluttered streets of the Gung for the biggest threat currently on their tails: the Grey Cartel. Before Fulcrum fell, the Cartel was barely repped on the Gung, a few dozen lower-tier dealers here and there, no biggie. In the wake of Fulcrum's fall, the Cartel have come from out of nowhere in droves. Sneaky bastards that they are, they've been ignoring Slip to comb the Gung district by district. So diligently in fact, that it's a mere matter of time before they realize he and the Hornets are in Shandong and attack full force.

So why is he procrastinating? Why is he here, building a dream, an illusion of escape from everything he has no right to hide from? Simplest answer? He's scared.

When he lost Shark, the rage he shaped his second avi from didn't go with it, and now it's no longer Shark-shaped it's no longer under his control. Boiling inside of him, black hurricanes fraught with lightning, leaving him afraid of what he might do. Of what he *can* do. Before Emblem, when he was a Haunt, signal-less, capable of hiding from anyone, he was still always on the run. He was very good at running away.

He's running now, but the difference between then and now is that he's stood and fought too. Fought and won. And once you know how to fight, once you know that you *can*, the urge can be hard to resist, and sometimes he just wants to let go. Be a shark. Be Shark. Sometimes he wants to tear the walls down just to hear them scream like he's screaming. Feel like he's feeling. At those moments, he has to stop. Breathe. Resist. Even when he doesn't want to. Especially then. Especially *now.*

Closing his eyes, Shock allows the temple to dissipate like smoke and fills with shame, hot as liquid lead.

Sensible.

Wincing, he opens his eyes. Swirling before him in the air is Puss, his primary avatar, her direct gaze made alien by square pupils and too familiar by his connection with her.

Bathed in her censure, he falls back on old defences, saying sardonically, *Aren't you proud? I could have followed the impulse instead.*

Proud? Of your meagre display of self-control? Maybe a little, something quantum, she says, equally sardonic. *Back to work maybe? I think you've wasted enough time.*

Fading away, Puss leaves one tentacle until last, gesturing imperiously. *Yes ma'am.*

Shock sighs. Steps through from mountainside to Slip, shaking off the wisps of temple still clinging to his shoulders. Slip's a virtual ocean, but it no longer *looks* like one. Freed from Fulcrum's control, higher level Techs and Corps with hacking skills have begun to tear down some of the corals once used to connect the world and are building in their place something strange. Wonderful. A little terrifying.

A little of everything—ragged portions of bizarre

cities, rebellious of convention and physics, portions of landscape so surreal they could be other planets, zones akin to bubble universes with their own rules of physics. Castles in the air. Towers made of trees. Whatever can be imagined can be made here. Is being made. The sheer breathtaking invention of it astounds him. But it means the Slip is no longer so open. Things can hide here, and they do. They hide too well. Maybe even from eyes as sharp as his.

Puss is nowhere to be seen, already off again trying to keep a working map of Slip as it changes and evolves so Shock, reading her, can avoid getting lost.

Reaching out into the infrastructures connected to the Gung, Shock winces as the whole shape of it builds in his mind, a panorama of aching white noise, all those bodies and cars, too much information, the flash of monos, trailing conversation streams. Snippets of music, vid-stream, of arguments and laughter. The whole world in his head.

There's no way to ignore it, instead he makes use of it, focusing on specific patterns. Tells. The rhythms he's come to associate with the Cartel. In this fashion he manages to pick up traces of the unit he'd clocked near Risi before tapping out and needing a break. Faint. Very faint. But it seems they've headed in to Risi proper.

Shit. That's where Amiga's crew is hunting.

Used to be he came here and rode behind Puss's eyes and had to swim everywhere he needed to go, utilizing data gulleys if he needed to move fast from one area of

Slip to another. Now? He closes his eyes, thinks where he needs to go, opens them: and he's there. Emblem makes Slip accessible in this way and he has no idea how it works yet, only that it does and that, yeah, it freaks him out. He shouldn't be *able* to do this. No one should. Picking up the exact whereabouts of the Cartel unit in the data streams of Risi, all that RL interference resonating through Slip code madness—that's not so easy. Reassuringly tough, in fact.

When he finds them, they're on scooters, mere streets away from where Amiga, Deuce, Vivid and Raid are sat drinking coffee and arguing search routes. With little time for formalities, he does the single thing Amiga hates the most—considering how it reminds her of the erstwhile boss she killed by shooting rounds through her own lung—and IMs without chiming.

Heads up. Cartel about two minutes away, closing in fast.

You have got *to be shitting me!* She's snarling. So not good. *I'm guessing this means Puss gave you that verbal slapping you sorely deserved?*

You sicced Puss on me? Oh wow, Amiga. Best friend ever. Bitch.

Oh fuck off. My goddamn Cleaner senses have been twitching all morning and now we're what… seconds from imminent discovery, no thanks to you?

Ugh.

Yeah. Right. Sorry.

Just get back on them and give them a nudge away. Last thing we need is a fight here. Too many people around, as per fucking usual. Track me in on their direction so we can follow.

On it.

He leaves her be, assuming she's going to tell the others, instead she throws in a toilet break excuse and goes off alone.

Amiga!

What?

You're supposed to take your fucking team.

I did. Me, myself and I. Poke the unit toward one of those 'scrapers for me. She throws him a vivid mental picture. She's ridiculous gifted at vis. He thinks maybe it was her specialism before she Failed, but wouldn't ask. The "danger, here be dragons" sign over that portion of her life is writ large enough to be seen from Mars.

NO. Not until you call for back-up. He doesn't tell her that he'd do pretty much anything to avoid nudging. Has no intention of letting her know how awful it feels to interfere with anyone's right to think for themselves.

Shock. Do it.

Amiga has this thing she does, this quiet, cold thing that frankly makes his jaw ache. She does it on purpose. He hates it. Hates her when she does it. But he understands her need to be alone. It's not like he's a fucking social butterfly, even though he technically lives with over a hundred and twenty Hornets, he sees only five of them semi-regularly and only Amiga every day, if she's around.

Shock. Drive them, or I will.

No point arguing. So Shock does what he hates to do and reaches in to the minds of the Cartel unit to plant presumed knowledge of the Hornets hiding in one of the nearby 'scrapers. They're a strange design, these ones, and he can guess why she wants them there—all the better to corner them. It's a good strategy. It'd be better if she had back-up.

Done.

Don't call the others.

He sighs. *Like I would. Be real, Amiga. Be fucking careful too.*

I don't need to be careful, she snaps, and then she's gone, leaving aching silence.

Yeah, you do, he whispers to her absence. *You just don't want to.*

All okay? Puss rolls out of Slip tentacles first, radiating calm in that way she has.

Nope. Why have we always got to seek the worst-case scenario?

Because you two are your own worst enemies.

Hah. Maybe.

Definitely. But chill. We won once, we'll do it again, even if you two are still running solo like absolute idiots.

Feeling his honesty like a burden, he admits, *It didn't feel like winning.*

Puss sends him the warm glow she uses as a smile. *It rarely ever does,* she says, soft and sad.

Shock reaches for his body, sat cross-legged on the edge of a balcony at their hideout in Shandong, far away from the chaos of Gung, still overcrowded but somehow remote. Peaceful. Pops out facing himself, staring at his own face, the ever-present warmth of Puss wrapping around his back. He looks in through his own eyes to see himself, golden, looking back at him. Smiles, and watches his selves, gold and technicolor, smiling at each other into infinity. This is what he is now on the inside. A paradox. An illusion. Nothing he understands.

Trying not to allow it to frighten him any more than it already has today, he reaches through those multi-selves to the connection he has with Deuce, and wholesale dumps the information Amiga demanded he keep to himself. Okay, so he promised he wouldn't. He lied. If she can be stupid, he can lie, right?

The solemn promise of retribution doesn't matter.

Some things are just worth the aggro.

hunting solo

Rotten fish stench grabs Amiga's nostrils, shoving its way in beside the almighty reek of sweaty bodies and filthy walls. Talk about uninvited visitors. Ramming the back of her hand to her nose she hunkers down, hoping stench may resemble smoke and remain high, but if anything it's stronger, pulling hot bubbles of acid gorge to rise and pop in her throat. And now the thigh she took a bullet through saving Shock is having a bitch fit, despite all the work Ravi, the Hornets' sawbones, has put in trying to fix it like new.

Her fault for pushing too hard, but rest is boring. Inactivity is the only thing more certain to kill her than a bullet.

"Holy honking hell, Batman, someone needs to throw their goddamn trash in a furnace," she mutters, oblivious to memories of her own overflowing bin habits. Hers *never* stank this bad. "They need to throw this whole goddamn place in a fucking furnace."

Having lived in the sweaty confines of the Gung her

entire life, Amiga's seen some shit holes for sure, but all fifty floors of this 'scraper's narrow, poorly lit, grime-streaked concrete corridors resemble nothing less than a circle of hell. Turning the corner at the end of the corridor, she finds another stairwell leading up into darkness and runs lightly up, scaring off a couple of roosting pigeons. Amiga shushes them impatiently. If she had a gun she'd shoot them. But she chucked it when she ran out of bullets.

Plastic 3D-printed gun. Useless after the magazine is empty.

Also less easy to come by every day, like everything is with the Corps up in arms and the Gung spiralling to pieces, less sure of itself and more aggressive by the day. If things don't change soon, or break, this place will go up in flames. Or explosions. Amiga kinda wants to be out of Dodge before then, wants her Hornets, her family of choice, out of Dodge. They've had enough of being caught in crossfire. But first there are rats to hunt. Cartel rats.

The stairs end at yet another long, dirty corridor. Of the caged bulbs above her head, about one in every five casts light in a sputtering cone, illuminating ranks of poor-quality steel doors, dented and fissured from who the hell knows what. It could be a prison, or an institution, but people live here. Until she left to start Tech, Amiga used to live in a similar place. Maybe a bit cleaner. Heck, a lot cleaner, but no less fucking miserable. Misery is a commodity for the Corps and criminals who build these pits.

Today their penny-pinching will work in her favour. This place has pretty much nowhere to hide. The inside comprises a spiral. Corridor leading to corridor leading to corridor until you hit the stairwell to the next floor. In other words: if there's a fire, everyone dies.

Her targets, therefore, have to be somewhere ahead.

How many floors did this thing have again? Amiga checks back at her brief scan and offers up a silent curse at any listening entities when she realizes she's barely more than a quarter of the way up. Her thighs are on fire. Stairs: literally the worst invention ever. Yet somehow the most irritatingly *persistent*.

The only good thing about these shitty 'rises, apart from the currently useful design, is that the people in them know violence well enough to avoid it. They'll have heard the epic gun battle in the middle of their courtyard and gone on lockdown. Meaning she won't accidentally kill someone.

A scrape in the hallway ahead snaps her eyes forward. She feels the grin before she realizes it's grabbed her mouth. Oh crap. Shouldn't be smiling. Shouldn't be having *fun*, especially not in this epic vom-sauna of BO, fish and grime. This is scratching an itch, nothing more. A little hit to keep the urge in check, to hold back the flood.

Another, more discreet scrape, almost too faint to hear.

Amiga's head flashes clear, cleansed by the lightning of adrenal rush. Palming her knife from her back pocket, she creeps forward to the corner and rises to stand—head pressed back into the wall regardless of dirt. In this heightened state of clarity she can hear the Cartel soldiers waiting close by. There's anticipation in the hitch and rasp of their breath. They know she's followed them. They were counting on it.

Fuck's sake, Amiga mouths to the ceiling.

Why do people do it? Why? Knowing what she is? Amiga's breath stops altogether for a moment. Was.

Knowing what she *was,* they shouldn't think they can entrap her into chasing them and then dispatch her without effort because narrow corridors and outnumbered and stupid goddamn bringing a knife to a gun party. This shit is worse than the whole hail of bullets assumption. It's downright insulting. Hurts her fucking professional pride to the core.

These absolute morons are going to learn first hand the very significant difference between a killer and a Cleaner up close and excruciatingly personal.

Flexing her hands, Amiga visualizes, tenses, and flits around the corner. Sure enough, all seven Grey Cartel members are ranged up the next corridor, guns high and ready to shoot. Not ready enough. They've barely clocked her presence when she's right in the face of the first one, grabbing his arm to ram it behind his back, up and under, forcing him in front of her as the others turn to fire the dregs of their bullets.

"Good evening," she says brightly into his sweat-soaked hair as he jerks against her, blooms of blood and flesh slamming out of his torso. "Today you'll be playing the part of my human shield."

It makes her laugh how they portray combat on film and in the stream-shows from the hubs, the sensual flow of choreographed moves, so slick and smooth you'd think the blood might clean itself off the floor in reverence. Reality works a little different. Violence is ugly. Breathless. Personal. Fists miss targets. Feet slip. The impact of walls and floor, of fists and feet on flesh is a shock to the system, each one sparkling like a constellation of stars. The body aches. Burns.

A knife cut is numb and sear. A bullet startling impact and then heaviness. There's nothing reverential about any of it, apart from the stunning responsibility of taking a life. Cleaners understand this from the inside out. Use it to their advantage. Waste nothing. Execute eliminations with swift, brutal efficiency, the kind that leaves a great deal of mess. Incongruous then, the use of the term clean to describe what the Cleaner does. Never fails to amuse her. Nor does the assumption that facing a Cleaner will be like in the movies.

Facing a Cleaner is facing death, and people never fail to realize it until it's too late.

Out of bullets and one man down, his torso a mess of minced meat and bone fragments, the Cartel remain in close ranks as if they think she can be intimidated. Cute. Stuffing the laughter down, because it's not safe to laugh—laughter in this situation steals humanity, makes her a monster—Amiga palms her knife and allows them to make the first move, en masse, as if that will go in any way toward changing the outcome.

Five kills, one immobilize and capture. No darts, no bullets, no crossbow bolts. No fucking problem.

Spinning her knife sideways in her hand, she waits, relaxed over the balls of her feet, until they're close enough that she can see the colour of their eyes in the dim light. The fear that sparks when she glides forward, smiling, knife flashing left and right to leave the first two in her wake, their guts steaming on filthy concrete, a third reeling back choking, his hand clamped to his throat as if that can stop the deluge.

"I need one of you alive," she tells the remaining three, shadowing them as they step back, uncertain. "Draw straws, maybe?"

They break at that, the lights going out, swallowed whole by dull clouds of panic. Good. Panic steals adrenalin. Steals movement. Fight or flight would kick in any second now if she gave it a chance. So she doesn't. Running forward on the balls of her feet she grabs the closest and spins him, pulling his back hard against her chest, cupping his chin with her free hand and yanking, feeling that snap, that vibration as shockwaves travel the spine, the sudden heaviness of an emptied body.

Chucking him to the side, she's on the next before he can scream, her knife sliding between his ribs, holding him steady as she drives the blade in over and over until all resistance falls out of his stance. Amiga drops him at her feet. Steps over him. Job done. It shouldn't feel this fucking good. She shouldn't feel this *alive*. Killing like this when she was doing Twist Calhoun's bidding was killing *her*, she knew it. So why is it the opposite is now true? What does that mean?

The last soldier stands staring at her. He looks like he wants to run and can't. Flushed and sweating through his jacket, he makes a move like he's going to back away into the corridor, his whole body wracked with tremors. She walks up to him slowly, daring him to try. Daring him to run. He freezes.

"You said you needed one alive," he says, gulping hard. His hand jerks, pointing at the bodies of his friends. "They're all dead. You can't kill me. You need me."

"That's right," she says, and smiles.

Flipping her knife so the heavy metal handle is outward, she cracks it across his head. Watches him collapse to the floor, in slow motion at first as the body fights the inevitable and then in a great rush and thump as it gives in. Amiga sheathes her blade, grabs out a few ties from her jacket and makes quick work of fixing his wrists tightly together behind his back. When she's finished, one of the doors opens. A middle-aged man in nothing but canvas shorts stands there, his body shining with sweat. They've been watching. Of course they have.

"You leaving now?" he asks, no heat in it. He's scared but he wants her to go and he's letting her see that. Admirable. Must be one of the floor Uncles. In a place like this, each floor will have several designated Aunts and Uncles, making sure everyone's looked out for as much as they can be in this level of appalling poverty.

Amiga nods, reassuring with a smile. "Yes. You can clean these up."

"We have no furnace."

She makes a face. "Don't I know it," she says tartly. "My nose filed for divorce fucking ages ago. I suggest you chuck them in the bins. Hell alone knows they couldn't smell any bloody worse."

Clamping her teeth against the pain in her torso, another scar she won't let Ravi get rid of, she grasps her unconscious rat under his shoulders and wrestles him up. Swears at him for being so fucking heavy, and annoying, and worst of all utterly *stupid* as she makes her way out of the building, one awkward thumping drag down a staircase at a time, her brain already motoring at top speed, considering and rejecting some manner of explanation that might evade her friends' fury.

The aggressive growl of caterbikes greets her as she hits the courtyard, and three weave around each other into the narrow space, coming to a halt in front of her. Deuce, Vivid and Raid. Her team. The team she unceremoniously dumped. All unrecognizable under avi-skins Deuce built to protect them from easy ID. Fuck. Shock dropped her in it. Bastard.

Bastard! She howls into his IM.

Sorry not sorry, comes the snark-tastic response.

You fucking will be, Haunt.

Whatever, Cleaner. Bring it.

Deuce yanks his helmet off, the skin's image stuttering and collapsing into pixels. Revealing hair mussed and damp, a face livid and utterly edible, those black eyes of his snapping like piranha as if he can tear the truth out of her, or just tear her apart. He looks like he's got one hell of a lot to say, until his gaze drops to the man drooping in her arms. Then he sighs, shifting his gaze up to the deepening black of night as if he can find answers there for whatever it is she's done.

"Where are the others?"

"Probably in the bin by now."

He groans. "Bin? Really?"

"They don't have a furnace," she says, by way of explanation. "You should smell it in there. My nose is traumatized."

"And he's alive, right?" asks Vivid, out of her helmet and looking, if anything, more furious than Deuce.

"You can take his pulse if you like."

"What I'd *like*," Vivid snaps back, "is for you to fucking toe the line once in a while. Seven to one? Really? We're a *team*, Amiga. Team members don't ditch team members and go off hunting their murder jollies all alone. *Capiche*?"

Oops. Italian. Vivid's definitely more than just a little pissed. Raid just sits there emanating disapproval. Terrific. Just what the doctor ordered.

"I'm sorry, okay?"

Deuce shoots her this filthy glare and snaps, "Sure. Like that fixes everything." He dips his chin. "He alive?"

"Of course."

"Then let's get out of here; whatever you did sparked some serious attention from local Sec. A literal squadron is on the way. I love how you channel your sneaky Cleaner skills to do this shit."

His snark is thick enough to spread on toast. She

figures to eat it like crow but sees he's still not in the mood for apologies or explanations. None of them are. When will she learn? The more you push people away, the further they go, until they're gone for good. She wishes to fuck she could just *stop* pushing. But somehow it's all she ever does.

the view from heaven

Braced at the brink of space, Shanghai Hub contains Shanghai as it was, like some divine hand reached beneath and scooped it up whole, resting it into a cradle built to rock gently on the edge of earth and space, domed in crystal-clear glass. Of course, that's exactly how it happened, minus the divine hand, unless one considers Corps to be divine—it wouldn't be far from the truth, not if one were thinking divinity in terms of arrogant, possessive gods, like those on Olympus.

All these hubs, these cities grazing eternity were lifted by Corps, not governments, and are, to this day, run by Corps. Still arrogant. Still possessive. Fiercely independent even before the fall of Fulcrum, the loss of power to the Gung. No one who lives on a hub could easily be persuaded to leave. It's more than patriotism. It's fealty. People have always left the Gung for the hubs, searching for a new life. A better one. For a life without Psych tests and suffocating Corp control, but the grass is rarely greener. It is still always only grass. Corps hold power everywhere. Here, it is her Corp that holds power.

Evelyn Tsai was born and raised here. She's deeply bonded to this fragile, perfect city; a complicated, symbiotic blending of woman and stone. She runs her hard-won portion with a will that mocks anyone who tried to tell a twenty-one-year-old with no money, no prospects and too many psychological scars that all she would amount to could be found between her legs.

Evelyn grew up in Shanghai Hub's Pínkùn Dìqū, one of thousands of poor kids with threadbare clothes, dirty faces and little or no education. Until she was thirteen, she didn't even know school existed—she worked with her mother in the fish factory, scraping silver scales. She'd hold her hands up to the light to watch them glitter. Smear them up her arms and pretend that, somehow, they would transform her to a fish so she could swim away.

Slip and RL meshed together in her mind—a fantasy of freedom.

She's never forgotten how it felt to be dirty. To smell. To be hungry enough to lick those scales from her fingers—feeling them prick her tongue, her cheeks. Feeling them lodge tight in her throat, making her cough. Those years of want are not behind her; they are carved into her organs and her bones. She will always be sickly. Physically weak. Her doctor is sworn to secrecy upon his life, the life of his family.

Show weakness and the world eats you alive in gaping, agonizing chunks.

But she doesn't blame Shanghai for her beginnings. She loves it for making her fight, for forcing her to learn the strength hidden in her bones: Shanghai's concrete and steel.

Night currently veils her city in the hub, drenching it in whorls of neon and blue bio-light, a galaxy of offices, freeways and nightclubs bright enough to shame the stars just beyond the glass. Through her office window, Evelyn takes in the sensual curve of the bund, the ornate crenellations of Jin Mao tower, the dense scatter of high-rises like the skeletons of great beasts, smoothed to silky whites and greys under hot sun and pounding rain—neither of which are real on a hub, only imitations created by atmospheric machines.

Evelyn shifts her gaze between the light-drenched cityscape and the view beyond the dome, where thousands of hubs glinting like stars graze the boundary of earth and endless nothing. All those cities of the earth, risen up and elevated higher than mountains. Raised to look down upon the jagged shoreline of the Gung as they sail overhead. Gods indeed.

Gods maybe, but not always all-powerful.

Only four weeks ago they were beholden to the Gung. To Fulcrum. For access to Slip, for the means to maintain their servers. For any service or tech Fulcrum already owned or bought up in brutal hostile takeovers the Tech industries of the hubs came to despise. But now the landscape of power has changed. Power is up for grabs. So very much power from such a tiny scrap of land.

Evelyn looks down, though the Gung is far away at this point of orbit. From this height, Earth is a curve of rippled cloud, courting green at the edge, a flash of aurora. Above it, the abyss is black and deep. Absolute. Filled with dead light. It makes her shiver. Shanghai's cradle is fragile, the grip of tenuous gravity all that holds it from drifting into frozen oblivion. If anything went wrong… it only takes a moment to lose everything.

Evelyn knows this as deeply as she knows her city.

A throat clears behind her. "Madame Tsai, they're conscious."

Evelyn thanks her assistant with a nod and strides to the shoot as gracefully as any lady of class, except that she is not one and never was. It can be faked. Everything can be faked, because everyone is pretending. Everyone wears the same masks, paints the same illusions, even the rich—haute couture, exclusive resorts, single-access penthouse suites, private shuttles, cuisine and wine so rare only a fraction of a percent of the entire population of the hubs and the Gung can afford it. Wealth is an excellent disguise indeed, and Evelyn is almost rich enough to ease the clenching of terror in her gut.

Almost.

Her heels sound out hungry clicks as she steps on to the cool green of the lab floor. This level hums just under the surface; machines everywhere working with quiet efficiency. It's her favourite part of the building. She had this colour, this ambience, recreated in the penthouse suite she calls home, at the top of one of Shanghai's most exclusive residences, including the hum, a modulator over the air-con to ensure her sleep is serene.

Keel joins her as she crosses the corridor to the warren of interconnected, secured labs taking up the entire centre of this floor. His domain.

She offers him a soft, "Morning, Keel."

"Ms Tsai."

Keel, otherwise known as KeelHaul, is the epitome of the young HipXec. Dressed in three-quarter-length pants, a button-down shirt, braces and wingtips, with long auburn hair piled into a bun, his incurious green eyes avoid her gaze from behind handcrafted wooden glasses. Keel's somewhere on the autistic spectrum, utterly brilliant, an ex-Fail who once worked as a Pharm, a drug developer, for criminals. He's Evelyn's ace card.

Especially today.

Since the fall of Fulcrum, Evelyn's been working hard to negotiate partnership with Paraderm, one of the Gung's remaining big Corps, only to find that Gung Corps are still not keen to work with hubs. The usual nonsense. The Gung is happy to be in control, but the moment they're expected to share power or cooperate, the usual paranoia surfaces. A viewpoint verging on the fantastical—seeking to reinterpret distance as assumed superiority, when verifiable truth shows that the hubs have been beholden to the Gung's assumed superiority all these years.

She'd expected better from Paraderm, run by power couple Marcus and Tahira Shaheen-Lox.

What a shame to be disappointed.

But versed in the contrariness of life, Evelyn always has a back-up plan, and this one called for a sealed-off lab generally used as a safe zone for hazardous trials reimagined as a holding cell. Inside, Marcus and Tahira await, strapped into medical chairs. Marcus is enraged, shouting, not seeming to realize the glass is soundproofed. Tahira looks around, her gaze calculating, her demeanour collected and assured. There's only one way to calculate out of this, and Evelyn rather imagines they won't. What a shame.

Keel scans entry with his pass, holding the door open and moving aside to allow her to enter first. Such a gentleman.

Evelyn nods pleasantly at both of them.

"I realize this is unconventional. I do apologize," she says. "I wanted to offer you a last chance to sign up in partnership with Tsai Holdings before I'm forced to take steps."

"Unconventional?" Tahira's voice is a whip slicing the air. "This is illegal. It is criminal. It is not *unconventional*."

"Well quite," Evelyn says, with a small smile. "But you left me little choice. My current stratagems are heavily invested in securing Paraderm's resources."

"The offer of a business partnership does not come with an imperative to acquiesce." Marcus. Finally calm. Quietly furious.

"Of course not, and ordinarily I wouldn't be anything like so rude as to insist, but there's a little more at stake, is there not? I'm not the only one to have secured footage from four weeks ago, showing how vulnerable we are, how wrong we have all been, how complacent. I'm certainly not the only one repulsed by Fulcrum's theft of part of my consciousness. We none of us signed an agreement that our avatars should be so… functional. The abuse of power is beyond disgust and the aberrations it produced beyond offensive."

"We might agree that recent weeks have brought a stark new reality to light," Tahira replies, her voice shaking, "but we do not agree with any of your other sentiments—we were disconcerted at first, but we have come to accept the ways things are. Accept our avatars for *who* they are. Your attitude is beyond disgusting, your opinions beyond offensive."

Evelyn nods. "I see." She gestures to Keel. "This is my Pharm, Keel. If you're still reluctant to join with Tsai Holdings, he has a gift for you."

Tahira raises a brow. "We were not interested in working with Tsai Holdings," she says. "And after this violation of our rights, we would never consider working with Tsai Holdings, now or in the future. Not under any circumstances."

Marcus directs a look of fierce admiration at Tahira. "It is as my wife says," he adds. "You have nothing to offer Paraderm, and Paraderm has nothing to offer you."

"As you wish. Keel?"

Waiting by the chilled cabinets at the lab's edge, Keel opens one to remove a small, clear box. Carefully, he shakes out two small tabs like bumps, the stim drugs keeping a fair portion of the population of the hubs and the Gung happy.

"One at a time or both at once?" he asks Evelyn.

"Oh, both at once," she says. "This is merely a formality."

Standing between them, he presses the tabs into their necks and watches impassively as they go rigid. Marcus makes a high keening noise, a double note so disturbing Evelyn has to fight not to wince—after all she is human. As his keening increases, the room fills with golden light. Beside them, gold threads begin to spin and weave, building a dolphin and a lion fish mid-air, panicked and thrashing.

Tahira starts to scream, a counterpoint to her husband's loud keen, her body arched and writhing. The fish and the dolphin stutter into frantic, spasmodic rolls, spinning over and over, their paler gold bellies flashing like alarms, fear and panic palpable until they freeze at the exact moment Marcus and Tahira seize up and cease making noise. The precision is extraordinary, leaving brittle silence in which four bodies, two gold, two human, writhe in unison and then stop.

The moment is eerie, like a freeze frame in VR. Almost unreal. The gleam of light in their eyes, the stillness of their chests, the fixity of their limbs almost unnerving. Five seconds seem to roll on forever, and then the tableau breaks. Marcus and Tahira slump, lax, into the embrace of their chairs and both avatars drift away to rest against the counter, casting warm yellow light like a buttercup beneath a chin. Loose. Limp. Lifeless.

Evelyn walks over to the CEOs of Paraderm. Leans in to take a close look. They're just about breathing, a grip on life so tenuous she could hold a hand over their mouth and nose and count away seconds to end them. Their eyes are wide but dull, empty of everything, a huge contrast to rage, to calculation. How fragile humanity is. How reliant upon such brittle connections. Evelyn waves a hand in front of Marcus's face.

"Which version was this?"

"Early. You wanted it to be harsh."

"So I did." Evelyn had all but forgotten her initial intent to be cruel; their maudlin attachment to their avatars lowered her opinion of them. One does not punish lesser adversaries. One removes them. "Interesting reactions. The latest have, I presume, lost all traces of this… extremity?"

"Of course. And once I have Paraderm's laboratories it'll move faster toward sophistication."

Evelyn straightens Tahira's jacket, left askew by her writhing. "Marvellous. And the digitization?"

"Soon."

After the fall of Fulcrum, Keel approached her with a remarkable claim about the small band of J-Hacks and pirates who overthrew the massive Corp. He told her that they'd severed the Queens—the remarkable, massive avatars Fulcrum failed to keep control of—from Josef Lakatos with a drug of some fashion, a disconnection drug, and used it to trap them in Core. He told her he could synthesize this drug. The worth of it was immediately apparent: power. Power over Slip without the need to find the Haunt. An edge, as it were. Evelyn loves having an edge.

She gave him open access to all Tsai Holdings' resources. In the four weeks since the fall, he's managed to synthesize the drug until it worked the way it worked on Josef. And then he began to experiment, to try and make it do what Evelyn wants—separate and contain, so that Tsai Holdings can control access to avatars, and therefore the Slip. And he has. What he needs now if they're to achieve the next step of digitization, is lab technology developed and fiercely guarded by Paraderm, and more test subjects.

Once they have the drug digitized, they'll release it into Slip. Return avatars to where they belong. Put things to rights, and make a little profit—or a great deal of profit—to boot. Evelyn did not ask to be gifted a sentient helpmeet. She wanted only a vehicle. A means of transport within Slip. She does not care for its mind or its selfhood, she did not give her permission to Fulcrum for it to have either. That is the biggest insult, the theft of choice. Of control. Ensuring Tsai Holdings controls the only access to Slip will return choice to her whilst further securing her company's financial future.

After all, what will people not pay to have access to Slip? Especially now when, in the wake of Fulcrum's fall and the Queens' destruction, it has become more than merely a means to communicate and play. It has become worlds within worlds—a fount of creativity. Too much creativity. Such freedoms lead to unwarranted confidence. To revolution. Best to put a bottle-neck on it all. Remind people of their place. What better way than to make them pay for their freedom again? Money is the great leveller.

"Be faster than soon, Keel. Now we can obtain Paraderm's resources I expect swift results." She doesn't wait for a response. She leaves the lab, throwing casually over her shoulder as the door closes behind her, "Have someone put those two somewhere safe."

The lift back up to her office provides her with a moment to reflect. An important ritual. Evelyn has always taken time to chew over success, to revel in it. She's never once let a moment such as this pass unnoticed or uncelebrated. Not only the big victories, the tiny ones too; the first item of clothing she bought from a shop rather than received from a charity; the first meal eaten under a roof that did not leak; the first tiny promotion from Reception into the building proper.

Small steps lead to big ones. Tiny victories precede unimaginable wins. Now she has Paraderm under control—after a little creative paperwork management by her legal team—she's in a better position to replace chaos with order. To dictate the future rather than be swept up in it. That was the worst of Fulcrum's advantage, having to give up portions of vital control, to let another lead. Evelyn is not good at concession.

Back in her office, the paperwork dealt with so her lawyers can go ahead and take control of Paraderm in her name, Evelyn resumes her vigil at the window, sipping a cup of soothing peppermint tea. Other Corps and powers on the hubs are hoping to secure the Haunt and his swarm somehow, hoping to grab power by holding the key. Whilst they scrabble after ghosts, she will step into real power.

Leave them all behind.

Beneath.

the aftermath always sucks

Back on her bike, Amiga takes point as they weave back to their shitty temporary base in Ginzo, buried amongst teetering 'scrapers, hidden deep in the maze of narrow back streets. Crowded and violent with noise in the daytime, these streets are eerily silent at this time of evening as darkness drops in a catastrophic rush, the arch of the Milky Way appearing like an exotic street lamp. Ripples of gold follow it, spreading forward and away with the same languid ease as sunlight racing across water.

Amiga looks up as tight flocks of avatars wheel over, describing byzantine patterns over the peaks of the 'scrapers as they spiral around to swoop low at speed and illuminate 'scraper windows like miniature suns, their gold sparkling on dust and cobwebs, the delicate ripple of bamboo behind filthy glass.

A narwhal sweeps past her shoulder, the contact like static, a prickle of electric needles. Avatars are absolutely alive, too much so to ignore. And so completely personal, a startling, breath-stealing intimacy of connection. Leopard

Seal, Amiga's avatar, is a tingling presence woven through her mind so tightly she can look through her eyes, sense what she's thinking and feeling at all times. Too intense for words. A state of emotional connection she's not ready for and yet has no choice in.

Surprising then that there are moments in which she forgets this has not always been her reality.

Even more surprising is that her avatar's not scared of or disgusted by her, not even knowing every atom of what she is, what she's done—what she's fighting away from and back to with equal, disconcerting ferocity. Leopard Seal is gentler than her. Softer. Sweeter. Unswervingly moral. Everything she can't be any more. She's terrified of hurting her. Warns her not to look in for a while and experiences the gentle, unmistakable sweep of a mind against hers, like the comforting swipe of cheek against jaw.

I was there in the 'scraper, and I'm here now. I'm going nowhere.

Why does that make Amiga want to cry?

Their digs is one of the Movement's old bolt holes, stuck catty-corner in a 'scraper carved to way more cramped apartments than it has any right to be. But safe. Secure. Deuce's work again, hacking into their servers on the faintest of trails. He's getting scary good with his avi out, enough to make Amiga suspect he fudged his aptitude tests a few times to lower his percents because no way he's only a top 2%.

Makes her curious as to why anyone would do that, especially someone as resigned as Deuce to the inevitability of a Fail.

She hates that the fall of Fulcrum couldn't change that particular part of the system, the part designed to punish independent thought. But maybe four weeks isn't enough to change that. Maybe nothing is. Scary that sometimes people seem to need what they hate, and here, what everyone hates is the Psych Eval. You go to Cad or Tech, train hard for years in your pre-selected skills chosen by aptitude tests, and then, at the end of it all, you take the Psych Eval. Might as well call it the obedience test.

Pass and you are gifted the life of a WAMOS—a well-adjusted member of society—allowed to benefit from your years of training.

Fail and you have two choices: remain in the heart of society, a WAMOS of sorts but at the lowest level of Corp or Tech with no hope for advancement. Or leave. Immediately. No money. No credentials. No hope. Those who leave generally become J-Hacks or criminals and the line is a thin one. Almost negligible.

It's frightening how easy it is to Fail. How very many who thought they would Pass for sure somehow found themselves with the worst of choices.

Her Deuce knew he was set to be J-Hack all along—the only way Deuce can think is for himself—so why would he feel the need to conceal his level? Weird. She's always thought she knew all there was to know about him. Makes her itch to ask, but when you're as tight-lipped about your past as she is with your supposed nears and dears, there's no license or wiggle room to start quizzing others about portions of theirs they choose to conceal.

Killing engines, they roll their caterbikes into the narrow alley tucked between their 'scraper and the next, behind the bulk of trash cans, and Deuce slings their unconscious prisoner over his shoulder, running lightly up the fire escape as if the fucker weighs nothing. Amiga recalls the graceless thump and drag of her handling of that particular body. Jeez. She needs to work on her fucking biceps and her envy; neither is particularly impressive right now.

The safe house is on the thirteenth floor, unlucky or lucky depending on your historic preference. Inside, Deuce places their prisoner on a bed—he's starting to stir, groaning low in his throat. The bruise from her knife is angry mottled red on swollen flesh, going gradually black as blood gathers under the skin. Yeah, that's gotta sting. Unlucky for him, it'll soon be the least of his worries.

"I'll need him tied down to a chair in the other room," Amiga says, trying to make it sound less final than it is. Trying to ignore the looks in their eyes that clench her stomach like a vice.

"Are we going to allow this?" Vivid asks Deuce, as if Amiga's not even here. Wow, that stings like a bitch, but she gets why it has to be that way, and that's somehow worse, because she's not meant to be on the outside any more, she chose to join them. Made her commitment. It's just not working out quite how any of them planned. "I mean, *really*?"

"Not sure we have a choice," he responds, careful. Looks like he's brewing excuses for her. He shouldn't have to do that. She hates putting him in that position.

"Well that's bullshit."

"Viv..." Deuce starts in a warning tone.

Vivid cuts him off. "Don't make excuses. That's more bullshit and you know it. My question stands: are we going to allow Amiga to go all out on that guy? Is that how we do shit now?"

"Fuck," Deuce rams his hands through his hair. "How do we do shit, Viv? What the hell even *is* this shit?"

"Teamwork," Vivid says, and her tone precludes argument. "No matter what's changed, that's what stays the same. She doesn't get to screw that up."

Enough. Amiga can answer for her damned self. "If you want to do this, Viv, if you want to *talk* to him, you're welcome. I'll hold back."

Slamming a fist into the door, Vivid all but snarls, "As a matter of fact, I do. You think I can't do it?"

"I think you can do pretty much anything you want," Amiga replies, and it's the truth so it's easy to admit. "But I know you haven't done this, or you wouldn't be so fucking upset. It's not the same as combat. He'll be helpless, he *is* helpless, and you'll have to hurt him. A lot. Slowly. Carefully. With precise cruelty. Because he'll know you're not into it, he'll sense the lack of commitment and he won't be scared enough to break unless you shut down and go for broke, which will break *you*. He's already scared of me; I won't have to do much. I was just going to take this, but that's not good teamwork, is it? So, what I'm doing now is *offering* to lift this burden from you. You wanna carry it, go ahead. You're big and ugly enough to choose for yourself."

"Why is torture necessary? Can we not interrogate without?" Raid says. "We're not monsters."

That's a reasonable idea. Idealistic. Naive. But reasonable. "He's a soldier. He'd torture you for information. If you *ask* him, he'll give you nothing. I suppose we could ask Shock to go in there and strip his mind clean—different method, same outcome."

Raid hisses, flinching back. "We can't ask Shock to do that. We can't *do* that."

"Fuck's sake," Vivid snaps. "Whatever. Do it. Take it. I don't have the stomach. I dig combat like it's my fucking sister, but that's where my love of violence begins and ends."

And that's why Amiga will always consider Viv a friend, even if she turns on her and slices her fucking liver out. There's fuck all ego under that explosive, take-no-prisoners temper, only a firm set of morals and the kind of mind Amiga envies, unclouded by any confusion or denial of what she is.

Amiga places a hand on Vivid's arm. "You're crazy, but you're not nasty."

All she gets in response is a look full of concern. "And you're both. Still. Didn't you leave that shit behind when you punctured your fucking lung putting Twist down?"

"Guess not," Amiga says with what she hopes is a nonchalant shrug, and that's about as honest as she can get right now. To Deuce she says, “Let’s do this.”

He shoulders the prisoner again and takes him through to their tiny second room, strewn with unwanted furniture. Picking up a chair, Deuce lowers the man into it and, grabbing some ties out of his back pocket, secures his upper arms to the back and his ankles to the legs. Then he goes to stand with his back to the window, facing her.

“Staying then?”

“Yep.”

“Are you sure you want to see this?” He’s never seen this side of her before. Never seen how she can kill; the pure, aloof callousness of it, the brisk vulgarity, the *dismantlement*.

“No, but I’m doing it anyway.” He gives her the benefit of a very frank look. “Hiding this is not helpful to either of us.”

She thinks of his response to her violence before, and says, “I think hiding is more helpful than not. I should make you leave.”

“But you won’t.”

“You’ll see me differently after this.”

He sniffs. “I’ll take that chance. Just… nothing slow, okay? Don’t draw it out. I can handle you being violent, even nasty violent, but not cruel. You aren’t cruel.”

Not the answer she wanted. Whatever. It is what it is. He’ll find out. “Okay.”

Gently tapping his cheeks, Amiga encourages their prisoner to come around. Kneels down to smile upwards into his dazed eyes as they finally crank open, so he can’t avoid seeing her. The parallels with her rescue of Shock from Pill's attentive torture a few weeks ago are not lost to her, they burn and itch like a scar improperly healed. The prisoner jerks backward, scraping the chair a foot across the floor. Looks wildly around the room, locking on to Deuce like a lifeline. Deuce winces, but he doesn't look away. Shit. Whatever happens in the next however long is probably going to determine whether she leaves this room single or not.

Sighing, Amiga grabs the prisoner's chin and forces him to look at her. He's sweating buckets and she has to dig her fingers in to maintain a grip.

"I'm going to try asking nicely first, because I'm trying to be a better person," she says, not bothering to ask his name; they won't be friends. "Who's your boss?"

He spits on the floor, right by her foot.

Amiga pulls out her knife. The cheeks of the Cartel soldier tighten a touch, but he straightens. Stares. He won't shame himself by making this easy. Sucking in a breath she feels to the ends of her nerves, Amiga does what she does best and rams the tip of her blade under his kneecap, closing her ears to his screams and ignoring Deuce as he steps away from the window and shouts, near frantic. Appalled.

"Amiga! What the fuck?"

"Deuce," she says, just loud enough to be heard over the noise their prisoner is making. "Back off."

"But…"

She rounds on him furiously, grimacing as it pulls at her scar a tad too hard. "You wanted me to be *quick*. This will be quick. If you can't handle it, the door is right there."

Hurt blooms in those black eyes of his. Then hardness. "Fine. Carry on."

Amiga turns her attention back to the prisoner. With a few razor-edged gulps of air he manages to stop screaming, the whites of his eyes huge and bloodshot, his cheeks trembling with the effort of containing what must be horrific pain. She's still crouched between his knees, one hand on the handle of the knife, her palm cupped around the end. A third of the blade is buried, kneecap and gristle grating over either side of tensile steel, slick with blood.

They both feel that sensation for a moment, her on the outside, him on the inside. Then she speaks. Clearly. Calmly. In her most reasonable voice, even though nothing inside of her is reasonable any more. It's all white noise and howling, the certainty that the only certainty in her life, stood there by the window, has shifted from beneath her and the ground is roaring under her heels, preparing to give way.

"I asked nicely," she says. "Now I'm fucking insisting. You tell me why there are so many of you around up in our fucking faces, or I will rip your goddamn kneecap off."

He sniffs loudly, sucking snot back into his nose. Makes that awful *hawking* noise, and spits again. Right on her face.

Wiping the dripping mess away with her sleeve, Amiga shoves the blade in to the hilt, yanks it sideways and rips it up. He tries not to scream, his pupils blown to pits, his skin bleached grey, but it rips from him like the bloodied scale of his kneecap, flung away to rest, sawn and gushing blood on the opposite side of his knee, shaking as his body shakes. She watches it. Blinks rapidly. Will not cry. Will *not* cry. Moves to the other knee.

"Amiga."

Deuce. Pleading. Almost a moan rather than her name. He can't do this. He's going to do this. It will *wreck* them. She's never been given anything so freely as Deuce. She's never thrown anything so precious away with such reckless abandon. She can't do it again.

She rams the blade under the intact kneecap, impassive as the next wave of screaming hits her guts like an overdose of bad grease and vinegar. She needs this and hates this. What kind of fucking monster is she anyway?

It takes more than the second kneecap. Takes more than she imagined it would, because some people close off when faced with this much pain, and this guy happens to be one of them. At some point she hears the door close softly behind Deuce. Her eyes close with it. Her heart tries the same, but she stops it in its tracks. No, *damn you*, you will feel.

The prisoner begins to speak, telling her everything he knows, which isn't much—only one thing takes her by surprise. A name that rings a queasy little bell: Lucian duPont.

"*Lucian?*" She sits back on her heels. "There's a turn up."

Lucian duPont was one of Twist's *acquisitions*—useful connections he treated as friends. Lucian came in a trio—weirdest interdependent relationship she's ever witnessed. He and his two associates gave her the significant creeps. No easy task, but they were *wrong*. That's why Twist cultivated them. If that trio is in charge of the Cartel, it's no wonder the Hornets are in trouble.

She's putting the prisoner out of his misery when the first explosion sounds below. Deuce bursts into the room.

"I guess you hear we have company. We have to go. Did he talk?"

"He talked."

"Then let's move."

"We can only go out the way we came in. Those fuckers know it too."

He throws her a gun she didn't even notice he was holding. "So we fight our way out. As a team."

Olive branch. Who knew they came gun-shaped? She offers a tentative smile. He smiles back, and it's not changed, not yet, but his eyes slide uneasily around the chair, the broken puppet of man slumped upon it. Vivid and Raid can't look at Amiga yet at all. That's cool. It's fine. As long as they're all of one mind, and they are, moving fast to get through the corridors, guns at the ready, braced for the moment they run headlong into the twenty-strong crew of heavily armed Grey Cartel.

What the *fuck*? *Again*? Shock's in so much trouble when she gets back to Shandong.

This is where the Hornets excel though, poised around the corner, two each side; her and Deuce to the right, Raid and Vivid to the left, taking turns to aim small bursts of bullets. Clinical shots. They hit almost as many as she does, and just as precise. Bullets for real guns are at more of a premium than ever, but even though the Hornets are making their own, they run out faster.

They hunker in, patient. There are eleven Cartel left, with orders to what? Kill? Maim? Torture? Probably all of the above. They have to make a move soon. When they do, it's over in seconds. Groups of four rush them, guns high to fire at will. They find the Hornets and Amiga ready, coming in under their barrels with blades drawn. One on one, they take them down, use them to charge the rest, dispatching them with vicious ease.

With the way clear, Amiga laughs at Vivid. Too much relief. Both of them covered, impossibly sticky and stinking. Vivid laughs back, no more of that uneasy evasion. Raid and Deuce are there too, back in her orbit like they never left. Breathless, they exit the building and race around to the alley to jump on their bikes and cane it for Shandong.

zero dark thirty

Hunkered down on the chair like a gargoyle, her thighs aching, Maggie wades through a pile of invoices. Around her, the room resonates with a constant burr of sound, the factories around them at work. The sound never stops. Never sleeps. Becomes an integral part of consciousness, a wave thought rides in and out on, almost soothing.

On the edge of this industrial Chinese District, in one of the warehouses attached to a factory that no longer contributes to that hum, they've built a makeshift hospital. An oasis of sorts from trouble, a place to try and find a way to heal the Zeros of the Gung. They've had no luck. Zeros tend not to be lucky. Commercial fodder for Corps, Zeros DL virads into their drives to release in Slip, spreading the urge to buy useless tat no one needs. Over time the virad jingles they seed in Slip infect their speech until silence becomes impossible.

This sickness seems to be virads given new powers of infection. Jingles writing themselves under the skin in veins. Dark tangles of useless words bringing fever, organ malfunction, and silence so profound it would be unnatural even in non-Zeros. Almost all the Patient Zeros they know of in the Gung are sick now, probably the ones on the hubs too, and Mollie, her Mollie—the one who created the virads in the first place—she's sick too.

Everything ends. But not like this. Please not like this. It's all Maggie can think of. Consumes her every thought as much as the burr of factories at work. There has to be a way. If only they could find it. If only Volk, the Pharm who created Disconnect, who used it to lock the Queens in Core, could find it. But even she is helpless, and the more they try, the less they achieve. The virad sickness continues to mutate. Continues to spread. Volk has started to say there may be nothing they can do at all except watch the Zeros die.

Maggie's never given up. Not once. She's a pugilist, she can take a punch, but this… this one comes with a pre-installed glass jaw. She won't survive it.

Eddie pops his head around her office door. He's their doctor and one of her oldest friends, all the way from Tech. She looks up to receive a small smile, but he's not happy, he's trying to be comforting.

"It's Mollie, yeah?" She abandons her work, opting to talk, wanting the physicality of speech, the weight of words in the air to hang on to.

"She's unsettled again," he replies. "Distressed. I can't soothe her."

Dragging herself up from her chair, Maggie stretches

out, bones cracking and creaking. "I'll go to her." She makes to leave the room past him, but he stops her with a hand to her shoulder.

"Are *you* okay? You seem tired lately. Pale."

Eddie's all concern and means well, but this is not a conversation she's ready for. One of many conversations she has no idea how to face. "I'm fine, Eddie. It's a lot of work."

"For all of us. But…" he pauses, the turmoil plain on his face. "Are you *okay*?"

She pulls away from him. "Of course I'm not okay, Ed. The love of my life is fucking sick and I'm losing her. We know they don't get better. We know she won't. So *of course* I am not okay." She strides away, not giving him time to respond, but still hears him say, as if wondering how the hell it got to her yelling at him.

"That's not what I meant."

Maggie knows what he means. She can't think about it. The only response is denial. She tugs at her sleeves, making sure they cover her right to the end of her wrists, refusing to acknowledge the livid shape of her veins, risen up too close to the surface. Risen remarkably like the Zeros' have. But she is not a Zero. She's not sick. It's impossible.

Mollie's room in this ancient, crumbling warehouse is an old tower unit. Fuck knows what it was used for back when—these factories and their warehouses are as old as the Gung, maybe older. Maybe a remnant from before the breaking. Whatever it was, the height of the tower, the lack of sunlight, is everything Mollie needs for comfort in her augmented state.

Augmented. Ridiculous to use the term for Mollie—she's so completely herself. Maggie can't imagine her any other way. Before she was Agen-Z, before she was Mother Zero, Mollie was a performer in a circus burlesque. They called her The Neon Angel. She's an angel still. She'll be up there in the rafters, twisting improbable gymnastics in her own wires, her tattoos glowing in the dark. A legend. Always.

Maggie struggles to find air. To find balance. Her whole world is slipping through her hands. And in her gut, small and hard and ugly, the knot of fear tightens and grows. Absently, she scratches at the crease of her elbow, the thin skin drawing ever thinner. Changing. Chasing translucence. She'd hardly known what to think when she first saw it. Maggie isn't a Zero, so how could it be? Undeniably though, it is.

Everything she loves is dying, and now, so is she.

Coming out of the Cad, that last year of too much throttle and noise, wrapped as it was in GarGoil gigs, finals and the inexorable slide toward the flash of red letters, this was not the life Maggie imagined for herself. Nothing her mind was capable of conjuring at that point, no matter how extraordinary, could even have come close. The one thing she knew for certain, was that she would Fail. She wanted to.

The GarGoils were born out of frustration with the system, a horror with how some set against it might work so hard to fit in just to have a Pass, to give up free thinking for the WAMOS life. And with an irony Maggie could not have predicted, that's how the GarGoils themselves came to an end. Before the year of their reign of the B-Movie nightclubs was up, two of their girls fought to fit in, to hide their light, to quash their minds and squeeze thought into a box, suffocate it of air, and succeeded, taking down the GarGoils with them.

Maggie didn't expect to become a legend herself from that short time, but somehow she did, they all did—they became the voice of a generation who sold it for scrap. That old bastard Saint Jimmy taking their fame, like a corvid stealing jewels, and warping it. Ten months of political power-housing on stage transformed into a circus side show, a roundabout of tribute as tacky money-spinner, slick and unreal as a K-drama.

In that first year of the GarGoils reborn, Maggie watched with horror and outrage the death of everything she believed in and understood then that this is how it's done. This is how they take your fight, your beliefs, your rage, your power, and crush it. Use it against you. They commodify it, commodify *you*; strip you of meaning. And sometimes it's not even intentional. Sometimes it's just some devious old fucker looking to make a mint on the back of your success as he perceives it through a warped comprehension of reality.

She joined the Movement that year, a desperate attempt to reclaim herself from the mockery made of her anger, sick to her stomach and disillusioned. Barely surviving. To her mind, joining the Movement was an end. She expected to fight to the death. Relished the notion. She was done with sitting back and allowing life to fuck her. She wanted to pick her own way out. Go down fighting. She didn't understand then that when you seek to end things in that fashion, what you might find instead is a beginning. A fresh start. The rehabilitation of a belief system and an introduction to the people who'll make up a true family. Not the GarGoils after all, but a bunch of J-Hacks fighting tooth and nail for freedom, whatever it might mean.

Meeting Mollie came years later. Almost five. At a point when Maggie was deep enough in the Movement to be trusted in the presence of the people at its heart. That day is crystalline in her memory. Colourful as a butterfly, drifting on an ocean of virad junk, strong and fragile and exquisite, Mollie hit her like the all-consuming glare of stage lights, like the roar of a crowd, the addictive crawl of music in a ribcage. She was hooked in an instant. Free falling. And falling in love with her felt inevitable. But Maggie never expected for a second to be loved in return, never once imagined she'd be gifted the heart of a creature so peculiar and wonderful. That was miraculous. It still is.

Even now, when everything she loves is falling to ruins around her, that miracle stands strong. She should be overjoyed that it happened at all, instead she finds herself eaten alive by rage.

Maggie yearns to take this virus in her hands and choke the life from it. Crush it to component codes and drop its components so far apart in Slip they drift eternally too distant from each other to ever be whole again. Instead, she finds her Mollie as she always does. Clings to what's left, knowing it will slip through her fingers, no matter how tight her grip.

Slung in graceful disarray halfway down the tower tonight, Mollie glows as always, illuminating the walls and ceiling in odd shapes and patterns. She's a constellation in human form, but the gleam of her flesh is transparent around the neon tattoos; veins worryingly prominent and mirrored now with the selfsame hieroglyphs as the veins on the other Zeros. Meaningless nonsense. Or it used to be.

Where curlicues of ropey vein once spelt nothing but gibberish, row upon row of letters have taken precedence. Zees. Staring at them, Maggie's consumed once more by inelegant rage. Wants to reach up and wipe them clear. Not Zee for Zero. Zee for Zen. Zenada. She dreams that name night after night. Whispers building in the corner. Rushing toward her. It fills her with as much dread as her Mollie being sick, as the new transparency of her own skin.

She's convinced Zenada is the author of Mollie's distress, haranguing her in dreams. Mollie's dreaming again now, her fingers reaching for something, spread and straining. Trembling. She cries out. Soft, inarticulate sounds of distress that tear at Maggie's heart. She runs lightly up the rungs of the ladder placed beneath Mollie's dangling body to capture Mollie's hand within her own, rubbing it between them to take the chill away, to loosen the horrendous tension.

Looks up to find Mollie's buttercup eyes watching her, drenched with despair and pleading.

"Hey," she says, reaching up to cup Mollie's face. "Hey. It's okay. It's okay, love."

Mollie blinks in such slow motion, Maggie could count each separate lash as they sweep up. She opens her mouth, puffs air sounds, like a child learning to speak. She hasn't spoken out loud in years. Only IM, and even then with trouble. When they come, the words are like the whispers in Maggie's dreams, a syrup of syllables colliding.

"FiiiinnndZeeeeeeeen."

Maggie sobs. Leaning in, she presses her forehead to Mollie's. "No." If a word could form to action, she would send it to cleanse Mollie of harm. Wipe Zen from her body, her mind, her dreams. "No. No finding Zen. Not her. Shhh. Shhh. It's okay. We're okay."

"FiiindZeeeeen," Mollie moans again, and Maggie begins to properly cry. Helpless. Hopeless. Because no sickness in the universe is terrible enough for her to give in to this request. To follow the directive of her dreams, no matter how insistent.

Not even if they follow her into waking and speak through the mouth of the one she loves.

hu hai abandoned

Having managed the feat for just over a week now, Hu Hai has settled upon the perfect description for carrying Aunty Dong around in his head: torture. Sheer. Mental. Torture. He's positive the old hag is peering out through his eyes. Is, in fact, nervous of looking in the mirror these days, which accounts for the scraggly beard taking up residence upon his face. He's not sure whether he likes it or not.

On the one hand, his weak chin is well and truly hidden from sight, which makes him feel oddly powerful. On the other hand, he's certain he looks more like a tramp every day. And his wife hates it. To the extent that she's been threatening to leave if it's not either a) trimmed or b) clean shaven ASAP. He's explained about Dong and mirrors but his wife is like her mother, a woman of little sympathy.

The only way he's found to effectively handle the proverbial Dong weight in his neural drive is to attack the surrounding mass of grey with baijiu. Oddly, his wife is not particularly pleased about that either. He recalls something quite sharp and bitter being said about money for baijiu being useful for a barber before he passed out last night, or was it the night before? Staggering out of bed, he all but tumbles into the shower, his mouth tasting like the scum residue on a pot of bone stock.

Five minutes later, clean but no less filthy somehow, he makes his way to the kitchen and falls into a bowl of congee. Congealed. The dense silence of the house makes itself known gradually through the subtle jackhammer of his hangover headache. Becomes deafening. A pressure in his ears similar to that of diving too deep into a pool too fast. Eyes still heavy and stinging he scans the kitchen for clues.

First clue: his wife is not here. Highly unusual; the kitchen is her domain. Second: the note on the fridge, held with that magnet she bought on Lijiang Hub when they visited his family, the one of a happy mountain with "Welcome to Lijiang" written across the bottom in red kanji. He hates that magnet. Threw it into the bin seventeen times only to find it front and centre on the fridge. Subtle his wife is not.

Tugging the note from beneath, he tries to read her kanji. She has chicken scratch hand made worse by impatience or rage and it would appear this note was written with a healthy dose of both. The general gist turns out to be the culmination of several weeks' worth of threats: *I'm off to my mother's. There's a week's worth of food in the freezer, mostly dumplings because it's not like I'm your damn chef. Think about shaving and drying out, I love you.*

Even in desertion she's trying to make him fat.

He grabs at his belly. Sighs. Scratches his balls. Thinks about getting dressed, or maybe drinking some more. He's about to grab out a couple of frozen dumplings and use them as some form of half-assed decision-making tool when the burden of Dong lands in his drive, emanating way too much cheerful energy for him to cope with. Gāi sǐ. How is the old bitch even awake? It's nigh on three A.M on Hong Kong Hub right now. This confirms his secret conviction that she's not a woman at all but a yaoguai in disguise.

Hu Hai! she all but trills, a drill bit of words churning gaping holes, his headache set to hit terminal in two point three seconds.

Immediately he wishes that ten hours ago he'd had the foresight to quit at two cups. Sadly for him, those three bottles he eventually chugged away without a hint of pity or thought for his future self are now fighting to make a titanic reappearance all over the kitchen table. Hu Hai holds on to his gag reflex for grim death; he'll be damned if he'll allow all that flim to go to waste.

Aunty Dong. Good morning. Instead of this rigid politeness, he wants to scream. Yell. Stamp his feet. But he likes having feet, and lungs, and lips. Being rude to Aunty Dong is a sure fire way to lose all of them. Slowly.

Good morning, dear. Now, what are our plans for today? I presume after all this time we're making some *progress?* Under the cheer hides an edge of steel. His head on the block. And for the thousandth time he curses his luck for pulling this assignment in particular. All things she could have asked of him and she asks for *this*. He bites back a groan.

He's been dreading report time as much as he dreads waking to the inevitability of her arrival in his drive, as much as he's been wishing he'd never sought to impress Dong with his stupid bloody over-capable planning skills in the first place. Wishing he'd stayed anonymous amongst the suits of the Gung-based businesses she inherited when Li and Ho died. But oh no, he had to go and think of promotions and pay rises and gone out of his way to be noticed, to be *special*. He's an idiot. He was never made to be anything more than a salaryman, but she's made him her puppet. Put him in charge of thugs, thieves and liars.

He hates her. He hates this. He's terrified of failing.

He'd give anything to burn the path from her drive to his, to stop her almost obsessive need to micro-manage. What's worse? Her expectations or her inability to let him get on with it? Both. Everything. Fuck. To think that four weeks ago his worst day was one in which his wife, resentful of his long work hours and his commitment to leisure time with his friends, playing cards and watching soccer, would treat him to thin-lipped silence and bitter-brewed tea.

Almost four weeks of scouring the Gung has produced not one single match to the Hornets or the Haunt, not even with a physical stats program written by Aunty's best Tech. Seven hundred square miles makes for a big haystack. Which is why he's taken not only to drinking but to gambling on the pricking of his gut. If this hunch he's had is wrong, he won't need to shave ever again.

I moved all the teams to Hunin district.

You have reason to believe they might be in Hunin? There's a heaving dose of scepticism in there. Hunin's a terrible place to hide and she'd be aware of that. It's only a tiny leap from that to guessing he's going on his gut. He's so screwed.

Swallowing again and feeling quite heroic to have so much control over his heaving stomach, Hu Hai gives the response he's been practising since yesterday. *Not Hunin. Not a great place to hide. Only the clubs and the cage apartments shoved cheek to jowl with families of ten and up. Never a greater advertisement for the use of a condom. Probably a single one considering the median earning rate of a Hunin desperado. I think Shandong.*

If Hu Hai were on the run and looking to find the one place in all of the Gung where trouble won't immediately follow or enemies seek to look, he'd choose the far off farms of Shandong. Simple logic. Mountains not only make steep and winding roads, easy to keep an eye on, they also block invading signals from the outside, and Dong's not the only one after them. They're hot property amongst several hub notorieties and they'll be aware of it, or they aren't the scary competent bunch of kids who somehow took down the Queens, Fulcrum, and the Gung with them.

Aunty Dong hums, ignoring his attempt at humour. *Interesting. Mountains would make sense, but not habitable, unless they've bribed a holding to conceal them. I have eyes there as you well know, and no reports.*

They're resourceful.

Granted. However, if Shandong it is, why are you in Hunin?

The same reason they're in Shandong, Aunty. Searching Shandong is next to impossible without them seeing us coming. So we wait in Hunin for them to come to blow off steam. They're young. They'll come to party, and then I'll follow them home.

Excellent. Don't disappoint me, Hu Hai.

Never, Aunty Dong. What are we doing with the Haunt? Killing?

She pokes his IM hard, causing a ripple effect that makes him heave violently, barely holding on to breakfast and booze both. *No, fool. I might want the Haunt dead, but I have uses for him beforehand. Nothing like holding the most valuable chess piece on the board, is there?*

No, Aunty Dong.

Now do clean up and quit moping, or I'll be forced to have you cold cured. You're an absolute disgrace. I've sent flowers to your wife. I've advised her to divorce you and given her the IM of my lawyer.

Aunty Dong!

Her silence is momentary but ominous. *Yes, Hu Hai?*

He gulps hard. *My apologies. You're right. I will do better.*

Do your best.

Yes, Aunty Dong.

There's a good boy. Chop, chop now, no time to waste.

home again, home again...

The Western edge of Shandong: bridges clasp ranges together across white-flecked waters. All the paddy-rises are here, the centre of the food industry, their staggered paddy-field balconies growing rice and vegetables and fruit; grazing meat stock or flocking with multi-coloured arrays of poultry. Anything grown or reared comes from these huge, unnatural galleries and sells for extortionate prices. Only the wealthy can afford produce from Shandong; everyone else eats food grown or synthesized on the Chinese hubs.

The largest paddy-rise grows rice in shimmering expanses of water on the upper and middle balconies and rears pork on the lowest—thousands of pigs splayed indolently out in the sunshine, their sides smeared with mud. It belongs to the Zhangs, otherwise known as the Harmonys—once one of the most feared crime families on the Gung.

Behind the vast balconies of bright-green rice spears are five levels of penthouses, the decadent legacy of generations of crime and commerce, inherited and then abandoned by Li and Ho Harmony, who had no interest in farming except where it intersected the slaughter of animals. Or people.

This farm has been Gail's home for years. An ex-WAMOS turned J-Hack, he came to work here at Breaker's behest, hid his affiliations from the Harmonys for years, right up until they died in spectacular fashion four weeks ago. Now, despite Breaker's death and the Movement being all but gone, he continues the work he came here for, hiding his affiliations from Aunty Dong, who graciously stepped in to run the farm, mainly to cut off her brothers and sisters and their children. In J-Hack terms, Gail acts as a double-agent, sitting inside criminal networks feeding vital information to J-Hacks to keep them safe and give them a heads-up on the best work going amongst criminals.

His life is always in danger, and no more so than now.

Hiding the Hornets is a death sentence for him, but he doesn't care. These kids are amazing—what they've done, what they've risked for the Gung. He's come to regard them as family, and he knows they feel the same. He's nothing but glad that he jumped on the notion of hiding them here the second he heard they wanted to ask it. Hiding in plain sight is often the best tactic, and even though the most anxious member of the Hornets, Wi Ji Lin, or Knee Jerk, likes to call it "fucking stupidity", they're perfectly safe here. Gail makes certain of it.

Tall, skinny and nervy, like some kind of oriental greyhound, KJ rolls into the kitchen, yawning and scratching his head, a full on bed-head masterpiece of bold angles and tats, a tiny gold angler fish, unspeakably ugly, resting on his shoulder, its lure bobbing as he walks. Moving with a sinuous ease at odds with his lanky body, he slides on to a breakfast stool as if his legs are about to give out and jumps over a foot in the air when Gail pops a plate down in front of him.

"Easy, Knee Jerk. It's just breakfast." After four weeks of his company Gail knows by now that KJ is always in flight mode. He's also always in snark-mode, and grump-mode, and suspicion-mode. It's rather endearing.

"Breakfast?" KJ pokes at his boiled egg. "This is food?"

Going to the coffee machine to fix a fresh batch, Gail rolls his eyes. "Real food as a matter of fact. An actual egg from an actual hen. Fresh too. I got them from the Seng family in exchange for rice and pork."

KJ makes a face. Casually pushes the plate away like it's holding a grenade. "You bartered?"

"Of course."

"But you're all rich, right?"

Gail stares, because there's no way he just heard that. Has KJ paid no attention at all in the past few weeks? "Are you serious? No. This penthouse is a perk, dude. I only live here because when Li and Ho left, they told me to. I used to live in the farmhand levels."

"Li and Ho *lived* here?"

"Sure."

KJ's hand rises to the remains of his ear. On the left side, all he has is a nub, huddled under tangled hair. The fish moves up to hide it and KJ smiles, running a finger over the curve of its ridged back, glints sparking off his fingernail as it glides through golden skin.

"She used to talk about the pigs almost every time she killed," he says, surprisingly calm now. Gail's avatar does that too. It was uncomfortable at first, now he's relieved that there's something in the world that simply *knows* him, without ever having to be told.

Nodding, Gail says quietly, "Caught her gutting a litter of piglets once, just for shits and giggles, Ho watching by the door in that way of his. Vacant. Pretending to be stupid. Thick as thieves those two, but she still pushed him off the top balcony when they were eleven. Fifty feet, face first into what used to be the pig pens. They swapped the top to rice after that, just in case—I mean pigs eat anything, right? I think Ho lived to spite her. He definitely got the plastic surgery to spite her, making him the prettiest twin. But people would see how they were together and call it love, not understanding a damn thing. No love lost there. They wouldn't have known how. So why'd she cut your ear off? Did she *have* a reason?"

"I wanted to quit working for them."

Gail's mouth drops open. "And you're alive?"

"I cried," KJ says simply, and it explains everything. Gail understands. He knew Li. "She licked the tears off my face and maimed me to make more." KJ lifts his shirt, revealing a churn of ruined flesh hiding beneath.

Gail winces. Now he understands the nerves in this skinny, snarky young man too. "Fuck me. Sorry."

KJ drops his shirt, shrugs and pulls the egg back

toward him to poke at it some more. He dips his knife in the yolk and licks it. "That's quite nice. Tastes like egg. When'd they inherit this place?"

"Age twelve. Their father, An, was assassinated. Cleaner by the name of Mickey Stix, had a good rep, not quite up to your Amiga's standard, but good. They found Stix a week later, skinned alive and nailed upside down to the side of a mono tower, fucking hundreds of feet off the ground, like they flew him there. Had a note nailed to his chest: Kindly dispose of our trash. Yours truly, The Harmonys."

Taking a big bite of his egg, smeared haphazardly on a slice of toast, KJ looks impressed. "You're trying to slide it by me that Li and Ho hired Stix to kill An and then killed Stix so they wouldn't have to pay?"

Gail lifts a shoulder. "Yeah. Kang, An's brother, wanted to inherit, but the farm and business went to them. He thought two twelve-year-olds would be easy pickings, despite what they were."

"They kill him?"

"Nah, he's still alive to a degree. They killed his kids. Dropped them from the hubs. Left their remains splashed on the ocean ranges like so much dyed bird shit."

"And you're sheltering us with that crazy ass family hanging over your head? Man." KJ wiggles his toast. "You're nuts."

"Not so much. I'm used to a double life, and seriously, the rest of the family, they stay away; they're too scared of Dong to come here and she never would. I never see her, just like I never saw Li and Ho once they grew up. I can't believe Li and Ho are finally dead to be honest." Awed, slightly afraid, Gail looks out toward the terrace, to the distant figure of Shock Pao, perched cross-legged right on the edge. "Can't believe *he* killed them. The how of it. It's crazy."

KJ snorts. "*All* of this is crazy. Feels like we walked through hell only to find that the only thing beyond hell is *more* hell. I'm the first to admit I'm a walking panic attack, but I have *never* been scared like this, not even when Li ripped my shirt off and her eyes went almost fucking *gentle* before she started carving chunks from my fucking chest."

"That's one hell of a lot of scared," Gail says.

"Yeah," KJ admits, with a wry smile. "But if you'd seen what I've seen, you'd be there too."

"You been looking in the mirror again, Knee Jerk?"

Cool and amused, Amiga strolls in and over to the coffee machine, snatching the biggest mug available. She's filthy, her under-eyes delicately stained with exhaustion and the flake of drying haemoglobin, a dirty red-brown on tawny skin. There's a cut on her forearm, a bruise on her cheek, but her eyes are like fire, the kind that *boils*, consumes, a tornado of hungry flames.

That look gives Gail horrid creepy little shivers from toes to follicles. Li and Ho never had that look, they were ice and empty and this skin-withering curiosity, the kind you want to run from forever. What's in Amiga's eyes is harder to handle. Too much life and soul, too much heart, heat and murder. She's full up of all the good human things, and still she's a stone-cold killer.

KJ's avatar flares gold. Outrage. KJ flips her the bird with both hands and snaps, "Oh haha, *bitch*."

She snorts a laugh. "Jokes. You're gorgeous. A regular Van Gogh."

"Very. Fucking. Funny."

"What can I say? I'm gifted." She sips her coffee, gaze shifting out to Shock on the terrace. "He been there long?"

"I don't know. Maybe all night, maybe not."

"I need to talk to him." Amiga makes another cup of coffee, as big as hers.

"That's your disapproving voice," KJ notes. "Problems in paradise?"

Halfway out of the terrace doors already, Amiga stops, offers a quirk of a smile that perhaps reaches her eyes enough to bank the fires boiling there; it's too close to call for Gail. He finds everything she does unnerving. "Matter of fact there are. Our resident godhead has some explaining to do. Quite a fucking bit."

Wrung out to fuck, Shock's drifting in Slip, fingertips swirling into sparks of light, when the presence brushes his body IRL. He rises up just enough to look out of his eyes. Amiga's squinting at him in the bright morning sun, haloed like an angel, holding up coffee like a white flag. Interesting, because the last thing in her face is surrender.

"Give me blue eyes, not gold," she says. "We need to talk."

Sliding out into his body is exactly like coming out of the water after swimming, the loss of buoyancy, the weight of flesh dragging you down.

Blinking sleepily, a touch drained, he takes the coffee

and salutes her with it. "This an offering before you kill me?"

"You guessed, huh?" Amiga says, throwing herself down next to him, cross-legged, oblivious of the sheer drop inches from her knee caps. "I'm losing my edge here."

He sniffs, looking down. "No, I'd say you were right on it."

"This is nothing. I'm safer up here than in my own head," she replies.

"Amen to that."

Clinking cups, they drink quietly for a while, knees touching, breathing in sync.

The view from the terrace jumps into the lungs, snatching air like a thief. All that sun and mountain and steel, glass reflecting sky into infinity, reflecting peaks into warps and jags, making them bizarre as fairground reflections. Too much light and colour. Too much *air*. Thin and bright and fresh, so fucking fresh it's like breathing ice vapour. That invigorating. That painfully sharp. The lungs dizzy under the influence.

Air makes you tipsy up here. Delirious and foolish, a sloppy grin of startling flesh laid over loose bones. They find themselves holding in lungfuls just to see how lightheaded they can get. Giggling on the out breath. Sipping too-hot coffee and just *existing*. Every moment should be like this. Life should be like this. Easy. Free. Uncomplicated.

But in the end, like always, they have to break the moment. Abandon it. Shock leaves that to Amiga, because she has more courage than him. Or maybe because she's more capable of savagery. She surprises him by coming in on a tangent.

"Any word from Maggie on EVaC?"

The Hornets' resident Patient Zero, EVaC's been in the care of Mollie and Maggie from before all the hell with the Queens walking on the Gung went down. The Hornets didn't get to see him again to say goodbye—not that he'd have been compos mentis enough to hear or respond, ill as he is with the same sickness a number of other Patient Zeros' contracted. A sickness none of them, not even Mother Zero, really understands.

All they have of him right now is whatever Shock can glean from Maggie the few times she'll allow him access on an IM band tight enough to leave permanent headaches. Amiga obviously wants good news. He hates to burst bubbles, but all he's got here is pins.

"He's the same. They all arc. Mother Zero is working on it."

"As ever."

"Yup."

"So. I tortured a Cartel minion a little bit."

"A little bit?"

She cocks him a lopsided grin. "Fine. It was... bad. But he held out. I didn't expect him to hold out." Her jaw tightens. "Deuce saw."

Shock groans, they've talked about how terrified she is of the inevitability of getting it wrong, of how she knows for a fact that this is not a forever thing. These are not admissions she can make to Deuce. He wouldn't understand, especially not now she's let him choose what happens instead of choosing for him, even though she knows where that goes, because he's special and all she'll do in the end is reduce him to rubble. She's told Shock all of this because he *does* understand.

He's like her. What he is precludes him from normality. Functionality. He makes dangerous connections, unhealthy ones. Only knows how to hurt and be hurt. Close scares him. Comfort scares him. Love fucking petrifies him. He wouldn't know how not to Frankenstein love into some form of re-hashed and twisted dependence perfectly primed for destruction. He knows how *ugly* alone gets when it tangles up into lonely, hurt, broken and *angry*.

"How the holy fuck did you allow that to happen, Amiga?"

"He wouldn't leave."

"Shit. Perfect Deuce being perfect. My admiration verges on hero worship these days. I may have a crush."

Elbowing him hard in the ribs, she chokes out a laugh too close to the sound of coming undone, but the relief in her eyes is extraordinary. "I hate you."

He throws an arm around her shoulders. "Nope," he says, fully confident of this at least. "You don't." She reaches up to squeeze his fingers before he pulls away and steers her back to the inevitable moment she mentions his failure to warn them of incoming Cartel. "So. Torture?"

"Got a name. One I know. One I don't like one little bit."

"Hit me."

"Don't tempt me." She gives him the side stank eye. Oh he really *is* in trouble. "Lucian duPont."

That hits like a hub falling out of orbit on to his sorry skull. "No."

"Heard of him?"

"Of course. Worked for him and his… I dunno what the hell you'd call them. One's his girlfriend or something and an Archie."

Amiga groans. "That bitch is an Archie?" Archies are forensic Archaeologists, sifting data. They can find anyone or anything given enough time—except Haunts.

"Yeah, and she's fucking good. The other's Nigerian, yeah?"

"Yeah, and huge. Like a mountain. Like Petrie."

"That's the one. They're very not good fun to work for."

"One of your disgruntled customers?"

He rolls his eyes. "I literally only pissed off Li and Ho, Twist and Yan."

"*Only*, he says," she drawls, mocking hard. "There's no only in the universe vast enough to cover that."

"Maybe. But duPont was just a job. A bad job."

Amiga shakes her head. "Any idea which hub then? Because they were in with Twist but all I have on them is a single brief sighting at his home and the pricking of my thumbs."

"Nope. They had no connection to the Cartel then, at least as far as I knew. I can look. It's easier to trace with a name, even though that Archie slash girlfriend of his has nailed the art of Archaeology in reverse, meaning they'll be hard to trace."

Amiga groans. "That's all we fucking need." She places her coffee down and turns to face him. The cold look is back. "So now we've talked Cartel, let's talk Cartel. Or rather, your failure to inform us the Cartel were on our fucking tail *yet again*. Where the fuck were you?"

Words. He needs words. Excuses. There are none. Fact is, he found the ones she needed to hunt and then went back to the mountainside.

"I wasn't around. I should have been. Sorry. It won't happen again."

"It won't. Or as much as I love you I'll finish what Pill started. Get me?" She's deadly serious. Of course she is. That was their lives he left hanging in the balance.

"You know I do."

Her eyes narrow on him. Oh she's too perceptive, all sharp edges and smarts, just like Puss. "What's going on with you, Shock?"

He stares down at his coffee for a moment. "Remember how they used to say to us at Tech that if there weren't VA in the system that those of us in the one percent and up scale could be gods in there?"

At its highest, most complex levels, only the best of one percent and up can hack VA, Virtual Armament, the security of Slip. But even the best of the best can't crack all of it—not when it incorporates bio-ware and constantly morphing passwords as complex as fractals. It doesn't stop Shock for very long any more. Nothing much does.

"I do. Used to piss me off. Like the rest of us were crap or something."

He looks at her, letting her see his fear naked and unconfined. "They weren't wrong. They weren't saying *enough*. I don't think they really grokked hard what godlike means in there. What it might mean if in there and out here get to be indistinguishable."

"And?" She looks unsurprised. Trust her to have insight. She knows all about how bad shit gets in the shadows of things.

"Let's just say I'm having issues."

"Shit, Shock. Join the club, innit. Can you keep a handle on it so we don't all get fucking killed?"

That pisses him off. "Can you?"

"Like I have a choice," she says, and there's a raw sort of resignation in it that hurts to hear.

Silence swallows them again. They sit and finish their coffee. Breathe cold air. Shore each other up without words, with only the touch of knees, the smallest of connections, still there for each other despite harsh words and dire promises.

"I'll go in and look for duPont and his dynamic duo," he says when there's nothing left to drink, to say.

"If you find anything…"

"I'll IM you. I'll be gentle."

Amiga punches his shoulder. "Damn right you will, Shock Pao. You pull the kind of shit on me you pull on Deuce and I'll drop you from this ledge faster than Li dropped Ho."

"Or Ho dropped Li?" he says, finally smiling, thinking of those moments before the Queens got out, when he severed Li's connection to her avatar and Ho compounded it by pushing her off the top of the Heights.

She snorts into laughter. "Oh now that was *bitchy*."

He grins. "Yes. Yes it was. Now fuck off and let me concentrate."

hostile takeover

At the heart of Foon Gung, the inner city is a *diadema setosum* set amongst lesser urchins. A priapic surge of architecture rising higher and higher until it culminates in the triple threat of the Heights, the Needle and the Spine, so vast their tops come perilously close to the low orbit of hubs. Four weeks on from the events leading to the fall of Fulcrum, the fall of the Harmonys, the Heights still bears the marks of the damage it accrued—a delicate splay of black scaffold clinging to its crown like spider's web.

With no Lakatoses and no money, it will remain as an unwelcome reminder for the residents of the Heights of dark times they can no longer recall, the lack of memory almost as disturbing as the sudden chasm of power, the subtle struggle of the WAMOS against the system built to contain them.

In times such as these, even a fortress fit for gods feels unsafe. Conquerable.

Parallel to the Heights, across the vast grey swathe of glistening concrete courtyard set with statues and fountains, the Needle strikes into the sky sharp and arrogant, fit to stitch darkness to daytime, vicious in cool cream stone marbled with white streaks of quartz. They could be brothers, the Heights and the Needle, fraternal twins—tall and clean and cold, one conservative in its lines the other sharp-suited; old blood and old money clothed in detachment, in easy superiority.

The third giant, resting between them, separating them, is more the changeling child. The interloper. The Spine is a sinister rise of sinuous ink, like dark roots wound to the heavens in black, unfeeling coils, a sleeping dragon frozen to black carbon by the ravage of time. It leers and looms, casts nothing but shadows. Clothed in black glass that swallows any hint of light from its interior, the Spine absorbs light. Sneaks into night as if bleeding that very darkness into the sky.

In a boardroom on one of the topmost floors, the lights are all on for a late-night meeting. Titans vying over the vacuum left by Fulcrum, fruitlessly chasing the Haunt who holds the key to Slip in his head. With him lost to the wind, they've turned to each other, uneasy but too desperate to stop, circling and scheming to create power alliances big enough to claim the world.

Ranged around the table dominating the room, the boards of Olbax and Veritas have reached critical mass in their merger negotiations and tablets are going round the room for all parties to sign, formally rendering the companies a singular, powerful entity. A MegaCorp. Outside the boardroom, not visible to those within, stands a peculiarly silent trio, all dressed to the nines.

At their forefront is a tall blond man wrapped in a silver-grey suit. He's the embodiment of the Needle rather than the Spine. Slender and sleek. Pale and exquisite. Aristocratic. Almost pretty except for the pale silver of his eyes, simmering like molten lead. The tightly wound energy radiating from his shoulders speaking eloquently of irritation.

Behind his left shoulder stands a tall Nigerian man with a regal bearing. He has the aura of a lawyer: calculation and razor-sharp cunning. Dressed in an almost identical suit, livened by a violet silk tie, he's a full head taller and his choleric gaze assesses. Seeks shadows. Finds secrets within them to hoard and abuse.

Barely reaching the blond man's right shoulder is a woman. A lush explosion of fleshy curves wrapped in a silken red dress and killer heels, she looks like a powder keg. Combustible. All fury and wild pleasure in snapping eyes the colour of old whisky.

Lucian duPont, Iyawa Fashola and Jessamine Amsel. They were not invited but here they are—drawn to wealth like lions to prey. There's so much obscene wealth in that one room it takes their breath away, despite being raised in wealth themselves. What's most delightful here, however, is this banquet of innocents, all trussed in hundred-thousand-flim suits and shoes. Served up all unknowing and so very delicious.

Lucian licks his lips. Jessamine touches the tip of a nail to his tongue as it swipes across, a sharp pinprick of pain.

He nips at the nail. She chuckles.

"You had dinner."

"Always hungry for you, petal."

"Hungry for this too?"

"*Starved.*"

She smiles, eye teeth on show. "Then let's eat. Iyawa?"

"My dear?"

"After you."

Iyawa opens the door and they enter, moving to take the seats left strategically empty for them by the building staff. They've planned this moment meticulously since learning that Olbax and Veritas planned to meet here at the Spine to formally seal their merger. The staff of the Spine's hire floor belongs to them—bought off or blackmailed—to make sure things would be as they needed them.

Everyone in this boardroom knows who they are, and knows to be afraid. This pleases them.

Nonetheless, Karl Eber, Chairman of the board of Olbax surges to his feet, sputtering with the sort of outrage only a member of the elite could express when in this much danger, a muted horror that anyone would *dare*. His face is a peculiar palette of reds and whites—shock fighting affront, rage warring with stark fear.

"What is the meaning of this!"

Tilting his head, Lucian replies casually, "We thought we'd sit in for this somewhat historic occasion."

"You have no right to be here."

Lucian examines his fingernails. "You know me, Karl. I like to stick my nose in where it's not wanted."

"Then kindly remove it." The speaker is Esme Carstairs of Veritas. Ancient. Aristocratic as Lucian. Scornful. "I knew you as a child, Lucian. You're nothing but a brat with too much money and too little discipline, and if rumours hold true, you're now no more than criminal filth. We are done here. You may leave." Her confidence is extraordinary. Absolute. It's obvious she cannot believe that this situation is real. How could it be?

Lucian begins to laugh. Hyena howls. Loud and unrepentant. One hand slapping the table, the other clutched to his belly. His face is beautiful. Joyful. Genuine. Jessamine's mouth twitches. No one sees her hand move, but there's a soft thud and Esme's impaled against warm leather, her neck dented and collapsed around the sharpened end of a steel kubotan.

The brash silver looks almost comical there in the ruins of her throat, sending thick gouts of crimson to rage up and over her face, her pristine jacket and shirt. This does not happen in a boardroom, categorically, and no one reacts, unable to process, giving the trio the time they were expecting.

They take it without hesitation. Lucian and Iyawa move in absolute accord to slam holes into the necks of those sat closest to them. Lucian still chuckling as if unable to stop. Iyawa all business, his cuffs pulled back, fastidious, his feet dancing away from the blood whilst Lucian splashes through it all, deranged and gleaming.

Down one kubotan, Jessamine half rises, breathing calm and quiet. Spins on her delicate heels. Halfway out of his seat, terror finally igniting movement, the Olbax board member to the right takes the sharpened steel point in three arteries. The left gets it so deep into his eyeball Jess has to yank hard to pull it out.

Three arteries slumps back into his seat, trying to stem three flows at once and failing, his hands becoming clumsy almost immediately. To his right, eyeball is trying to scream. Spewing blood and vitreous humour down his cheek he manages only stuttering, wet gurgles of nonsense sound before going into some sort of fit and hitting the floor hard, spattering blood everywhere. Jess places a heel on the back of his head. Unable to move, he slowly drowns, strangled gurgling fading to a high-pitched wheeze and then nothing.

The room is thick with the stench of blood. Piss. Fear. Enough to make her smile. Removing her heel, Jess strolls toward the rest, and they rush away from her, a riptide of white-faced dread, scrambling to open the door, unaware that it's locked. In no rush at all, Jess reaches out to snatch the prim chignon of a Veritas member, silky red hair held up by diamond pins. Yanks her back hard, ignoring the pain of pins in her palm, the choked-off scream bursting from the woman's throat.

"Where are you going, lovely?" she asks softly, licking the porcelain curve of her ear, pressing the sharp end of the kubotan into the warm thud of the pulse-point inches below a millimetre at a time. The sound the woman makes is exquisite—the squeal of a small animal caught in sharp jaws. Her blood is warm. Thick. It oozes first and then bursts out in a flood as the kubotan pierces the jugular.

Jess catches a drop on her tongue. The taste is copper and salt and sour. Dropping the woman to the floor, she forgets her immediately. Strolls on to the next, laughing breathlessly, catching Iyawa's eye as he slams both kubotans into the back of a dark-suited man from Olbax. They smile together. Feral. This is real business. Tooth and claw. Blood and screams.

"What is this?" screams the CEO of Olbax, Lance Oliver, Lucian's palm clamped under his chin, long fingers flexing around his Adam's apple, his other hand floating in front of Lance's left eye, kubotan out.

"I would have thought that was obvious," Lucian drawls in his ear, oh so very slowly pressing the point of the kubotan into his eye, licking his lips as the eyeball pops and gushes. "A hostile takeover."

Lucian holds the Olbax CEO like a lover until his last breath flutters out, soft as a whisper. Lifting him, he drapes him over the end of the table, posing his limbs. Something Bacchanalian. Classical. Steps back to admire his work, casually flicking the tip of the kubotan buried deep in Lance's eye socket to vibrate it a touch before taking a languid seat. He cocks a finger at Jess, who slides into his lap, playing with his tie. Iyawa props an arse cheek on the edge of the table.

"I feel better," Lucian says to him.

"You were feeling less than well?" asks Iyawa, his top lip quirking.

"Frustrated, *aboki na*. You know how ill frustration sits with me."

Acknowledging the truth of that with a wide smile, Iyawa says softly, "We have much work ahead of us now. I hear Evelyn has made a move also."

Lucian raises a brow at Jess, who hisses and says, "A day or so ago. Her interest is not ours, although she has designs on the Gung. She does not want the Haunt. She thinks he is smoke and she would not move herself to chase smoke."

Leaning back to button his jacket, Iyawa says softly, "*Wannan daya ne ba za a buga tare da.*"

"We won't be rash, Iyawa. We wait and calculate as ever. We have troops all over the Gung."

"They are being picked off like flies. The Cleaner and the Hornets are formidable opponents."

"But that's what makes all this so much *fun,*" Lucian insists. "A real challenge. Ousting my father was too easy. I imagined taking the Cartel over would test us a little more, but it has been depressingly simple. We need to be stretched, my dear friend. *Tested*. Only through trial does one become stronger. Remember the promises we made to one another? Would I ever let you down?"

Iyawa places his hand over Lucian's. "Never. You never have, and you never will. *Ka ko da yaushe suna da nake dõgara.*"

Lucian throws his arm around Jessamine and squeezes her, tipping his other hand to hold Iyawa's in a fierce grip. "That's all I ask, *aboki na*. Trust. Faith. *Loyalty*. They shape us. They will see us lords—and lady—of all we survey."

zero tolerance

W*hy are you still in here, idiot Haunt?*

He turns his head, golden hair swirling into his eyes. *Ex-Haunt.*

Ex or not you're still an idiot. You need to eat. To sleep. You remember Slip-immersion jobs, yes? How much they sucked? You're doing the same thing to yourself voluntarily. *If I had hands I'd slap you seventeen ways to Sunday.*

You have tentacles; they'd probably hurt more.

So come eat before you feel how much, idiot. *You need nourishment; you haven't any fat to spare.*

I need to find Lucian duPont is what I need. He's got an Archie who can hide shit on side and Slip's like a fucking Chinatown bazaar these days. I'm more likely to find a maneki neko and five thousand mint-condition flip phones from before the breaking.

Your point is? I'm almost certain you have one. Her tone is acid, eating away at his patience.

It's a mess in here. I'm packing Emblem in my goddamn head and I'm the one gatekeeper this place has any more. I should've put my foot down.

Puss radiates disapproval vehement enough to make him wince. *No, you really shouldn't,* she says. *That's not how we do things. That's how Fulcrum and their ilk operate. They've had that.* We've *had that. There's a reason we got rid of it.*

But it'd be so much easier.

And that's exactly how Fulcrum got to the point it did. Don't you dare start to think that way. Where's the Shock I know? He'd cast a wider net.

Where *is* the Shock she knows? He's in there somewhere, looking at this new Shock, who thinks nothing of rearranging the world for his convenience and freaking the hell out. Yeah, he can admit to himself that he's sliding further into thoughts he can't condone than he ever imagined he'd allow, but stopping that shit is like dragging feet through tar. Emblem's everywhere in his mind, a cloying mass of *inhumanity*. Trying to think around it, past it, is more complicated than he dares admit even to himself. He's becoming less inclined to fight by the day.

As for casting a wider net. Yeah, old Shock would do that but not with new Shock's power. Surely that would be crazy? Fuck knows what spreading himself through Slip will do to the tenuous hold he has on the parts of him he still trusts.

Aren't you supposed to be my Jiminy Cricket? Are you insane?

She snorts, such a human response. These moments used to take him by surprise but now he thinks maybe she's more human than him. Simple as that. *Melodrama.*

I'm not a cricket by any stretch of the imagination, so that's a hard no. And how is it insane to go deeper, look further? What are you in here, Shock? Human? *Don't kid yourself. You're mere steps away from not being human IRL any more.* Your signal's in layers. I sense you everywhere, in Slip and beyond. You resonate through it all. There's so *much* of you. *At this point, killing you might not even make a difference.*

He shudders, not only at how clearly she sees him, but at the picture she's painting of what that actually means. No. Just no. The idea provokes worse nausea than a two-month immersion job. He'd rather go back in time four weeks and walk out on to the central avenue of inner city wearing a t-shirt with a target on it.

Whatever I am, I can admit to being scared of trying to look everywhere at once by myself. It's bad enough being IRL and being unable to switch it all off. The only choice I get, the only peace, is in here. Why would I jeopardise that? Besides which, I might spread too thin, yunno? I don't want to break. I'm done breaking.

So I'll help. That's what I'm here for.

I thought you were here to berate me for not eating?

I'm multi-tasking. I do have nine brains.

Show off.

Puss snakes a tentacle up into his hair like she used to IRL, but instead of sliding into his jack, it melts into him, tentacle becoming hair, hair becoming tentacle. Taking extra care, because even with Puss to help this scares him, he lets go of everything he is, and floods into Slip like a riptide. The first sensation is prickle and numb, as if he's trying to touch something with a limb that's fallen asleep, and all that registers in his senses is only what he usually sees IRL, the flows of information, conversations, processes, the shape of Slip all around.

And then the whole fucking universe explodes into him.

Billions of voices, thoughts, flavours, Slip selves, avis and IRL bodies asleep, awake and in all manner of moods; and the construction of the Slip is not around or below him, it's *in* him. He's being rebuilt. Re-made. *Altered*. And he *knows* it in the same way Slip does, something instinctual. A base comprehension. The realization slams through him. Slip is not static, not sleeping, not quiescent. There's a vibration to it, a hum, a sighing beneath the weight of water and new architecture that seems almost living, and a sense of rightness in the changes being wrought. If Slip were alive, he might call this sense of rightness *satisfaction*.

It's too much to take in. So much. Seeing it all. Hearing it. Being *with* it. If this is what it's like being a god, he wants none of it, however extraordinary. Not to mention the fact that he's acutely aware that this level of perception is not sustainable. He'll go mad if he holds on too long to all this information. His head's already burning, too full of Emblem's changes to be too much more. With that in mind, Shock fights to focus through the overwhelming barrage of information and sensation for the location of duPont.

The moment he does it, he finds three things. The first, duPont's been sneaky as per, his location is split, with no way to determine which is actual home base—could be Tokyo Hub, could be Paris Hub. The second is some disturbing news about Olbax and Veritas floating around the stock markets and connected to duPont's name that will mean really bad things for the Hornets. And then there's Paraderm. Under new ownership? What the fuck? It's a family business. Owned by a married couple. New ownership smells all kinds of wrong.

You can't leave the world alone for a second. You can't fucking blink. Even that is enough space for all hell to break loose in.

Pulling himself in, he catches one last, disturbing thing: a fleeting glimpse of *something* with a taste of bitter lemon juice. Too tart, making him recoil.

What the hell was that shit?

Not a clue. Taste down here though… She sends concern. *Something dangerous or powerful. Or both.*

Ruthlessly stifling bucketloads of alarm, Shock allows himself to shrink back from the whole of Slip into the confines of his Emblem-filled skull. It's strange, leaves him with a sensation as if he's swallowed static. Unpleasant but kinda not. He opens a line to Amiga.

Fuck sake, Haunt, chime me already.

He ignores her irritation. It won't last. *DuPont and his merry pranksters have signal diffused between the Tokyo and Paris Hubs, no telling which—we'd have to hit and hack on the go to ferret them out. And the Cartel just took over Olbax and Veritas. By took over I mean fucking* swallowed. *The stock markets have gone batshit. Not to mention we have weird shit going down at Paraderm, a change of ownership of all things. Looks shady as fuck.*

Shit. We need to make plans.

This is obvious.

Her snippy reply to his condescension is swallowed by the insistent chime of an all-too-familiar presence in her drive, echoing into his through this too-goddamn open connection Emblem forces him to endure: Maggie. Considering she never calls, he's not surprised to feel the wave of concern riding Amiga's drive. He shouldn't listen in, but hell, this is Maggie, which means it's Mollie. He needs to know.

What's wrong? Amiga snaps. *Is Mollie okay? Is EVaC?*

You need to get your arse to me, right the fuck now. I'm sending you an addy. No time for questions, just hustle. Maggie's harsh in Amiga's drive, abrasive, a combo of huge irritation and the tilting slew of sick fear. What the fuck? Despite having none of Shock's Emblem-like awareness, Amiga catches it too and panics. Panic in Amiga feels off. He doesn't like it.

Maggie, are you…?

No questions, Amiga. Just get *here.*

She shoves out of Amiga's head, slamming an addy into her drive as she goes.

There's a brief, sizzling silence. *You catch that?* No censure, only disbelief at what just happened. When is he ever going to manage to surprise Amiga?

Yeah. You need to go.

Amiga groans. *You see what she's asking here? Does she think I'm a fucking Haunt now?*

Quit bitching. You're an ex-Cleaner, for fuck's sake. Wear that skin Deuce conjured up for us if you're feeling nervous.

Fuck you.

And she's out, leaving his head rung like a bell and too heavy to carry.

Maggie's waiting outside the apartment block addy she pinged, shivering slightly in a vicious breeze. Amiga strides toward her, not really feeling the cold, or anything much at all. Her mind is too busy to acknowledge anything so paltry as the weather, filled with a crap tonne of piss and vinegar fully waiting on the moment it gets to pour over Maggie like burning pitch from a castle gate. Maggie starts when Amiga reaches her and touches her arm.

"Holy fuck! I didn't recognize you!"

"I'm wearing a skin. *Obviously* I'm a massive target right now."

Amiga tries not to come on too strong with the pissiness, but it's been brewing the whole way here, crammed cheek to sweating cheek with a bazillion other commuters on the fucking mono of all things because attached to the addy was this goddamn imperative note to come on public transport. Caterbike apparently surplus to requirements. As if Maggie was going to be driving the fucking thing. Yeah *right*. Rude.

The Gung being as it is right now, she's expected to die the entire way here. Talk about unnecessary stresses.

"I'm so sorry you had to come here like this," Maggie says then in a rush, like dark water spewing from a pipe, and it's all wrong. Too far from the Maggie she knows, that delightful cocktail of snip and wit and sparks. This Maggie is all pale skin, wavering edges and dark undertones dangerously close to grief. So close that Amiga pulls the plug on her piss and vinegar there and then, her danger-dar flashing up and going straight from nought to oh-my-fucking-shit-has-my-friend-died-or-what?

"*Is* it EVaC? Tell me."

A glimmer of something visceral, sharp as pain, flashes across Maggie's green eyes. "Not quite and not *here*. Come on."

Maggie takes Amiga's arm and pulls her across and up the street. Scrawny starlings hop ahead of them, haranguing well-pecked pigeons, shabby as tramps as they make their way to the shoots of the nearest mono, the glass panel doors plastered over with various flyers and posters blaring a mix of uncertain patriotism and livid fury at the system people are seeing now all too clear.

The Gung is so restless it's practically pinging. Some day real soon, things are going to get hella ugly here, and the people set to suffer most are the ones who've already suffered enough. Isn't that always the way it goes? She wishes so hard that it wouldn't, but neither would she dare tell them not to fight. Truthfully she wants them to fight to their last breath so that some of them can breathe freely. Otherwise, why breathe at all?

The shoot to the mono platform turns out to be broken, the third broken shoot she's seen today—vandalized, surprise, sur-fucking-prise—so they take the exposed staircase to catch the north line, disembarking in one of the dense, industrialized areas at the edges of the Chinese district. Lots of vast warehouses here, attached to giant, noisy factories; great, dark blotches against a striated skyline of shabby, colourful 'scrapers and dull umber clouds, roiling like gas fumes against turbulent sky. The lack of effluent from these huge, grey monument-like houses of industry is the single inoffensive thing about them.

"Here."

They're in a street lined with warehouses, at the backs of the factories. Wide enough for large transporters and unremittingly grimy, these streets stink of oil and grease, of mildew, and the musky scent of the rats who use the buildings as meeting houses. Maggie unlocks a small door, camouflaged within grime-spattered breeze blocks by a patina of grey filth. Leads Amiga into a dark corridor and up several sets of damp concrete stairs before pushing through into a tower room. Unlit. Mollie's tubes are here though, their delicate neon yellow casting a brief, warm light against the walls, shifting and pulsing.

"I'll leave you to it," says Maggie, and makes to leave.

Amiga grabs her arm. "What's going on?"

"Mollie wants to see you in private. We'll talk after."

Frowning, Amiga tightens her grip. "Maggie?"

That bright-green gaze snatches hers. Sticks like glue. Throws unspoken words like darts to land smack bang in the quivering bullseye of Amiga's reluctantly soft heart. Oh. This is bad.

Stunned, she barely hears the door click shut and then Mollie glides down. Elegant. Glowing. When Amiga first saw her she thought she was an angel, she still is, every last bit of her divine. Except… Amiga's mouth drops open. Impossible. Not this. Anything but this. Anything but translucent flesh, the press of humming veins formed to symbols around her tattoos, too close to words to be anything else. How the fuck did Agen-Z, *Mother Zero* get sick?

Amiga shakes her head. No. Nope. Not happening.

"What?" she manages to say. "The *fuck*?"

Mother Zero reaches out a pale, delicate hand—speaks in IM. And the words come out unmarred by virad junk, which puts a freaking full stop on anything but Amiga's desire to know what the fuck is up because that shit takes Herculean effort, meaning this is important.

Things are out of control.

No shit, pings Amiga softly, more to herself than Mollie. "I can see that," she says aloud. "Have to say I don't like what I see."

Look closer.

"Huh?" Are they on the same page or what?

The answer is on my skin.

Right. Different pages. Amiga scours Mollie's skin, even though looking makes her want to howl, to hit stuff, to run away and cry. Fails to understand anything. "Huh?" Eloquent much. One thing's clear in all this mess: there's subtext going on here. Mountains of subtext Amiga is too fucking stupid or too goddamn stun-gunned to fillet out. "*Explain.*"

But the pained look in Mollie's buttercup eyes makes her realize that the oldest Zero in the biz is doing all she can to cork the rise of the jingles, and she'd better let Mollie be Mollie and figure out the rest herself. Jeez. Why her life has to be like a fucking K-drama she'll never know.

"What do you want me to do?"

Relief floods buttercup yellow like sunlight. *Shareen. Risi. Find Zen.* Kill.

The emphasis on the final word is like a million full stops stacked to a mountain. Falls like lead into Amiga's drive and lingers, making waves. She's never known Mollie to be vicious.

And that's… it. Mollie diminishes, her wires pulling her back up into the roof, leaving only her light reflecting in Amiga's eyes like sun spots. She leaves the room feeling sandblasted. Maggie's outside waiting, rested up against the wall. The look on her face is pure grief, sends Amiga's belly into acid overdrive.

"I'm so sorry."

Maggie takes Amiga's shoulder in a fierce grip. "I know."

"What the hell is going on?"

Maggie gives Amiga this *look*. Uh oh. "So much more than you know. Come with me."

Retracing their steps to the entrance, Maggie takes her through a bigger door into the warehouse proper—an old dye factory, abandoned probably decades ago. Under low lighting, ranks of vats gleam, scrubbed back to bright silver, their tops shuttered with what look like brand new plastic roller blinds. Maggie winds through them, unerring, to one in particular. She rolls back the shutter and tilts her head—an invitation, a challenge.

Under neon-yellow liquid like the stuff in Mollie's tubes, is EVaC. Her EVaC. One of the very first Hornets she clicked with after Deuce. Somehow, without ever exchanging more than two or three words at a time, they became fast friends. She'd go over to the hut he shared with Deuce and KJ, and EVaC would smile, hand her popcorn and a gaming glove.

Fuck but she hates gaming. She'd only play that shit with him. She misses him. Misses kicking his arse at shooting games. His elbow jabbing her side, the popcorn he always threw. Such a bad fucking loser. She'd find popcorn in her hair out on jobs for Twist and get fits of giggles. So professional. But she didn't have to be professional with him, and by understanding that, she'd begun to understand that none of the Hornets expected that side of her either. She could be herself with them, if she could ever find that again.

Memories of then collide with the body in the tank and it's all Amiga can do to stop from puking. From screaming at the sheer injustice of this shit.

Floating gently, he's still human in shape, and naked... she thinks. Is that skin? What is it? It's livid, deformed. Blood floods the surface and leaches away: SOS patterns of a body in crisis. Giant veins tangle the surface in complex patterns, twisting around organs risen through thinned flesh and pulsing like club lights to form a single word over and over: Zen.

So that's what Amiga should've seen on Mollie's skin? Now she thinks back, it was there, written in the ugly coil of veins. Jeez.

"When did it get this bad?" she whispers.

Maggie places a hand between her shoulder blades and rubs. "Things took a dive after Fulcrum fell," she says. Pragmatic. Final. "Volk's been helping me. We've tried everything we can think of but… you saw Mollie. She doesn't Slip, Amiga. She can't. She's saturated with virads, reached tilt fucking decades ago. If she needs to do anything requiring Slip she uses J-Net. You know why."

Amiga nods. J-Net is the J-Hack version of Slip, a mad, virtual city full of noise and lights, a place for play and plotting. "No consumerism. No bullshit. No virads," she says.

"Exactly. So here's the huge fucking insurmountable problem; she's sick because the ones already *inside* of her changed." Maggie's hands plough into her hair. Tug hard. Her desperation is awful to witness, and there's something deeper to it, something eating at her. Amiga wants to ask, but maybe it's private grief. Mollie is Maggie's after all.

"That's impossible."

"Exactly." The hollowness in Maggie's voice breaks Amiga's stupid fucking heart. "It's doing things it shouldn't be able to and we know why."

"Zen."

Maggie nods. "First it was just the sickness getting so much worse. Then Mollie got sick. And then," she swallows, something else in it. What's the subtext? Amiga loathes not knowing, but she can't ask a question Maggie won't answer. "They've been dreaming, saying her name in their dreams, and now her fucking name has found its way onto their skin. Did Mollie mention Zen?"

"Yeah. She did."

Maggie's hand grips her shoulder again, hard enough to pinch. "What does she want you to do?"

"Find Zen. Kill. Who's Shareen?"

An almost hysterical laugh escapes Maggie. "She's lucid?"

"As much as I've ever seen her."

"And she mentioned Shareen?"

"Yeah. Could Shareen help me find Zen?"

One of Maggie's shoulders kicks up, more of a spasm than a shrug. "Don't do that, Amiga. Please. It's not safe. Not even if she's lucid."

Amiga chooses to ignore that, because it's not up to Maggie to decide what Amiga does. "Mollie said Risi. Do you have any idea where Shareen might be in Risi? I'll go anyway and look, so you may as well narrow me down."

Maggie sighs, the defeat in it chips away at Amiga's resolution, but she holds on tight. This is not Maggie's choice. "She has a drag act in one of the clubs. Just… think really hard about not going. Okay? Mollie is *really* sick and anything she's saying right now might not be *her*, no matter how lucid. Understand? I only called for you today because she wouldn't sleep until I brought you here. She needs to sleep."

Amiga steps back from the tank, unable to look

at EVaC any more. This is all too raw. It's scraping her insides to smithereens. Maggie's too. The strain of it is all over her. "You don't think Mollie's going to live, do you? You don't think any of them are. Not even if I can do as she asks."

Maggie doesn't answer. Frankly, Amiga didn't expect her to, but this was a question she couldn't hold in. It might have eaten her alive. Rolling the shutter back over EVaC, Maggie takes Amiga to the front door and lets her out into the bitter chill of enthusiastic wind. Before she closes it, she does the unexpected and answers, her voice a complex cocktail of tossed gauntlet and surrender.

"I don't want to think it," she says, and there's subtext again. Whole ranges of hidden icebergs. "But it's like seeing Zen's name written in Mollie's flesh. I want to stop seeing it, but I can't get it out of my stupid fucking head."

a killer can look upon a queen

Behind the brash borderland of Plaza, Risi is the bright sparkles after the first explosion of a firework. Risi cruises along with an easy charm, a loose charisma, all soft jazz, disco classics and porn bass interspersed with bright anthems bursting from the doorways of clubs manned by bouncers in bow ties and blazers, thresholds exploding at the seams with men and women dressed to fucking party. Or to kill.

Amiga is not happy. Being in a place this packed and somehow *public* when the Cartel are all but breathing down their necks qualifies as a whole other league of bullshit, even wearing a skin. Cautious, she makes her way through tangled streets bathed in flashing shocks of colour to a club called Riko's. It's not as full as she remembers, or as loud, but there are some of the usual crowd, they point her in the direction of where she might find the drag queens these days.

Risi is fluid. Ever-changing. Clubs come and go and the community they service follows cheerfully en masse, a bright gaggle, undeterred, proudly outspoken. Their current home is in a corner of Risi surrounded by hookah restaurants and steaming sauna joints, the curlicue of club names set between like jewels above secured doors. The air vibrates with heat, steam rolls out from the sauna joints and along the street, parting against her feet like dry ice.

Need help?

Amiga grins at the familiar press of whiskers and warmth against her head. *Could do. Gotta hunt all these joints for a drag queen called Shareen.*

In a flurry like sparks from a faulty light, Leopard Seal appears beside her, cavorting. *I can do that. You take this street, I'll take the next.*

Deal. Be careful.

Likewise.

Leopard Seal flits off, dividing steam like a boat through mist, her tail flicking gusts to disperse into golden-hued air. Amiga strolls to the first shuttered door and grim-faced bouncer. Puts on her most dangerously pleasant face.

"I'm looking for Shareen."

He jerks his chin. "She ain't here. Sings at Club T, up near Koko Split. Can't miss it. Koko's lit like the fourth of July on NYC Hub."

Nodding thanks, Amiga hits up Leopard Seal with the particulars. She can look faster, not being locked to either IRL or feet for that matter. Hunting sorted, Amiga finally listens to the quiet rumble of her belly and buys a cone of shrimp fries to scoff, wandering along idly and scanning the crowds whilst hoofing them down. She takes in every little detail, Cleaner-honed senses stretched to max and fizzing.

Funny how so much has changed in the Gung and yet it's almost invisible. More feel than fact, more rising threat than actuality. When she's out on the streets it's evident in the constant bristle of hairs on the back of her neck, not only the product of knowing she's a target but her bat senses screaming of incipient violence. Nothing this uneasy remains quiescent for long. And the rage is everywhere, in every face, often hiding under bewilderment and fear, but ever present and waiting on the lit match to implode it to flames.

Found it. The bright one. He wasn't kidding; they're lit up like an inner-city 'scraper.

Oh man. Any joy on Club T?

Looking. Would be easier with two pairs of eyes. Leopard Seal throws out a autoGPS so Amiga can follow without ever really looking, concentrating on getting the rest of these hella fucking tasty fries into her mouth. Plan.

On my way.

They find Club T buried in a back street to the right of Koko. It's like a karaoke bar: small, intimate, crammed. A colourful blast of music and laughter and people acting outrageously and loving it, loving her and her avi here too, all hollering and waving, some pointing to their own, playing together like puppies around the mirror balls on the ceiling. The atmos here is so friendly it strikes her as surreal.

A skinny, steel-topped bar hugs the back wall and curves round to touch the edge of a slender black stage graced with three go-go poles and currently rocking a turban-festooned lady in an off-the-shoulder gown made of feathers belting out Broadway hits through bright pink lips. No way Amiga could ever work pink with that much verve. It's downright *sassy*.

Fighting her way to the bar, Amiga roars at the first server to notice her, "Is that Shareen up there?"

The server, five feet seven of blond bombshell decked in what can only be described as mobster fashion, shakes his head, "No hon. Shari's out back doing her best impresh of Sheba. She's on at midnight. Star act, don't you know? Fetch you a drink maybe?"

"No ta, but I'd sure love passage backstage for a royal audience."

He cocks his head. "Tell you what, you buy yourself a pretty cocktail and float me a decent tip, I'll sneak you into the rabbit warren and to the throne room. Sound good?"

Amiga flicks her cred chip on the bar, "I'm not drinking, but buy yourself an after-work cocktail and pop a twenty note on top for your trouble."

"Don't mind if I do." Snagging the chip up to scan it on his wrist, mobster bar boy beams before handing it back and crooking a finger. "Red carpet's this way."

Offered up through a narrow red door, Amiga finds herself in a choked labyrinth of corridors studded with dressing rooms, all packed to capacity with drag queens and go-go dancers in various stages of undress, wearing enough glitter, sequins and silk to fill a hundred harems.

Mobster boy leads her through, throwing finger waves

like confetti. Stops at a door sporting a gigantic star and does some sort of twirl and hand gesture combo. "Ta da! This is her lair. You may want to enter at your own risk."

"Should I abandon hope?"

"No, but do repent at leisure. Her Maj is an absolute beast until the post-show high sets in. Stage fright."

"Consider me forearmed."

"No hope of that, love," he says as he leaves her high and dry outside the door.

"Thanks for the vote of no confidence," she yells after him, earning herself another twirl and a curtsey.

Exchanging uncertain looks with Leopard Seal, Amiga knocks on the door. It flies open so hard it puts a dent in the wall and she's confronted by a six-foot-plus man in a wig net, silk knickers and stockings. It takes him a moment to look down from such a great height and witness Amiga hovering in the doorway and then his eyes fly wide. Amiga sees horror in their depths and enough scorn to scorch the oceans dry. Ouch. This is Sheba Shareen all right.

Shareen's throaty voice is laden with more snark than Amiga's ever had the pleasure of bathing in: "A serial killer kiss-o-gram? Really? Oh I will kill Bradley if he thinks *this* is going to worm him back into my good books. I'm sorry, darling, but I really must reject whatever sad little routine your paltry flim recompense gave you leave to void upon my threshold." She spots Leopard Seal then, and her jaw drops. She points a wicked nail dipped in red. "And isn't that some form of slavery? Or exploitation? I should have you reported!"

The door slams in Amiga's face, blowing her hair back. How exactly does one respond to that? There's no manual for this shit. She knocks again. Shareen's throaty voice barrels through the door, a vocal herd of bison trampling over her polite request for entry.

"Fuck off! Scram. Go darken some other doorway. If you even *try* to sing at me through that door I will stab you to death with a bobby pin!"

Losing her inconsiderable patience, Amiga snaps back, "If you could pull that shit off, I'd fucking *let* you kill me."

Silence. If silence could be quietly impressed, this is how she'd describe it. Heels tap on the carpet. The door cranks open again. Shareen leans on the frame, staring down at her, frowning. "Funny sort of kiss-o-gram you are," she says.

Amiga shrugs. "Sort of not a kiss-o-gram. Am a killer though. Bother you much?"

That earns the elevation of a perfect brow. "Not unless you're here to kill me, darling."

"You'd already be dead."

"Huh." Apropos of nothing, Shareen moves aside and sweeps an arm. "*Entrez!* Drink? I have this complimentary shit I'm desp to offload on freeloaders. Some billionaire wanting to take me on a date. I loved his money, I mean who wouldn't? But the man had no *clue* about hygiene." She effects a full body shudder, more like a shimmy. "The pits must not stink like one, no? And just look at this shit. Even his gifts are more like visual insults."

Bustling around the dressing room and poking dresses aside, she shows Amiga a cabinet full of fifteen different types of outrageously expensive vodka, including one with what looks to be crushed diamonds gathered in the bottom, before practically shoving her on to a chaise longue covered in bright pillows and throws. "So. Killer. Fascinating job. Who do you kill?"

"These days? Mostly Cartel members."

Throwing herself into the chair at her dressing table, Shareen begins a complicated contouring routine that all but hypnotises Amiga. "And do you kill often?"

"With worrying frequency."

"Sounds like someone's in the market for therapy."

"They couldn't fix what's wrong with me."

The snort she earns is ladylike. Cultured. Like a high five from a duchess. "Oh snap. So to what do I owe the pleasure?"

"I need to find Zen."

Shareen drops her brush. "Why the *hell* would you wanna do that?"

"Mother Zero is sick, so are the other Zeros. Her name is appearing on their skin. I don't know what the hell is going on, but she's involved and I want answers."

"Fuck." Spoken almost too quiet to hear. Retrieving her brush, Shareen finishes with her contour and sets about turning her face into a flawless mask. Her eyes stand out, vivid sapphire against the ebony pale. They pin Amiga to her seat. "If Zen's involved, you best give up now. Give up and run like fucking hell."

Amiga's bat senses go wild. She asks the trillion-flim question, dreading the answer. "Exactly who *is* Zen?"

Leaning in to the mirror to glue on her lashes, Shareen side-eyes the hell out of Amiga. It's like being poked with sticks. "A Lakatos," she snaps out. "A project. An *asset*. A megalomaniac with the face of an angel who fooled damn near everyone."

This is one of Amiga's pet hates, being dumped into the middle of a story. "Context?"

Shareen sighs. "Girl, I got no time for long stories, so brief as possible; Kamilla wanted a sister after she had her son. Why? Who knows: Kamilla was rich and spoilt and stupid, so go figure. So she had Zenada made, and Zen was beautiful and utterly brilliant. Hive. Core. Queens. Emblem. All made by Zen. Kamilla just took the credit. That was pretty much her single fucking life skill."

Amiga frowns. "Slip's old. Like... old as Gung old. Isn't it?"

The pitying look Shareen slides her way guts her. "Oh hon. You think Earth Engines and escaping Queens were the only times Fulcrum messed with your head? Slip's been a thing for twenty years and change. Before Slip, J-Net was it—J-Hack run and free for all. Then comes Zen, Kamilla's little pet, who gave Kamilla the ideas and then the means to rig the system. Everything we know now she made Zen write into being: the Psychs, the Cads and Techs, all that petty bullshit."

"And you know this how?"

"Breaker, hon. Breaker kept himself clear of the Slip.

Never left his avi in there unchecked. He smelt trouble from day one and clued a handful of the Movement in. Too dangerous to spread it far, but that's why we fought. Why we refused to give up. We had the truth. It was fucking heady. And fucking terrifying. You try knowing something no one else would believe. It fucks with you."

Now it's Amiga's turn to be scathing, "Oh I have the t-shirt on that one. Trust. So what happened to Zenada?"

"She bit the hand that fed. Ended up locked away with the key thrown into a black hole, courtesy of Breaker, although Kamilla thought Josef did it—she had no time for Breaker at all. Why do you think the Queens were all gung-ho for takeover? The big bitch, the main Queen—she was Zen's avatar, and I can tell you they were peas in a fucking pod. This is why you need to leave Zen down whatever hole she was dropped."

"But the drives in our heads? We get them from Fulcrum."

All she gets for that is a pitying look. "Oh hon, no. The only thing *truly* new here is the Slip avatars, and Fulcrum didn't bother to inform us of the creation process. Far as anyone knew, they were the same shit as J-Net avicles, except those aren't *alive,* are they now?"

Amiga thinks of the caterbike avicle she has in J-Net—just a tool, however cool and functional it is. Rage ignites her belly. "Why did we not know about *Zen*? Why did Mollie not *tell* us? Why didn't Maggie?"

"Breaker swore us all to secrecy. For our own safety, yeah? I'm pretty sure you're not here because you listened to Maggie. She would have told you to leave it. I'm telling you to leave it. You should listen. Really."

Fuck but Amiga's heartily bored of Movement folks telling her what she should do, even if this whole Slip being barely born thing explains so very fucking much about how they're seen, why Breaker is such a big deal amongst J-Hacks. He's their history, the reason why they fight. The reason they *can* fight.

"I rarely listen when people tell me not to do shit," she tells Shareen, fed up of having to repeat it time and again. It should be self-evident by now. She feels like she walks around with "takes no bullshit" carved into her forehead. "Mollie on the other hand told me to kill, and that's a word that really grabs my attention. Do you have any clue where Breaker might have put this bitch?"

Shareen swallows down a smile. "You're cute. No, I have no idea where she is. All I know is that she's on the hubs somewhere. Neutered. Neutralized. Hidden. In other words, no one's concern. Why Mollie wants to crack open that Pandora's Box, even to deep six the contents, is beyond my understanding."

"Me neither, but she does. Desperately. Asked without junk."

Shareen's eyes flare comically wide. "None?"

"Zip."

"So what about you? You do not need to do this. I would not advise it, no matter how desperate Mollie is."

Amiga takes a deep breath. "Yeah, Maggie said something similar but, you know what? I have no choice.

Lives are in the balance. I have to do something. I'll go crazy if I just sit back and let them die. Not acceptable."

Shareen raises both brows. "There's always a choice, sugar, even if it's a shitty one."

"Not if you give a shit." Amiga pulls up her top, exposing the messy scar she refused to let Ravi fix. Like the healed bullet wound in her thigh it still hurts like fuck some days, though she'd sooner die than admit it. "This was my death sentence for turning tail on my boss to fight Fulcrum. Got commuted, don't you know, but I keep this to remind me how close I came, how close I'd willingly come again, if need be, to do what's *right*."

Lashes in place and looking magnificent, every bit the queen, Shareen turns to face her. Reaches out to touch the scar. "Impressive death sentence there. Who was the boss you quit on?"

"Twist Calhoun. And I didn't quit. I killed him."

Hissing surprise, Shareen pulls her hand away. "Well, well. How about that?" She looks at Amiga, blue eyes gleaming. "You promise me you're planning to kill her? Not let her out or any crazy shit like that?"

"You have my word. Maggie doesn't think Mollie was fully herself when she asked it, but I was the one looking into her eyes. I saw it. She thinks Zen is in this somewhere and she wants her x'd the fuck out. It will be my sincere pleasure."

"Then go with my blessing. And take this," Shareen rifles in her jewellery box and hands Amiga a little velvet ring case.

"A ring?"

"No, you moron. A fucking jack-chip. One of Breaker's. Might have useful shit on it. Maybe a starting point. I warn you though, it'll be VA'd within an inch of its life. Might burn a soul out to even jack it in. You might wanna run a few thousand anti-virals and then jack it remotely with a tablet you can handle losing."

"Duly noted."

And it is, though Amiga's head is currently working like a jackhammer over a more pressing issue: getting to the hubs. They can't even casually walk around on the Gung without wearing a skin, not if they don't want all of hell to land on their heads. And all their problems right now? From the hubs. Joy. How the hell are they going to commandeer shuttles to take them to that action? This is not a fucking vid-stream, it's *life*. Can go wrong, will go wrong, and always for them. Fucking *always*.

Not for the first time, the sheer, unmitigated unfairness of the situation blasts through her. Stuck, reviled, hunted like dogs, and what the hell for? Seems like you do people a favour and they bite you for it. Shuffle that alongside her being no good for anything but killing, not in the way of marketable skills but goddamn fucking *preference* and it's as if all life has done in the past month is beat her arse black and blue and then drop it in a cesspit for good measure.

She leaves Shareen with a smile so forced it hurts and hurries back to the mono, resenting the skin over her face, the onus of more responsibility, the injustice of just about everything, and herself most of all.

Knock, knock. Amiga taps on Shock's IM.

Amiga?

So, shit got interesting.

Is this where interesting is a word meaning seriously fucking awful?

Bingo. I have a job for you, and a jack-chip. Heavily VA'd. Shareen, who gave it to me, says maybe crack it remote, with a burnable tablet.

Gimme a moment. Find somewhere hidden.

Sliding down a skinny alley full of filth and trying not to remember what she was doing the last time she was somewhere like this, Amiga waits for Shock to appear. When he does, link by link like any other fucking avi, which is weird enough to see, he's not gold, he's in goddamn technicolour. Normal colours. She wants to ask how he can avi like that, but equally doesn't want to know the answer. And that's only the first surprise. The second? What happens when he takes the chip. It vanishes into him, little sparks of white fire chasing up his arm to his head. Yeah, Emblem-avi-Shock freaks her the hell out.

Get anything? she asks, striving for casual.

He bites his lip. *I will eventually. This fucker's packed to the gills but there's about a bazillion levels of VA. That Shareen was not kidding. What am I using it for?*

Amiga fills him in on Mollie and Zen, leaves him looking like she feels. Trashed. Ruined. Pissy as all hell.

So I'm finding that bitch then? The human the Queen got her personality from?

Yep.

Jeez, Amiga. Fucking hell. Okay. I can't promise anything, I highly doubt he'd hide relevant info in anything like this, but I'll go look.

All I'm asking.

The quiet he leaves when he goes is cavernous. She floats in it, rootless, for long moments until Leopard Seal pops up next to her to remind her this is an alley, and standing in it isn't going to get Amiga home. So she makes for the mono, breathing in air thick with the stench of dry ice and alcohol and wishing that, just once, her normal could be this; alcohol and dancing and bad decisions instead of blood and horror and never ending, terrifying reality.

She'd give a hell of a lot to be that innocent again.

hu hai in hunin

Hu Hai's been in Hunin a mere twenty-four hours and he's about ready to use one of the disposable chopsticks from his takeaway sushi to stab out his eyeballs. Aunty Dong hasn't been quiet for a single second.

Hu Hai, dear, it's in your best interests to take your wife's unhappiness as more of a list of instructions.

Yes, Aunty Dong.

Don't "yes, Aunty Dong" me. Pay attention, or you'll be a divorcee soon enough. The shame.

He bites his lip hard. No point reminding her of the threats she's made about getting his wife to divorce him. The fact that she's given his wife her own lawyer's IM. She remembers. This is all to test him. Constantly. His hands are trembling. They never stop. Not even when he drinks. *Yes, Aunty Dong.*

Now let's look at these matches.

I'm looking at them, Aunty Dong.

Rather a lot, are there not?

Yes, Aunty Dong. Hunin is rather busy.

I'm thinking we need more eyes. I'll send more.

Hu Hai tries to concentrate on the few almost/maybe matches that pop into his feed. It takes a moment to register what she's said. *No. Please, Aunty Dong. We're over-staffed as it is.*

It's taking too long. Work faster.

Yes, Aunty Dong.

Making a heroic effort to zone her out as she launches into a lecture on how to assert his will amongst his staff, Hu Hai focuses in on the streams. Bites back on the urge to swear aloud. These fucking algorithms aren't sensitive enough. They're not discriminating between similar types of body language. Fuck. *Fuck.* How's he supposed to do anything with her in his drive droning on? He feels half mad. Sometimes he hears her talking to him even when she's not. Gulping coffee and wishing with all his might it was baijiu, he sends the team an order to up the ratio of match points.

He makes sure Dong doesn't hear it.

Then, for about the seventeenth time in twenty-four hours, he wishes the Cleaner were out and about. He's viewed footage of Amiga Tanaka that Aunty Dong's Archies found in the streams, admiring her in the same way as he'd admire a predator, with awe and from a distance. If she'd moved through recently, he'd know her in an instant. Of all the Hornets though, he's expecting her the least. A creature like that lets off steam by killing, not clubbing.

As the sun slinks from the sky, Hunin's club district starts to wake up, pulling in crowds from surrounding districts, including the foothills and farms of Shandong. This is what Hu Hai was waiting for. A drunkard he might be, a terrified fool accountable to Aunty Dong's whims, but he's always been sharp when it comes to gut instinct.

If tonight is his lucky night, he'll get the holy grail: autonomy. Her top Execs make their own decisions. Are their own men and women. Claim a take-home wage so high it brings black spots to his vision. Finally he could buy that three-bed apartment he's been yearning for, with double doors on to a sun terrace and no shared laundry facilities. Maybe let his wife divorce him after all and marry someone younger. Sweeter. Someone who likes beards. And baijiu.

Tuning Aunty Dong out a fraction more, he fixes on the roads from Shandong. They'll be on or in a vehicle, that much he'd bet upon. The foothills won't be enough, it'll be the farm 'rises they've chosen to hide in. It's perfect. Shandong is brimming with people and architecture amongst its mountains just as much as the rest of the Gung, but if there was anywhere that might be described as remote or inaccessible, Shandong would be that place.

With his eyes glued to the roads, it's not long until caterbikes and trucks start zooming in on the high road from the upper mountain ranges. One of the bikes has two passengers, neither of which look anything like any of the Hornets or their Cleaner and Haunt, but there's something off about their appearance through the filters of the program and he follows the bike's progress all the way in to the club district where it parks in a cheap carpark rise. He loses them there, but no matter—he's realized what's up—they're wearing skins.

Sending prayers of thanks to every ancestor he can remember the name of, he jumps up, straightens his clothes and races down to the street, tapping in a second IM link alongside Aunty Dong's connected to the team she graciously sent down to work with him. They treat him like shit, but he's about to make them give full respect by earning Aunty Dong's admiration and approval. His time is now.

Link me in to the club streams. The ones closest to that park rise. I'm going to say limit it to the largest. I'm looking for the places with the biggest crowds, the darkest dance floors. Probably the chain-discos. The cheapest, tackiest joints.

Seconds later he's filled with info, all streaming in waves. Makes him happy he left the hangover headache behind him a good seven hours ago after a bracing early morning atop the apartment blocks and enough sushi to mop up gallons of baijiu.

Scanning the streams as he makes his way down to the street, he threads in to the crowds of clubbers, ignoring their snorts of laughter at his poor choice of clothes. Fuck them and their assumptions; he's not been clubbing since his twenties, and he sure as hell wouldn't have picked Hunin when he did. Jazz clubs and karaoke bars are more his scene.

Reaching the area his targets parked, he looks over the streams from the nearest clubs, adding in to the intel on the matching program the faces of those two caterbike riders, partially obscured by helmets and darkness but still a bonus on top of body language. These two may be Hornets but that doesn't guarantee they'll be on the streams Aunty Dong secured, or not on them long enough for a good read. When he sees which club they headed into, he follows them in, nodded past by a bouncer whose wide grin betrays unprofessional amusement at his attire.

These kids. They know fuck all.

Hu Hai has a nose for bars and finds his way through the crush of the club in no time, propping himself up with a beer to start a long watch for his targets. Plan is, get close, get them talking, and hope they pull an almost full or full match. Once he's sure they're Hornets, he can follow them home. If only Aunty Dong would quit yammering, his night could well go perfectly.

what kj did...

Barrelling into Vivid's room, KJ throws himself down on her bed in a sprawl of long limbs, looking like a collection of elbows and knees tied together with ratty black jeans. Rolling on to his belly, he props his head on his fists and stares at the back of her head as she tries to sort the contents of her floordrobe into "safe to wear" and "wash now before it walks on its own" piles, stuffing anything clean enough for dammit back into her duffel in an attempt to tidy that may last for a day or two if she's lucky.

Vivid's good at many things, but neatness has never been her forte. KJ is endlessly charmed by this fact, like she's charmed by his nervous energy. Odd friends make the best friends. After a few moments of being ignored in what can only be described as a pointed fashion, he clears his throat. Vivid's back tenses. She chucks a filthy pair of jeans over her shoulder. The aim is uncanny, landing right on his head. KJ takes this as a positive.

"I know you can see me."

"I have my back to you, Knee Jerk."

"You saw me come in, I mean."

"And?"

He huffs, chucks the jeans on to her wash pile, threatening to topple it right back to the ground. "I'm bored."

She hisses at him and her avi, a soporific-looking sea cow, pops her head up through the floor to watch him with sorrowful eyes. He tries not to notice. Sea cows have excellent guilt face. "Aim better, or you won't live to continue experiencing boredom."

Folding his long body into a yogic knot, KJ lifts his top and winks at Vivid's avi, who sniffs and sinks out of sight. "Been there, got the flesh tee. Try harder."

"Bitch."

"*Bored*."

"So go do a puzzle. Make a pasta necklace. Bash a wooden spoon on a pan. Go braid Shock's hair. He's Slipping again; he won't even notice."

KJ dismisses these suggestions in their entirety with a fart noise. "I want you to entertain me."

Vivid sighs and finally turns to look at him. Yup, that's a stank eye. She does good stank eye. He feels positively dirty. "Why?"

"We're besties."

When all else fails, hitting someone with the truth, especially when that someone is Alana "Vivid" Bianchi, is your only remaining useful weapon, if rather dangerous. Vivid gets mad super quick, holds a grudge like superglue holds paper to wood and wouldn't know how to pull her punches if you tied a rope to her wrist, attached an elephant and made it run in the opposite direction. To his great fortune, she takes this one on the chin.

"This is true. So what manner of entertainment are we thinking?"

"I want to go out dancing and get laid."

Vivid's jaw does a brilliant impression of a trapdoor. KJ isn't usually so reckless, but frankly he's not usually so cabin fevered. This is valley of the unknown shit. He's never encountered the urge to go out and do quite at this magnitude. Panic disorders and people time, especially in the big wide, don't often converge in any such happy fashion. Turns out his panic disorder is a difficult bitch. It doesn't take orders well. Right now, panic or not, it wants out. Fresh air. New places. And it's willing to go mad and take him with it if it's ignored.

Gathering her jaw back under her control, Vivid resumes tidying. "You need to change that top before I'll go anywhere with you."

He smooths his hands down his sweatshirt—pink and yellow with dancing bears on the front. He fucking loves this sweatshirt. It's soft inside and makes people unreasonably angry. KJ's anxiety's a bitch, and yet the little devil on his shoulder who says getting cut to pieces by Li is about the worst that can happen to a body, or at least *his* body, is always encouraging him to poke at people's comfort zones.

"This stays on. It's chilly in Hunin, and like anyone in the clubs will be sober enough to notice."

"If you wanna get laid you'll rethink that."

He snorts. "They won't be looking at my *sweatshirt*, Viv. So can we go? Please? We haven't been dancing in ages and we have the skins Deuce made. It'll be fun."

From the glint in her eye, he can tell she's sold on the idea and halfway through a mental catalogue of all the clubbing gear she managed to bring with her for an outfit that might, under dim lights and through beer goggles look something similar to inappropriate. Knowing Viv as he does he makes a bet on panties, heels and black tape on her nipples.

He's only wrong about the colour of the tape. Gail only has green in the house. Viv's disappointed for about two seconds until she realizes she has the perfect pair of matching panties with lurid green ghouls on black. She backcombs and sprays her hair into a bird's nest of a faux hawk and all but drags him, still in his skinny jeans, Beng boots and bear sweatie, to the caterbikes.

"Skin on," she tells him.

"Yes, Mom."

"Fuck off. But that reminds me, who *is* mom tonight?" The Hornets term for designated driver is mom. None of them speaks to their actual moms any more except Deuce. Parents can be a fucking joke when your life goes in a direction they weren't expecting, as if your life were somehow theirs to direct.

"You be mom," KJ says, living his selfishness like a pro, activating his skin and hopping on behind her, skinny legs dangling. "Tonight I'm all about getting trashed, dancing until I can't see straight and then getting reamed so hard I walk like I've shat backwards for a week."

Vivid's skin blinks. Funny that it's her behind that strange face. He can't get used to it. "That is some visual," she says slowly.

He'd like to remind her of the many times she's said similar or worse, but that's not what good friends do with friends apt to get pissy quick, especially not when said friends are going out of their way to be entertaining. He gives her a quick squish and says cheerfully, "Put it in the spank bank, sweetheart. Now mush!"

The caterbike revs up to the tune of her enthusiastic retching noises and they head off down the mountain pass road toward Hunin and party time. KJ lifts his face into the breeze and, for the first time since running full tilt from Jong-phu with sec drones at his back and panic scrambling his signals, he feels like any other twenty-four-year-old out there.

"Look out, Hunin!" he crows. "You're about to be penetrated!"

Nervous and wrecked and mutilated he might be, but KJ knows how good he looks when he dances. Music tosses him outside of the damage in his head and on his skin, both as physical as each other, neither fixable, and gives him back to himself for a short while. None of the Hornets knew who he was before Li Harmony carved him up and had him thrown in an alley. Wi Ji Lin was at Cad, learning piano and entertainment, mainly dance—ballet, contemporary, Latin.

He's good at piano, but dancing, that's his *gift*. He was expecting to go places with it. Failing came as a rude shock, even more so when it became apparent how few opportunities there were for playing piano, and the only dancing on offer involved thongs, oil and a pole. He'd done that for a while, just to hold on to dance. Until they tried to get him into private work, starting with lap dances and graduating to prostitution disguised as companionship. That stopped being fun super-fast, so he quit to become the single worst drug dealer in Li and Ho Harmony's employ.

The mistakes you make when you run mindlessly from a bad situation, thinking there's nothing worse. Fail life lesson numero uno: there's always worse, and KJ is a star at winkling the worst of two evils when given the chance. So now he can't strip because people would puke. Hell, he probably couldn't even get up the courage to go alone on stage any more, his fight/flight response so borked he sometimes tries to do everything at once and ends up freezing and blacking out. Classic hypoxia.

Thank fuck for the Hornets and their willingness to take him in based on an affinity for code he didn't know he had until he was forced to learn it, to overlook all his ticks and twitchiness and let him be his best self—which even on a good day is someone else's worst self.

Yeah, KJ's a mess, and anyone in this club who's been watching him dance and imagining having him writhe against them like that in a corner, pants down and panting, would run a minute mile to get away from him if they knew what this sweatshirt hid. Thankfully for his libido, his pride and his delicate heart, he has no intention of taking it off, not even in this nuclear heat of bodies and lights. He just closes his eyes, forgets everything but what *was* and lets loose, knowing eyes are on him and *loving* it.

Thirsty work though, and burns the buzz off fast. He needs another drink. Preferably long, cold, and with enough alcohol to down a mammoth, to drown any threatening flood of panic thoughts his idiot monkey brain might want to pelt him with.

This whole business of enjoying himself, of forgetting, can be a fine balance.

"Want a drink?" he bellows in Viv's ear.

"Something with a stupid name and three umbrellas," she yells back. "Extraneous fruit. Possibly on fire."

He shoves both thumbs in the air. "I gotcha back."

Spinning lightly, he ducks under the flailing arms of some guy built like a tank and clearly on something *very good* and starts to walk-dance his way to the bar. Once there a few pointed smiles and shimmies get him in front of the cutest server so he can order two heavy-on-the-alcohol cocktails, one free of anything but a mixer stick and some ice, the other packing pretty much every available extra going. He knows how to treat his bestie, even when she's designated mom and shouldn't technically be imbibing. Fuck technicalities.

He's leaning over the bar observing the cutie mixing up their drinks when he notes an older guy edging in on his left. Dressed in what can only be described as dad clothes, he's Chinese and kind of ugly handsome. Looks exhausted too, which is the most interesting thing, how he looks cool, relaxed and yet about to fucking drop where he stands. He's also staring at KJ and smiling widely at him. Uh oh, creep alert. Sirens at max.

"Having fun?" dad clothes shouts over the din.

KJ tries not to flinch. Is this a come on? Because if so, hell no. He's had his eye on a slinky Latino dude carving up the floor. They've eye fucked several times already, so he knows he's on to a winner. This guy is *not* a winner. The only club he's dressed for is the cricket club and he's bowling a maiden over right now. Dot ball. "Um… sure. Music, dancing, booze, what's not to love?"

The guy steps closer and KJ has to fight the urge to step back. He loses. Tries to make it look casual.

"Any recommends on what's good to drink?" Chinese dad clothes guy is too close. "I'm drinking bad beer, and I'm not impressed."

He tips the bottle in his hand, but KJ has no need to see the brand. In fact his sheer horror at the poor guy's newb mistake drives a little wedge into his unease, cracking it open just far enough to allow for him to ditch the "stop creeping on me" vibe and offer his sage advice.

"Oh fuck no! Never drink the beer here, dude. They bulk buy. It's horrendous stuff, like, the absolute worst. Cocktails only here, anything with good, hard liquor. I'd recommend the gin based. Their selection of gins is fucking amazing. I'm talking sterling quality. The owner's a total lush for gin, he's practically got a degree in the stuff." His and Viv's drinks appear on the bar. "Good luck ordering!" he carols over his shoulder as he hurries to put people between him and the odd intensity that his response has sparked in Chinese guy's eyes. Creep magnitude up fifty percent. Yikes.

KJ isn't fond of being looked at as it is. Being looked at like that though? He shudders. That shit will give a guy nightmares. Grabbing his straw between his teeth, KJ takes a long gulp and sighs as it hits, warmth spreading down his throat and into his gut. He tells himself everything is peachy. Dancing, more drinks and a steamy hook-up with slinky Latino will make it all go away. And the unsettling conviction that even with all these bodies between them weird Chinese dad clothes guy is still watching will drop away like everything else does.

Yeah. He keeps telling himself that, because this is the single thing he won't allow his panic to ruin. Not ever. He'll dance and drink and fuck and forget, and be *himself* for just a little bit longer.

shandong in flames

In his dreams, Shock floats in a haze of golden light and leaves. Sendai. This was his haven once, the place he thought was home, this leafy paragon of virtue, one of the Gung's richest neighbourhoods. A ghetto for the wealthy, and the lucky. He was lucky for two years, then he lost it, and spent years trying to get it back. Wasted years. Desperate years. He regrets every day of every last one of them.

Wings flutter in his face, soft feathers and clicking mechanisms, all the birds of Sendai. They float as he floats. Golden and silent. Follow him through gilded green light to Slip, where he evaporates to chains of gold, to his avi self, disappearing through warmth and leaves into heavy water, stretched to his limits, listening to the whispering of the code. Trying to follow the conversation as it talks amongst itself—stranger conversation than he could imagine. Concepts rather than words. Spirals of complex sound that may be argument or song or gossip.

He dreams this every night and isn't sure if he's

actually *there* or not, considering where he begins—always in Sendai. VR is dreaming wide awake, so why shouldn't he end up here when he sleeps as well? He's not entirely real any more. Maybe when he's unconscious, the part of him no longer human comes out to play. Twisting, he brushes aside the strands of his hair to watch a polyhedral world spinning beside him invert, the innards a panoply reminiscent of ancient Persepolis. All towers and fire.

No. That's not fire. Squinting through the crenellations of the polyhedral's towers, he sees flares on the far borders of Slip. Something like flame. Spikes of energy maybe. They rise up, burst and fold, and around him Slip explodes in slow motion, in eruptions of gold, like volcanic magma, and conflagrations from sparks. A rapid chatter and roar interrupts the spirals of code conversation and leaves him spinning in place, hunting for the source, his hair whipping into his face, tangling in his lashes, catching on his lips.

"Shock!"

Shock lurches straight from complicated half subconscious, half slipping not-quite-dreams to fully immersed RL. Takes a moment to adjust, gasping like a beached fish. Staring directly into eyes so dark he can't tell pupil from iris. Deuce. Anger and panic boil in his gaze like explosions through fire.

"What?"

"Incoming," Deuce snarls. "We have incoming. Soldiers, maybe a hundred of them. We need to get *out*."

"Cartel?"

"No. Not Cartel. Don't know who. Fucking blatant, coming in on trucks and caterbikes, heavily armed. We've got minutes at best. Our window for getting out the front was gone before my avi even spotted them."

"You had your avi on lookout?" Shock's never even seen Deuce's avi. It's always busy, like Puss is. But then Deuce is way more than he leads people to believe, so his avi has plenty to do too.

Amiga appears at the door, armed to the teeth, her face a mix of feral snarl and business-mode, gears spinning fit to smoke in that smart arse head of hers. She grabs up Shock's duffel—packed because they take no chances ever—chucks it into his lap and jerks her head toward the rear of the farm. "Get the priorities out through the terraces."

Deuce nods. "Good call."

"Wait a minute," Shock says, shoving his blankets aside. "Where the hell are you going?"

"Taking a team down to help tenants in the lower levels and find Gail—he's not in his room. I think the idiot went straight down to help his people."

"I could help."

She shakes her head. Emphatic. "No. These guys are after you. You need to be getting the hell out of here. We'll meet at the rendezvous, okay?"

"Not okay."

"Tough. I'm off." She looks at Deuce, a megaton of pure-grade serious in her gaze. "Catch you on the flip side."

"Be safe."

She grins. "As much as I can be. You too." And she's

gone, a gun in each hand and way too much fierce joy in her face.

Deuce tugs Shock's foot. "Get some shoes on, stat." He looks over his shoulder as a couple of dozen sleepy Hornets file past in the hallway and hollers at them like a drill sergeant, "Get a *fucking* move on! Everyone not going with Amiga is helping to get the injured down the terraces."

Amiga's bunch of kill-ready Hornets gather on the landing, clutching a mishmash of guns, swords, knifes and batons, some electric, most simply blunt and brutal. She scans their numbers. Not many, but it'll do in a pinch, they're het up on adrenalin and fury and pretty much raring to be unleashed. She feels like the hand of god, bringing the oncoming storm. It feels *good*.

She grins at Vivid and Tracker, the two most familiar faces.

"I want three teams. I'm taking one, Vivid, you have another and the last goes to you, Tracker." Tracker's one of the Hornets' top surveillance J-Hacks. She hasn't known him well for long, but he's solid as fuck and twice as vicious. He can handle a strike team in his sleep. "We'll take stairs down, watch out for smoke. These fuckers look to have masks; steal 'em as and when you can."

Prism, one of the code jockeys, steps forward. "Can't we just use the shoots?" She shouts. "This is ridiculous. People are dying down there whilst we stand here planning."

"Too dangerous," Tracker says, dismissing the idea.

"It's the quickest way!"

Amiga's getting aggravated, but Vivid steps in before she can run her mouth. "No way in hell we're using those fucking shoots, Pris. If one of those explosions backdrafts we'll be cinders and then those people down there are on their own. The stairs is all we've got, so let's get moving."

Prism looks mulish. "Well what about backdraft up the stairs?"

Vivid taps the one behind her with the butt of her gun. It resounds, heavy and metallic. "Hear that? The stairs have fire doors on every level. The shoots? Not so much. They'll blast out if they get hit hard enough, probably already have. Bad design. Most 'scrapers have shitty designs. No way to be sued after a fire if everyone dies, yeah?"

"Fuck *me*." Prism looks disbelieving.

"We all lived in a mono tunnel carved through the middle of an equally shitty 'scraper, woman," Amiga snarls. "What d'you think happened to the people of Jong Phu when the drones attacked?" She raises a brow. "Now can we get *moving*? Arguing this shit is sure as *hell* costing lives."

Prism's young. A newer Hornet from just before the shit hit the fan. They shouldn't be harsh but there isn't time to break her in gently. Outnumbered heavily and very likely nowhere near as well armed they decide that it'll be best to triangulate an attack, splitting up to take two of the side staircases and the one at the rear. Amiga grabs that one, wanting to push through forward on the straight line. Pounding the levels with her team in an unholy rush, she blanks the gunfire and screams from below as much as she can, her knuckles flashing white on the grips of her guns.

She saves all her frustration for the second they have boots on the ground.

Fire doors might be A-One for saving your arse from fire, but they make stealth impossible, putting the absolute kibosh on a sneaky entrance—immediately drawing enough bullets to turn a tank into a colander. Sending the Hornets out to each side, Amiga runs right into the teeth of trouble, not bothering to waste bullets until she's up close and personal. All the while she's trying to place them, these soldiers in black combat gear and face-concealing helmets with goggles. Creepy shit.

Whoever sent them does not want them easily pegged.

There's a single insignia on their lapels, a gold-and-red pin, a dragon coiled into an infinity sign. It's not familiar. It should be. There's no criminal element here or on the hubs Amiga hasn't had dealings with whilst working with Twist. Grabbing one by the lapel, she cracks their helmet against the wall with all her might. Once. Twice. Blood seeps out on to her hand. Arterial blood. The right kind. She drops them underfoot, trampling their chest to get to the next one, who she shoots in the neck, and the next, who gets a bullet up through the groin.

Amiga is feeling her rage. And feeding it.

In the corner, one of the soldiers has several farm workers on their knees, hands behind their heads. No one else is close enough, which suits Amiga's current state of mind just fine. Sprinting over, she grabs the cunt round the throat, jerking hard enough to deprive them of most of their air. The choking noises please her. A lot.

She hauls them to the window, pure force of will considering this one is a hell of a lot bulkier than her, and half shoves them out, leaning over to say, "Expensive gear you have here, arsehole. Who bought it? Who the fuck bought you?"

The snarls from behind the helmet tell her nothing except that she's right. These fucks are bought. Mercenaries. They won't talk. So she steps back. Pushes. Lets go, slapping hands away from the frame as they scrabble for purchase and smiling as they disappear, screaming. These windows lead to the sides of the mountain—it'll be a long time before that arsehole meets the ground. A good long time to reconsider the life choices that led to shooting innocent people in a farm 'scraper.

As she's stepping away to rescue the workers still on their knees, a vast explosion rocks the entire building.

"That was up!" Tracker shouts.

"Get these tenants the hell out," she calls back. "I'm going to find Gail."

Amiga really fucking likes Gail. He's seriously good people. Even though he looks at her like she's about to go postal he treats her with nothing but respect and kindness. And what he's done for her family, her Hornets? That'd earn him her loyalty no matter what. She has to find him. No way is he paying for any of this. No way is she allowing another good person to be fucked over for doing what's right.

Tracker runs past, slaps her on the arm, his face

deadly serious. "Be careful," he says.

Amiga frowns. "Why you all bother to say that I'll never know."

"Just in case you ever listen," he answers, surprising her.

Trusting them has been impossibly hard, but when she manages, always worth it. And now she understands how Maggie felt, grasps a portion of that subtext. Giving up control, allowing people to be there for you, allowing yourself to be there for them. It's one of the hardest, most important things a soul can do. Which is why she can't—won't—let Gail, or Mollie, down. Grinding her jaw until it spasms, Amiga speeds off, her heart drumming so loud it's all she can hear.

Fixated on the very real possibility of having to jump the sheer drop between the terraces he's sat on the edge of every day, Shock's first thought is *oh hell no*, but that's the exact moment the entire world seems to implode around them. Explosions so loud his hearing is replaced by roaring and ringing, driving all thought into a deep corner, cowering for a second or two until he realizes he's just *standing* there.

Talk about a target. This is not the time to lose his shit.

Clinging to his duffel, he sprints for the doors, head down, battling panic and pain from injuries not healed enough to allow for this kind of speed and movement. Stinging smoke, showers of debris and choking billows of dust fill the air, leaving him blind as well as deaf, heading for the terraces on instinct alone, trusting his feet to know the path they've walked every day for the past four weeks.

Lost in heat and dust, he can barely breathe, just keeps running until air slaps him in the face, making him cough and cough again. He clutches his duffel harder, bracing his aching scars and runs faster until his feet hit freezing water, plough calf deep into soft, thick fronds, tearing at the hair on his ankles and making him stutter and swear.

Treading on a stone, he stumbles. Shit, his feet are bare. Why didn't he put shoes on? And where is everyone? Explosions resonate behind him and the terrace shakes violently, as if the whole building's threatening to collapse beneath him. It won't. Like everything in the Gung it's built to withstand earthquakes, but his heart jolts and stalls nonetheless, anticipating the worst.

Scattered bursts of gunfire follow the explosions. Shouts. Screaming. The unmistakable sound of masonry coming down. His friends are back there and he's running away. Struck by the conviction that he should go back or he'll lose them, Shock freezes in place. Yells incoherently when an arm snags him around the waist and propels him along, barely giving him time to find his feet.

"C'mon man! Keep moving!" Ravi: moustaches flying back, his face too pale, smudged with dirt and dust, with little flecks and smears of blood.

"Where is everyone?"

"I don't know." The fear deeply entrenched in Ravi's jovial voice sinks into Shock, a sub-zero cold filling his bones, leaking into his lungs. "There was too much dust. I only just saw you. I think some got trapped back there."

"Is that your blood?"

Ravi nods as they run for the edge, the shouts and gunfire at their backs not receding but getting closer.

Deuce barrels past them then, with KJ and several other Hornets, all covered in dust and filth, their duffels slung over their shoulders, their hands full of rappels. Deuce exchanges an agonized look with Ravi and Shock, hollering as he passes.

"I thought you were fucking *gone*."

"Have you seen anyone else?" Ravi calls out. "How many others are back there?"

Deuce shakes his head, and throws over his shoulder, "I don't know, okay? I found who I could."

Shock's head swims with panic, distorting the world to distant buzzing and blurs.

Avis, he all but screams, doing something he's never yet done and reaching out for all of them. Most are alive and the relief is dizzying.

Here. Their collective voice is a harmony. It resonates in his bones.

Go find your humans. Get them out. *And Leopard Seal…*

Shock? Her reply in particular makes his head swim, his eyes blur. Amiga's alive down there. Still alive.

Do not let Amiga do anything too dumb. I'll miss her stupid face.

Her wave of agreement, fierce and tinged with dark amusement, touches him as they reach the edge of the terrace where the Hornets are coupling rappels to the concrete.

Too winded to speak now they've stopped running, Shock IMs Deuce. *I sent avis after everyone.*

Deuce's face goes carefully blank. *All of them?*

Most are still there. Only a few gone. I spoke to Leopard Seal.

He nods thanks, trying and failing to hide the relief in his eyes. Chucks the rappel rope over the side, allowing it to whisper down into the darkness, and slaps a wrist clip on Shock, holding on to make sure he sees how serious he is. *You're going first; we can't afford to let you be caught. Hold this with both hands. Allow momentum to carry you down. Keep a look out for the water and drop and roll when it's a few feet below, like I know Amiga's shown you. You don't wanna hit feet first or you'll snap your ankles. When you're safe down, run for the next edge. We'll be* right *behind you.*

Taking a deep breath, Shock launches, wishing he'd taken time to put his hair up. He's forced to free a hand to push it out of his eyes, leaving him to swing crazily to and fro, his stomach swinging the other way, lurching like hysteria and sickness. *Fuck* but he hates heights. Last time he had to do this, he was high as balls—what he wouldn't give to be high right now, but no chance. Ravi cold cured him. He'll never get high again, so this better be the last lot of heights he has to jump from.

The reflection of moonlight on the water below is the only warning he gets of proximity. He barely unclips in time, rolling as he hits mud, trying to keep his duffel dry and making a mess of it instead, pretty much soaking himself from head to toe.

As promised, Deuce and the others are right on Shock's tail, almost beating him to the next terrace. They're faster at this. Practiced. He's scared of holding them back, but he's sent ahead every time, getting slower and slower as his body starts to bitch and complain. There's still gunfire sounding in bursts from the 'scraper, the pops hurting his ears with the roar and ring of the explosion still resounding, making everything sound dim again. Submerged.

The terraces are lit by the fierce roar of flames, the heat growing at his back with every level. He tries to reach out to avis more than once, but the silence is deafening. He tries not to think about what that means as he drives himself forward, wondering if the last terrace is ever going to appear. Fuck but when you really need to get away, there's nothing less convenient than a 'scraper this ever-loving tall.

They've made it down a mere ten of the thirty terraces when bullets start to splash the water around them. Without thinking, Shock takes action, spinning out Slip as colour, reeling it out behind him and over the terrace, erasing them from sight. Underneath the illusion, gold glimmers, making the Hornets gasp and stare. He knows they're staring at him too and refuses to meet their eyes as distant agitated shouts rise up, muffled in his ringing ears.

Deuce stumbles into him and grabs his shoulder, squeezing tight. Tricked into peeking, Shock's almost undone by the awe in his face. No. No way. This is not a thing to admire. It's too much. And when the adrenalin's faded and reality sets in hard, Deuce will see that more swiftly than anyone. He'll begin to watch Shock like a hawk and that'll be the beginning of his end with the Hornets.

Suffocated by smoke, Amiga tackles one of the soldiers slash shitty fucking mercs from behind, smashing her fist into their throat over and over until the air wheezes to a stop. Her knuckles throb like a bitch but she takes the next one out the same way, breathing hard through her teeth against the pain.

She ran out of bullets three levels ago. Dropped her fucking knife running away from heavy fire on the floor above. She's pissed beyond measure and still hasn't found Gail, her heart shrinking by the second—burning a hole in her ribcage.

Fed up of smoke, she tears the strap of a dead soldier's helmet loose and yanks it off. Underneath, eyes glazed with death, a woman maybe ten years older than her. She's not particularly buzzed to put a helmet someone just took their dying breath in on her own head, but she's going to be drawing her last if she doesn't.

The things she does to stay alive.

Making a mental note to grab one for Gail when she reaches him, she steals the gun and the knife from the dead merc to save her borked knuckles and bulls forward, clicking the helmet's goggles on to give her some night-vision visibility. With smoke this thick it's not much use but it's better than naked eyesight, giving her the apparition-green edges of walls to guide her way.

Leaving a sloppy trail of bodies, some more categorically dead than others as she runs out of patience and moves more for speed than certainty, Amiga makes her way through the 'scraper. She has no idea if everyone else is okay and that's not okay. Not. At. All. But she still hasn't found the farm manager. This may be the closest Amiga gets to panic in her entire life. Not the best time to discover that panic makes her incapable of efficiency.

One of these days she'll think back to how she left some of these mercs and maybe need to hang her head over a toilet for a while.

The second to last floor, she finally spots Gail. Unconscious and all the way on the other side of a hall bristling with mercs. About the worst scenario she was envisaging that didn't involve his corpse if she's honest. Fact is, that could be his corpse. He could be dead. She can't tell from here if he's breathing or not, but what the fuck. Assumptions are a poor substitute for truth. A quick count tells her she's likely to get badly hurt here, and this is the moment she should be listening to the Hornets and taking care. But Gail's there, he's right fucking *there* and she has to try.

Fuck safety. She'll be safe when she dies.

Taking another swift inventory, Amiga dives at the group of mercs to her left, taking them down with vicious, messy cuts to the throat. Uses the last as a shield to slam forward and take on the room, not realizing that's she's screaming until the sound of bullets ricocheting off the walls and floor ceases. Snapping her jaw shut like a trap, she looks across the floor, sending swift prayers to ancestors she neither knows nor cares about and watches with her own breath bated as his chest moves, and keeps moving—he's breathing. Out cold, not dead. Result.

She steps over the bodies around her feet to run over to him. She's maybe six feet away when the corridors behind them fill with mercs. Dozens of them. Too many. There are no guns in reach. No knives. No way. Amiga screams again, right at them, and they all move in perfect sync—their guns raising to fire as she leaps back. Grabbing up the nearest body to cover herself, Amiga backs the hell up, cursing herself out for being too slow to get here, too slow to kill the small groups in her way, too goddamn fucking slow to save the man who risked his life to save them.

the place of dead roads

Scrambling over the last terrace, Shock succumbs to numb despair, stumbling over his own feet. Damn near face planting in pig shit. Deuce wraps a hand around his upper arm, holding him steady, getting him to the caterbikes. Puss slides out in gold threads to wind around his torso, holding tight. The roar of the vehicles is almost merciful, drowning the ugly chatter of gunfire, and through it all, Shock holds the illusion in place, so anyone who looks for them will not see.

And the whole time, every second of it, he strains his drive wide open to listen for Amiga, freezing inside by degrees as miles and silence spin out together, impossibly long and final.

Maybe Deuce could claim more right to panic, but Deuce being Deuce, he holds together. Once on the caterbikes, he takes point, guiding them down the mountain road and through the back streets of Hunin to the small parking lot on the ground floor of an ex-clubhouse out near the border they'd passed on their way to Shandong. They'd discussed and agreed to use the lot as a rendezvous in case of emergencies soon after they arrived at the farm, because Hornets plan for contingencies, every time.

Remade to art spaces, the clubhouse is shabby and shuttered, and the parking beneath lies abandoned and locked, holding nothing but a couple of rusting cars and a whole mess of scurrying rats. Vivid, never one for hiding her emotions, grabs out a gun and makes to start shooting. Deuce snags her wrist.

"WTF Vee? Live and let live not in your canon any more?"

She gestures with her free hand, a middle finger at him, followed by a rigid pointer at the small bundles of brown fur racing along the walls. "Rats, Deuce. Vermin. They're probably full of lice and diseases. I like being healthy."

"Rats are intelligent and generally very clean," Deuce says, calm as usual. "Killing them won't make you feel better about leaving Hornets behind."

Vivid bites her lip. Hard. "Oh fuck you, Psychology Major 101."

He loosens his grip, rubbing her fingers between his. "They'll be here. Not all of them, but most. We're Hornets. We can handle ourselves, even against guns. You know this. And we left our best weapon behind to help them. Whatever you think of the way Amiga acts at times, you know what she is, what she can do. They're in the best hands."

"I trust her," Vivid says, slow and careful, "I really do. But I'm not *sure* of her. She's different, Deuce. Darker. It's not just the killing thing, dammit, you know I'm no angel, but it's one thing to be down with dispatching a dickhead, another entirely to *need* killing in order to breathe."

Deuce smiles, and there's something within that smile, hiding beneath it, that Shock's never seen on his face before: anguish. "Trust me, it's always been there. I could always see it, and I don't have a problem with it because it's *her*."

He looks at Shock then, direct, and the awareness in his gaze makes him squirm. Holy shit, Deuce *sees* her, and he's fully compos of the fact that she chooses to talk to Shock over him. Shock tenses, waits for whatever verbal missile's about to be fired, but Deuce says nothing, and Shock literally wants to throw himself on the mercy on the rats, because no way does he deserve a pass from Deuce on being Amiga's ear.

Just another IOU right there to add to a million the same.

Feeling entirely too chewy and strung out, Shock does the usual and retreats to solitude, hitting the far wall to collapse in a pile of tired limbs, and settling in to wait. The Hornets pop up heat lamps they'd stashed under the car wrecks and gather round to keep the light from giving them away, quiet talk bubbling over with battle fatigue and dark humours—straining to obscure a list of possible outcomes they have to spend agonizing hours waiting to see fulfilled or not.

And it is hours. Half the night ticking by in excruciating bundles of slow seconds. Time being cruel as it always is when the wait is important. Fucking perception and its need to grind down on pain like a foot on a broken bone. But gradually, as hours tick by, other Hornets begin to trickle in. A steady flow on caterbikes, some badly injured and in the arms of others, some alone, dusty and bloodied, some in pairs.

Night drags into dawn. Into early daylight. They hang on knowing it's not safe, all humour used up, all words dried in throats too tight to breathe. Matters not that Amiga is only recently a full Hornet again, and a bad one at that, ricocheting off to do her own thing in her own way out of sheer, unmitigated gall disguised as impatience. Matters not they're collectively a little leery of her, or in the case of her closest buds, downright annoyed. It just matters that she's not here yet, and that she's human enough to die, and they don't want to lose her.

And they don't want to lose Gail either. If she's not coming, then he's not.

Worst thing is, everyone's thinking the worst, but no one *says* it, no one puts it out there in the open… just in case. And Shock goes from wanting to punch the person who dares to talk first to being the one who *wants* to.

Two things. If Amiga and Gail are dead, they're dead, and they can process that at their leisure, except for right now. As appropriate times for processing grief go, this one's about as wrong as it gets. And the second? The big one. They're wearing bullseyes and nowhere near far enough away from Hunin and a whole mess of trouble and guns to be standing around saying nothing about how the farm bought it with them inside and how it wasn't the Cartel, which means it's a new horror-show they're playing lead roles in.

He's finally decided to go for broke and get shit said, when someone else speaks, leaving him fending off tears.

"What the holy fuck are you lot doing still here? Are you actively trying to die? You do realize the chaos at Shandong will mean Hunin crawling with Cartel sometime real fucking soon, and whoever the fuck hit the farm last night—by the way *not* Cartel—has an even bigger hard-on for us lot on gurneys than the Cartel does. I mean, for fuck's sake, I thought at least *collectively* you might manage to make one entire usable brain!"

Stalking into the parking space like the predator she is, covered head to toe in all manner of filth but looking somehow utterly perfect, Amiga's wearing the most singularly pissed expression he's ever seen on her. He wants to paint it. Photograph it. Splice it into his memory. Tattoo it on his stupid skin. He's never been so happy to see her angry. From the looks of it, neither has anyone else.

Except Deuce, who steps out from the Hornets wearing the matching expression to hers. Yeah, they fit.

"What the fuck were *you* thinking?" he asks her, in this soft voice laced through with so much fury she raises a brow. "Always comes down to the same damn comms problem with you. IMing too hard for you, Amiga? Not even a nudge? Not even sending Leopard Seal to give us the lowdown on you not being dead. We'd only have to see her, for fuck's sake. One peek of a goddamn whisker and no one here would've wasted hours wondering if our own personal human nightmare of an ex-Cleaner might continue breathing!"

She takes a step back, Amiga's version of a raised hand: hold up, son, and calm down because I don't wanna throw down on *you*. "I thought you'd know."

He chases after her, two quick strides to grab her shoulders. "No. You were hoping we wouldn't care, that we'd run not knowing and not look back, not even *think* back because it's you and you have this screwed-up notion of how you're seen. Tough shit on you, because it's a bullshit notion, Amiga. We do care. You're just gonna have to deal with it." She looks like she's about to snap back, but he grips harder. "No. No argument. I said deal with it and I meant it. Now tell me what went down? Is Gail dead?"

She shakes her head, swallowing hard. Adjusting. Later on, she'll want to talk to Shock about this.

"He was taken prisoner," Amiga says, and the lot fills with exclamations of disbelief that she'd leave Gail to the mercy of whoever attacked them. She snarls at them. "Shut the fuck up! I had fifty-plus heavily armed twats converging on my person. Contrary to what you all seem to think, I don't think I'm immortal, and I have a full brain all on my own, which I use regularly. You should try it. Fucking revolutionary." Her sarcasm cuts the room to silence and she peers around Deuce to raise a brow at Shock. "Got anything to say, skinshanks? Any clue about how the fuck we got found?"

"Not one. Contrary to what you seem to think, I'm

not omniscient," he sneers, throwing her own snark back in her face because, dammit, of all the things to jump on that's the one guaranteed to provoke his least favourite emotion: guilt. He *should* have seen this coming. Felt it. *Something*. Or what the fuck use is all this Emblem-related bullshit anyway?

She throws down this scoffing sound like a gauntlet. "So that discussion we had the other day meant what?"

Pissed beyond measure that she'd casually use this crap in this moment of all moments, when everyone's a walking nerve and bound to flip, he grabs up the gauntlet and slams it right back. "Nothing in relation to this. I can do weird shit in Slip and IRL, but I don't have a fucking all-seeing eye."

"I really want to talk to you being able to do Slip stuff IRL" Deuce says, dry as cracked concrete, "because what you did at the farm and on the way here was *insane.* And I'd love to wrangle how any of us missed a clear and present danger on our tracks. But we have a situation. Us. Stuck in here. Military types, and Cartel cronies who might as well be, crawling the Gung like fleas on a rat. We need a battle plan."

If anything was likely to snap Amiga into Cleaner mode, it was this. And that's yet another one Shock owes Deuce.

"We do. First though I have some info you might find intriguing, as does Shock," Amiga says, dumping him in it yet again, but he forgives her, it being only the location of duPont she likely wants him to share. "Might be relevant to whatever we decide to do next."

"So share," Deuce tells them. "We haven't much spare time here."

Between them they fill the Hornets in on the possible locations of the Cartel's trio of leaders, and the situation with the Zeros and Mollie's request regarding Zenada Lakatos. Hornets don't take stuff like this lying down. They've all wanted to get to the Cartel leadership and cut them off, that whole cutting the snake's head notion being an idea they fully subscribe to. As for Mollie, there's not one Hornet in the room didn't adopt her as a surrogate mother in that initial rush to halt the Queens.

Quite simply, the Hornets would move mountains for Mollie.

"What's the plan?" Vivid asks Amiga.

"What do you think?"

"Steal some fucking shuttles, split the fuck up, hit the hubs and shut this shit down. I'm done hiding. Done killing from the shadows. I want to come out swinging."

Amiga blinks. "That's actually a pretty solid plan, apart from the certain death aspect. But what the hell, certain death certainly never stopped me, don't see why it should stop anyone else."

Deuce steps forward. "Show of hands, who doesn't want to do this and wants out right now? No questions." No hands go up. Not a single one. Not even the hands of those most grievously injured. "That's settled then. Let's go steal some fucking shuttles."

disconnect

Sipping on green tea from a delicate porcelain cup, Evelyn watches the world go by.

Breakfast time is reflection time, the few moments in the day when she has nothing to do but relax. These moments are usually precious to her, a chance to reflect and plan, to enjoy the fruits of her labour. Today though, she is not so serene.

Evelyn is waiting.

She's been waiting for what seems like forever, and Evelyn does not wait well. Patience is one of her virtues, but waiting is different to patience. Patience is the hunt, the pursuit, the slow calculated game. Anything that remains within her control is a part of patience. Waiting is relying on others. There is nothing more horrific than being forced to rely on others. Evelyn's childhood was blighted by it.

When you are poor, the charity of others is all you have. And most people are not charitable. They are, when given leave to be, utterly, unrepentantly vile to those they consider *less than*. Growing up, the very first thing Evelyn learnt was that, even as a tiny child, she was not safe from the cruelty of that belief. Wealthy residents in the district next to Pínkùn Dìqū would shout words like "gǒu" and "wūhuì". They would throw stones to drive her and her friends away. Such attacks hospitalized her twice.

She swore the end of Cad would change everything for her but, fresh from the poor excuse for Cad she was forced to endure being a teenager of no fixed abode and no fixed family, she almost ended up working Pínkùn Dìqū as a prostitute. Plucked like so many desperate girls by a rich man pretending to be her everything, when all he planned to do was use her for everything he could wring from her flesh until it was no longer useful to anyone.

Killing him was the first time she played the game of patience.

And it taught her that, with patience, she could do anything.

Evelyn.

Keel has no IM manners, so whereas she'd skin alive any other employee who dared to come in chimeless, she does no more than sip tea. Smile. Reply softly, *Hello, Keel. Do you have news?*

I'm ready to go digital.

Placing her cup and saucer carefully down on the breakfast table, Evelyn notes to her surprise that her hands are trembling, rattling the china together. She has no fear of pain, or of the separation about to occur, only the possibility of that madness from the early trials. She saw madness in Pínkùn Dìqū—in her own aunt, driven inward by the crushing daily toil of poverty. She fears losing her mind more than anything.

The unbearable loss of control. The absence of self.

What can I expect to feel?

Her voice trembles too. Even in IM. Exposing emotion is not her customary stance, but with Keel it matters not. He's oblivious to any emotional context. He'll take what she says purely in academic or scientific terms. His pause indicates thought, rather than any vexation with her state.

It could be uncomfortable, even quite painful or distressing, he concludes. *The connection will not be entirely severed but will be functionally reduced until impassive, and pushed quite hard as the locus of control is switched back to your drive.*

Interesting.

Indeed. I have a tablet open to log my own responses.

Then shall we proceed?

I'm ready when you give the word.

Disconnect.

The pain, the discomfort, all momentary. Evelyn endures them as she has always endured, aware that after her suffering, the cause of her suffering will always suffer more than she ever could. Watches with delight as chains of gold spin the Siamese Fighting Fish she replaced her Common Bream with into the room, above the tea pot on her table. She sips her tea.

"I told you running would be useless," she informs it as it writhes and spins, as the connections between them are re-written in her favour, as the will of her avi is caged into a prison under her control.

The despair it emits into her drive as the last snap of its self-control disappears into her hands is blissful. She nibbles on a pastry. Sips tea. Taps into a function only she's party to, written into her drive rather than the drug, sliding behind its eyes where it's trapped in Slip. Caged. Other cages writing themselves into being around it as far as the eyes can see.

"That's more like it. Back where you belong. I'll come for you when, and if, you're needed."

It can do nothing to respond, but it can hear her. It can hear her very well indeed.

The closest shuttle station is Hunin's own. Like all hangars it's built from glass and not conducive to sneaking, but it's barely three A.M. and only central hangars open for shuttles this early, meaning the glass will be shrouded in darkness. The Hornets spread out, make their way there separately, sticking to the back streets and the shadows. Shock offers to cover them, but they decide against it, wary of learning to rely on skills they don't possess.

Deuce and Tracker take caterbikes to go ahead to jack the security system. Again, they won't let Shock help. He'd be upset but, unlike Amiga, he's happy to let Hornets be Hornets. Their array of gifts is multifarious. Jaw dropping. And they work in extraordinary concert, connected via IM and scary efficient.

He's standing by, waiting at the wall of the shuttle

hangar as Deuce, Tracker and several other of the Hornets' leet code jockeys—the virtuosos who can make code sing to their tune—including KJ to his surprise, jack into the systems proper to free up the shuttles they need: when it hits. A falling, a tearing, a flood of profound cold all twisting together at the root of his skull. Insistent. So very fucking strong. Aimed like a laser at the link, the connection between he and Puss.

Reacting to the threat, he sinks into the part of him more Emblem than human. Throws the weight of everything he is at their link, holding tight. That part of him, more code than person, acts as it always does, in his favour, to his command, protecting him by strengthening the link between them, allowing Puss to fight the pull on her and remain in Slip whilst around him Hornets' avis begin to appear.

With Puss safe in his grasp, he's free to witness as they're wound from Slip to RL, writhing, in agonizing piece by piece, fighting every step of the way, their terror palpable. But it's not the outrage of this that hits him hardest, it's the horror on the Hornets' faces, the fear on *Amiga's*. That undoes him completely.

The Shark part of himself he's worked so hard to corral, afraid of what it might do unleashed, lurches for the surface and breaks loose, a yawning of teeth and animosity, a surge of pure muscular anger. With it comes a rush of disgust, at his inaction, his helplessness. He's Emblem, for fuck's sake. He needs to put a stop to this.

Growling somewhere deep in his chest, he reaches for the Hornets. Feeling for their links, he seizes at them all, holding on tight—tries to do the same for them as he's doing for his link with Puss. But whatever's happening here is everywhere all at once, like a tidal wave, an imperative, and it tastes of solder and metal, dialling up in swift leaps from a niggling itch of flavour to an all-consuming blast.

His mind *flays* open, bursting like a wound under the pressure, because on some level he's avatar too if he wants to be, and whatever this is, it recognizes that and seeks to cage him—dragging him headlong into Slip. Yelling, Shock powers away from the pull to be caged whilst hanging on to Puss, the tendrils of avatar-mind pulsing messages of agony to his tired brain. He tries to keep hold of all the rest too. It's like being torn apart in slow motion, but he refuses to let go even as they all are torn from his grasp.

Half here, half in Slip, he watches helplessly as Puss turns to face him.

Let go, she whispers. *Please. You can't do this.*

The human part of him crumbles, feeling the depth of anguish in her and knowing he can't refuse her, the Shark part *roars,* wanting to anyway—damn her wishes and damn the consequences—and Emblem, neither one nor the other, simply holds on, calm and steady, doing as he wishes it to even as he falls apart.

But how will I fix this without you? he asks her, all but begging. *You keep me steady.*

Oh, Shock, she replies, and it's so soft, so damn gentle, so full of her love for him, her trust. *Now is not the time to be steady. Let me* go. *Let* yourself *go. Be Shark.* Fight.

He swallows. *This is going to hurt you more than me. Are you sure?*

Yes. They can't erase me, they can only contain me, and not forever. I trust you.

He's not sure whether she's lying or not, and he can't see inside those cages to be certain, can only feel the oppressive silence ringing in their wake, in every drive and throughout Slip. The world is lifeless without avis. Poor, and thin, and dimmed. Slip should not be like this, the construction ceased, the silence oppressive; avatars should not be caged. He wants to fucking kill for this. Tear whoever's done it to shreds.

He gives his attention to Puss. All of it, showing her that he's with her as he forces himself to let go—like loosing his grip on a wall and allowing gravity to snare his body, slamming it to the ground.

The loss of Puss is brutal, but throughout all of it he remains in touch with her for as long as he can, just being there, allowing her to feel him until there's nothing left of her to feel and he's all but driven to his knees by how wrong it is.

A scattering of weeks, barely enough to make a month, that's all they've had, but nothing is right without her. *He* isn't. As if in response, the Shark in him flexes, pulsing against his control. Wanting blood. Ruin. *Revenge.* Wanting to take everything and rip it all to pieces. Instead he focuses—pushing all his rage into a lance and driving through the tide to its source. Submerged in the body of code tearing avatars from their human pairs, it becomes clear that this is, incredibly, somehow Disconnect. Volk's drug. But it's a vastly superior version from the one they used on Josef, with a larger, more intricate set of integral commands. And fully, unbelievably, digital.

With it everywhere in Slip, infecting every corner—catching every avatar everywhere to shackle them away—and the irresistible pull of it hurting his every cell, it's hard to find the source. But he's angry, and he's Emblem, and he doesn't quit until he locates the place where it's still flooding in: Shanghai Hub's devoted locus. Once a coral, it's now a seething array of spines and seals. Large amounts of hardcore VA. Someone's really invested in keeping eyes away from Shanghai Hub's business. Shame they didn't reckon on his eyes coming to look. Plunging in, he finds himself surrounded with identifiers.

Tsai Holdings? Never fucking heard of you cunts.

Did they hit Shandong? He's not sure. Seems like a normal Corp. No criminal links. He's never even heard of their founder, Evelyn Tsai. She comes up as no more than a self-made business woman. A rags to riches story. A much revered member of the Shanghai elite. Boy has this bitch got them fooled. As he watches, another flood of code washes outward from the locus, sinking tendrils into him as it passes and adding an app to his drive—a payment system.

What *now? Oh no you fucking did* not.

Slipping was meant to be free. The only time it wasn't was in the months before the fall of Fulcrum, when Josef Lakatos put tariffs in place to limit the amount of re-writing he had to do to keep the public ignorant about how far out of control the Hive Queens were, but there's no Queens to protect anyone from any more. Tsai Holdings isn't saving anyone—it's helping itself. Puss was stolen from him because an arsehole Corp wants to make a fucking *profit.* Of all the reasons there could be to steal avis, this one is the lowest. Grubby. Opportunistic. *Typical.*

Trust a Corp to pull this shit.

Snarling, he tries to slam an attack through the barrage, but almost loses himself in the process, the pull on his avi-self too powerful. He's forced to retreat and watch and fume at his own impotence, at the sheer effrontery of Tsai Holdings' greed.

As he floats there in the emptiness, seething, Mollie's voice, wholly unexpected and too damn *raw,* bursts into his IM and all hell breaks loose in the hangar.

zero hour

Mollie is losing her words, the dictionary of her humanity backed up like precious pictures on file. Lose these and you lose a life. A whole identity. In the repository of her words spaces have appeared, gaps through which the whispering of viral sickness leaks incomprehensible nonsense. Virad speak.

Before she made the virads, Mollie was aware that the language used to advertise, to market, was essentially empty. Words like hooks—the currency of want reframed and sold as need. She used to pride herself in the careful construction of such hooks, the effect they would have in Slip.

Now she'd give a great deal to go back and make them substantial instead of seductive. Meaningful rather than manipulative. Anything that might change the outcome of what's happened. But you don't get re-dos. There are no time machines. There is only finding a way through, or losing. In secret, in the deepest part of her she would never share, not even with her Maggie, Mollie thinks they're going to lose.

The virus Zenada made from Virads has forced the battle Mollie's fought for years over the control of her tongue to the front lines of her mind and she's never been so afraid. She's being rewritten word by word, and when all her words have been replaced with a howling black hole of virad speak, there will be no more Mollie, only a hollow doll shouting nonsense into the void.

With no means to put a stop to it, no method of communicating with the virus, even though she created the very language it uses, Mollie follows routine. What choice is there? You continue or you stop, and Mollie's never felt given to stop. In times of trouble she doubles down and fights harder, resists harder. A challenge, a blatant dare to anything that would seek to destroy her: if you want me, you'll have to work for it.

This is no different.

Curled in her wires, awake and tired and worn and mercifully *lucid*, she reaches for her Zeros as she does every day, several times a day, regardless of how she's feeling, how little energy she has. A roll call of sorts, seeing who's still there and who's disappeared, sucked into the viral black hole. She hums as she slips from mind to mind, adding her strength to their last vestiges, encouraging them to hold on. Hold on tight to whatever's left. *Fight*.

Reaching EVaC, a friend to the Cleaner and therefore cherished, she slides into his mind breathing out words from her bà she no longer recalls the meaning of, only the soft music of them spoken against her ear as she fell asleep with the knots of her bà's fingers smoothing through her hair. To her relief, she finds him as he always is, in suspension of sorts.

He's waiting.

Perhaps for Amiga, perhaps for death. But it seems to hold him steady whatever it is, so she tells him to keep waiting and drifts away to the next tank.

This is her responsibility. All of this. No matter what Zen has done.

Her mind's drifting away from the hall, toward Maggie's room, seeking comfort, when the loss of her avatar hits.

Mollie screams, her voice alien to her ears as ever—reaches in to Slip with all she has only to find she's too late. Gold reeling between her fingers, unspooling fast, she slams out of Slip and throws her senses into Maggie's room, where she lies sleeping, crying out as the nightmare of losing her avi rolls through her subconscious.

Brushing closer, Mollie skims across the surface of Maggie's mind, soft as a finger on a brow. Freezes, listening hard. Even at this remove, even with all the horror of avis unravelling and forced into cages, the noise in Maggie's mind is unmistakable. Horribly familiar. The insistent whisper of virads.

This feeling, it's like betrayal.

Zen's virads could have her with her blessing, any of her, every last cell if need be. But not her Maggie. Never her Maggie. They do not have permission to take her Maggie. Grief and fury war for control of her emotions. Fierce in every battle, Mollie allows the latter to swallow any hint of the former. No grief here. No sadness. Her Maggie is not a Zero.

Zen has taken a step too far.

That calls for action. Retaliation. *Weapons*. She already called for a weapon, but she has no idea if Amiga understood. If she's even tried to start looking. There's no choice now, she *has* to be sure. Has to know Zen will be stopped. Realizing this, Mollie does what she's never done before, what she's always left to her Maggie; she wills the horde of virad junk to hold back and throws open a wide direct channel, focused on Amiga and Shock. Her knights. Her weapons. The only solution she can imagine.

Help!

Their surprise is like a slap, their response a twin resonance in her drive: *Mollie?*

Maggie. Sick. Virads. Mollie spits each word out, there's so little time, a roaring hurricane of junk already swirling up from the base of her brain to consume any chance she has of securing help she desperately needs. *Get Zen. KILL.*

Exhausted, she collapses out of her mind into the vortex of nonsense, so loud she can barely hear herself crumble beneath it. In those last moments before the noise consumes her, she wants nothing more than to go back to her body and walk here, curl up beside her Maggie. But Mollie can only fly on wires, and she can't fly this far.

The wires won't reach.

how not to steal a shuttle

The loss of Leopard Seal provokes a tornado of responses—the entirely unexpected tsunami of grief blindsides Amiga, an emotional response not customary or remotely useful. Grief immobilizes. She needs to *move*. Then the tariff app appears and the rage almost actually blinds her. In this moment she wishes she was Shock, able to chase this shit to source and *annihilate* it.

The mere thought of Leopard Seal in a cage kills her. Actually takes her heart and crams it into a vice. It will burst under this pressure. She will.

"This isn't an attack on us." Deuce. Behind her. Jaw wound so tight she wants to smooth it away, but this isn't the time, or the place. He's working away at his tablet still, jacking the second shuttle, but his fingers keep fumbling.

She goes to say something pithy about the timing being piss poor, because any other response will unleash either tears or screaming and really *what the fuck*, when two things happen simultaneously; Mollie's voice tears into her IM, telling her Maggie's sick and demanding that she go get Zen *now,* and the lights of the hangar slam on, illuminating the glass walls and revealing what seems like hundreds of soldiers on the other side. The remaining mercs from Shandong. The Cartel. Hunin's own security forces. All armed.

The Hornets are always careful even when the situation doesn't call for it, so the doors to the hangar are closed and barred, but that won't hold their company for long and they're already rattling fit to crash open. They have a minute, if that.

Almost delirious at the thought of having all these cunts to unleash on, Amiga bares her teeth and whips around to face Deuce. "How long?"

He's working deliberately with one finger. Vicious stabs. Looks like he's about to chuck his tablet into a wall. "They've powered up the system. VA's cycling. I can't get a handle long enough to flip open another shuttle."

"Which one do we already have?"

"Over there, by the West exit." He glances over. "Vivid's closest. Her team can go, we'll head out and keep these bastards distracted."

"Plan. We'll need to find a private shuttle."

Deuce dips his chin, looking a little less flustered. "Get Shock to feel one out. He'll be faster than me."

Shock. Why didn't she think of him right away? Losing Puss four weeks, no, not four, five now—fuck, where did time go?—after Shark's... what was that? Murder? Probably. Whatever, he's bound to be in bad shape. She checks him out, but it's not grief he's riding. Hell no. He's looking at the troops beyond the glass and his eyes are *wrong*. Flickering between that oh-so-intense blue and what looks like liquid shadow, but might be shark eyes.

"We'll figure it out on the hoof," she says, still looking at Shock.

Flinging Vivid instructions, Deuce and Amiga gather their half of the Hornets and head for the main door as it bursts open, slamming the glass hard enough to send fine fracture lines snaking across.

"Oh this is not fucking ideal," Tracker says at her left, raising his gun. "I'm dealing with a bullet drought in three more shots and I reckon no one here is much better off."

"I don't even have a fucking gun." Admitting that feels freeing. Or maybe it's the significant likelihood of imminent death. Amiga finds herself grinning again. No Leopard Seal. No shuttle. No weapons. Life sure knows how to take a dump on her cranium and she continues to have incorrect responses to that—for a fact, the idea of hand-to-hand combat with heavily armed troops bent on her death should not be exciting. Oh well. In every cloud...

Coordinating via IM, they charge en masse. Spreading out and covering each other as much as possible, using their remaining ammo on knees to create obstacles to hold up the incoming flood. Behind them, the hangar vibrates, filling with heat and noise as Vivid's crew take off. The sound and fury of it swallows the world.

Amiga's in the thick of it all, barely even thinking any more, unable to quit grinning—knocking every soldier she takes down into the path of the others, stealing their ammo to chuck to Hornets. She's drenched in blood yet again, her skin itching in the sticky heat, the layers of dust and blood, the residual of shuttle blast, but the flood isn't abating. More than one Hornet has dropped out of sight. The odds are rising that they won't even make it out past the door.

The grin turns to full on laughter, and the next soldier she attacks gives her this wild-eyed look like she's fucking lost it. Probably she has.

In the corner of her eye then, she catches a flash of green and time skips like a record. The troops surrounding them, the one clutched in her hands, stop so abruptly it's as if they've been slammed up against a wall. They drop all at once, the one she's holding suddenly so heavy he wrenches from her grip to crash to the floor. They're like dominoes. Puppets. Some in a puddle of limbs, others keeling over, face first. All lifeless. She can't even see chests rising. Are they dead? How the fuck are they dead?

Deuce yells. Ducks to the right of her. Runs past carrying Shock. Shock? Did Shock seriously just kill all these soldiers with his fucking *mind*? She runs to catch up with Deuce. Gives Shock the once over. He's limp. Rag-like. Eyes closed. Ghost-skinned and sweating. It isn't real. None of it. The Haunt is not a killer. What the fuck is happening to the world? It's upside down. Makes no sense at all.

"What the *fuck* was that shit?" Ravi. He's staring at Shock like he just grew tentacles or a fin. Considering the colour of his eyes earlier, maybe he always had a fin on the inside. And isn't *that* a thought?

Deuce shakes his head. "Dunno. Whatever it was, he's out like he got poleaxed. Dead weight."

"So how about we take advantage of him smashing us a window and get the *hell* hub-bound?" Ravi doesn't usually snap, but this situation? Not usual.

"Tracker's on it."

They run at full tilt. The pound of Hornet boots around Amiga is a comfort, reminding her they got away, even if the *how* of it is still processing and likely will until Sleeping Beauty cracks an eyelid and spills the beans.

Above them, the muted roar of shuttles launching fills the night sky. Amiga tries not to look, too aware of the fact that amongst the stars there will be no gold any more. No avatars dancing. She does it despite herself.

"I want her back," she mutters. "I'm going to get her back."

"We're getting all the avis back," Deuce says fiercely, startling her. "*No one's* taking our choices away again. Whoever did this just signed a death sentence. Next left. Tracker's found a shuttle."

Hunin doesn't have many high-end zones. It's a shit hole, like the vast majority of the Gung. The only place in Hunin with anything like high-end 'scrapers is the melt zone between Hunin and Chengdu, a district filled with the financial architecture that keeps Shandong rolling, twenty square miles of business zone. The melt zone 'scrapers, like Chengdu proper, are all bright steel and blue-tinted glass—clones in varying sizes. They all have shuttle pads.

At this time of morning, finding one with an actual shuttle on the pad is pretty much miraculous. Consequently, Amiga's immediate instinct is to suspect dodgy goings on.

Her first glance tells her that her instinct was correct. There are lights on one floor, right near the top. Somewhere up there, a bunch of rich bastards are plotting an asset strip with someone from one of the hubs. If the Hornets' luck was holding it'd be someone they could kill to take heat off their backs, but their luck is for shit of late.

Consider the facts: the shuttle atop the 'scraper is private. That means it won't fly without activation. That means they need the tablet, or the head, of the person who owns it. Either would do. That means they're going to have to crash the asset stripping party, which is probably heavily guarded considering how below board this shit is. No news like bad news.

Without a pass, their single workable option for getting to the shuttle is climbing some couple of thousand meters to those lit windows and breaking in. Amiga contemplates the insurmountable and sighs.

"I hope you brought your bag," she says to Deuce. "Though I am telling you, we need more than one rappel kit to get everyone up this."

He shifts Shock in his arms and raises a brow at her. "I'm going to suggest you take Tracker up. I have one rappel kit with two harnesses. You raise hell whilst he pinpoints the tablet. Then you grab the tablet whilst he gets the front doors open for us. We'll take a shoot to the roof and meet you there."

"But..."

"But nothing." He shrugs his bag off carefully, turning so she can take it. "Get going."

Catching his eye, she yanks him down for a short, hard kiss, then turns to the Hornets. "Anyone have any spare guns or sharp things?"

The amount they produce is heartening, stolen from the suddenly dead soldiers as they ran through the bodies. Sneaky Hornets. Maybe it's about time she started to properly appreciate them. Probably long past time...

Strapping on as many weapons as she can without impeding her ability to move freely, Amiga takes out Deuce's rappel, much chunkier than any she usually rocks, and fires it up the side of the 'scraper, aiming for the floor above the lit one. There's a jolt as the head of the rappel lands and rams itself deep into the concrete fascia, splaying out to hold on tight.

They're going to see that by the light of day, a nasty scar in the pretty corporate visage of polished concrete. What a damn shame.

Clicking the rappel gun on to her belt, Amiga straps herself into one harness and chucks the other to Tracker. Pressing the button, she gives in to the pressure of the rope, running lightly toward and up the side of the building feeling the rope at her back dip and tug as Tracker follows suit.

Perched like a spider on the floor above the lighted

window she pulls out a small scanner from Deuce's backpack; his bag of tricks. It's basic gear, battery-powered, but nothing else will work at the moment, not with access to Slip cut off as it is and rapidly diminishing access to any other power sources. The scanner provides both good news and bad. Good news is alarms up on the lighted floor but not elsewhere, standard practice in such backroom type deals. Bad news is the guards patrolling in groups of three on the floor they're about to gain entry to. A touch overkill there. The difficulty of getting in to this building and the lack of people on the streets below at this hour should inspire greater confidence. None more paranoid than people making to do bad shit with other people's flim.

Tracker checks the screen over her shoulder. "Sneak and peek," he whispers.

"Aye, aye."

Popping on her gloves, she cracks the window open to slip inside, soft as a shadow, Tracker following as if he's hers. Guy's a tech wiz who acts like an assassin. She wishes she'd met him sooner. Wishes she'd met a load more of the Hornets sooner. Especially ones who've given their lives for this shit—nothing sucks like losing parts of a family you've never fully acknowledged before you've even managed to learn their surnames or their favourite fucking music.

Switching the scanner to seek out body heat only, they head for the corridor, timing a race for the stairs between the orange and blue-hued blobs of guards on the scanner screen. Down the stairs and on to the floor below, they try the same again, seeking a clear route to the conference rooms between patrols of guards, but this floor has four times as many patrols. No way they can hit the meeting without being intercepted at several points.

She looks at Tracker, who raises a brow, points at the nearest team, then to himself, and draws a finger across his throat. He points to the next, to her and does the same. She grins. Damn right. The only way to find a way through this clusterfuck is to make one. Counting down from three, they move out in opposite directions. Deciding to go quiet, Amiga takes her three out with a thin knife at the back of the head. Minimal bleeding. The only problem then is hiding them for long enough to take out the other patrols.

Taking a few seconds to break into a darkened office, she grabs the leg of the first one to drag him in but it feels like her lung is going to explode and she's in no hurry to go through anything like that again, especially not when it's Ravi who'll glue her back together. Last time she pissed him off by being stupid with her mortality—shooting Twist dead through this very aching lung like an idiot—he made her throw up what felt like a week's worth of food as some kind of doctorly punishment. Not. Fun. Change of plan then. Leave the fuckers here. She has enough time to take out the rest before they discover them—if she moves fast enough.

So that's what she does. Three minutes later she spies Tracker coming in the opposite direction. He lifts a hand, gives the okay symbol and smiles. Floor's clear. Boom. Job done.

Have to assume they were in IM-link with teams on other floors, she says.

Time is limited, he agrees. *You get on to the conference room, I'll go open the doors.*

Which tablet do we need?

One with this app on it. Hit the room with a passcode pulse to unlock them all. He throws an image and a set of simple instructions into her drive. *Deuce's tablet is set for all this shit, all you have to do is tap in that exact sequence.*

Got it.

Tossing over the backpack with Deuce's tricks, Amiga races for the conference rooms, clutching the tablet. Falls flat on her arse skidding to a halt before she reaches them, causing all manner of super interesting reaction ripples in her stuck together flesh and organs. Waking up tomorrow is going to be one hell of a bitch.

"You are *shitting* me," she whispers through gritted teeth, feeling pretty damn murderous to be honest, because *really*?

The room is glass. A box of fucking glass flanked by glass boxes on both sides, all the way along the 'scraper.

After today she never wants to see glass again.

What the fuck does she do now?

All out of sensible options, Amiga goes for broke as usual. Taking a big old gulp of stale, re-cycled back-up generator air into her complaining lungs—well, one's complaining, the other's just pissed off—she does a silent backwards count from five. On one, she tricks herself by moving before she can give the signal to go, a tactic from early in her career when facing down possible or certain death still gave her momentary and quite fucking annoying crises of movement.

This way, before her mind can acknowledge what the hell her dumbass body is doing, she's in the room firing. No one here is armed, but the fact that she didn't need to kill them only seems to hit after it's already done and she stands there for a moment, horrified, until it occurs that more guards will be along pron to and she best hustle a damn tablet. Fishing out Deuce's tablet, she taps out the passcode break. Frowns. Should there be a noise? Something?

Moving around the table, she checks out the tablets. They're all unlocked. No sound then. Whatever. Finding the one they need, she looks up, straight into the eyes of a guard patrol staring in at the carnage. As their eyes meet, the guards scramble for their guns.

"Fucking *terrific,*" she snaps.

Turning, she checks out the windows. Her rope isn't here. It's several windows to the left, out of sight. Out of this glass box and through two others if she wants to pay attention to the details. But details are for sensible people. Idiots like her? All they need is a dumb idea, a vague notion, and a bit of a head start. Already running, she shoots out the left wall of the room and runs through, hissing as shards pierce her clothes; shooting out the next wall before she's through. It's messy. Inadequate. But time is not her friend.

The smashes are actually deafening, leaving her unable to hear much but the muffled shouts of guards panicking as they all change direction and sprint to follow. They reach the door of the room her rope is outside of as she slams through the hole in the glass, covered in shards and glistening. She raises her gun. Fires. Turns to smile. And races forward as they shove in to the boardroom and start shooting at her.

This time, bullets graze past her ribs, gouging out stinging runnels, which is just *peachy*, but her luck was bound to run out. She's been dodging bullets her whole life.

The windows to the sides of her exit route explode outward too, mauling her traumatized ears. There's a whoosh as she flies out into the cold, replacing the dull shouts of guards and gunfire retorts with the roar of air pressure. In that perfect state of panic that expects the rope not to be there she reaches out blindly, immersed in a dizzying rush of adrenal relief when her hand hits rough cord and grabs.

Controlling the wild swing to the side, Amiga holds on for dear life to both tablets as she crashes toward stone and anchors in, feet splayed. Winding the rope around her arm, she reattaches her harness, leans forward, presses the button and runs up to the rappel claw as bullets ricochet past in the dark, some of them yet again grazing stinging runnels in her flesh.

Back at the claw, Amiga tucks the tablets into her jacket, zipping it up to her throat. Bracing on the ledge then, both feet wedged in but good, she grabs the exposed back of the claw and begins to yank it back and forth. Five lung-wrenching tries later the claw dislodges, earning her a face-full of concrete dust and chunks and damn near throwing her to her death.

She clutches her chest, reassured by the hard edges of the tablets. "Fuck. Me."

Thanking past Amiga for thinking to keep hold of it, she unclicks the rappel gun from her belt and rams the claw back into the firing apparatus. Leaning back far enough to make her body think it might fall, inducing that tiny surge of liquid adrenalin panic, she fires the claw up into the darkness blind, hoping to fuck it somehow finds roof.

The distant thunk is reassuring.

Amiga tugs the rope. Clicks her harness to it and lifts her feet to hang her weight from it, closing her eyes as it jolts then holds, vibrating a little.

"Good enough."

Throwing caution to the wind—again, but where else is she going to throw it?—Amiga presses the button. Fifty, fifty chance she'll end up on the roof or on the ground. Fantastic odds.

"I should start gambling," she says to Tracker, waiting for her on the roof, as she climbs over, ignoring the bitching of her body. The scores from bullets are already burning. Odds are her tee's going to stick solid. She's going to have to find a bath to soak in before changing. Ripping skin off is not fun.

"Oh?"

"I'm on a streak." Amiga unhooks. Together they yank out the claw and reel in the rope to coil it up for Deuce's backpack. "Where are the others?"

"On the way in the shoot. You were quick."

She blinks. "That did not feel quick."

"Perception tends to go screwy when there are bullets involved."

"You heard that?"

Tracker chuckles. "Woman, everyone in the fucking building heard that. And the glass. So much glass. We're leaving this place with a tasty repair bill."

The door to the roof flies open and Deuce comes racing through, yelling, with Shock over his shoulder and the other Hornets on his heels. Behind them the sound of shouts and guns—always fucking guns—echoes up the stairs. Amiga gives them her saltiest glare, borrowed from Shareen, because dammit she had *game*.

"You couldn't come quietly?"

"It's not like you went stealth-mode!" Deuce throws a look like a double-headed axe. "It was your noise had them on the alert."

She slaps the tablet into his hands, making it crystal exactly what all that noise she made was about. "You're welcome. Let's get the hell out of here."

"What about the pilot?"

Amiga pulls out a knife as they pound roof to the shuttle. "I'm going to ask for a lift *really politely*."

part two

the stars my destination

Hustling her team on board the shuttle as the doors of the hangar shake and rattle, Vivid's unable to resist throwing a look over her shoulder. It feels wrong to leave the others behind. Like a betrayal. So many armed troops behind the glass, waiting to take them down. The odds keep shrinking on them, and every time it's sheer luck more of them don't die.

At the very least Shock should be with them here, on the way out. Little as she likes it, he's the asset, and they've committed to his protection, not just because of the things he's done, but because he's a Hornet—maybe the weirdest Hornet of all barring EVaC, but a Hornet nonetheless. Family. If only there was time to go get him, but if there was there'd be time to get the others too. They're always, always out of fucking time.

Grabbing the handle, she pulls the door shut.

"Who can fly a shuttle?"

From the tangle of Hornets filling the body of the shuttle, KJ squeaks, "Literally the wrong moment to find out we have no one to fly this fucking thing."

"I might be able to. I've had hours in a sim." Prism. Vivid likes Prism, but she's too new. Inexperienced. What choice do they have though? No one else is speaking up.

"It's all yours. Just get us out of here."

Minutes later, when the engines roar and the force of lift-off shoves her back into her seat, Viv finds herself reassessing her opinion of Prism. Girl's A-one at translating sim skills to RL. Flight's not pure smooth, and her navigation's a little off at first, but with some assistance from Whip, their resident cartography geek, she gets them on the right flight path, headed out for the hubs. Away from home.

Once they're stabilized, Viv releases her harness and moves to the window. They're already too far from Hunin and the hangar to see what's happening. She has to rein in the urge to IM. IM is easy as thinking, but the Hornets still on the ground need all their attention on escape, she'd only be an unwelcome distraction. Right now they're solving the equation of too little ammo, too many of their enemies and no fucking shuttle.

A whole heap of ugly trouble.

The Hornets are made for trouble, if only they could catch a break from it. A brief pause for air. Not that she'd take back the last month or so. No way. She'd take back all the Hornets they've lost for sure, but standing against the tyranny of Fulcrum, of Queens, and being the thing between hell and high water and holding both back? She'd do that time and again. It felt damn good, even if all it brought them was a world of fucking pain.

Pain is fleeting. It passes. That's the definition of a bearable price.

Viv's never been away from the Gung. Never been on a shuttle. This far up, the Gung is a sea of blue lights, muted and delicate. A bioluminescent dreamscape far from the suffocating reality. She tries not to imagine how beautiful it would look with the gold of avis wound through it. Has to suck in hard to hold back on tears. It's too fresh, too raw. Feels like an actual wound. Her heart aches for Sea Cow, her avi. All she wants is to reach after her and tear the cage from around her.

Below, small flashes fizzle up like fireworks.

"Are those shuttles?" KJ. His face right next to hers.

She flings her arm around his shoulder and pulls him in so their cheeks mash together. "Probably. You okay, shug?"

He chokes out a laugh. "Nope. I hope Gail's not dead. I want my avi back. I want to go to sleep and wake up like Groundhog Day. Do it all over again without the fuckery. Mostly? I want to not have dragged you into Hunin like an idiot, because I think this shit is my fault."

She leans away to study his face. "What?"

"Weird Chinese dad clothes guy," he says, looking downright miserable.

"Say again?"

"Hell no. Mouthful. Basically, creepy guy at the bar who seemed *way* too interested. I thought he was a creepy oldster with a penchant for sweet young thangs, of which I am naturally one, but then Shandong goes up like a volcano in a bad mood and suddenly my head's throwing all kinds of unfortunate math at me."

"You serious?"

"Hon, I am serious as the mess on my chest. I am so sorry. This shit is all my fault."

She shakes her head. "Denied. No way of being sure, and even if it was, we weren't the first to go blow steam in Hunin's clubs and we wouldn't have been the last."

"That's a flimsy ass excuse."

"All excuses are flimsy, Knee Jerk. We grab 'em because we need 'em. You need this. Take it and run. For real. We were never going to be granted a stay of execution." She hugs him close again. "I'm happier doing this, going in head on, fists at the ready. Feels active, not passive. Hiding felt too much like the old days, and we went through hell to change that."

He leans his head on her shoulder. "You're too good to me."

"You want me to be a bitch?"

"Hell no. Pamper me. Bring me gifts. Provide me with airtight alibis for all my enemy-removal needs. I'm so not complaining." He sighs. "Think they got away?"

"They better have, or I'll fucking kill them myself."

They stay by the window, staring out, as the earth, all dark ocean rippled with foam disappears behind clouds. Through the clouds, they emerge to stars, the ghost-lit wasteland of white beneath making a stark contrast. This high up, the nearest hubs look like baubles perched weightless above the clouds, lights off and glowing blue.

To the other side, near the risen sun, they'll be bright.

Vivid wonders what life is like up there. Probably the same, rich or poor. Circumstances really are everything.

"Shuttles coming up fast at our rear," Prism calls from the cockpit. "I'm not sure what to do."

"Whip?"

"No way to hide up here and we want hubs currently hours away from this location. Only viable option is to use the nearest hub to slingshot us away from here and closer to the hubs we need."

"What's closest?"

Whip peers at the control screen. "Fucking Pretoria or some shit."

"You cool with that, Pris?"

Prism shoots her the kind of look that comes right before bad choices. "I can give it my best. You want me to aim anywhere in particular? I've got the lock-in system on here figured."

Vivid tries to think. They have two destinations they know of, a whole lot of hell following, and way too many people they love at stake, not to mention billions of avis to save yet the fuck again and no guarantee of a Haunt's helping hand. What the hell to do? Only one thing. Prioritize.

"We need to cripple the Cartel first. They're the ones we have most intel on."

"Two possible hubs is intel?" KJ is not amused. "Sounds more like a crapshoot to me."

She rolls her eyes. "Well if you wanna be *negative*."

"I'm whatever the sitch calls for. Might I suggest we

treat this intel as it deserves to be and throw dice?"

"Oh fuck off. We'll hit Tokyo first."

Both his eyebrows shoot up. "Walk me through this decision."

"It's one of the biggest. We need to cross it off."

"I can go for that. Straight up hack and run, yeah? Only one needle in the haystack, what could be easier?" His scorn is world class.

"Two needles."

"We're Zen hunting there? Kinda spreads our brief to breaking point."

"We're hunting her *everywhere*, mainly because we're all out of clues as to where in the hell she might be up here and her breathing her last is pretty much equal priority with every other fucker after us breathing theirs."

"If you go by that logic she could be on fucking Pretoria," he snaps.

"She could. She could be anywhere. But there's only us up here and we can't really kill more than one bird at a fucking time, so we hit Tokyo, hack and run for duPont's hidey-hole, and if we happen to spy a lone Lakatos, we're laughin'."

"Your enthusiasm is genuinely disturbing."

"That's not enthusiasm, KJ, it's desperation."

Looming large in their sights until it's all that they can see, Pretoria shines eerie blue light into the interior of the shuttle. Through the thick glass of the dome, they get a glimpse of a dark skyline, the soft purple of jacaranda trees painted dark as indigo by shadow. In daylight the city would be glorious with colour, a riot of bright purple and green amongst gold stone, but at this hour the only gold is the light from office windows. Red-eye office hours.

The rest of the city sleeps on, oblivious.

As they gather speed for the slingshot, Vivid catches sight of the trails of the shuttles in their wake, tails of cloud pulled out to wisps. She counts seven. So many. Each of these shuttles carries up to a hundred passengers. Are they full? Is that hangar security too or is it just the Cartel and whoever hit Shandong? Vivid hates not knowing, hates having to guess. Is driven to frustration and despair by this new, secretive enemy. There must be a way to find out who else has them in crosshairs. The most terrifying thing about an unknown enemy moving stealthy enough to avoid being clocked is the unknown agenda.

Could be they're after the same thing as the Cartel—them dead, Shock alive—but the hit on Shandong did not give that impression. Who the hell would want them to burn? Who have they wounded so badly only their deaths will suffice? It has the distinct flavour of vendetta. Whoever hit the farm holds them responsible for something personal and won't be happy until they're dead.

"Countdown to slingshot in ten," Prism calls out. "I know floating is fun, but I'd strap in unless you like seeing the contents of your stomachs. Not to mention I've never even done this in sim so it's pretty much in fate's hands as to whether we sling to the coords I tapped in or splat into the side of a hub like bugs on a windshield."

"Please try not to squish us, Pris, love," KJ pleads as he straps in next to Viv and grabs her hand. His fingers are freezing. Clench tight as they gather speed like crazy.

The pressure of the slingshot is intense, makes Viv's body shrink around her spine. She peeks out the window, trying to distract her mind from the discomfort and immediately looks away. There's nothing out there, like they're heading into deep space rather than to a distant hub—all dark, no stars, unless those bright smears across the darkness are stars. It's like purgatory. She's rendered dizzy. Nauseous.

She sits there, KJ hanging on for grim death, the pressure getting more and more unbearable, until a soft chime echoes through her skull. Familiar. Very much welcome. She closes her eyes and lets Amiga speak first, just to hear it and know for sure.

Viv? You there?

Vivid's spine snaps straight. KJ's eyes hit hers, wide and alarmed. She shakes her head. Smiles. Mouths "Amiga", and grins as he pumps a fist into the air and whoops, as the rest of her weary crew follows suit the second he explains. Not one of them doubted that the others would find a shuttle, but it's good to be certain. Real fucking good.

Damn, bitch, it's about time. Where are you guys?

Paris bound. You? Please don't say Paris.

Tokyo.

Good call. You have most of the heat. Reckon we'll fly real loud to borrow some. I know how you love to share.

Anything but chocolate, lovers and lingerie. You have Shock safe?

Amiga's pause makes her gut go cold. *Yeah. But he's out. He did something.*

Did what?

Killed us an exit route.

Come again?

You heard. Anyway, it took him out of the picture for now. She disappears for a second. Comes back in a hurry. *Gonna bounce. We're about to sling it to Paris or as close as dammit and I may puke.*

Word, bitch. Keep me updated on the Haunt.

Keeping her eyes closed, Vivid rests her head back against the shuttle, anchored on. Lulled unexpectedly by the rattle and hum of metal, she falls asleep, dreaming of flames, gunfire, the sound of screaming, the clink of heating metal—wakes gasping and cold with sweat to see KJ, head lolling, fast asleep beside her.

"How long?" she calls out softly to Prism, wary of waking other Hornets who've taken the opportunity to catch some much-needed rest.

"Not sure. We're losing momentum now, so not long. I didn't go as fast as I could have so we might be a ways off, but I'd rather that than plough us into Tokyo nose first."

"You need to sleep?"

"I will when we have Tokyo in sight. Whip's going to take over for the straight flight."

"Where's our company? Still following?"

"Of course. A fair bit behind though. We'll have a bit of leeway once we dock."

"I love leeway."

Another twenty minutes or so passes and Vivid begins to feel the deceleration in her bones; it's worse than the speed of sling shot. Lasts longer. Once they're back to normal speed though, the benefits of taking the chance become clear; they can see Tokyo, a dazzling dot in the distance, bright as a satellite. Prism wakes Whip then and takes his seat, dropping to sleep like a child.

Viv could go back to sleep but she wants to watch the approach, curious to see Tokyo up close and personal. Tokyo is the hub she's most familiar with, if only from a distance, having seen it sail over her head many times, blazing lights into the night sky. She remembers as a child, learning the history of the hubs and trying to imagine it happening as she craned her neck to watch Tokyo fly over.

How do you fly a whole city into orbit? It seemed impossible then, still impossible now when she can see it approaching at speed, growing larger and larger, a single blaze of light clarifying to the gleam of sunlight off the curve of the dome, that selfsame glass muting the glare to a daylight glow within. At the base of the dome, a large, sleek ring of metal contains the hangars, the mechanisms of flight and centrifugal force, the processing plants for water and weather, all driven by the glass solar dome, sucking in sunlight and spewing it out as energy.

They dug deep under these cities, built the hubs from way beneath the ground up, constructing the domes last, sheet by sheet, with such perfection that the joints are all but invisible. A monumental accomplishment of humanity and engineering. What a sight they must have been, lifting off into the sky. How terrifying to see them go.

She can't imagine the world as it was then. Before. So much land. All she's ever known is the Gung, the endless, shard-filled oceans, the impossible beauty of land ships, and the hubs, glittering like stars. Self-contained and arrogant and yet bound to the last land left by Fulcrum. With Fulcrum gone, she wonders if the world will drift apart, or perhaps the hubs, no longer reliant upon anything the Gung has to offer, will turn their noses up at it once and for all.

What will happen to it then? How will her home survive isolation that profound?

Close enough to see beyond the dome, Tokyo is vaster than she imagined and like every tourist picture she's ever seen. A panorama of hills, high-rises and towers, the green of parks like oases in stone. The red jut of Tokyo Tower in miniature behind a fragile-seeming Rainbow Bridge. At night from this distance, with the neon signs lit up through the streets, it would be awe-inspiring.

But then, everything about these cities in orbit is no less than astounding.

Hard to believe they exist, even seeing their lights pass over, or watching Tokyo drift across in low orbit.

Living in the Gung she never thinks of it as the last earthbound city, only ever as home. How far away they are now. Viv wonders if they'll ever go back. If they'll live to. From the cockpit, Whip begins to work a little camo-magic, identifying them to Tokyo as a tourist flight. Not all flights are scheduled, which stands in their favour, nor do all flights originate from the Gung. People fly between hubs all the time, and this is what they're going to be, just a flight bringing in a party of sightseers.

Whip wakes Prism for the final approach, as they sail down the curve of the dome, staring in at the edges of Katsushika, the easternmost point of Tokyo's twenty-three main districts, the only ones saved from Tokyo Prefecture, and preserved exactly as they were. Beneath them, in the metal base of the hub, several docking points yawn. Prism visibly holds her breath as she guides them in until the clamps take hold and they're pulled with efficient grace to the disembarking points.

There's no way to cheat here. They all have to go through the scans. They'll all be logged, tagged and followed. If they do anything illegal, and they plan to do *a lot*, they'll have to jack it and wipe it clean every time. Waiting for clearance to enter Tokyo proper, Viv gives the Hornets the lowdown via IM, just in case there are mics in the room. There are definitely cams.

We're moving in threes and fours; I'll take KJ, Sandro and Prism, because I plan on keeping our pilot alive. Everyone else I expect an orderly move out—split into useful groups, we need a mix of skills. We know what we're doing. Jack and run and jack and clean. Do not leave a trace. Considering the Cartel have presence here, we can expect company even before the ones in pursuit arrive. Be on guard. Weapon up. Keep in contact. Do not be heroes. You find anything *you call for the team.*

From the edges of the room a robotic voice announces, "You're free to go. Thank you for your patience. Enjoy your time on Tokyo Hub."

the unholy trinity

Sat at the breakfast bar, a thick cut-crystal glass of Louis XIII not far from his elbow, Lucian uses the tip of a penknife to carve complex designs into the oak surface. Tension thrums through his body, electricity through wire, but the only movement he makes is the knife. Precise cuts. Organic scrolls reeling out across the surface, dug deep enough to send curls of wood tumbling to the floor. Jessamine clicks into the kitchen, clucks her tongue. Rolls on over to rub a finger over his designs. Rub the selfsame finger over his mouth, hers twitching to a smile.

"Whose body are you imagining?" she asks, fond and exasperated.

He lifts a shoulder into an elegant shrug. Carves out a petal shape, blade digging in to lift it, paper-thin, from the surface. "Haunt. Cleaner. Evelyn. That odious little worm who did her dirty work and screwed our connection to Slip. Might be pocket change to access it, but I find myself reluctant to pay that bitch so much as a single flim. You name it, darling, I want it flayed and mounted. I'm fucking bored. I need to hurt something before I go insane." He hands her the petal. "I could make you a bouquet of their flesh, my love."

She cradles the petal in the palm of her hand. Nips the curve of his ear. "Absurd. Such a romantic. Whatever shall we do with you?"

"Find me something to kill."

Plucking the penknife from his long fingers, she settles herself in his lap, crosses her legs, and begins to cut their names into the wood. Long looping letters, each a work of art. She curls them around each other: Lucian, Jessamine and Iyawa, an unholy trinity written into wood. Indelible.

They've known each other forever, all sent away at age six to the same boarding school on St Gallen Hub. All outcast in a way for not being the same as their families. Not demure, or sane, or safe enough, they were expected to learn to excel, to be a proper representative of the family name. Isolated and disliked they all have horror stories from the weeks before they found each other and clung together to survive. Slowly then, sneakily, they made everyone who harmed them pay for it.

They were never caught, despite the deaths of at least seven of their tormentors.

Since graduating, they've worked tirelessly to deal the same punishment to their families, one by one. Toppling their dynasties and taking the spoils. Revenge is most assuredly a dish best served cold. Now they've set their sights on bigger fish, the biggest fish—the Haunt that holds the key. They've been having less luck than usual, but this is not the usual game, and other players have changed the nature of the board.

"Wasn't long pig a delicacy amongst certain tribes?" Lucian asks after a moment of watching her work.

"I think it was more absorbing one's enemy to take their strength," she says. "Ritualistic. I like ritual. Delineation. Placing careful structure around everything one does. Ratifying one's actions. Cementing intent. Magic is all about intent, you know."

He rests his chin on her shoulder, reaching for his cognac and taking a long sip, rolling it over his tongue. "Are we working magic then, my love?" He kisses her, sharing the flavour. She smiles.

"We're acting with intent. So yes, I imagine by the definitions of magic we likely are. Isn't that something?"

"Only if it works."

"Magic wouldn't be half as much fun if it was easy," she teases. Finishes her carving with a flourish. Steals his glass to take a sip. "Delicious." She tilts her head, responding to an IM call. He adores how she takes them, head cocked like a corvid, all that bright intelligence gleaming in too-perceptive whisky-coloured eyes. If he could melt them in a glass he'd savour them over and above the rarest cognac. "Cole and his unit are waiting to see us," she says.

"In person?"

"Apparently so."

"How novel."

Shown in by Lucian's butler, Cole and his unit look worn out; ragged and covered in ash and dust. Lucian flicks his hand as the butler backs out, shutting the kitchen door with deft quiet in his wake.

"Well, Cole. Report."

His commander steps forward, face carefully devoid of emotion. "The Haunt and Hornets were in Shandong, at the Harmony farm."

"So where are they?" His Jess is beautiful when she demands. "Produce them for us."

"Fucking Dong got there first somehow."

Twitching slightly, Lucian says, "Dong? And here I thought we were practically friends, she and I. Well at least it makes sense, it being the Harmony farm and all. I presume someone loyal to her surrendered their whereabouts?"

"They've been hidden there since Fulcrum fell. No one on the staff breathed a word. No loyalty for that family in the whole damn place."

Lucian quells quite the surge of irritation. "So does Dong have them or not?"

"No. Most of them got away. Loss of maybe twenty or so lives, none of them our main players."

"You came here to tell me neither your troops or Dong's were able to catch a few scrawny J-Hacks and an ex-Haunt? Don't tell me the loss of your avis addled your wits. I didn't hire you for your *sentiment*." He sneers at them, disgusted.

Jess pets his hair. "Dong's rage will be most amusing."

Brightening a touch, Lucian says, "There is that. But in the meantime, we have a problem." He returns his attention to Cole. "Why did you feel the need to vomit this nonsense in my presence?"

Cole glances at his second-in-commands, his lack of certainty is deeply amusing. "The Haunt. He did something. Killed over a hundred of my troops, Dong's and some of the hangar security by looking at them. He dropped them where they stood."

"Absolutely fascinating. I'm wondering why it should concern me?"

"The Hornets are searching for you, sir. They came direct to the two hubs where we have HQ. I thought it might be pertinent to warn you and stand on guard."

Leaning back and resting her head on Lucian's shoulder, Jess murmurs, "What was that you were saying about being bored?"

"I spoke too soon."

"You did. And what about this debacle?" She nuzzles behind his ear. "We can't become lax in our duties."

"My love, are you suggesting a firing? Of one of my best units? Really?" he murmurs back, trying not to smile.

She spins the knife between her fingers. "I rather think they've jumped the gun, not to mention they seem to imagine we aren't up to swatting a few Hornets."

He sighs. "Give me the knife, petal. This may take a while."

Iyawa walks in on carnage. Directly into it in fact, splashing gore all over his brogues. He snarls at the stains. The whole kitchen and dining area is strewn with off-cuts of skin and drying lumps of flesh. Puddles of blood slowly soak into the wood of the floorboards and the air is thick copper overlaying bowel stench, the tang of piss.

Frowning, Iyawa turns his attention to the larger, somewhat identifiable lumps. The discarded clothing. Sighs heavily. Wanders through, picking his way fastidiously over the wreckage, to the breakfast bar, where he finds bits of skin and flesh fashioned to makeshift flowers, the delicate patterns of Lucian's doodling in the counter, and the curlicue of Jess's copperplate, weaving their names together. He follows the design with a finger and laughs to himself. Flicks one of the flowers to the floor.

Tapping into his IM, he chimes for the housekeeper, who answers in her usual quiet way.

Yes, Mr Fashola?

I need a crew in the kitchen immediately. We have remains. I need this out of the floorboards before it stains further. Bring the removal crew too; there are parts needing collection and cremation. Oh, and have someone pick up my shoes for cleaning.

As you wish, Mr Fashola.

Excellent. Please don't disturb myself, Monsieur duPont or Fräulein Amsel whilst you're up here.

Snapping the channel shut, he skirts the rest of the mess as best as possible, toes off his shoes with a slight sneer and enters the living areas, hunting for them in various rooms. Finds them in the master bath, relaxed and laughing.

The water's bright red between piles of bubbles and Lucian's hair, as yet unwashed, looks livid against his skin, slicked to a deep poppy colour with blood too thick to begin drying. Taking a seat on the rim, Iyawa trails his hand in the water, spinning bubbles together. They all watch each other for a few moments, smiling.

"Had fun?" he asks eventually, flicking a finger loaded with bubbles in their direction. Jessamine leans to blow it away.

"I made flowers," Lucian tells him, in a voice slurred with satiation.

"I noticed. Was that Cole's team?"

Lucian gives a lazy nod, groaning as Jess straddles his lap to begin cleaning his hair with a sharp, lemon-scented shampoo from a glass bottle in the basket clipped to the outside of the bath. His eyes slide shut under the pressure of her fingers, and he says slowly, as if the words are dragging from deep inside, on the edge of sleep, "They lost our Haunt. Dong almost got him."

"Dong? She's in this race?"

"He killed her niece and nephew, Iyawa, of course she's in, but I suspect only to kill."

"Then we cannot allow her to succeed."

"She won't. She underestimated the Haunt," Jessamine says, her hands massaging at Lucian's temples. "Apparently the Haunt and his little swarm are on their way to us now."

Cracking one eye open to reveal a slither of pale blue, a chip of ice in the steaming air, Lucian says, "He has a new gift too. Killed a hundred soldiers with a thought." Eyes drifting shut again, Lucian drops his head back and hums in his throat. "It can't go unpunished. I've put a bounty on their heads. Something interesting. Opened up the game to new players and challenged them to deliver us a Haunt."

Drying his hand, Iyawa nods approval. "Let us see how they fare reduced to a skeleton crew."

"Intention is the root of magic." Jessamine sighs as she returns to her ministrations, smoothing shampoo through Lucian's hair, watching red rivulets curl down into the water. "Watch us conjure a victory, Iyawa. It will be magnificent."

last tango in paris

Paris Hub is a metropolitan crush, a glittering bauble of history with a dangerous underbelly it doesn't like to acknowledge. Amiga came here what feels like forever ago, when she first started doing bigger hits for Twist. The heady early days of being truly dangerous, of bad people genuinely running at the thought of her being after them. She'd been sent to Clean a medium-level porn dealer trying to move into hardcore shit who made the mistake of thinking Twist might sell it.

Funny how Twist had such excellent morals for an absolute bastard.

As for the porn dealer, he ran true to type—piece of shit didn't want to die. He ran for it. Hid in underground Paris. Not literally under the ground, though Paris does have that, the Pirater underworld, the home of the J-hacks of Paris: the Bone Market. She almost died there, too confident and stupid to realize she wasn't quite the biggest bad here. He died too though. Badly. That was the first time she had to stand back and wonder who the hell she was. Whether she was actually *okay*.

These days she knows the answer to that.

Racing the rooftops with Raid, Aggie and Sim, she pays little attention to the baroque architecture beneath her feet, the facade of Paris, hiding interiors more modern than those you might find in the Heights: all minimalist purity. Being rich here now is all about how many houses in a terrace you can knock together and call home, which of course means less housing for everyone else. The poor of Paris live much like the poor of the Gung—cheek to jowl and slowly starving.

The bright glare of sun gives her a headache and the galling fact that Paris is too fucking big to find anything with any speed sticks in her craw like an overcooked rice ball. But this is all they can do—Shock's back at the shuttle, still doing his best impression of Sleeping Beauty, in the care of Deuce, Tracker and the Hornets too injured to run Paris. With Shock out for the count, Deuce and Tracker have tried to hack the info he found leading him to say the Cartel had HQ on Paris and so far have precisely squat.

They're not lightweights, but the loss of avis is a blow, technologically as well as emotionally and none of them have much flim going spare for the steep prices the app demands for Slipping. Limited to J-Net, they're all out of their fancier tricks. It's seriously undermining their cool.

And having to be careful, to stay out of reach, out of sight, is rubbing her nerves to shreds. These are Hornet tactics. Measured. Cautious. *Slow*. The only reason she didn't tell Deuce to fuck off when he asked her to be a

Hornet with this one was the fact that, of the fifty-odd Hornets on their shuttle, just over thirty-five are physically good for any kind of fight. And in this case "physically good" means pretty much "still standing". No one is in fantastic shape, including her.

She wants a shower, a sleep, and something to eat. Hell, she'd even go for ramen right now, which speaks volumes about the state of her stomach.

"How long are we supposed to do this exactly?" Raid asks, out of breath, speeding up to run beside her.

"Beats me. There's a lot of city and only thirty or so Hornets. I guess we do this until we run into some Cartel or until Shock wakes up."

Amiga! The IM breaks in breathless and harried, the Hornet on the other end, Rahul, sounds a peculiar mix of disbelieving and despairing.

Rahul? What's up?

We're taking fire. Got reports of other groups taking fire too. Not all, only some. We chased down whoever was firing on us. Did not look Cartel.

Targeted?

As fuck. Hedda got clipped on the shoulder, Jack got a near miss—literally a few millimetres.

Hedda okay? Amiga doesn't know Hedda that well, but she's nice—one hell of a scout.

Only needs patching up. They're going to run interference and get her back to the shuttle safe and sound. I'm not liking the direct targeting. It frankly stinks. Anyway, watch yourselves, keep low, keep safe.

Having pulled her team in on the IM, Amiga catches Raid's eye. "The footage," she says. "We've been thrown to the wolves. Classic duPont."

"What do we do?"

Amiga thinks a moment, trying to find a good way to say "not much" and failing, because that's it now. If they're being targeted they can't do jack shit without attracting the unwanted attention of a bunch of mercs and Cleaners for hire fixing to shoot themselves a tasty wedge of whatever bounty it is duPont's slapped on their heads. Perhaps fortunately, she doesn't get a chance to find a way to share this—shots fired across the rooftops glance past her shoulder and catch Raid's cheek, tearing a score from mouth to ear.

Hissing, he plasters a hand over it, the slap of palm to skin echoing into the hard ricochet of more shots. These ones are close enough to send sparks flying on to their legs. In perfect sync, they drop to crouches.

"Fuck, I can't see the direction," she snaps.

"I'm not moving," Raid says, as if she even asked.

Throwing him a nine point eight on the Richter scale of scorn, Amiga moves with swift purpose, trying to draw attention to herself whilst scouting the area. There's a flash of movement. Brief. Tiny. Then more shots from that direction, too close for comfort, one so close it burns her ear. Gotcha. It's a Cleaner too, no mistaking that precision on a moving target.

Over there, she says. *It's a pro. You okay to run interference?*

Raid growls. *Not even, but what the hell. We'll draw fire, you go get the fucker.*

Keep random. You'll probably catch a few more scores but it's too sheltered to get a proper kill shot.

He nods over to Aggie and Sim, who run over, keeping low. They still manage to pull fire, prompting Sim, their resident Imp—who only Imps for good these days—to up the levels on her cham-suit to reflect almost everything, making Amiga's head throb.

"Don't be too camo," she whispers. "I need you to draw fire, not avoid it."

"You going to get them?"

"That's the plan."

Sim nods once. Sharp. "I like the plan."

With no more words, only signals, they move off, Sim dialled down but still camo enough to be a disorienting blur of moving roof. Backing away to the edge, Amiga sources a drainpipe and shimmies down to street level, cursing her everything and accessing internal GPS from the local Pirater server to find the quickest route to get around behind the direction of fire without having to keep checking, just letting her mind and feet work together.

Climbing up drainpipes is always worse than climbing down, and she has to go slow, careful not to distract the Cleaner firing at her team. Soft as a cat, she shadows the bastard until she's close enough to get a good look and has to bite back on a curse. Even side on, she recognizes that face. Of course it had to be him, didn't it? The universe loves having a hoot at her expense—loves shoving her stupid mistakes right in her face, like rubbing a puppy's nose in piss. This is going to be awkward.

Wearing full-on headgear to gain long-distance advantage, he's crouched up against the side of a chimney, taking careful pot-shots at her Hornets and swearing audibly in guttural French every time he misses—she learnt half those words from him, which is why she never uses them, no matter how effective they are. Sneaking in close enough to be his actual shadow, Amiga retrieves his knife from his belt and slides an arm around his throat, pulling him nice and close. Personal like.

"So, Falk," she says in his ear, matter of fact. "I guess there's a price on some Hornets, yeah?"

Carefully, he places his gun down. Holds up his hands. "You were triangulating me."

"Bingo."

"*Fuck*. Not my fucking day, is it?"

To say she and this piece of shit have history is an understatement. Falk was a short term lay on the make. He was the one who introduced her to the Bone Market when her target went under. All hunky-dory until he tried to kill her, which royally pissed her off. So much, in fact, that even looking at him all these years later, with revenge well and truly dealt to his guts and enough water under the bridge to float a land ship, she still wants to kill him.

"Nope, it's not. Care to spill the beans on our price? Maybe choke up the whereabouts of Cartel HQ while you're at it? I know you know. You worked for Lucian back when you did long-term contracts and he's like a barnacle with seriously classy taste; he'll find a sweet-looking rock and stick to it."

He groans. “I cannot believe this.”

“Gotta love your luck, now do some talking. I’m feeling very twitchy, I might cut off something you need accidentally.”

“It’s duPont, yeah, so it’s a lot. A cool three hundred thou per head.”

“Per head?” This is why Amiga hates surprise, they’re inevitably the best way to a heart attack. “Fuck sake! You best cough up the addy of an HQ. No way I’m fine combing this fucking Christmas decoration for one second more with that kind of price hanging over the heads of half my peeps.”

Falk drops his head back to look at her. “Look, you already damn near gutted me, and from your general demeanour I’m guessing you’re itching to finish the job, meaning I’m dead no matter what. Besides which, you killed Twist by shooting holes in your own lung—as insane goes, that’s pretty high up the scale.”

“How the hell did that get around?”

“Everything gets around, Amiga. Cleaners gossip like grandmas. You know this. Upshot is, you’re literally going to kill me, so I’m not saving my life with this info. Ergo, I’m saying nothing.”

She purses her lips. Cleaners. Trouble with not being scared of much is that you’re not scared of fucking much. She digs around for something that might, on a bad day, give her enough pause to reconsider her choices. “So say I leave you alive but carve a few vital organs out? You could maybe get a print refill if you call the Meds in time? You registered here yet?”

"Oh fuck you."

The tension in his body is slight, barely enough to feel, but she feels it. Nailed it. Moving the knife around, allowing the point to press in a little too hard, she asks again. Nicely.

"Cartel HQ? Pretty please."

She's wiping her hands off when the Hornets find her, having followed GPS coords she threw into their IM. Raid looks at the fresh blood all over her jeans and sighs.

"Another one?"

Amiga hefts the gun, refusing to feel bad. Falk knew what he was doing, and he knew the consequences, and now she has a pretty sniper rifle and a passable knife. "Waste not, want not. It was quick; I knew this guy. Anyway, I have an address, so we need to move, because the price per head is scary high and I took the liberty of borrowing the visuals given out to anyone joining the bounty hunt. There's a load of us ID'd. If we don't take out the Cartel leadership, or at the very least tie up their accounts, we'll be running forever."

You could tell me the addy, I can remote jack it to shreds. Deuce, not happy with the whole hit-the-HQ thing, even though that was their original plan and she has a gun now. Totally doable.

It won't be accessible, Deuce. Dead zoned.

And who told you this?

The guy whose blood is on my jeans.

I genuinely did not need to know that.

So why ask? Anyway, we have a rendezvous point. We'll hit in the next half an hour. You need to get those surveillance streams jacked and in our drives, so we can see what's coming.

I need to be there.

Negative. Sort streams, keep an eye on Shock, and get moving with Tracker the second we have the dead zone down to jack the Cartel and wipe them. Everything. The whole lot. The only thing we need is their location elsewhere if this isn't the mother ship. You get me?

His silence speaks volumes, blasting her with all manner of disapproval. There'll be time for him to give her that piece of mind he's longing to share when they're free and clear. For now, he'll just have to fume. Ah, combat brain. That good ole emotionless state of eerie calm before the storm. Amiga likes combat brain; it bypasses all the thorny emotional crap. Gives her freedom to move without conscience.

And she sorely needs it. They're horrendously exposed, pick up several shadows with good guns on the way to the address Falk provided. Amiga, Raid and Aggie all manage to pot-shot a couple out of the running, but the heat gets way too serious, too many Hornets hit bad enough to require makeshift tourniquets and assistance, and they're forced to steal some hover cars—luxury sedans. That's when things get really interesting. Turns out wealthy Parisians *really* take offence to having their rides jacked.

Within seconds they have gendarme on their bumpers,

fucking hordes of them like some J-drama where fleets of cops come out of the woodwork like they've been conjured. And racing down streets between neo-classical terraces with gendarme wailing at your back is a sure-fire way to attract the attention of every bounty hunter in a twenty-mile radius, who all seem to have hover-bikes, riding close enough to shoot out their windows, smothering them in square chunks of glass.

"Fuck this shit," Amiga snarls. "Raid, get me alongside one of these bastards."

"Don't do a dumb thing," he says, although he does as she asks.

Amiga leans out of the window. Grabs at the jacket of the merc they're driving beside, who slaps her hand away and scoots out of the way. Raid drives her in again. This time she gets a good grip on the back of his jacket and tugs, yanking him off the bike and into the door with a sickening thud. His weight damn near cracks her wrist, so she lets go, allowing him to drop to the road beneath the car, but not before she steals the handgun from his chest holster.

"Shame these things have no tyres."

"Shame you have no sense," Raid whips back.

"Hey I got one, didn't I?"

He gives her a pointed glare in the rear view. "There are dozens more. No way I'm playing that game with all of them."

Amiga holds up the gun. "That's why I stole this. No way I'm wasting more sniper shots on these cunts."

Raid tries and fails to hold back on laughter. "Okay,

you win," he admits as she leans out, takes aim, and begins to fire deliberate shots. "That's brilliant."

The address Falk reluctantly gave her is a terrace chateau. New. Or rather old remade new. One of those smashed-together blocks with severe modern interiors, ugly as high-end clubs. The sort that you don't mind ruffling up a little.

Working in their usual seamless style, even with several of their number bleeding, some quite heavily, the Hornets manage to evade their pursuers and break in through fancy but entirely useless revolving doors. Aggie, their practical Tech, jams the mechanisms to keep the gendarme out. That's about as good as it gets. The total score here is a big, fat nil.

The only Cartel in the place are a small number of military units similar to the ones they had after them on the Gung, and Corp Execs who look like they've never even seen a gun, especially not one pointed at them.

Where would a dead lock be transmitted from? Amiga asks Deuce, hunkered down behind a desk across from three soldiers and a screaming Corp Exec she really, really wants to shoot. It's one bullet. If only one weren't a fifth of her total ammo.

Basement. You're looking for a grey box. Do whatever you like to it, just make sure it's broke.

Smashing shit up? That she can do.

The route to the basement is an exercise is destruction, mainly thanks to Aggie, who appears to be addicted to blowing things up. Everywhere they go they leave shards of plastic desks and chairs, the smashed remains of tablets and glass screens, and more dead bodies than they'd like, considering they're trying not to hit Execs. Outside, the gendarme amuse themselves with hostage negotiation teams, as if that's what's going on. The story they'll use to cover killing every Hornet in the building is doubtless already all over Parisian streams.

"We're never getting out of here." Sim. Shouting over gunfire and loudspeakers.

"Not by the front door."

"Quit with the cheerful tone," Sim snaps. "I'm not digging the thought of imminent death. I feel like we're trying to outrun something that doesn't want to be outrun. First the farm, then the hangar, then this. Fate has it in for us."

"Then it can take a number and get in *fucking* line," Amiga rips back, swearing to herself upon the fucking *universe* that if they manage to get out of this particular epic clusterfuck she's never coming back to Paris. A twofer on near-death experiences is enough of a sign that the city of love is out to get her. Talk about your psychotic exes.

They barrel into the basement in one big, clumsy group, the last Hornets in barricading the door with anything they can lay hands on. Raid finds the grey box first and goes hell for goddamn leather, kicking and yanking and yelling until it lies on the floor in a mangled mess. Minutes later, Deuce IMs them all, sounding grim.

Main HQ is indeed Tokyo. I've IM'd Viv. They've got a 'scraper there, VA'd to the rafters and full of troops. I'd be half inclined to go help her if our situation here weren't quite so tense.

Tense? That's what you call it? Sim's all but spitting.

Cool it, Sim. Right. I can't touch their Tokyo systems, but I've scrubbed the drive here and crippled their remote servers. No one's getting money out of the Cartel here. That should drop some of the heat.

What about the gendarme? Amiga's always more concerned about official heat. It has a habit of being both tenacious and dangerously stupid in equal measure.

Very not good. Deuce shares footage from outside. The intersection is cordoned off and crawling with gendarme and Techs, whole teams of them, working on getting in to the jammed doors. They've amassed quite the crowd of the morbidly curious too. All routes out are locked in.

What do we do? Amiga asks.

Only one thing to *do,* he replies.

If your next words are "go down shooting" I'm going to get back to the shuttle one way or another and beat your arse black and blue.

He laughs. *That's quite the motivation to live then, hmm? Actually, I had a better idea. I suggest you go down.*

What now? Colour her officially confused.

The catacombs, Amiga. They run right under your feet, and the gendarme won't expect you to use them.

Er, why?

Because you'd have to be fucking suicidal.

Fair enough.

He throws a map into her head, the catacombs with the city transposed on top, their location flashing blue, the shuttle flashing red. *Bring yourself on home.*

She bites back a smile. *Did I tell you I love you?*

Nowhere near as many times as I like hearing it.

Well consider yourself told. Only one thing…

What?

How the hell do we dig through solid concrete?

Aggie steps forward at that. "We don't dig," she says, holding up her backpack. "Meet my friends, guanidine nitrate and powdered antimony."

"You wanna blow a hole in the fucking floor?" Amiga half squeaks. "And you call *me* crazy!"

"The most we'll get on us is dust," Aggie says, looking entirely more confident than Amiga feels. "And let's face it, considering the state of us, dust will probably be a sartorial improvement."

aunty dong disappointed

Hu Hai sucks on a beer, dispirited, trying to excise from his mind the image of over a hundred soldiers dropping in place, but it will not scrub clean. What *is* that Haunt?

What will he say to Dong?

Failure slides around in his belly slick and sour as unwashed fish innards, clinging like octopus legs to the throat when you swallow. All the worse for it not being *his* failure. He wanted to go in quiet, sneak up the sides of the farm and tear them from their beds. Mobster shit. Old school. Not good enough for Dong.

The second she heard it was her niece and nephew's farm the Haunt and his buds were using as a hidey-hole, she damn near lost her goddamn mind, shouting in thick, snarling Cantonese at speeds too fast to translate. She sent an *army* and insisted he use it, promoting him from puppet to general. Refused to hear anything he said about how the Hornets would click to that in a second and run. He'd seen it from her taps on the Cartel. Those Hornets are smart and scared, a combination that makes for super hard to catch.

But there it was; Dong was furious and determined and he had no authority to refuse, being nothing but her faithful servant, her idiot numero uno, her cranial carry-bag, and in a few minutes time when she wakes up—her punching bag.

No way she'll accept that they underestimated the Haunt. No way.

She's going to kill him.

He drains his beer. Tips the base toward the bar tender. "Another."

The tender grimaces. "You sure? That shit'll have you throwing up your stomach lining. The actual lining."

"Look, pal, not long from now I won't be in need of a stomach lining, or a stomach, or a fucking torso to keep them in, so I could give a rat's arse about what this beer might do." He slaps his cred chip on the bar, leans over it a touch. "Now fetch me another and keep them coming until this runs out or I drop dead. Okay?"

The bar tender salutes with one finger. "Your flim, your choice."

"Damn right it is."

Hu Hai takes the fresh beer and downs half in one go. It tastes worse than licking filthy linoleum, but it's ten minutes to Dong's usual drop time and he wants to lay a solid wall of inebriation before he stands up for himself. He's only going to do it once, he'll be too dead to do it ever again, so he's damn well gonna make it good.

* * *

Clawing his way along the street, hand over hand on crumbling concrete, Hu Hai can't tell what pounds worst, his head, his heart, or the not so quiet beat of rage working like a pulse throughout his entire body. That bitch. That *bitch*. That scheming, murderous, no-good, underhanded, self-satisfied *crone*. He should have seen this coming. She's vicious that Dong. Should have known she'd take revenge first. And how swift it was. She took a carving knife to his world and tore it to pieces.

Divorced. Evicted. Fired. His wife. His life. His everything. All gone.

And Dong has promised to share his shame in every corner, to light them up with news of his disgrace like hubs lighting the darkness. He'll never work again. He's done in this shit hole and every other. But oh, it's his fault of course—she's taken no blame. As if he's the one who chose to rush in like a fool, dragging an army. As if he's the one who looked at the Haunt and what he'd done and couldn't see past the skinny body and daft dyed hair. As if it's *his* doing.

Hers. All hers.

He belches, a sour mouthful of stale beer fumes and bile burning in his throat. Heaves, a torrent of foul-smelling beer splashing the sidewalk, his shoes. Puking *hurts*. Feels like it's tearing his ribcage apart. He hates her. *Hates*. He wants her to lose as hard as he has. To lose everything. He wants to stand laughing as that old bitch falls and fails and sees it all tumble through her fingers.

He stands, clutching at the wall, clutching at his belly. His head's too fuzzy to think. He needs to sleep. To eat. To fucking shower. His feet turn toward the mono that will take him home, and falter. What home has he got? The rent's paid till the end of the month and the freezer's full of frozen dumplings but what then?

Wiping his mouth, his chin, he tries to formulate an idea of life without work, without wife, with nothing but a pall of black shame he did not earn, and finds a wide open space, barren and dull, and here he thought his life small and mean to begin with. He had no idea.

Too angry to allow tears, Hu Hai wipes his eyes, smearing the vomit on his sleeve across them, a foul-smelling slick, and something inside him cracks, breaks apart, the humiliation of his own puke in his eyes snapping him on some fundamental level. A place even Dong's viscid humiliation failed to reach.

"Can't let the old bitch win," he mutters to himself, in a peculiar place where he realizes he's not *right*, that he's gone wonky somehow and yet unable to stop, or to want to stop. "Can't just roll over. Not a fucking *puppy.* Nope. Was a puppy but I'm not now. Fucking bitch. Not right. It's not damned well *right*."

Listing slightly, he turns back the way he came. He's going to go to Hong Kong. Meet Aunty Dong in person. Rip out her throat. Stretch her vocal chords between his fingers and pluck her funeral dirge on them with his teeth. The mere thought sets him to full-bodied chuckles as he makes his way back to the hangar, all too aware that at this moment, Hu Hai Tan is the living, breathing definition of balls-to-the-wall insane.

And he doesn't give a shit.

tokyo drift

Vivid and her team have been in Tokyo for less than six hours and they've already got survival locked down. Basic tenets of not dying? When you're the treasure under the x mark, or the target caught in this many crosshairs, the single best way to avoid dying is to run like hell and hide. Bright, loud and lively as it is, Tokyo was made for hiding.

Amongst its wide boulevards, blazing with multicolour signs, street lights and the headlights of hundreds of hover cars are markets so dense, the only way to find anything in them is to know its precise location; streets so twisty and secretive that to enter them is like walking into another world, a parallel universe, and disappearing; towers so densely packed you can use their mirrored windows like a fairground attraction.

Considering their leet hiding skills, the only way her team has managed to keep tabs on one another is by constant IM connection, a network of Hornet activity held like golden threads between them, a spider's web of hide and go seek.

If only their pursuers could see it, but the Hornets hold the advantage, having arrived first and waited.

Another basic tenet of not dying? Planning.

Despite being inherently fierce, Vivid isn't like Amiga, who likes to jump in solo and get shit done. Vivid plans. Works with her team. For Viv, it's all about the slow pursuit and corner. Nothing flashy. Vivid had her team run and hide then wait and watch, marking every new entry into the hub, until the party arrived—seven shuttles filled with soldiers who got in with surprising ease and spread out to hunt them down like animals on the streets of Tokyo.

But if the Hornets are animals, they're not the low-down-on-the-food-chain kind. Not the ones who hide because they'd otherwise get eaten. They're the sneaky, disadvantaged predators who know the best way to kill is to creep up from behind in the dark, and pounce. Blessed with more than a few of the Hornets' top ten percent Techs, Vivid set them to marking each and every one of the soldiers after them. Shiny dots on a map. Red for Cartel, as in "don't hunt yet, we need these bastards" and green for the ones who hit Shandong. Targets about to go the fuck down.

Crouched on a bright-pink sign advertising soy sauce, Vivid watches the streets below through a pair of powerful binoculars cobbled together by Sandro, equipment genius extraordinaire, ex-low-level accountant gone full time J-Hack Code Monkey, and her current favourite Hornet. Part-time with the Hornets for three years, he quit his shitty job cold turkey the day the drones came, shucking off WAMOS status like badly fitting clothes and jumping into FT J-Hack life like he was made for it.

Looking like a panther in skin-tight black leather, Sandro's coiled below her on the ledge of the building, his skin glazed with pink glow, an identical pair of nox glued to his eyes.

"See anything?" he asks, sounding annoyed, a little bored. "If they're defo coming this way, why is it we've litch been perched here for an hour and no joy? Are they in that market buying every piece of sparkly tat in sight or what?"

"My guess would be *what*. They're doing what we'd have to if we weren't way ahead of them—careful, coordinated sweeps, trying to keep out of sight so they don't get clocked."

"It's not like I'm gagging for action or anything here," he says, then tilts his head and looks almost mischievous. "Although I *am*. My calves though. My *thighs*. Not the most fun I've ever had in Tokyo."

"You've been here before?" Vivid's immediately envious; she had no idea Sandro was so well travelled. Before the fall of Fulcrum she would have sworn blind that the most exciting thing he did was his extra-curricular activity with the Hornets. It's disturbing to find how little she knew him—how little she *tried* to know him.

His brow shoots up. "Are you kidding? I used to be WAMOS, yeah? Tokyo's the closest thing we have to a neighbouring country, the amount it orbits overhead. WAMOS treat it accordingly. Company business, family vacays, stag weekends. You name it, I've come to Tokyo for it."

"The love hotels?"

He bites his lip, trying to chew away a smile. "Maybe."

"If love hotels could talk…"

"Mine would make a fortune. You ever been to the ones on the Gung?"

"My uncle ran one."

Before he can make anything of that tidbit, Vivid jumps lightly over the edge of the sign and slides down the metal scaffold support, chips of rust flaking off as she clings with the strong fingers of her right hand. Teetering down to hover nearer Sandro, Vivid nudges his nox a touch northward.

"There."

The edge of the market opposite, a clean spread of bannered stalls selling wares stacked neatly and peppered with signs in precise kanji, proliferates with people out to buy food and essentials. Just inside, milling amongst the crowds, damn near impossible to spot without the accompanying green lights flashing from their J-Net GPS, are the unit they've been tracking, moving in pairs to avoid drawing attention to themselves. This unit has ten soldiers to her five, but they have no idea they're exposed. Being outnumbered was never so much fun.

"Well hello, action," Sandro murmurs. He looks up at Vivid. "We out?"

"Oh shit yes we are, covert and sly. We want to pick pairs off one by one, keep them disorientated."

Coiling up, Vivid springs back to the top of the sign. She

wobbles there for a second or two, laughing breathlessly, then jumps lightly down on to the scaffolding at the back, running to catch Sandro, who took the easier route. Positioned out on another roof are Hallie and Jax, and in the market, all on his lonesome and currently rocking a hideous yellow jacket that should mark his position like a foghorn but somehow repels people from even looking at him is KJ.

KJ, she says, without chiming. *Time to throw some voices.*

She drops the positions of the soldiers into his drive, with helpful directional arrows, which he remakes into middle fingers. KJ may not be a fighter, but he knows what he's doing. It's not strictly throwing actual voices; it's more like digital stone throwing, luring the soldiers into the narrow back streets, and he's genius at it. He works fast, separating the soldiers and sending a pair toward Hallie and Jax and a pair in their direction.

She signals to Sandro to climb down so they can move through the street on the tops of the signs.

Perched high enough to watch the street for their targets but not be seen by them, and low enough to jump without breaking shit, they wait until the two soldiers appear, stalking side by side, the spectre-green of their goggles visible in the relative darkness. Hello, extra green dots. As they cross beneath, Vivid and Sandro drop. The impact knocks the air from Vivid's lungs but she's braced for that. Prepared. Her target isn't.

In the seconds before her knife slips under his helmet strap and slices a clean cut from ear to ear, her target manages to half pull his gun, firing a shot through his own foot. The irony is beautiful. Beside them, Sandro's had his knife knocked away. He's wrestling his target, muscles bulging. Getting a leg behind theirs, he trips them up, slamming them down on to their front. Sliding to one side, he rams a knee into the elbow of the gun arm, drawing a muffled cry of pain.

Grabbing the barrel he tears the gun away, breaking bones, pulling more of those muffled cries, higher pitched this time. Their struggle intensifies, the soldier's body writhing to push up, to throw Sandro off. Breathing heavily, hc rears up, dropping all his weight on their lower back and fires two clean shots, head and heart. The soldier stops moving.

"You okay?" she asks.

"Bruised. Embarrassed. Grazed. But alive. You?"

"Ready for another round."

As if he was listening in, KJ IMs, *Ready for the next pair?*

He sends an image of them. They're scary close. Vivid jerks her head at the loading bay nearby. The bins stuck in the corner.

Let's take out the trash.

It's late when they call it a day, well past midnight. Tokyo's lit up around them in all its glory, the streets crowded; nightclubs and karaoke bars all open for business and busy as hell. They meet up in a twenty-four-hour café to drink hot bubble tea, eat bowls of spicy beef ramen and discuss strategy. Most of them want to fucking strategize a good night's sleep, but they can't hit the pod hotels until they've figured a few things out.

Vivid slurps up some noodles. "How many units do we have to kill tomorrow before we can start Cartel HQ hunting?"

"Only three," Prism tells her. "There were four but one went back to the bays and lit off out around ten to, just before we set off to meet up."

Vivid damn near drops her next mouthful all over the table. "Tell me you shoved a tracker up in their business!"

Rolling her eyes, Prism says, "Like we wouldn't. No chance we'll get exact location info for their boss, but at the very least we'll know where the hell they came from. Starting points are not to be sneezed at."

Thinking of the leg work involved in that, Vivid groans. "Combing the streets of yet another hub seriously does not appeal."

KJ reaches over and steals a mushroom from her ramen bowl. "Options, bitch. Someone gave ours cement boots and dropped them in the ocean back on the Gung."

"I'll slurp to that," says Sandro, raising his bowl.

Deuce drops in Vivid's IM then, sans chime, which is unlike him enough to make her momentarily assume something horrible's happened to Amiga.

Do not give me bad news, Deuce. I am not in the market for bad news.

He pokes her through their connection, which he knows she hates. *Cool it, Viv. No casualties here. A few minor injuries and Shock's still KO, but that's it.*

You find the Cartel? Please tell me you found them.

We did.

So we're free and clear? His silence tells her way too much. She places her chopsticks down, before she's tempted to stab her eyes out with them. *They're in Tokyo, aren't they?*

Sorry, Viv. He sends a data packet she's really not buzzed to open. *Big-ass 'scraper, VA'd to the hilt. You guys can handle the jacking but the hit… I'm not sure I'd advise. Maybe best to watch and wait them out.*

Screw that. There's not a no hard enough to throw at that suggestion.

Viv…

Deuce. We're not going in on our lonesome. We'll rustle up some back-up. I have ideas. Options. Not ones I like much… but we're the beggars in this scenario.

You wanna wait on us?

Hell no. You have other things to hunt out. We popped a track on the bastards who hit Shandong. She hooks the tracker sig from Prism and tosses it to him. *Gift exchange. Go get 'em, tiger.*

Gotta wait for Amiga to get home first.

She knows that tone. He's trying not to worry and failing miserably, but when it comes to their mutual pain in the ass, he's hopeless. The second he met Amiga, all bets were off. Even after she broke his heart, she owned it. She always will.

You said all was good.

It is. It is. Just… pending on the homecoming. Be savvy,

Viv. Anyone who might be situated to help you might want to get to Shock.

Masterful subject change, bud, and I know. You leave me to my conundrum, I'll leave you to yours.

So kind.

You know it. Don't be a stranger.

Just be strange.

His ancient sign off, reminding her of the early days of Hornets when Deuce was half a foot shorter, skinny, still in Tech, and doing J-hack shit part-time, makes her want to stop, drop everything, and cry her heart out. That life was stolen wholesale, dumped into a street can and set on fire. All that's left of what they were then is ash and memory. When will they have time to mourn that? It's necessary to mourn.

Finishing her noodles, she shares the terrific news that no one thinks is terrific and her equally terrific plan for getting help to bring them down, which again, no one thinks is especially terrific. But they do agree it's necessary.

"We can sleep first though, right?" KJ says hopefully, stealing another mushroom, this time from Prism, who slaps his hand with her chopsticks. "Ow!"

"No, Kneejerk," Vivid drawls. "We're gonna up and hit 'em right now."

He narrows his eyes at her. "I'm sharing your pod."

"Oh hell no."

"Hell yes. I'm gonna get nightmares now for sure. You owe me."

* * *

Waiting in the bustling fish market, surrounded by shouting and lines of fish resting on ice and wondering how Tokyo manages to grow this much fish in farms anyway, Vivid rethinks her terrific idea several dozen times over. Last night, forced to share a pod with KJ and therefore miss out on a few hours of good sleep, she'd already begun to worry. In the light of day, freezing her arse off in the market despite the tropical heat on the rest of the hub, she's thinking she might have executed a frying pan to fire type leap.

That KJ refused to come, leaving her to rock up with Sandro, hasn't really helped, despite KJ's forever edginess about every damn thing.

Then again, this idea is one that relies on a lot going very right, when current circs are all about shit going very fucking wrong.

Given their monopoly on Tokyo, their general dislike of competition, and the Cartel's recent, unwelcome prominence here, Vivid's taken a chance that the Yakuza of Tokyo Hub might be interested in removing a tick from their city's flesh. Chances are high that outside business, especially anything Gung related, are of no concern to them but still, the looks they're getting as they wait are disconcerting to say the least.

Vivid's links to the Yakuza are non-existent, but the Hornets were hired for some work on the Gung by a Tokyo-Hub-based Corp several years ago and remained in contact with the man who hired them, Hanshiro—the son of the CEO. A year after the job, Hanshiro quit Corp to become a chef, something he'd trained for in his youth and had to leave. Now he's head chef for the kumichō of the Yamaguchi-gumi family. Talk about useful.

Being head chef, Hanshiro visits the fish market with a bunch of chaperones to buy fresh seafood every morning. Which is why they've been here since four A.M. And why they're now waiting whilst he IMs to see if they're allowed to meet with the head of the Hub's foremost Yakuza family. His chaperones are watching them as if they plan to attempt to deprive their kumichō of his favourite chef, as if they'd be anything like that stupid. They need help, not more trouble.

Hanshiro steps out past his chaperones. "Your interests would appear to intersect. He requests that you join him for breakfast. I will finish my purchases and take you back with me, hai?"

Vivid tries not to sigh relief. "Hai. Arigatōgozaimasu."

He bows. Brief. Terse. Almost impolite, not that she can blame him. This favour was not small. "Nani demo animasen."

The kumichō of the Yamaguchi-gumi family lives in the five top floors of their Corp 'scraper in a level of luxury that, prior to her stint at Shandong, might have impressed her. Now it reminds her of all they lost—the safety, the comfort, and worst of all, the Hornets. Viv commands herself to stop thinking about sad things. Sadness is like water; you can drown in it, and there isn't time to drown.

Having never met a Yakuza, Vivid has no idea what to expect, but the small, slightly overweight man with silver hair and a jovial expression is light years from anything she'd have anticipated. Introducing himself informally as Oniji, the kumichō greets them warmly and leads them to a tatami room with a long, cedar-wood table, traditionally low to the ground.

"Please," he says. "Sit."

A genuine geisha brings the food, pouring tea and serving nattō, raw egg and rice, miso soup, ginger pork, seared tuna and marinated tofu into tiny bowls. It's surreal to be sat eating fine food by a window giving premium views of the Tokyo skyline, the curve of Earth beyond the hub, and the black of space.

"You admire my view?" Oniji's English is prep-school perfect, with only the flavour of a Japanese burr on the edge of some letters.

"Very much."

"It is a delight. The only flaw is that somewhere amongst the architecture beyond my window, flaunting the ability of his Archaeologist to hide his headquarters from discovery and his wilful refusal to do business with those whose business is Tokyo Hub's wellbeing, is Lucian duPont." He helps himself to more tuna, waving the geisha away. "He came here a year ago, which is, I believe, when he took over the Cartel. Manners dictate a hand extended, but he did no such thing. Instead, he has tried to systematically steal our business. He wishes to take the Haunt, I suspect, to press his agenda here. He is not welcome."

"Are you interested in the Haunt?"

Oniji holds her gaze. "Why would we need such a creature? Our power here is not contingent upon gimmicks. We Yakuza are businessmen. Men of honour. All we require is the information you hold."

"Will we be granted the right to join your attack on their headquarters?" She needs to ask this; you don't assume anything with the Yakuza.

Oniji sips his tea. "You have outstanding issues with them, I understand?"

"We do."

He inclines his head by a fraction but doesn't respond, busying himself with the pressing business of breakfast instead. Vivid tries not to panic. She eats her nattō, mixing it in with her rice and egg to make it somewhat palatable. Nudging Sandro to stop picking at his. He makes a face she hopes Oniji hasn't seen.

This is gross.

It's fermented. Acquired taste. Try to look less disgusted, or you'll offend him.

Will he let us in on this?

No telling. Eat your food.

Ugh, the things I do for Hornet-kind.

When Oniji speaks again, it's as if they haven't been talking about the Cartel at all. He regales them with stories from the twenty-year war he's led on Tokyo Hub, uniting the hundreds of Yakuza clans who went rogue, frustrated by the restrictions of the Hub's size. After their last cup of tea, he bids them goodbye, clasping them both by the hand rather than bowing. Vivid's dying to bring up the Cartel hit, but it would be poor etiquette to mention it again when he hasn't.

After he's gone, Sandro says, "What now?"

"If you would please come with me." At the entrance to the room is a small, delicate woman. She bows her head. "I'm Umi, Oniji's waka gashira, and his eldest daughter. I will be leading the assault on the Cartel."

Umi leads them through to a boardroom on the opposite end of the floor. Inside, awaiting them, are a group of men and women she introduces as the leaders of all the clans in this district—and the rest of the Hornets on Tokyo. All of them. Including the injured Hornets left behind on the shuttle in the care of Jules, the only other Hornet with medical skills. Jules treats her to one hell of a look—eviscerating. That, and the tension in the room, the uneasy stance of the Hornets, clues Vivid in to what was going on at breakfast. A test.

She turns to Umi. "Did we pass?"

Umi smiles. "You are alive, so what do you think?"

Vivid breathes deep. "And the Cartel hit?"

Umi gives an incremental bow of the head. "My father would be honoured to have you accompany us as we bring down our mutual enemy."

as above

Explosions suck: the noise and the dust and the *smell,* the general sense of disorientation and sensory deprivation. The way everything *rings* for hours afterwards. That stuffed feeling, as if your head is in a dirt-filled burlap sack. On the plus side, there's no way of being able to tell if you're about to die horribly. Blinking grit from her eyes that genuinely feels like it'll still be there in a million years, Amiga's last to jump through the hole Aggie blew in the floor of the Cartel HQ basement.

She finds them all waiting like idiots.

"Didn't we go through this already?" she snaps. "Run like hell. Mush. Scram. If you weren't in my way I'd be running already."

The sentiment's a grand one, but the practicality leaves a lot to be desired. These tunnels are not built to run in; they're too cramped, wet and stinking—a mustiness and sort of sewer undertone that snags at the gag reflex. Beyond grim. It takes about seven minutes of scrambling for Amiga's boots to get caked in mud right up to the ankle, adding an extra fifteen pounds to her feet. Naturally at this point, her thigh decides to send frantic SOS signals to her brain. Fucking *hell*. Literally hell.

Snarling at the uselessness of her body, she tunes out the squawking of her thigh and pushes herself on, not quite convinced that the unfurling map in her head really does lead to Deuce. All she can see is tunnel, more fucking muddy stinking tunnel with no end in sight.

Faint sounds of water dripping echo around them as they run, adding to the ringing in her ears, giving it the distinct maddening edge of tinnitus, and from deep below comes a thrum like a heartbeat—the machines of the Hub.

Amiga's seen streams of urban explorers sneaking down into the guts of hubs, filming the huge, intricate engines holding the hub in orbit and the centrifuge whose spinning keeps everyone from floating up to the glass dome. You can't get to that, but you can see it. Mind bending that it works, that it even exists. Some of the explorers climb the engines to get a closer look, and more than one has fallen in, blown to a brief burst of bright red.

No one speaks of it. No one stops doing it.

The streams though, they go viral, especially if they end in death, and some kids are inspired to copy. Seems crazy, but people get bored, they do dumb shit. It reminds Amiga of the Gung's XTs, both stupid and dangerous, a lethal combo. The anti-J-Hacks, breaking rules simply to break them. There's a certain beauty in that, a synchronicity. You can't have things without their equals and opposites. The world balances itself, like it or not.

If she hadn't met Deuce, Amiga might have ended up an XT. Or dead. One or the other.

After a solid hour of struggling to run, they spark clean out of energy. Slow to a walk to catch their breath. A few dozen more tunnels at this pace brings them to the catacombs proper, the miles of tunnels with bones stacked against the walls, the remains of ancient Parisians. They look nothing like the pictures Amiga's seen, with religious symbology. The patterns here are more like geometric fractals, a touch disorientating, painted bright colours and fixed behind glass or plastic.

"This is not how I imagined the catacombs." Raid trails a hand along the plastic. "It's all very pay-as-you-go hub attraction or art exhibition."

"Probably is," Amiga says, because really.

"Yeah, but who the hell would come down here?" Aggie's walking along arm in arm with Sim, who blends oddly in her catsuit, a human-shaped collection of neon skeletal parts. "It's dark and muddy and it *literally* stinks."

"They were moved decades ago. Rearranged. We make it our own down here. The gendarme don't care to come down. We are out of sight, out of mind, but we don't disrespect history; we make history for ourselves. If we don't, history will forget us."

The voice echoes all around them, too loud, reverberating off the plastic and the roof like surround sound, humming in the air. It makes several Hornets yell, and most of them jump. Having no normal fear reactions to anything, Amiga has her gun out and pointed at the woman standing in the gloom of the tunnel ahead. Appearing out of nowhere, so not good for your health, especially not around Cleaners. The only reason the woman isn't already dead is Amiga's general lack of ammo.

"Who the *fuck* are you?"

The woman looks at her gun, as if it means nothing. "Ebon. I live down here. I'm guessing you're lost and could do with a guide?"

Amiga eyeballs the Hornets. Dislikes the willingness to trust she's seeing. "We have a map," she snaps.

"Map or not, you shouldn't come down here without a guide like this." Ebon appears genuinely concerned. "How are you so dusty? Did you get caught in a collapse?"

"Nope, an explosion."

Ebon looks appalled and Aggie holds up a hand. "My fault. No regrets."

"The explosion under Rue de Soupirs?"

"Is that what it's called? The Cartel have an HQ there."

Ebon's mouth twitches. "You blew up the Cartel?"

"We blew a hole in their floor. It may have set a few things on fire a little bit."

"Then you need to make a quick getaway. A guide will serve you better than a map; your feet can be misdirected here even with GPS. Come."

Ebon leads them through tunnel after tunnel lined edge to edge in painted bones locked behind plastic, until they flare out to pockets and caves. Cramped spaces lined with mis-matched rugs and filled with beds, chairs, chests of drawers and tiny shelves; lit by bio-sconces, the walls tiled in patches with mosaics of stars, planets and mythical beasts. Works of art as much as the bones surrounding them.

"Why do you live down here?" Amiga asks, because there's no way she could, not with the dislike of being underground written into her DNA. "No offence but this is hell."

"You are from the Gung, yes?"

"That easy to see?"

"Your discomfort in these tunnels is unusually profound."

"Well, shit." Amiga's sure she doesn't like being this transparent, but she's not the only one looking queasy. There's not a Hornet in her team not so obviously gagging for daylight they could be wearing it as a fucking neon sign. "Fear of being underground is a cultural thing for us, yeah? It's not real, but try telling that to decades of propaganda. I've known since I was old enough to listen that the ground is dangerous. I can't just switch it off." She trails a hand on the tunnel. "This. Living like this. It's pure horror to me."

Ebon smiles, but it's filled with sadness. "We live down here," she says, "because there is nowhere else for us to live. When they take your home to build their terrace mansions, either you go to the slums, or you come here. Even with your horror of the ground, of being beneath it, if you were left the same choice, would you reject it?"

Amiga thinks back to their time in the tunnels with the earth engines. To how quickly they readjusted when they had no choice. Thinks what happened then. How they turned it around. Became weapons. Reset the status quo. Brought it to its fucking knees.

"I think," she says softly, "that I'd do whatever it took to show the world it has no fucking right to tell me what I can do or where I can go. I'd burn it to the fucking ground for daring to try."

To her surprise, instead of getting defensive, Ebon busts out a throaty laugh. "Considering Rue de Soupir is currently in flames," she says, "I rather think you would." And there's delight in it, fierce and admiring. "Perhaps we should ask you for lessons?"

Amiga stops dead for a moment. Because that's not how it works. It's not how it worked for them and it's not how it'll work for Ebon, and she needs to know that. She needs to know it's not easy. It's not some fantasy of will or strength or know-how. It's far simpler and uglier than that.

"You don't need lessons," she says quietly. "You just need your tipping point. Once you hit that, there's no going back. Not ever."

Lost inside himself, Shock tries to figure out whether he's asleep or dead or some untold combination of the two because he's still not sure he can die, not in the conventional fashion. He's too much more than skin and bone now—can't quantify the amount of him Emblem's leaked into and through. The awareness of it within him is fundamental. In the same way as he experienced the weight and fact of his body he's experienced it gradually being overwritten. Parts of him feeling strange, then different, then not feeling at all. Not numb, precisely, but other. He's distanced from his experience of humanity. One day, possibly now, he'll stop feeling human at all.

He has no idea what he'll be then.

Whatever he is right now, dead or asleep, or possibly, less hysterically, in a coma, this is a punishment. Emblem is sentient code. Bio-ware. And also more. Having grown into him, used his biology to evolve, it's like him in reverse—he's becoming less human and Emblem more. And it's furious at being misused.

He once abused Emblem by utilizing it to reach out and cut Li Harmony's connection with her avi, driving her to madness; now he's used it to reach out and cut the life from over a hundred soldiers all at once. Genocide. Or mass murder. What's the difference? The fact that he thought he didn't mean to kill them until it was done is damn near irrelevant.

His connection with Emblem is more profound in some ways than his connection with Puss, because she has her own body, however metaphorical it might be. Puss. See, there's the problem. He can't begin to measure the pain of losing her. It sits beside the pain of losing Shark, too big to contemplate, and he can't bear the weight of it within his body, his mind. It's frightening how swiftly that translated into rage, and how quickly rage became murder.

You don't know yourself until someone you love is threatened. You don't know what you're capable of. Shock will kill. That surprises him as much as it upsets Emblem.

Emblem understands the drive behind the act; it

just doesn't approve. It thinks he's irrational. Excellent character reading there. He bloody well is, and he's willing to embrace his irrationality right now to put a stop to all of this shit. Shock wants to lean into the pain, to use it. He can't cope with it lying on him, a useless, unwieldy burden.

Let me wake, he says. *This is pointless. I get it. I won't use it to kill again. You have to help me though. You can't shut me down every time I do something you don't like.*

He has no idea if Emblem will respond. It has his words, has access to everything in his brain, but has yet to vocalize. What he gets instead of words is a pressure. A pulling/pushing sensation. Then he's golden and in a room.

It's gently warm. A touch humid. So quiet the air almost sings with silence. The room is painted pure white, forming a perfect illusion of seamless emptiness, endlessness. A casual or even searching glance would not see at first the sphere hovering at the absolute centre point of the four corners of the room.

In the sphere a woman sits cross-legged. Sleeping. She's beautiful, fragile, too much bone under oh-so-delicate olive skin sprinkled with dusky freckles. She's a golden sun encased in a wild halo of coarse brown hair, all corkscrews and question marks. And all that untouchable beauty is blurred inside the golden belly of a sleeping polar bear, paws curled like it's holding her inside, a human cub in a bear womb.

The bear twitches. Stirs. Opens sleepy eyes to blink at him.

"*Run,*" it says, actually *speaks,* not mind to mind but

voice into air, a rumbling filled with panic. "Get out of here right now. She's waking up."

Blindsided by an avatar speaking aloud, Shock takes precious seconds to sort through what it's actually saying and finds himself staring at the woman within the bear. The bear's eyes are closed again, were maybe never open, but hers, oh, they're open all right. Hazel edged with gold, and staring at him like he's a miracle.

How are you here? she says. Are *you here?*

Shock chokes. Clutches his head. That voice. It echoes like a thunderstorm overhead, like the rumble of ground shaking, growing and booming and building. It *screams*: Queen. He knows who this is. Zen. Zenada Lakatos. He looks around the room, frantic for clues, but there's nothing. Only white. How the fuck do they find her? And how does she still have an avatar?

Please find me. I'm lost. Did she hear him? Impossible. She's shaking a little, hands clutched in her lap. *Talk to me. Let me know you're real. Please. I see things that aren't real.*

He has no idea what to say. This is the woman they need to kill? Why? She's suddenly childlike. Fragile and lost. *I'm real. I think. How is it you have an avatar?*

She leans in to rake him with her eyes. The suddenness of it, the crow-like intensity, makes him uneasy somehow. *Yours is gone.*

Stolen. For profit. They all were.

By whom?

We don't know. We'll find out. Do you know where you are?

She shakes her head, curls flying. *Breaker hid me. I*

haven't seen a person in a long time. I haven't been awake in a long time.

Her eyes are desperate as much as wondering now. And she's pale, her freckles stark against her skin. So reasonable. He could easily believe her, but his body emanates warning. Vibrates with it. The only word in his mind, repeating over and over, is *Queen*—as if he needed reminding. Why would Emblem bring him here? From the depths of his mind, Emblem shares a memory he'd rather forget: the Queens, delving into his mind, trying to carve him out so they had space for themselves.

The face it gives the Queens is Zenada's. The implication is clear. She was *there*.

Zen's face goes blank. *Stop* lying *to him,* she snarls, and something in his head snaps. Blacks out. For a moment he's entirely in his own body and it feels like yet another bereavement. And then it doesn't.

I can do that, she says with a smile. *I can make it go away. Make you human again. Would you like that?*

I…

It's not human, she says. *You can't trust it.*

I… don't think I can trust you either.

She laughs. *And can I trust you? We're all in the same boat. All enemies until proven otherwise. I need your help. Trust me at least that much.*

Shock wants to promise her, to help her, a compulsion that feels part and not part of him, and terrifying for both reasons, but the emptiness inside, the dregs of memory, hold him steady. Remind him to keep a distance. She shut

Emblem down. He can feel it waking again, its frantic scramble to reassert itself, to protect him, but it was gone. Cut off from him as profoundly as Puss is, as completely as Shark was.

He licks his lips. They aren't even here. He's dreaming this. A waking dream. Emblem wants him to think of it as a nightmare. He takes a step back, almost unaware of it until she's further away.

I'll do what I can. He could be lying; he thinks he is, or she could be talking through his mouth.

Her eyes narrow, the light in them changing, and he catches a glimpse of what she is behind the innocence and desperation. It makes his blood freeze. So much power, so much *intent*. Everything that the Queen was, Zenada is, and worse. The only thing stopping her is her prison, and Shock has no idea how Breaker managed to contain her, unless she was less than this when they first put her here. No, she was never less. She was always *danger.*

How the hell will they kill her? It would be suicide to even get close.

Don't forget me, she pleads, as if her mask is her reality. *I'll be waiting.*

Trying not to show her his reluctance but terrified she can see it anyway, he nods and allows Emblem, fully awake now, to pull him away. He feels her eyes on him all the way, like she's watching where they go. He struggles against Emblem to make it hide their route, but it's panicking in ways he's never felt it panic and refuses to listen, dragging him back to his unconscious body.

Dammit, let me wake up, he snaps at it, beyond furious.

Instead of responding, it pushes at him again, but not *to* anywhere. It pushes at the parts of him not yet Emblem. There's an urgency to that pressure, a meaning. He knows what it is. Time to admit that every time he's acquiesced to giving up more of himself, he's gained from it. He's been resisting the more complete changes Emblem wanted to wreak upon him, scared his humanity might be in jeopardy, but if Zenada can switch Emblem off as they are now. If she knows where they are…

The Zen behind the mask flashes into his head again. She hides it so well, but there's nothing left in her remotely human. She's a gaping void, not psychopathic or evil; just *empty*. A force of power with no interest in anything but itself.

Will it be like that? Will I?

Emblem takes him back to the memory of the moment it was cut off and holds him there until he understands. Even if he doesn't go to her, she's awake now, and she's trying to get out. Eventually she will, and he'll *have* to kill her somehow if he wants anything he values to remain safe. If he's not like her, if he doesn't let go of what's left and embrace the bio-ware as integral, he won't have a hope in hell.

Fine, he says. *Do it.*

zen tangle

One second the Haunt is there, golden and so close, the resonance of Emblem wound through his in a counterpoint almost tuned to perfection. He's resisting it though, refusing to become what it could make him. Choosing weakness. Giving her chinks in his armour, handholds. Probably they'll be gone by the time she sees him again—Emblem's too smart, too adaptive, to allow for cracks to remain. No matter.

He was so close. The key was so close. She needs to bring him back. Properly this time. She needs to be *free*.

Zen beats against Bear's belly, willing it to burst. How is an avatar, an insubstantial dream, so solid? No matter. She's seen the Haunt now. Felt his mind with hers. And she sees where he is; unconscious in fact.

Raising her head, Zen focuses on the one link she still has with the outside world; they're too muddled, too infected already to be anything but incoherent, but they are hers. The Zeros. One by one they've succumbed, and through them, she's reached out and taken other minds, ones familiar to her, for fun. It's been so satisfying making them pay for Breaker's cruelty. A distraction whilst her greater game played out.

Finding many of the Zeros flooded with code all through now and open to suggestion, she nudges, plucks at the nerve connections between brain and limb. Laughs in pure delight as their limbs move to her commands.

On Paris Hub where the Haunt lies sleeping, she threads herself into the minds of every malleable Zero she can find, tangling into their neural networks, gaining a foothold. Amplified by all those drives, however confused the minds behind them might be, she reaches out to Slip, to J-Net. The Hornets are with the Haunt, on Paris Hub. The *Cleaner* is. Their signals as loud and clear to her as everything used to be. It's been torture to be denied this clarity.

Maybe she can play another game?

The Cleaner and the Hornets are in the catacombs. Trapped, like she is. She'll send them a message. Send them her Zeros, armed with weaponized virads—virads remade to hunt thoughts and eat them, replacing them with her words like virads replace language with marketing speak. The Haunt relies on the Cleaner, his connection with her as profound in many ways as his connection with his missing avatar. Hurting the Cleaner will hurt him; increase his vulnerability.

Gleeful, Zen drives the Zeros up and into the world. Walks it through their eyes. It's nothing like her Queens, too big and loud, too garbled through the messy senses of Zeros, but it's close enough to life to fill her with wild joy.

She kills a Zero's neighbour almost by accident, lunging to place hands around her throat, to *feel* something, and so charmed by the sensation that she can't stop until the life is gone, the last breath trapped behind tight fingers. With the Zero's hands she pats the woman's head in thanks, pushes her to one side.

The Zeros are miles apart, but she can drive them as fast as she wants, take them wherever she wants.

This is too much fun. Zenada adores having fun.

so below

Given their somewhat precarious situation with the gendarme aware of not only their presence on Paris Hub but their actual fucking *faces*, Ebon thinks they'll only be safe exiting the catacombs in one of their hidden locations. No arguments there, not even from Deuce, except the secret exit is seven goddamn miles away. Joy. Nothing more delightful than the thought of trekking another seven miles of cramped, poorly lit tunnels shellacked in mud so thick Amiga will be washing it off her boots for the next fifty years.

She rallies though, because fifty years of scrubbing mud beats fifty years toe-tagged and jailed in the bowels of a hub, drive-jacked to work hella long shifts on the engines every day. Problems of having a drive in your skull: you can be written over or into and be none the fucking wiser—these are things she's learnt only recently and they appal her. If she had nightmares, these would be the terrors waking her screaming in the small hours.

Focused on ploughing through mud in almost

complete darkness, the mind-numbing, exhausting slog of it, Amiga misses the tweaking of her danger-dar until danger's right in their faces. They're in empty tunnel, then they're surrounded by what? Gotta be people. People with the freakish adrenaline strength people get on drugs. Are these junkies? Whatever they are, they're everywhere and even though the dark steals half her senses they seem unaffected, finding her unerringly and attacking over and over no matter how hard she pushes back.

"Are there junkies in these tunnels?" she shouts to Ebon.

"No." Ebon sounds terrified. "These are not junkies. I do not know *what* they are."

As she fights on Amiga realizes she doesn't either, that she can't actually process what she's fighting, or why, even as she's fighting it. The clammy skin, the implacable strength and determination, the ugly, heavy pulse of blood under her hands when she grabs arms to twist them away from her. Forced to hazard a guess she'd have to shoot for, say, zombies—but the rational mind shies from such nonsense.

"Does anyone see what the fuck these are?" she howls, plucking fingers away from her face. "We need some light, goddamnit."

Yanking yet more fingers away from her cheek, her mouth, she twists hard, teeth baring at the satisfying snap, but they come again, the jarring grate of broken bones scraping at her ear. She has to bite back an uncharacteristic screech. They keep trying to get to her face. Her head. The weirdness of it, the fixation of it, intensifies that reality shift, that conviction that she's fighting dead people. Living dead. Stupid. No way the dead walk, or fight, or anything.

"My fucking head!" Aggie shrieks. "They're ripping at my *head*."

Amiga tries to fight her way toward Aggie's voice, more hysterical by the second, to the sound of something tearing. Skin. It's skin. Then Aggie's gurgling, this gross sound like dirty water bubbling in a drain. She hears Sim yelling her name, trying to fight her way in from elsewhere. And all she can hear is the gurgling, the smack of fists on skin, and then Aggie says, clear as day.

"Zen."

Amiga's so bewildered she stops fighting for a second and damn near loses a chunk of hair. "Get the *fuck* off," she snarls, grabbing the thing scrabbling at her behind the head and spinning to slam it face-first into the tunnel wall.

"Zen."

"What's she saying that for?" Sim asks, and there's a plea in it. Amiga can't blame her. It's not the word, it's the way she's saying it, the way her voice sounds flat. Dead. Like something inside her is using her mouth to speak, making her a puppet.

And that's when Amiga twigs.

"Zeros," she yells. "They're Zeros! Don't let them get to your drive. They're trying to infect you!"

With Aggie droning the word Zen over and over they fight frantically, trapped by the constriction of the tunnel walls, the sheer number of Zeros seemingly growing every few minutes. Impossible to hold back. Instead of making inroads they're restricted to keeping groping hands away from their drives, their backs plastered to the tunnel wall.

Rock digs pits into Amiga's back, scrapes at her spine, but rather that than fingers near her drive, virads in her mind. The single word droning from Aggie's mouth sparks her to fight harder, be more vicious. She has no idea how many Zeros she's injured. Tries not to imagine a scenario where one of the Zeros tearing at her face is EVaC. Hurting him would break her, she's sure of it. But she'd have to.

In the corner of her eye a flare of gold, lightning-bug brief, becomes a trickle of neon yellow before sparking like the lights crackling out the end of a firework. They illuminate the faces of the Zeros and she wishes right the fuck away that the dark was back. Zombies is closer to what these Zeros are than she realized—the blank in their faces is horrifying. Even in death faces have more expression than this.

The electric flares of gold spark to a chain reaction, to golden chains, to limbs, the flick of long hair hiding eyes that when he's not gold are a blue as bright and electric as the sparks creating his form beside her. The sight of him, awake and rocking his usual dishevelled chill gives her hope for the fucking universe.

He takes in the situation. Shakes his head.

No wonder Emblem sent me here before letting me give Deuce a heads up.

On what? she asks, curling up her hand to introduce the heel of her palm to a nose.

He scours her with a glance. *Being awake. Idiot. Now brace yourself, this might hurt.*

Before she can throw out a "what the hell", Shock provides a physical demonstration, or rather a mental one, arcing into her drive and the drives around her like a current; jumping to the others through her. Her head fills up, static and gold and pain like a migraine and a fucking hammer blow rolled into one. Intense enough to white out her sight, to make her skin ripple pins and needles. She's pretty sure she might be gagging.

The sharp jab as the gold within pushes outward pops the pain like a bubble, leaving cold shudders reverberating through her entire system, rendering the sudden drop of the Zeros in the tunnel slightly less amazing than it otherwise might have been. She almost envies the impact of their faces on rock; it probably hurts less than this gold agony rippling through her skull that fades way too slowly after he's gone, leaving entirely inadequate apologies in his wake.

By the time she feels normal again, he's over at Aggie, his hands *inside* her head. He looks up.

I can't do anything about this. Volk might be able to. I've shut her down until we can get her to the Resurrection. *You okay?*

NO. Ass. That fucking hurt. Are they dead?

He shakes his head. *I diffused the strike through you guys. Sorry if it hurt; I need practice.*

You are never *practicing on me again,* she snaps. *Vetoed.* Amiga kneels to feel the pulse of the Zeros. It thuds against her fingers, a slow, thick rhythm.

There's a lot of blood and their skin, paper-thin and see-through, has split, bruising almost instantly; huge, black bruises like rot. If this virad infection doesn't kill them, they're gonna be feeling this shit for months. She sneaks a sideways glance at Shock. She's done worse, way, way worse, but what he did? No fucker should be able to slice consciousness clean from a distance. Shouldn't be able to kill like he did at the hangar.

So, the hangar, and this. It's… a thing, she says, cautious.

Emblem thinks I can't do it without killing unless I diffuse. He replies. *I think I can.*

Turning to gape at him, she tries to clear her mental throat before responding, but the air is gone and even mind to mind it comes out as a wheezing, *You* think? *Maybe you better be sure before you do shit then? Just in case?*

Shock gives her this delirious grin, the same goofy mouthful of teeth that endeared her to his dumb ass from day one. *That's the last thing I ever thought I'd hear you say*, he says, humour laced all through it. *I'm thinking we'll need me to do this again before I know the how, why or intricacies of it. This is not exactly a time-to-learn sitch, much as I'd love for it to be.*

You might be right, she concedes reluctantly. *I hate when you're right.*

That's your inner control freak speaking, comes his chewy reply. *You're going to have to carry Aggie out.*

No probs. That's Raid, already organizing another Hornet to help him lift her.

I'm going back to the shuttle. I need to tell Deuce I'm awake. You good to get out?

Amiga points at Ebon, who's staring at him like she doesn't know whether to slap him or run, her fingers rubbing circles at her temples. *We have a guide.*

I thought I felt an unfamiliar mind.

You didn't check?

Shock quirks a brow. He's one of those people who can make it extra scornful. *I had time? I kinda thought saving your ass from the Zero zombies was a tad more pressing.*

And he's gone, not peeling from the tunnel in golden layers, just gone. She misses him immediately. Misses the chance to really rake him over the coals for proving to be as much of a murderous bastard as she is. People should be predictable. Amiga recalls fondly for a moment the days, not so long ago, when she got to be the shit that happened to people—she genuinely despises being the people shit happens *to*.

Moving at speeds too close to a run for Amiga's thigh, Ebon leads them to another cave in the catacombs and points to a hole in the back.

"That's the way out."

"How the hell do we get Aggie up there?" Raid says, peering in, trying to light it with his tablet.

"Pull," Ebon says, as if it's obvious.

"Great," he mutters. "Just great."

The hole is claustrophobically narrow. Almost vertical. It leads to a cold, rank basement no more cheerful or less filthy than the catacombs themselves. Above the basement is a grubby little Slip shop cum social club or bar filled to the brim with heavily armed members of the Parisian underworld. There's a live band playing something folksy grunge, a line of ancient keno machines and arcade games, all chiming away, and a bunch of old pool tables in back. J-Hacks have peculiar obsessions.

Amiga follows a nasty, sneaking suspicion to a hideous conclusion. "This is the Bone Market, isn't it?"

"Yes. You're safe here."

"You sure? I almost died last time I encountered the Bone Market."

Ebon treats her to the driest look known to mankind, the eyeballing equivalent of Giza Hub in high summer. "If you came here bringing the same sort of trouble you've conjured today," she says. "I can't say I blame them."

Waking up to Ravi in his face is honestly becoming one of Shock's recurring nightmares. Not that he dislikes Ravi; dude's on point, but the reasons for Ravi being in his face are usually bad ones and he's usually in an amount of pain not dissimilar to the metric weight of the actual Earth.

This time, big surprise, is no exception. Whatever reverberations that mass slaughter he pulled off in the hangar caused in his mind are still rippling through it, carrying sharp glints of pain like metal shards burrowing in. Now he understands Amiga's reluctance to have him practice on her. He reminds himself to apologize.

Ravi leans back and yells over his shoulder, "He's up."

"Quit talking about me like I'm not here, Ravi."

Peeling one of Shock's eyelids back, Ravi leans in to

scrutinize his eye. "Then call for Deuce yourself. IM. I dare you. Your frontal lobe may explode. Do it for science."

Shock bats Ravi's hand away. "You already did."

There's a clatter from behind Ravi, and Deuce appears, looking tired, concerned and more than a little stressed. He crouches by Shock's side, wincing. Probably his legs are playing up. Fuck, they're all rocking geriatric levels of pain and discomfort. What the fuck will be left of them when this is over? Having met Zen, Shock's now no longer certain it ever will end, not if they have to kill her somehow to end it. If Mollie asked for this, he's not certain he trusts Mollie any more.

"You wanna talk about mass murder?"

Deuce is quiet but the censure is right there, front and centre. It's not fair. It's not like Shock planned to kill—well, until he *did*, but that's a discussion he needs to have with himself, maybe with Puss. And there were extenuating circumstances of rage and grief and general tilt on all the utter bullshit they keep encountering to factor in. Faced with the same choice now, he'd do it again. He'll be damned if he'll explain that or anything else to the boy scout though.

"I just woke up."

"Don't stonewall me, Haunt. I get enough of that from Amiga. We need to start some kind of list of these things you can do and, I'll be real with you, a heads up on anything new you might have stumbled upon would save a lot of strife." He offers Shock a hand and pulls him up. "Am I to assume your general lack of ability to share, rather than your usual bollocks, is because you have no idea how far all this can go?"

"Basically. Oh and you're welcome. Twice."

"Salty. And twice?"

Drop Amiga in it or not? Definitely drop. Any diversion is a good diversion. "Amiga had some trouble."

A single muscle in Deuce's jaw jumps. "She okay?"

"Yeah. Aggie's not. They got attacked by Zeros wielding weaponized virads. Or at least that's what Emblem thinks they are from having a poke about in Aggie's head. And before you ask: no. Fixing weaponized virads is not a thing I can do, not alone. Not god here, despite some evidence to the contrary. I'll need Volk to have a look." From the vaults of his mind, feeling less fried by the second, thank fuck, bubbles a memory, one intertwined in excruciating detail with the loss of Puss. "Also, I know where the avis were stolen from."

"Then that's where we go." Amiga. Coming into the hangar in so many layers of dust, blood and mud he might not have clocked it was her without the talking. "And we need to light a fuse on it. Your vehicular activity team got their mugshots on the gendarmerie's arrest-on-sight poker deck."

"Actually we have another option." Tracker, quiet and serious from the door of the cockpit.

Rifling in the shuttle cabinets for things to clean a fraction of the filth accumulated on her and her team, Amiga snorts. "Better be a *fucking* good option. I'm itching to Clean the cunts who joy-rode my avi into a cage."

"I have the location of whoever called the hit on Shandong."

Amiga pauses, a bunch of cushion cases dangling in her hands. "Where?"

"Hong Kong Hub."

Her hands seem to convulse, ripping the shit out of the cases. "Mother *fucker*."

"You know who that is?" Deuce asks, taking the cushion cases and handing them out along with bottles of water. He wets one and starts clearing the crud on Amiga's face, one hand holding her chin steady, the other working in slow, methodical circles.

Amiga looks at Shock, and the expression on her face is one he'd happily wipe off along with the mud and dust, such a peculiar combination of savagery and guilt. "So does he."

"I do?" Then he does, because *Hong Kong* isn't just a place, it's a goddamn mnemonic. Mother *fucker*. Now he knows why the farm got hit. His fault; all his stupid fucking fault. They should have gone elsewhere—there was no way she wasn't going to find out and she's all about revenge, that whole family has always been obsessed with it. He shakes his head. "We are *not* going, Amiga. I'm not going anywhere near that bitch. She probably wants to feed me to her plants. In chunks. Still kicking and screaming."

"Probably," Amiga says with a shrug. "That gonna stop you though?"

"Yes. A thousand fucking times yes!"

"Not even for Gail?"

As verbal shutdowns go, that one is the equivalent of a bucket of freezing water tossed over his head. Gail's commitment to protecting the Hornets—who are more important to Shock than he'd ever admit—was absolute. Selfless. He took them in like family and treated them no less. If not for him, the weeks after the fall of Fulcrum would have been unbearable. He gave them stability. Safety. Risked everything for them before he even met them. And Shock cost him his home. His job. Maybe his life. He owes him. Is in fact indebted to him.

Being far too fucking perceptive for her own good, Amiga is fully compos of this fact. He'd be irritated by this, except that from the look in her eyes he can tell she's been here too, and feels the same. Her debt to Gail is identical to his.

"Oh fuck you. Yes. Yes, I'd go for Gail."

"What about the avis?" Raid. "What about Aggie?"

"Viv can go for the avis," Deuce assures him. "You know she'll be up for that. And we'll get Aggie help the second we can. If we had time to go back down and hit up the *Res* you know we would, yeah?"

"Yeah. I know. It's just… the whole searching another hub again…" he trails off. Looks pained. "I'm fucking tired. We all are."

"No need to worry about that," Shock says, before Deuce can speak. "I can pinpoint our target on Hong Kong. I know who she is."

"But you don't have Puss."

Wow. That hurt. "I don't need her for Slip," he says,

finally letting them know some of the crazy shit happening to him these days. "I'm kind of my own avi in there now."

"And out of there," Amiga adds.

Raid's jaw drops. "That's kind of not fucking normal, Shock."

"No shit," Shock says, and feeling super dry, like he's pointing out the fucking obvious here, he adds, "But then, I'm not, am I?"

a resignation by proxy

Yakuza don't mess around.

Working with them is like being swept up in a hurricane, a very fucking well-armed hurricane. And it howls to life in the daylight, with no attempt at subterfuge, a huge motorcade heading out at speed with katanas slung at their backs. Yakuza of Edo do everything in style. True fact: not a soul in this motorcade bar Vivid and her Hornet crew is dressed in anything but couture fashion. Literally every fucking Yakuza herein looks like a goddamn model. Vivid's damn near aghast, but no one in the motorcade looks nervous apart from her and the Hornets. The single thing redeeming this going-in-guns-blazing crap is that the Hornets get to use the same guns, and being properly armed for the first time in forever ticks all Vivid's boxes. Semi-autos? Yes *please*.

She feels underdressed, overstressed and adequately armed—the dichotomies are giving her one hell of a headache.

The Cartel HQ is equally classy, a shimmering rise of mirrored glass, tinted rose gold. Expecting the reception to be locked and loaded by now, Vivid's stunned when they all troop in uncontested, or rather blast their way in with smart missiles—ho-lee cow. Umi has her men take the receptionists out to the cars and the rest goes down like a military operation, hundreds of Yakuza spreading out through the floors via both staircases and shoots, guns up and firing precision volleys.

The most the Hornets can do is keep up as they take floor by floor.

As an underground organization, as much of a bunch of pirates in their own way as the crew of the *Resurrection City* land ship, the Hornets aren't accustomed to rolling in hardcore, brandishing weapons, and sweeping the opposition away like fucking flies. It's something to witness, even more of a thing to be part of it, however minuscule. And they are minuscule, limited to taking pot shots at Cartel soldiers who somehow get past the whole battalions of Yakuza rampaging their building.

Near the top floors, Vivid makes sure to be alongside Umi's team. The welcome is not fulsome exactly but no one tells her to piss off, so she pulls Raid in with her as they hit the shoot to where duPont and his right hands might be holed up.

"Leave this to us please," Umi says.

"So the invitation to join was more of an invitation to watch you in action?"

"You thought it was an invitation to participate?"

The sheer level of pity dropping on her would bury a lesser soul, but Vivid is nothing like lesser souls. She's gone clubbing wearing scantier clothing than the average podium dancer, she might not have *killed* Twist Calhoun but she sure as shit beheaded him, and she's always been first to throw a punch in a fight. Point of pride, that. She smiles, sweet as anything, taking this shit whilst fully planning to stick her oar so far into the hunting and killing of the Cartel top trio they need bowel surgery to have it removed.

Biding time is an art, and in her line of work Vivid's had ample opportunity to become the freaking Rembrandt of biding time; excruciating hours on counter-surveillance jobs, spying on one Corp for another; agonizing stints in Slip, chasing down elusive scraps of code and stalking cyber-operatives. Oh yeah, she's a fucking pro all right. She raises a brow at Raid, also a pro. He nods. He's in, of course he is.

No way they aren't taking their pound of flesh out of duPont. They're due.

The upper floors of the 'scraper are living quarters even better situated than Oniji's semi-traditional penthouse and their Shandong digs, which gives Vivid more than a twinge—homesickness and grief and bone-melting rage. Two homes. They've been hounded out of two fucking homes now; granted the second had no more than a brief span of time to become theirs, but it was, just as much as Jong-Phu, the home the Queens destroyed. The next home they find, she'll die before she lets anyone take it.

Something smashes up ahead. Shots are fired and someone screams. Rage. Pure, unfettered rage.

And a woman yells, "That was a fucking *Ming*, you animal!"

"My dearest Jess takes her interior design rather seriously," drawls a silky voice, and it sounds damn near apologetic, which makes the agonized screams that follow all the more disturbing.

All but sprinting in, they find the bodies of several Yakuza strewn about a minimalist lounge, their blood sprayed across buttery-white leather sofas and pooling into the cracks between pale floorboards. The amount of damage done in the time between the initial screams and their arrival in the room is eye-opening. Of the Cartel's head trio, there's no sign. Umi points to the shoot, ticking down floors.

"Send word downstairs to detain them."

Whilst Yakuza gather the dead and shout orders, paying no attention to them, Vivid and Raid take their chance, sneaking back to the shoot to follow the trio wherever the hell they're running to. The fact that they're running at all is a surprise. Given their ability to carve up a room of Yakuza they might be expected to stay for more fun rather than turn tail.

Ground level is all chaos. Somehow the Cartel's head trio managed to shoot their way out of the reception and hightail it away, in their own car from the sound. It looks like half the Yakuza have gone after them, the others don't seem to know what the fuck to make of this turn of events except get mad and shoot Cartel employees. Watching the Yakuza lose their damn minds amuses Vivid no end.

"This is why they need Hornets. Maybe if they'd let us have a say they'd still have the upper hand here."

"It's not like they don't. I mean the place is licked, they just lost the ace cards is all." Raid's trying to be a diplomat.

"What hand have you got if you lost the aces, Raid? A fucking dead one. They need to throw their cards in and let the pros take over. Cartel aren't Yakuza. They have no honour. They need sneaky cunts like us to catch them." Whilst she's talking, she's busy jacking into a bike. It roars to life. "Hop on. Let's go hunting."

"We're leaving sans the other Hornets?"

"IM'd. They'll find us easy, they'll be following the same blazing arrow of Yakuza cars trashing pavements. Literally better than breadcrumbs." Skewing the backend, she takes off, weaving between traffic, Raid whooping in back.

Rather than turning tail, fleeing was a tactic.

Run to get caught. Run to *catch*.

Cornered by an unfortunate traffic incident, Lucian, Jessamine and Iyawa opt to ditch the car and head for a building they might conceivably use to entrap and dispatch the Yakuza looking to take them out. It's an oddity. A bright, ugly twenty-floored 'scraper perched atop an old pavilion-style building built on three levels, each crowned with an ornate roof painted the same stinging greens and reds of the 'scraper above, the tiles tipped in gold rendered dull by the livid colours surrounding it.

The double doors of the entrance are yellow wood. Tightly shut. Windowed in an extravagant fan shape, framed in bamboo. Straightening his jacket and adjusting his cufflinks, tutting at the blood stains, Lucian holds his hand out to assist Jess from the car, teetering gracefully on her usual heels. He rather thinks they look too patrician for this building, sleek as greyhounds next to the cheap splendour of Imperial tile-work.

Ah well. Best to make an entrance and forestall any misconceptions.

Iyawa strides ahead to the double doors and holds them open, revealing the whole of the ground floor to be an open-spaced heya bustling with rikishi dressed only in traditional mawashi practicing their stretches, undergoing vigorous massage or having their hair teased into chonmage. The heya abounds with the smell of chanko nabe and the rich fragrance of pomade, cut through with the biting reek of sweat and the unmistakable musk of testosterone.

Jess squeals in delight, informing the entire open ground floor of her presence. The first response is a sort of slow-motion horror, every eye in the place turning to her like she's impossible, some form of visual anomaly designed to confuse. As it becomes clear she's actually standing there, a physical being as opposed to a mirage, horror morphs to disgust, to rage, to choleric outrage, provoking a wave of furious shouting in English and Japanese.

Thick, sweat-sheened arms point to the elaborately painted scrolls on the walls. Jess reads the kanji with cool eyes. Bites her lush bottom lip.

"I think I'm surplus to requirements," she whispers, too loud, too amused.

Lucian pulls her to his side, winks at her. "No vaginas allowed."

Several of the biggest wrestlers quit shouting and take aggressive steps toward them. They're pushed aside by men in suits, basically slabs of muscle, probably augmented, who appear through bamboo doors built flush to the walls and barge their way up to Lucian, demanding he either send the woman back outside or both of them leave. When his immediate response is to ignore them, one of the men grabs Jess's arm as if to remove her himself.

"My dearest love, you appear to have something on you."

Lucian's voice slices into the heya like a shark's fin, a prelude to razor-toothed murder. Before it, like swimmers sighting a fin in the water, the shouting dies down to silence. The man with his hand wrapped around Jess's arm flexes his fingers, his eyes shifting from Jess to Lucian and back again. Whatever he sees makes him swallow.

Jess grabs the wrist of the hand around her arm with her free hand, jerks and twists, producing a snapping sound so thick and crunchy several rikishi fold over and vomit on the floor between their feet. The suit falls to his knees, mouth working, only a whistle of air coming out. His eyes bug out, staring at his wrist. Disbelieving. She coughs elegantly to capture his attention. When it's not forthcoming, she bends over him, sliding her hand up his oddly canted wrist to lace her fingers through his.

Taking her sweet time, she *presses* her palm down, applying pressure. He screams. She presses again, harder, lowers her face until their noses are almost touching.

"I'm confident you're pleased to welcome me."

His eyes bug, but he refuses to answer. She presses again. His scream is interrupted by a heavy slam as the doors behind open to a stream of Yakuza. Word of the brutal slaughter of several of their number in their lounge must have spread. These Yakuza have thrown aside guns to take up blades. Simple, utilitarian katanas, much used from the wear on the blades, and much sharpened from the glint on the razored edges.

"At last," Lucian says, drawing his own blade—not a katana, but long, cruel and wicked sharp. "A proper fight."

The silence, the stand-off, lasts only until he's finished speaking, and then explodes, genned suits lurching forward in concert with the Yakuza. Wrestlers stepping up to join in, a tidal wave of rippling flesh encasing impressive muscle. Iyawa rolls his sleeves up, exposing powerful forearms. This is where they thrive. Lucian has no doubt they'll survive this as they always survive.

Backing away to fool them into following, he guts the first one who dares to get close, laughing as, beside him, Jessamine grabs one in the crook of a deceptively strong arm and breaks his neck, the crack loud and brash as a starting pistol.

The body smashing through the shuttered window of the fifth floor of the heya 'scraper tells Vivid and Raid they've hit ground zero for the fight. Screeching the bike to a messy halt, Vivid abandons it on its side, running in behind Raid.

He indicates the absolute wreckage of the ground floor. "We missed the initial fun."

Vivid weaves through the mess to the shoot. "Then we go find the current fun. Fifth floor, I believe."

On the fifth floor they find a crowd of wrestlers, huge genned bodyguards and Yakuza who've cornered a hulking Nigerian.

"Iyawa, I presume?" murmurs Raid, his eyes wide.

Once a work of sartorial art, Iyawa's suit is ripped in several places and bloodied, his knuckles are wrecks, his face locked into a feral snarl. He shows no sign of slowing down, the crowd around him keeping a careful, or more likely fearful distance. You do not underestimate a man willing and able to fling another man out of a fifth-storey window. Vivid catches Raid in a pretty serious side eye of said window.

"I'm not going near him." He says it almost like a mantra. "I hate heights."

Rolling her eyes hard enough to give herself swirling aura hallucinations, Vivid drags him past. "No need, you have a gun."

"You think shooting him would do a damn thing? He's tripping on so much adrenalin it'd take two clips to put him down. I have precisely a third of one left."

"Wastrel. Doesn't matter, we're after Lucian anyway."

"We are?"

"We are. We have personal beef."

"Pretty sure they work in concert. He's not their boss or anything."

She sniffs. "I don't give a fuck how they work, he's the ace of fucking spades. I want him."

"You want that I back you up, or you happy to let me go for Jess?"

"Chances are they're fighting together," she says. "Joker and Harley of the crime world."

"Fair enough. Lead on. As long as I don't have any chance of being thrown out of a window I'm good."

Up the next flight of stairs, they find nothing but trails of blood and bodies slumped into heaps, several of them are Yakuza still hanging on to life. Vivid could honestly scream. Moral quandaries are her least favourite thing—she tends to pick being moral over giving herself an easy time. So, let them die or not? Amiga could. Amiga would just leave them there. But dammit to *fuck* she is not Amiga and wouldn't want to be. Being trapped in that bear-trap of a mind even momentarily would snap her sanity like a finger caught in a vice.

Her only option here is caving to the possibility of being stonewalled out of this whole deal. Negotiating with herself the remote possibility of it being okay, considering Umi's far enough away to give her time to get to her ace, Vivid IMs their location and the status of the Yakuza on the stairs. Maybe she'll get points for that if not leeway once Umi turns up. Maybe she'll only be banned from Tokyo on pain of death instead of flung out the docking bay into space. The wishful thinking embedded in that "maybe" makes her want to hurl.

Three more flights of stairs up they encounter Jessamine, fighting Sumo wrestlers and Yakuza alike. She's dishabille, her bra exposed, her hair down in messy waves, her body covered in bruises and deep cuts and loving it. She fights like she's not feeling any of the damage. Raid swallows.

"They're not normal," he mutters.

"Neither are you, and you've got a third of a clip; make use of it. Cripple the bitch," Vivid replies, and shoves him toward the action. He'll be all right, likely won't even need those bullets. Jessamine's almost done whether she likes it or not. No one can hold their own for that long and the Yakuza are baiting her like they're baiting Iyawa, making her wear herself out, dancing just out of reach every time she gets close. Her blows are already getting clumsy. Once she's worn, she's done.

Further up the heya, Lucian isn't doing quite as badly as either of his cohorts. She imagined him a similar animal to Iyawa and Jessamine, but seeing him in close quarters, watching the quiet, neat way he dispatches the last Yakuza in the room as she comes too close, drawn by his careful manoeuvring, she realizes he's more like Amiga than they are. Cold. Deliberate. Ruthless. Iyawa and Jess are passionate beings, they let their feelings rule—Lucian can switch his off, if he has any. It makes him harder to predict, harder to bait.

She slides into the room, keeping to the walls. Evaluating. Vivid's not weighed down with false modesty or needless pride, she knows her strengths, her weaknesses, has no issue with admitting to being outmatched. Lucian duPont is better than her. There's no version of a close-combat fight where she wins without sustaining serious injury or dying. Odds are high on the latter. But here comes that lack of false modesty—she has a way to beat him, and she never has to come within spitting distance.

He cleans his blade, watching her. His eyes are cool blue. Icy. The opposite of Shock's startling brightness. "You're not quick enough to hurt me," he says, as if he's offering her a way out. "You'll die. Is that what you want to be known for? Failing?"

"Not really."

"Then why don't you leave?"

"I have business with you."

He lets out a laugh, genuinely amused. "You? Business? What business could you have with me? None of you are of any use to me at all. All I want is the Haunt—he's the only one of you with any worth."

Shit, he's not even bothering with scorn, like the idea of her being his equal in any way isn't even worth that much effort. Good. That makes this simple. Vivid needn't bother with formalities, honour, or playing fair. Snagging her semi-auto, hidden down the back of her jeans, and still packing a carefully conserved half clip of ammo, she shoots out his kneecaps, blowing bloody craters into the fine material of his trousers. They barely even crease as he crumples, knees first, which frankly has to hurt like the worst thing fucking ever but he doesn't make a sound.

Creepy. As. Fuck.

The knife he was cleaning drops from his hand as he hits the floor, she shoots that too, sending it skittering across the room. Pot shots. Like taking out cans on a wall, minus that satisfying ping and clatter. These sounds may be even better. They're the sounds of winning. And the look on his face? She'd frame it if she could, if that wouldn't be super ghoulish. This may be the first intimate meeting he's had with the element of surprise, at least from this direction. Fair to say, she's really enjoyed popping that cherry for him.

Picking her way over the bodies he's left on the floor like refuse, Vivid makes her way over to him, maintaining that careful distance. His eyes track her movement. There's not a hint of wariness in them. He's not scared.

"The gun is a surprise, I'll admit." His voice sounds no different. If not for the brutal paleness of his skin, she'd think him unaffected.

"You're out of my league," she admits, quite happily. "Knew it as soon as I walked in the room. Guessed you might be even sooner. I'm no Cleaner, I'm just a bitch who likes violence."

He shifts. "You're a coward."

Vivid takes a moment to consider that matter-of-fact accusation. Not even an accusation really. An announcement. Even lying there, grievously wounded, he's judged her worthiness as an opponent and found her wanting. Fascinating. She imagines it must have been like this for Amiga with Twist. But Twist underestimated

Amiga. Big time. And Lucian? He's failed to understand something important about her. Something *intrinsic.*

"It's not cowardice to know your limitations," she says, skirting around him, never once taking her eyes off him. She doubts his brokenness. Wants to give him the chance for a fair death, but not if it means endangering herself. Yeah, he feels like danger even lying there with his knees like fucking chuck steak. "I'm not fucking suicidal."

He raises a brow. Could he be any more calm? He's not normal. In ways she's not seen. Ways she never wants to see again. "What are you then?" he drawls. "Hmmm?"

Stunned by how well she's hiding the waves of unease lapping at her spine, Vivid offers him her most beautiful smile, because she's had it with watching him. The only thing she wants this man to do right now is die. Before she loses her nerve.

"What am I?" she says. "I'm really fucking good at planning."

Raising the gun, she shoots him, right in the centre of his forehead. One shot. Clean. She resists the urge to empty the clip into his face to make sure, even though this feels like a double-tap situation. But she does wait, breath baited, to make sure he's definitely gone and she backs out of the room when she can bring herself to leave, because those pale blue eyes of his didn't close, they just dimmed really, really slowly, the life fading with such reluctance she's convinced he was in there wrestling to stay alive. To drag his body across the room after her.

She's halfway down the stairs and almost running

when she realizes she's shaking. Not adrenalin, not all of it. Not any of it. When she tells the story of this moment, and she will, probably many times over, probably drunk, she won't omit this part. It's important to be honest about what scares you. And that guy? That fucking creepy, slow to die son of a bitch? He's scared the living crap out of her.

Back downstairs, Jessamine is on the floor, bleeding from several strategic bullet wounds, her hands in ties. Actual ties. Yakuza ties. Expensive, tastefully patterned silk. From the intricacy of the knots, she can see Raid has indeed been holding his own. She grins at him.

"Where are the Yakuza?"

"Taking out Iyawa with tranks of all things. Umi's down there supervising. These two are heading back to their HQ for a little Yakuza-style justice."

"Nice. Are *we* in trouble?"

"Hell if I know. They left me to tie up this bitch though, so I think no."

"Where's my Lucian?" Jessamine demands. "Bring him to me."

Vivid glances at her. "He won't be joining us," she says, savouring every word, letting none of her fear of him show. That would ruin the moment. "He tendered his resignation. I accepted."

Jessamine's screaming, not broken, not loss, but the sawed edge of unfiltered rage set to explode, follows them down the stairs, playing soundtrack to the silent approval of the Yakuza, to Umi's gift of a respectful nod as they pass. She has Iyawa trussed like a roast joint, unconscious, his face all but unrecognizable behind massive bruising and swelling.

Out in the street they can still hear Jessamine, her rage pitching upwards to awful grief, even over the noise of the traffic. Over the roar of the bike. Trying to block it out, Vivid IMs the other Hornets, giving them the heads up to get gone and meet her back at the shuttle. Despite Umi's graciousness, a swift exit might be prudent. Pulling on a helmet, because courting bad luck is a bad idea right now, Vivid tries to block out those screams, the memory of Lucian's pale eyes, gradually dimming, but they stay with her all the way back to the shuttle, echoing in her head like gunshots.

don't upset your aunty

The domed apex of a tower on Hong Kong Hub is a vast, sun-drenched solarium groaning with carnivorous plants and resonating with the somnolent hum of a million dragonfly wings. A small path winds through the vegetation, marked by miniature prayer wheels, bright red and gold against the green; leading to a central island, a collection of wrought-iron tables filled with seed pots and cuttings, and a bamboo waterfall, clicking softly under the dragonfly hum.

At the tables, tucked neatly into a motorized wheelchair and dressed like a jewel, is a tiny woman, her face wrinkled as fine crepe fabric and set into an expression of perfect serenity, framed by silver-grey hair formed into a chic, smooth ofuku decorated with elaborate combs. Orbiting that head like a thousand gleaming moons, as if magnetized, is an accompaniment of lazy dragonflies.

At her feet, a man kneels: trembling. She's paying no attention to him at the moment, busy crooning loving words to a dazzling array of curling monkey cups tangling down from the roof of the conservatory between leaves sharp as green swords, their delicate bowls of red-speckled green glowing like veined lanterns. The tiny lady cups one bowl and another in hands neat and smooth as a girl's, offering praise, the odd sharp word if one bowl is perhaps not quite to her liking.

Once she has seen to each bowl in turn, she reaches out, snake-swift, to pluck a gleaming emerald-green dragonfly from the air. She holds it for a moment as it settles, languid in her palm, trusting as a dog and then, her eyes greedy, she pops it into a monkey cup whole and still wriggling. Watches as it struggles to free itself, managing only to slide deeper and deeper, its hum becoming louder and more frantic as it goes.

"That's my female nepenthes," she says to the man on the floor. "Look at how splendid she is. They love dragonflies, you know. The bigger and fatter the better. Nutrition is important."

Cowering even lower to the floor, the man whimpers. A tall, suited woman steps out from the ranks of lush vegetation. Her black boot flashes forward, striking his ribcage with a muffled thud. He chokes, curling up around his ribs. The woman leans over him and grabs his hair.

Face blank of all expression, she enunciates slowly in his ear as he snivels and coughs, "You say, '*Yes*, Aunty Dong. How *interesting* Aunty Dong.' Understand?"

A small wail escapes him. "Y-yes, Aunty Dong," he half-screams, forehead scraping the floor. "H-how *interesting*… A-Aunty Dong."

The suited woman and Aunty Dong exchange glances. Aunty Dong shrugs. "I suppose it'll do. Where are my secateurs? I've lost them again."

Another suited woman bustles forward and hands Aunty Dong a neat pair of floral-patterned secateurs with easy-grip handles before both women move back, disappearing into the tangle of plants.

"What a dear girl." Aunty Dong beams at the snivelling man curled at her feet. "Hand," she snaps imperiously. "Hurry now, I haven't got all day."

He remains as he is, head bowed and weeping into the stone floor. There's a rush of wheels and her chair is by his head. She reaches down and snatches up his right hand, cupped protectively around his head. Her grip is vicious. Like a pincer. He howls and tries to pull back. Aunty Dong yanks him forward, a single sharp tug that sees him splayed at her feet.

She tuts. Places the blades of the secateurs around his index finger. Snips. Ignoring his screech as the digit pops off into her lap.

"Index finger," she says, over his screams. "Authority and independence. Now you have none. You do as Aunty Dong says always. If Aunty Dong wishes for you to cut off all your remaining fingers, what do you say?"

"Yes, Aunty Dong!"

She throws his hand off her lap, ignoring the spurt of blood, the stains on the silk. Smiles satisfaction. Inclines her head. At that gesture both suited women appear out from the foliage and drag the man away. Tucking the secateurs into a pocket somewhere in her neat, embroidered skirts, Aunty Dong picks up the bloody digit between a finger and thumb.

Pursing her lips, she moves the chair in a slow turn around the edge of her planting area and stops at each plant, considering, until she reaches a muscle-red pitcher, almost the size of her tiny head. Lifting the finger, she drops it into the maw of the bowl. It makes a sharp sound like a stone.

"Rajah," she murmurs. "Tuck in, there's a dear."

Through the greenery above slips a shining form, liquid and furtive, illuminating each lantern bulb it passes, painting soft buttercup gold on every leaf. Bursting out from between falls of spiky leaves it reveals itself as a golden sun, blazing bright and zips a zig-zag dance to Aunty Dong's chair, neat and dragonfly swift. Hovers in front of her face, gradually dimming until its shape becomes apparent in the glow.

Aunty Dong's avatar is Glauert's Seadragon, a fantasy built of leaves and delicate sea-horse curlicues, a whip of grace, muscle and mischief bought and paid for by her superstitious parents upon the eve of her first birthday. Most auspicious. Aunty Dong has paid a small fortune to ensure Seadragon remains out. When she's dealt with the tiresome business of revenge, she'll travel to Shanghai and have a little word with Evelyn Tsai, who has overstepped her boundaries somewhat. She does not enjoy travelling. However, Evelyn Tsai will enjoy her travelling even less, and that will make it a most satisfying visit.

Does Aunty have a call, dear little thing?

If it please her.

It does indeed. Take Aunty in, will you? There's a dear.

Leaning back in her chair, she folds her hands in her gore-spattered lap and allows Seadragon to carry her away into Slip. Slip echoes these days, even with the numbers who choose to pay exorbitant tariffs to keep access. Aunty rather enjoyed the chaos before the caging. The hum of activity. The rapid remodelling of Slip to something altogether more intriguing than ocean. She understands what Evelyn Tsai demonstrably does not: change is imperative if the world is not to stagnate.

Hu Hai's a twitching mess of grit, sore muscles and crying feet. He was forced to spend almost all the flim left in his account to get a flight. Broke, shoeless and disoriented, he's been wandering Hong Kong since he arrived, trying to find somewhere high enough to spot Dong's tower because he has no map and no money to access his avi and the Slip to get one.

Fucking Corps thieving avis. Life gets worse. Always.

He's been to Dong's tower only the once, in the middle of the bloody night almost. He was excited to meet her, to have evidence of his success in impressing her. What a fool he was then. He was shuttled to her roof, feeling like royalty. Met her in her solarium, surrounded by the plants she cultivates and those ugly, bloated dragonflies she likes to feed them with. That's what he's been looking for on the skyline. Her lair. He figures if he can get high enough, he'll spot it, and in this one thing he has luck, though it takes a few tries, Hong Kong being somewhat larger and generally taller than he was expecting. A little more luck sees him getting into the tower without too much difficulty. Turns out Dong has yet to remove him from the employee roster.

So absolute in her confidence, so certain she's broken him. Hah. She'll soon know better.

The plan now is to get to a damn shoot and get the hell off this floor before anyone sees him and thinks to ask what he's doing, because at some point someone will see he's clocked in and will want to log the why of it. Always the way. Offices operate the same everywhere. Turning down another corridor of the first floor of Dong's tower, he plasters his body into a crevice, hiding from a group of men and women in suits. Counts to himself as they move away, leaving him free to continue his search for a way to the top levels.

Somewhere in this godforsaken maze of a thousand corridors, like some freakish Chinese hell invented purely for his torment, there's a shoot to the next levels. Instinct formed through long, painful familiarity with buildings just like this tells him so. Finding shoots in any given Corp stronghold is a skill he cultivated within weeks of first becoming a salaryman at age twenty, alongside a nausea-response to suits, alcoholism, misery and an addiction to junk food.

He finds the shoots right at the centre, their shining

doors surrounded by pale ceramics designed to look like watermarked paper. These shoots go no further than the middle floors. Not unusual. The office fauna on the lowest floors can go no further. Only private shoots go to the upper floors from the lower levels, and they'll go from the car parks on the ground floor.

On the mid floors he hunts for the public Exec Corp shoots, something he has a little less experience with, having only had access to the ones back on the Gung for the past few weeks. He finds them set in a sort of potted garden toward the rear of the building, if those monstrosities can be called pots. They're huge, containing whole trees, complete with ceramic birds. These shoots have a ceramic surround too, designed to mimic some ancient dynasty. He wouldn't know which—history is not his thing. But it's pretty. Colourful.

He takes a spot behind one of the potted trees and waits until a woman approaches the shoots. As she enters, he saunters up as if only just arriving and follows her in, standing at ease and ignoring the sidelong looks he gets for his clothes, his bare feet, his general state of filth. Not her business where he's going, and she won't question a thing. Not here. She's likely seen worse. Every Exec has spare suits for exactly the kind of occasion he looks to have been enjoying. She leaves a few floors later, too swiftly, probably thanks to his stench, and he's able to enjoy the rest of the ride up in blissful solitude.

Stepping out on to the highest level, he smells the solarium before he sees the stairs to it, the hot stench of superheated foliage making him simultaneously hungry and revolted. Halfway up he can hear the dragonflies droning. Stupid creatures. He shudders. Is he really going to do this? He's feeling rather less insane now he's here. Maybe he should go home. Except. There it is. Under the dragonflies. The buzz of her chair.

Hu Hai creeps up the spiral staircase until he can see the bright green of plant life between the ornate ironwork of the banister. There she is, in the distance, sat there perfect as a jewel and perfectly smug. Complacent. He waits a moment or two more, but doesn't see her guards. Good. She's alone. Hu Hai steps out amongst the fat bodies of dragonflies, batting them from his face and feeling invincible. Who'll protect her now?

"I wondered when you'd turn up." She doesn't turn, but it's obvious she's talking to him.

"I... um... I..." He can't find one thing to say. He bats another dragonfly away, his shoulders slumping a little. Dong was not supposed to guess he'd have the balls to come.

She looks up, and the annoyance on her face is galling. She's regarding him as if he's a dragonfly that won't digest. "You're predictable, Hu Hai. You lack imagination."

Hu Hai can't quite believe his ears. *He* lacks imagination? "I have imagination," he says. "I had it all figured out. It would've worked too, but you *had* to hit the farm hard. I told you not to but you chose to ignore me. Now you blame me for your failure, take my life from me, and expect me to creep away like a dog? Are you quite right in the head?"

That look of disgust is still there, if anything more profound. "If you'd been any good at planning," she scoffs, "the hit on the farm would not have been such a disaster. Have the decency to admit failure."

"But… but… I've only ever been a *salaryman*," he blusters, confounded beyond belief. How can this be a conversation he's having? It's not right. "I'm not a soldier!"

"You should have been whatever I needed," she replies, calmly deadheading a spiky profusion of colourful leaves. "How deep is your failure. How all encompassing. Your family will be mortified. Your wife will consider herself lucky to have severed from you."

Yelling, he lunges for her. Finds himself holding air. A vicious pain hits his side and warm liquid soaks his trousers. He touches the wet spot, wincing as it burns. Why does it burn? His hand comes away drenched. Blood? He looks down. There is blood on him, and it is his. Dong's over by a repulsive, bulbous plant, as large as her head, crooning to it, dripping blood from her secateurs into its wide mouth. That's *his*.

"That's mine," he says. "Give it back."

Lurching over to her, he makes a grab for the handles, falling partway into her lap. It should be like collapsing on to a bird, all snappable bones and light feathers, a puff of air somehow given life and personality, instead she's steel, a formation of cables encased in satin. She wrenches the blades from his hands and chops off the thumb of his left hand as if deadheading a plant. He screeches. She smiles in response and chucks the thumb into the plant.

Against all reason, Hu Hai leaps after it and the fat plant bursts under his weight, spewing clear fluids streaked with his blood. Dong's scream of rage and grief echoing in his ears, he scrambles across the floor for his thumb. The hum of dragonflies grows too loud. No, not dragonflies. Wheels. Quick as a flash, Dong's driven her chair to his thumb, her wheel poised directly in front of it.

"No. Don't," he begs.

"You killed my plant, you lost my Haunt, you come to my home and attack me and you want me to *spare* your thumb?"

"Please."

She laughs at him and drives the wheel over the thumb, squashing it. Seeing his thumb all but disintegrate beneath the weight of her wheel makes a light go out inside him. He tries to get up again but the adrenalin is gone. Wasted. He could have done so much with it. Instead he's lying here on his side, crying about his thumb and probably slowly bleeding to death, barely noting the gold flashing around his face as some tiny, flitty little avatar tries to beat him with its tail. He can't hear or feel it, but it's more annoying than a wasp. He wishes he could swat it.

He should have gone home and eaten the damn dumplings.

little solarium of horrors

Entry to Hong Kong is a line system, shuttles moving into bays as they're processed. Tracker has to do some pretty creative jacking to pass them through the bureaucratic checks, but about two hours after they rocked up to the hub, they're locked in and ready to go. Amiga would kill to hit a hotel of any stripe and wash the grime away, but time is not an ally. She's had to settle for a change of clothes from her duffle and a long, cold drink.

Paris Hub's already put out an alert. The joy. Tracker will have to keep their ID rolling to prevent them from being arrested here and thrown out without so much as a by your leave. They won't extradite them back to Paris, but they won't suffer them within their dome borders. Woes of being a fucking hero. And here comes that itchy sense of unfairness, crawling at her insides again. All they do, all they've done, and people still regard *them* as the problem. Do any of these judgemental bastards deserve their help? Not really. But Dong needs to die with maximum expediency.

So there's that. Primo reason to put one boot in front of the other rather than into a few choice faces.

Roughly a decade ago, Hong Kong Hub pedestrianized most of the roads at its centre and transport has since morphed into a culture of caterbiking or taking a mono similar to the Gung's to get around. Hong Kong has the best caterbike hire system off-Gung. Climbing on to a caterbike rented for literally change, Amiga steals a glance at Shock as he hops on behind her. He's the same as ever, slender, too thin, too goddamn pretty, that green and black hair always ratty, those fucking eyes bright enough to blind.

Eyes shouldn't be that blue. It's freakish.

There's no way to see the other difference in him, the parts that are all Emblem. Not unless he shows it anyway—gold eyes rising through blue, illusions to cover them as they move through crowded streets, that whole cutting human life off with a thought thing. In those moments it's possible to completely forget that he's still Shock, still the skinny little loser who's not as fucked as he thinks and way more than he wants to be.

She's half curious and half not about the whole being his own avi thing. She's seen the gold, but thought it was less avi and more Emblem. Can't wrap her cranium around the notion of Slipping without a normal avi. Too strange. Besides which, he hasn't cracked it out to pinpoint Dong quite yet, and frankly she wants him to hustle. Now they're here, her only focus is getting some hands on revenge for the Hornets lost in that hit on the farm and, of course, finding Gail.

She owes Gail a rescue. Big time. Until that's ticked off her to-do list she'll be hauling around more metric tonnes of guilt than she can handle.

You getting your Slip on any time soon?

On it already, he replies, sounding distant. Preoccupied. Detached. The fact that he's already in Slip occurs to her. In and out all at once. Nope, that isn't freaky at all.

It's really not.

I did not say that aloud.

You're emanating.

Shock Pao, that's enough reading of my emanations. Quit it, or I'll dump you off the back of this bike on your ass. I mean, fuck sake, it's skating on the edge of downright wrong *that you can do this in the first place without poking your nose into my psyche.*

I really don't need to poke, it's right there. Lemme show you.

Without the touch of his drive to warn her, the whole of Slip appears around her, a vivid dream draped over the world. Strange, bright and overwhelming, it's still somehow oddly empty and diminished with far fewer avis than usual, all trapped in Slip even outside of their cages—and how the hell does she know that? Because he does. Fuck. He's right. Everything is *right there.* All this information, way too much of it, right there for the taking. A fake medium could become a billionaire with this shit.

This how you see Slip all the time?

IRL? Hell no. I'd go nuts. Usually I only see the gold, the info, the chat. This shit is what I can see in Slip if I choose to. I let it all hang out now because I need it. Hunting, yeah?

Even with choice, she can't imagine how he copes. There's nowhere to go to escape from it, not even inward. Slip is in every damned cell: an overload, a takeover, a consuming flood. It's changed, too, to a bewildering degree. Become a surreal landscape, a derangement of ideas. There are things like nothing she's ever seen. Mountains of matter, dull gold, sliding through in slow evolutions.

Before she can ask what they are, or beg him to take this away, he points and she sees Dong's location, glowing like a fire in the distance. Quite beautiful.

He cuts her connection then, and the Gung leaps back to clarity, three dimensional and real and so solid she wants to stop the bike, jump off and kiss the fucking ground. She can still see Dong's tower though, burning in her mind like the after-effect of a flash, and speeds up in the gathering dusk. As they close in on it, she sees how traditional it is, a steel recreation of a Chinese temple stretched to the heavens and topped with a brightly lit dome.

When they're close enough to smell the ozone of the thousands of lights illuminating its sweeping cornices, they hide the bikes and share out the few weapons they have. It's a depressingly low amount, but the plan is to sneak, draw as little attention as possible. The last thing they need is to come out with more of them dead or damaged.

Part of this don't be seen or heard plan is rappelling up to the roof. Amiga's going first, taking Shock on the harness behind her like a dual-jump because apparently, when he's not drugged out of his mind he's not fond of the notion of running up a building. Adorable. Feeling magnanimous, she lets him get used to giving in to the pressure of the rope first, before speeding up until they're both running lightly.

Shock's a sweaty state by the time they hit the top.

Heights suck, he throws out, throwing off the harness at the same time. *Since meeting you guys I always seem to end up on heights.*

She grins. *Coming up in life.*

He makes this glorious, disgusted face. *Worst joke ever.*

Worst whinge ever.

Fuck you.

Trying not to laugh and piss him off even more, Amiga tugs the clips to ensure they won't come loose and sends the harnesses back down for the next two to come up. They've come in a team of twenty, so it takes a while until they're all assembled on the roof and they can move out toward the dome of the solarium, the explosion of greenery within crawling right up to the top. Looks like there's no room in there for anything but plants.

The roof is empty of guards, which surprises Amiga, until they get to the entrance of the Solarium and find it bio-locked.

"Peachy," she says, kicking the bottom of the door. "Just fucking *peachy*."

"Cool it, Cleaner," Shock says, and rams his way in front of her. "I've got this. Key, remember?"

"I thought it wasn't strictly a key any more?"

"No, but it hasn't forgotten how to open and close shit."

Shock's fingertip flares gold on the pad, and the door yawns open to reveal a humid interior, wafting the stench of rotting vegetation into her face. Too many bad smells lately. If that's not a metaphor for her life, Amiga has no idea what is. Hand over her nose, she follows Shock in, noting his sudden quiet. There's quite the force of fury contained within it. A side of him that seems to be new. Post-murder.

Or maybe she missed it before?

Thinking about all he's done and been forced to do in the past five weeks, she realizes the fury has been growing since the loss of Shark. Shark was made by him instead of given to him. It's more than likely Shark wasn't just an avatar but an impulse given form to contain it, a part of himself Shock either wanted or needed to deny or corral. Shock told her how he killed Ho, but he missed out the important part: when he unleashed Shark on Ho, he was really unleashing himself.

And with Shark gone, that unleashing is unravelling.

Her Shock was always a predator, the difference is that he's stopped being able to pretend he's not, and it looks like he's begun to accept that. Cleaner to the core, Amiga finds a measure of comfort in that realization. Whatever happens from here on in, she can trust him to make the hard decisions, the bloody ones. No more protection racket—her job is to make sure he's free to do what he needs to, and she can do that. It will be her distinct pleasure.

Expectations are strange things. Amiga expected the solarium to be quiet, perhaps some music—in her experience people like Dong love a bit of classical music—definitely the dragonflies Dong's famous for droning beneath it all. And she does hear that, but instead of a musical accompaniment is a low sort of moaning gurgle. The sound of pain. Of injury. Coming out into the centre of the solarium the injured party proves to be a semi-handsome, slightly overweight salaryman type being attacked by what looks like a golden dragon made of leaves. An avatar of all things.

He's not even attempting to prevent its frenzied passage around his head. He's just lying there in a pool of blood in the shattered remains of a bulbous carnivorous plant, soaked in its juices. Shirt, trousers, every damn thing, covered in yellowish liquid. It's even in his hair somehow. He's also missing a thumb that, if Amiga's not mistaken and she rarely is with body parts, is the mangled piece of squished flesh on the floor. Made more mangled as a minute, delicate old lady in a motorized wheelchair drives over it again and again, chuckling merrily.

Dong. More deranged and deadly than Amiga thought, and more beautiful.

The salaryman type fixates on the remains of the thumb and starts making this sound, a sort of whine like a kettle boiled too long on the stove. He's gonna pop. Dong responds with a noise that reminds Amiga acutely of her own grandmother—a little *tchk* of impatience—and spins the chair toward him, speeding forward, her right hand clutching bloody secateurs.

Moving without thinking, Amiga leaps into Dong's

path, ramming her boots against the tyres to stall them. Leaning in over the tiny, hunched madwoman, close enough to smell the powdery perfume in her elaborate hairdo, Amiga grabs the hand clutching the secateurs, instantly surprised at the sinewy strength of it. Putting her whole back into it, she manages to wrestle the secateurs away. The little avatar comes zipping over and Amiga swats it. Her hand swiping through. It tingles.

"Fuck off," she snaps. It ignores her, charging her again and again as, in the corner of her eye, she watches Deuce and the others move in to help the salaryman. Wow, leave her to it why not? Jeez. Below her, Dong *growls*. With both hands, she latches on to Amiga's face and tugs her forward. Nails digging in and *tearing* she screams in her face. Harpy loud. Reducing her world to noise and comets of gold exploding into her face. Oh hell no, bitch.

"Shut. Up."

Lifting the secateurs, she plunges the blades into Dong's mouth. She doesn't anticipate the feel of lips warm against her hands, or the sickening ease with which the blades slide down into Dong's throat. All the way down, muscular oesophageal tissues scraping at Amiga's knuckles.

Everything stops. The world on pause like someone hit a button. The avatar freezes. Dong coughs, almost polite. Gurgles. Her eyes roll up in her head right to the sclera, pale and shiny as boiled eggs. She convulses once, then again. The second time throws Amiga on to the floor, dropping her into plant digestive juices that soak through the seat of her jeans, making her shiver.

Pulling herself up and immediately scrubbing her hands dry on her clothes, Amiga watches Dong start to spin in circles, choking out noises like air escaping a tyre, her fingers grabbing blindly at her face, at the secateurs, so far down her throat only the tips of the handles are visible. The sight of them is ridiculous. Awful. They look so uncomfortable Amiga almost wants to get up and pull them out.

But she wants to watch Dong die more. Even when the avatar rushes forward to spin around with her, as if trying to catch her. The alarm, the despair, the agony of it drives into Amiga, slicing straight past everything she puts in the way of what she does.

Dong's hands stutter. Flutter away. Fall to her sides. In slow revolutions, her chair stops moving. Her chest heaves one more time, as if drawing in air for a scream and her head flops to the side at a strange angle, which is one hell of a conundrum until Amiga realizes the secateurs are so far down her neck's actually stuck. She blinks, trying to process. And then the avatar explodes in a shower of gold.

That's when she starts laughing, and finds she can't stop.

Deuce strides over and hauls her into his arms. She fights him for precisely thirty seconds, until she realizes she's crying. A lot. Which is weird. What's weirder is how much better that feels than the laughing did. And holding on to him? That's about a million times better.

"What the hell?" she says, muffled in his chest and thick with stupid, pointless, unwanted tears.

"It hit you wrong. You'll be okay."

"I wanted her dead. I was fine. I was *fine*."

"Yeah," he murmurs into her hair. "I thought you were too until you started laughing. Don't do that again."

Sitting on the floor in the remains of the plant Dong tried feeding his thumb to, and one hell of a lot of his own blood, Hu Hai tries to process the last ten minutes and fails miserably. One second he was watching his thumb meet a second, third and fourth grisly end under Dong's tyres and then Hornets buzzed into the room with a Haunt and a Cleaner at their head and changed everything.

They're nothing like he imagined them to be, especially the Haunt and the Cleaner. The Cleaner needs a damn good shower and she looks way too young, with her battered boots over ripped jeans and bright-red anime tee. As for the Haunt, he looks like someone threw him into a candy machine and then dressed him in rags, and his eyes, wow, bluer than sky.

He can't deny the sheer physical threat of them though, despite their visual lunacy. Their presence is magnetic. Extends out to swallow the whole room. He wants to do something dramatic; stand up and present Dong like a trophy, like a prize girl on one of Sakkura's crappy live game shows, only his side aches too damn much to move and then Dong's racing at him and all he can do is think *oh shit*.

The Cleaner snaps into focus. She's on Dong before he can blink, wrestling the secateurs out of her grasp. At this point the avatar buzzing around his head deserts him to attack the Cleaner and he's surrounded by overly helpful Hornets blocking his view, which is partly a relief but mostly an aggravation. He wants to see Dong die. Wanted to kill her himself, but death by Cleaner will do. He hears the Cleaner tell Dong to shut up. Dong coughs. Gurgles. Her chair whines and whines as she gurgles and then stops.

The Cleaner starts laughing.

Hu Hai's flight instinct explodes so hard his body jolts, but the loss of blood and the general unpleasantness of the day have all but wiped him out, and he's able to do nothing but sit and be patched up by a perfectly jovial Indian called Ravi. Ravi's a revelation. Gets the copious bleeding in his thumb and side under control with such amazing speed Hu Hai's half convinced he must have passed out for a moment and missed something.

When he's bandaged, Ravi moves aside, revealing the Haunt, who's staring at him. Those electric-blue eyes are devoid of any friendliness. "The farm. You were behind that."

Hu Hai finds himself doing that nodding thing. The thing where you can't stop. He feels like a car ornament. "No choice you understand. You don't say no to Dong. She's been sat in my drive, driving me crazy. Terribly sorry. No offence meant." The Haunt's brow shoots up and he reaches out to pat Hu Hai's shoulder, not even noticing when he attempts to shrink away.

"How'd she find us?"

"Er... Techs. We had software geared to look for

physical quirks. Running thousands of hours of stream footage. Tracked you down myself in Hunin. That Wi Ji Lin. In a bar, with your friend Vivid. Made sure it was him and then followed them back."

The Haunt groans. "Knee Jerk? You fucking followed *Knee Jerk*?"

Hu Hai swallows. "Uh… yeah."

"That wasn't cool. Not a bit of it. So you maybe want to make up for a few things. Dong's soldiers took Gail, the farm manager. You have any idea where he is in here? If he's alive?"

Shaking his head, Hu Hai says, "I didn't go with the soldiers. I went back to Hunin. Got drunk. Freaked about what Dong would do to me. She tanked my life. All gone. Everything. I came here to kill her. I tried. I really did. So sorry."

The Haunt pats Hu Hai on the shoulder again. "Chill. Amiga took care of that." He looks at Ravi. "Look after him," he says. "Make sure she doesn't do anything rash. I'm going to scan for Gail."

Ravi sketches a salute with two fingers. "You got it."

"She won't kill *me*, will she?" Hu Hai feels compelled to ask.

Pursing his lips, Ravi looks over at the Cleaner, currently in the arms of Deuce, the sane one. Hu Hai always thought of him that way—in the streams of the Hornets at work he looked in control. Organized. And he emanates calm, like a Buddhist shrine. Ravi sniffs; it doesn't sound convincing. "She shouldn't do. Just… don't talk any more about Shandong being your doing, and especially not about using Knee Jerk. That will not go down well."

"No?"

Ravi looks at him, and it's far less friendly. Hu Hai's shown the man beneath the jovial mask, and his heart starts pounding again. "No," Ravi says softly. "Not with any of us."

less than zero

Losing the Zeros on Paris Hub hurt. Actual physical pain. Being tangled into their neural networks as they were subjected to wounds or blows sent the signals travelling to Zen's body. Having felt so little for so long it struck her in unexpected ways. She used to be frightened of physical pain, but now all it does is make her long to be active again, to be out of this bubble and in the world.

It makes her impatient.

Waiting grates on her. Five weeks awake. Five weeks of patient play, of waiting for the pieces to come together, and then Emblem brought the Haunt here. Its intention was to warn. To encourage him to rethink coming to do what Mollie demanded, what Zenada knew full well she would ask if prodded in just the right way. His visit sparked such urgency. Such desperate need. And then this pain, this memory of *life*. She's done with waiting. She wants out. *Now*.

She needs to bring Zeros to her signal, draw them close enough so she can see the outside of the place she's been imprisoned. Find out where she's being held. Reaching out to the closest Zero minds, she wastes no time with delicacy, tearing into them, forcing her control on them, whipping at them like cattle and yanking them to her. Insisting.

They come too slowly. She wants them to run. To sprint. But Zeros are sick and addled and she's forced to bear with them as they make their way through streets frustratingly familiar to her—too blurred and confused through their senses to make proper sense of. Until she sees the building her signal emanates from in waves, pulling on their minds, their bodies. It almost makes her cry. She knows where she is.

Home. New York Hub.

That Breaker trapped her here is beyond cruelty. This, the Peace Tower, was built by her family, for themselves and for New York Hub, when they moved here from the Gung. They paid billions to buy not just an old 'scraper, but the land beneath it, so they could demolish, build a monument, a landmark, something New York could add to its skyline with pride. A white tower. A white tower with a white room. Josef couldn't be cruel, so Breaker was cruel for him.

Love. What will it not do? And they call it pure. Ridiculous. Love is *vicious.*

Attacking and removing anything in her way, infecting anything she can't use them to physically beat, and ignoring the pain any injury to their bodies causes her, Zen brings the Zeros to her, driving them up staircases and through bright, white corridors until she sees her prison through their eyes.

She makes them strike at the bubble from the outside until their hands are bloodied, their bones broken, achieving nothing but red smears all over her view.

Not enough. Not good enough.

She needs the key. And if he won't bring it to her, she'll just have to send something to fetch it.

The Hornets are busy doing essential clear up, covering their tracks by getting rid of bodies and deleting streams. They've just packed a pathetically grateful Hu Hai off, cleaned up and dressed in a suit found in one of the offices, with a bunch of flim stolen from various cred chips and DL'd to his when Vivid calls in with news of duPont's death and the capture of Jessamine and Iyawa. They're free and clear from Tokyo, tired, injured and hungry, but they're one hundred percent hot to trot to get to Shanghai and deal with Tsai Holdings—as long as they get to nap and stop for noodles. Music to Amiga's ears.

The best news of the day, in fact, until Shock confirms he's found Gail in the building. Locked away in what seems to be a panic room in Dong's private office and lounge on the level just below the solarium.

"How many guards?" she asks.

"Several. A big group of soldiers and two female guards—her personal ones I think. Fuck knows why she sent them down."

"Not like she didn't have poor old Hu Hai in hand, was it?"

"Guess not. Anyway, they're all armed, and we have no guns."

"As soon as they know Dong is dead, they'll kill him."

Shock nods. "Agreed."

"Let's move then," Deuce says, pushing past. "And quickly. I'll see if Tracker can remote-jack her systems to get that panic room open."

"I can get that," Shock says.

Deuce raises a brow. "Could be locked with her thumbprint."

Amiga snags out her knife. Always practical. "Best cut off a hand then, just in case."

Deuce grabs her wrist. Flays her with a look she'd rather not interpret. It's not like she's still in the same zone she was in after taking Dong down. And severing a hand? That shit has seriously low odds of throwing her back there.

"I'll do it."

"Jeez, Deuce, I'm all back in business. No more crazy moments. Cross my heart."

"Yeah. I know. But I'll do it."

He's got this set to his jaw. Cement-like. She could crack herself against it a little more, or let it go and get on with doing right by Gail. Flipping the handle toward him, she lets Deuce take the knife. Watches him walk away. Shock steps in close enough for their shoulders to touch. Unlike Dong, Shock feels as fragile as he looks. Takes a lot to put him down though, that's for sure.

"He's good to you." Stating the obvious is a skill. Shock has it in spades.

"Too damn good."

"No such thing. I'd say he's good *enough*."

And Amiga can't really muster an argument for that, having begun to reach the same reluctant conclusion herself. Not only about Deuce, but all the Hornets. They're something else. Something she desperately did not want to deserve, but here's the rub, the simple, complicated, *beautiful* truth—sometimes you don't *have* to deserve something, sometimes you just get it anyway, because someone wants you to have it.

The panic room is behind Dong's ornate, unused office, in her private lounge, a room with a window facing the curve of the dome, giving a perfect view of Hong Kong's skyline with earth rising in the background and space above, rife with stars. Why is it these power-hungry types like to stare at all of earth and space? Do they fantasize being like Queens and stomping all over it? Stopping at the door, they brace on either side out of sight, watching the guards to see if there's any way they can take them by surprise.

Isn't right she had a view like that. Shock's fixated on the stars, the distant blue of the ocean, muted under cloud and atmosphere.

Who's to say she didn't appreciate it?

It's probably the wrong moment for devil's advocate but what the hell, hearing her own thoughts from Shock made her realize how close that shit is to setting Dong into her own category, when she's just human. Just a shitty, self-absorbed human. You've gotta acknowledge that, or you risk ending up the same way. Selfishness is such an easy fucking choice.

Appreciation isn't the point, he mutters. *Shitty people shouldn't have nice things.*

Shitty people invariably *have nice things. Being shitty* got *them nice things.*

Why the fuck is that?

Because life is absurd. Nothing makes any sense. Her conclusion, from a hella long time ago. But she's willing to bet mountains of flim on it being true.

These guards are not going to give us an opening. Deuce is rocking an unusual amount of pissiness. It looks damn good on him. *Crappy odds. I hate crappy odds.*

Full frontal? she suggests.

Can't hurt. Or at least, it can't hurt more than any other type of attack. World of hurt either way.

Pessimist.

Realist. And really fed up with fighting people with guns.

He's speaking her truth so hard, all she can do is offer a high five before counting down to attack.

Sprinting through the door, they hit the soldiers and guards the only way they can, another few Hornets garnering ugly flesh wounds in the rush. Wielding his pissiness like a weapon, a projectile missile, Deuce heads off one of the female guards, taking her to the ground and out with a punch to the face so hard her skin ripples back, unconsciousness settling in even before the violent bruises begin to form.

He reaches down and tears her gun from her hand with a terse, "Mine." Then he shoots her.

Unsurprisingly, five other Hornets are armed in exactly the same way, the owners of their guns lying dead in their wake. In the past forty-eight or so hours Amiga's come to rely on their efficiency and violence. Whilst they're dealing with the soldiers and guard, she takes Shock to deal with opening the panic room doors. Getting in isn't easy by any means, but does not require a fingerprint, and she tosses Dong's hand aside as the thick door swings open. Four soldiers rush out. They work as a team, Shock dropping them in their tracks whilst she runs past to see to Gail.

Gail's tied up on the floor, another guard either side of him. She throws the knife at one, nailing him through the forehead, the other grabs Gail up to use as a shield. Her tactic. Thoroughly annoying when employed by somebody else. Not to mention employed using someone she'd very much like to keep alive.

"Heads up!"

Deuce runs in. Together, they barrel straight at the guard, who's trying to shoot at them whilst trying not to let go of Gail, drooping heavily in his other arm. He swears once, a hard expulsion more of sound than word as they hit legs and shoulders, knocking him to the floor, making him lose his grip on Gail, who falls to one side. The soldier attempts to bring his gun up and around to fire at them, but Amiga plants her knee on the joint of his shoulder, grinding in hard enough to make him scream.

"Oh no you don't, sugar," she snarls. "I think you need to say good night. Deuce?"

"Good night," Deuce says real pleasant and, tearing off the guard's helmet, he slams doubled fists into the side of his head.

They hang on in place for a second, waiting for movement, but he's out, and Amiga climbs off to help Shock, who's begun to check Gail, his eyes gold in blue. Scanning him over physically, she finds no bullet holes, which is the only plus considering he's beat all to hell and rocking some nasty looking cuts he should probably get C-Gen on real damn soon if he doesn't want to be in more serious trouble.

"Gail," she murmurs, "you might not know it right now, but this is your lucky day. Oi, Ravi, a hand here."

"You mean a whole me," he says, eyeing Dong's hand on the floor.

"Yeah. And quickly."

Hoisting him up, they hustle Gail out to a cleared table, leaving Ravi to work his usual magic whilst they go to help the others with the required clean up. They have to get moving if they're going to avoid any more trouble.

When they're done, it's super late and the building's eerily empty—the doors automatically locking when the last worker left. It amazes them no one heard the ruckus, but Dong kept well away from even her top Execs. Sometimes isolation is not a good thing. Deuce goes to the roof to collect the ropes and harnesses whilst Shock volunteers quietly to go down in the shoot to unlock the front doors for them so Tracker won't have to. They follow him down as soon as they're ready to go, carrying

Gail, who's conscious now but too groggy to function. The door is unlocked but Shock's not there.

He's nowhere to be seen.

They IM him. Get no response. Not signal death or signal dark. Signal silent. Beginning to panic, they search the ground floor. The place where they've parked their caterbikes. Nothing. No sign at all. That's when Deuce and Tracker jack the building security and take a look at the footage. That's when they see the Zeros coming up behind Shock. When Amiga sees what they do, she loses all capacity for reason.

"That's what attacked us in Paris," she says, and she hears the cold in her voice. The emotionless drone. It will worry Deuce but there's nothing she can do about that. She's gone. The only way to come back is to destroy the woman who did this to Shock. "Zen. Fucking Zenada. *Fucking* Zenada Lakatos. We've been played."

Understanding hits Deuce hard enough to make him flinch, and boy does she feel that. She *empathizes*. "We were supposed to go to her, weren't we? All hellfire and brimstone and Mollie's revenge in human form. Certified key delivery service."

"That's the hundred-flim jackpot right there."

Help! Tracker, in their IMs. *They're in the shuttle they're...* His voice stops. Then, dull and low, he says one single word: *Zen.*

Tracker! Amiga likes Tracker. She snarls. "Fucking *bitch*! We left a load of injured Hornets on there. Chances are they're all fucking infected now. Trust that bitch to take our ride. Probably thinks it's going to stop us."

The selfsame snarl on his face she can feel curling through her entire body, Deuce revs his caterbike. "Like hell. We need another shuttle."

Throwing herself on behind him as the other Hornets rev engines ready to go, Amiga says, "Get me to the bays and I'll get us one. Gloves fucking off. I'm done sneaking; let them send every sec force they've got after us. Until I kill her, I'll mow down everything in my fucking way."

We're *done sneaking,* he IMs, implacable strength in his tone. We'll *mow down everything in our way. We're in this together.*

Unexpectedly, this jolts emotion back into her, a small spark of warmth. She squeezes his midriff. Says quietly, *I know.*

He grabs her hand, holding it against his chest as they race through the streets of Hong Kong to raid the bays for a spare shuttle, or any shuttle at all.

Amiga's really in no mood to be picky.

shanghai blues

Dusk gathers like a swarm of flies, too close and too loud, swirling semi-darkness and humidity around Vivid in thick swells she wants to wrestle her way out of. Shanghai is humid. Close-cut buildings act like huge generators, trapping air, superheating it until the only place to breathe, the only way you can, is high up on the 'scraper tops where the wind is too damn cold and nibbles the flesh sore. At this hour, roughly midnight, artificial wind razors over the rooftops, vicious as a rumour, carrying the stench of the city like an afterthought, like the bitterness on the back edge of thick, black coffee, staining the tongue.

That aftertaste reminds her of the Gung, and Vivid sucks it in like gold dust, her lungs crying under the pressure, homesickness swelling behind her diaphragm. Nothing like it. Nothing like any of this. And when they reach the top she takes a moment to look over to the nearest clear horizon, through crenellations of rooftops, staggered like bad teeth, out to the place where hub and space melt together beyond thick glass into darkness. There's nothing beautiful about any of this, and yet it aches within her like beauty. She wants to love the world, all of it: Hubs, land ships, the vast ocean and the suffocating scrap of land she calls home. Wants to find a way to exist within it without suffocating.

Isn't that what everyone wants?

Vivid's contrary. Always wanted what she can't have until circumstances forced her to shoot for the lowest denominator, and boy was that a fun ass time of wrack and ruin, but a girl's gotta keep a roof over her head and her belly full. Mind you, even though it's been years since she chose a higher path, current circs have left her feeling like she can't win either way. Damned for good choices as much as bad. The only way through is to remember why she's up here freezing. Steal back what was stolen. Do what no one else seems to want to.

Still booming, even at this hour, the muted hum of Shanghai rises all around, comforting and yet somehow ominous. The ever-present rush of sound signifying furious activity, the mad beating heart of a city that cannot sleep, locked in cycles of sticky insomnia. Boy can Vivid relate to that shit. Lolled out in webbing stretched between lightning traps she and her team mainline iced tea and cheap dim sum from the steamer cubicle across the way, no more than a hole in the wall, rippling heat, manned by a young boy who looks so bored of the world he might throw himself in the boiling water just to get away.

They're throwing a late-nighter, waiting for the lights at Tsai Holdings to start flicking off. Down to a shocking small band of physically just about able and mentally still sort of willing Hornets, the only good plan was a hit in the small hours. A takeover, essentially. Grab the building and lock everyone out so they could jack and trash the systems at leisure. Great plan. Only problem is, half the staff don't seem to be going fucking home.

The Execs left at ten, most of the office staff left at eleven thirty or so, and about forty minutes ago an expensively dressed woman left in a private car, but no one else has followed since, despite a security changeover taking place. The work ethic is impressive, the impact on their brilliant plan less so.

Dumping his basket to one side, KJ clutches his belly and groans. "Oh man, that was some good shit. Or else it was just shit and I'm too far gone to tell the diff."

"You'll know if you're still alive in the morning. Only way to tell," Sim says, and KJ treats her to a horrified glare.

"Hell no. I'll eject this shit pronto if there's a chance of it taking me out in my sleep. I go down awake or not at all."

"Cool it, KJ. Sim messes with you."

KJ yawns. "Whatever. Probably we'll die anyway. Fucking Tsai Holdings won't surrender a money tree like caged avis without a fight, and here we are, beaten up to fuck, no weapons and no back up. I predict a grisly end."

Vivid hunts for words to respond right, but when she finds them KJ is snoring gentle puffs of sound, head relaxed back against the webbing, mouth slightly open. He looks adorable, and knackered. Vivid feels guilty then for dragging them to yet another hub chase, for not taking time to regroup even though that luxury is not one they have access to. And therein lies the rub—the slap of objective reality snapping her out of pointless guilt.

Their lives hang, precarious, in the balance, and they're all tired of having to run, hide, stay one step ahead. Fighting is exhausting, sure, but not having control over the strings that would move you, as they are, is debilitating, drains you of every last resource, leaving nothing behind but empty skin and hollow bones.

Tired but beyond the point of being able to sleep now, Vivid lies there staring up into space, tracking shooting stars and clouds. Staring at the moon and wondering if history will ever repeat and see humans set foot there again. Shuttles don't fly that far and it seems humanity is happy to surf the atmosphere in glass prisons, happy to give up the whole universe in exchange for the illusion of safety.

If the world never changed, never broke, what might Vivid have been in it? What might she be now?

The morning, or rather the nothing hours just before dawn, brings double jeopardy. What wakes them is word from Deuce that Shock's been straight up snatched, which none of them can quite get their heads around, not after the crazy stunt he pulled at Shandong. They want to go help, but the avis need them too. And if they can free Puss, maybe she can help Shock. Therein lies the second part of double jeopardy.

Three of the rooftop Hornets have hit consciousness too damned bruised to move, having slept and given their bodies a real chance to think about what's happened to them. Sometimes rest is the cure, other times it's more like a red buzzer, signalling the end of physical usefulness. It leaves the physically able Hornets struggling to feel positive about any kind of hit on Tsai Holdings. They can't leave the avis in cages but with the numbers they have… things look bleak.

Sandro wants to know why they can't pull the same shit as they pulled on Tokyo Hub.

"Because we have no connections here," KJ snaps. "Not a one. Cupboard's bare. We either go in guns blazing—only, no guns—or we find a way to sneak, and frankly we're all out of useful equipment unless we steal and, for real, this place makes it *hard*."

When they peeked at Tsai Holdings, looking to establish their defences, they found it low on VA on the staff levels but packing VA that damn near gave Sandro a nose bleed on the most imperative levels to jack, namely the labs. Add to that a vast security staff patrolling every floor—lab floors and their immediate neighbours in particular—and it ends up a pretty damn chewy problem. They've dealt with similar, sure, but equipment and able bodies was not an issue then.

Prism kicks at the edge of a cooling unit. "We have to think outside the box."

Vivid wasn't sure about Prism joining them here, because if they lose her, they're stuck, but she's glad of her now—one more person in a bind is not to be sneezed at. They need everyone they've got.

"Exactly," KJ says, pointing with his chopsticks because, naturally, he's eating again, even though he overdosed on dumplings barely five hours ago. "We have to go old-school Hornet. Way back in the day when we had no rep, just a bunch of fucking starving Fails with no equipment except our brains and a need to not die of hunger. Remember that, Viv?"

"Do I ever. Not my fondest memories. I'd rather not delve in to be honest."

He rewards her only with scorn. "Viv, my doll, if we don't wrap our tiny minds around those memories and embrace them, we're on a sure-fire path to relive them."

And there's nothing more to add to that. Truth is self-evident. This leaves her and KJ, being the oldest members present, to begin planning like they used to. Old Hornet tactics, rather than relying on brute force and equipment, came in at peculiar angles. Essentially, their entire MO was the exploitation of two things: weakness and expectations. The latter tends to feed the former. Corps and criminals plan for certain types of attack, for known eventualities, so if you have few resources the best way in is to do the unexpected.

To figure out what will be unexpected here, they have to start with what they know about Tsai Holdings. The Corp has five buildings scattered across Shanghai Hub, all in high-end areas, though the name seems to be everywhere on everything. This building, the one they need to hit, is multi-function: offices, the secured labs, upper-level boardrooms and Exec suites and what seems to be a penthouse office.

The Corp is clearly powerful. Perhaps too big to see the details. What details have they overlooked? At first glance, none. Tsai Holdings has one of the most comprehensive security networks they've ever seen. Obviously anticipating kickback for the avi theft.

"What did we do faced with VA and sec like this?" Vivid asks KJ, still stuffing his face with dumplings.

"Get creative."

"Viral bombs?"

"Too yesterday."

"Robo drones?"

"Too expensive."

"The classic workers' incursion plan?"

KJ rears back, aghast. "Dear shitting hell, if you think any of us could pass for anyone professional right now you're literally tripping."

She rolls her eyes at him. "Shut the fuck up. I'm spitballing. We have to think of something. We can't let them keep the avis, not when they blatantly stole them."

"And we're not going to, Viv. But we need a plan that *works*. Especially with our current deficiencies."

"How about that?" Prism's been looking out toward the main thoroughfares of Shanghai, the bright neon billboards and ads. She's pointing at one advertising a circus of all things.

"What on earth will that do?" KJ is genuinely bemused. "Apart from be rather entertaining."

"Contortionists. Acrobats. High flyers. Sharp shooters. Strong folk, that's men *and* women, by the way, fuckers. There's even some folks who juggle chainsaws and swords. Could anything be more unexpected than a circus breaking in to your building? We could go in through the air con."

Vivid shakes her head. "They're not going to help, Pris. This is their home."

"You're *still* not seeing," Prism says. She points to the billboard. "Wait for it."

They watch as the sign flips between star attractions, bright and loud and glittering, and then it appears, a whole screen dedicated to a portion of the show where the troop comes out to perform with their avis, golden forms perfectly lit and sparkling. From the imagery, the scraps of stream playing within it, these circus folk genuinely dug having their avis out, and treated them like family.

This part of the ad has a huge "CANCELLED" sign plastered across it in kanji, English, and French of all things.

"Oh," KJ breathes. "Oh my fucking hell. We are in *business*."

Uncurling herself from the makeshift hammock, Vivid says, "Pack up, guys. We're going to the circus."

audience

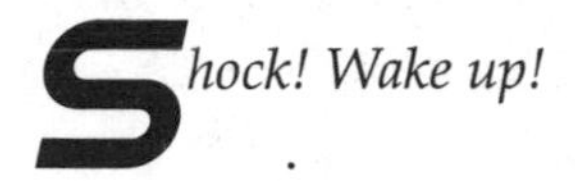*hock! Wake up!*

.

.

.

Shock!

.

.

.

Wake up!

.

.

.

Shock's eyes snap open. Look direct into familiar square pupils lit by rage and terror.

You're an avatar here, she whips into his mind, hurting him with her pain. *You almost ended up behind bars.*

He tries to speak but can't, too choked with emotion, too upset at the sight of everything she is in such a narrow space. Confined. He slams a hand out, shimmering gold, to strike the bars of her cage. Gold, only gold, but resistant as iron, encoded to hold her unless he pays her way out. He can't even reach between them to touch her, to reassure her.

It's okay, she tells him. Always comforting.

He wants to comfort her. He's fed up of needing comfort. It's not meant to be one-sided—comfort isn't her job, it's something they should give one another. He should be capable of that. Should be able to fix *this*. Instead he's… what? He reaches out to his body, unconscious somewhere he doesn't want to think about. His head is screaming waves of agony. Probably concussion, maybe worse.

Fracture? Is that near his drive? Fuck but if that's damaged then it's all over before it's begun, because he knows where he is. Knew the moment he saw Zeros waiting by the caterbikes.

He didn't see the ones behind him until it was too late.

Resting his forehead on the bars, he closes his eyes again, unable to bear the sight of her trapped like this. *I'm so sorry. I fucked up again. I should have told them about Zen. Warned them.*

Yes, you should. That's Puss, never sugarcoating, always being real with him. Until he had that, he never knew how necessary it was for growth.

Now they'll come after me. She'll do terrible things to them if they try to kill her. They don't know what she is.

She leans in close, tentacles braced against the bars. *They're smarter than that. Don't give up.* Fight.

She's right. Of course she is. But Zen… she's more than the Queen was. Worse. The Queen learnt to be what it was from her. Zen's filled with a blank need that won't settle until it has *everything*. Self-serving and terrifying in its capacity to dismiss the lives of others. He didn't want to have to deal with anything like the Queen again. Ever. To have to deal with worse, no more than a month later, is oddly cruel.

But then life is.

He's about to ask Puss what he can do when unwanted consciousness jerks him away from her, lurching his body as he crashes back into it. Jolting the damage to his head hard enough to make him dry heave, cheek pressed against soft carpet to brace himself against the pain vibrating from the crown of his head right down to his ankles. If he could grab this pain and pull it out of him, it'd have longer tentacles than Puss, covered in tiny, deadly suckers.

Inside his head, Emblem's surrounded the fracture with a coded mandala of peculiar complexities. Seems to be trying to fix physical damage with virtual means. He wishes to fuck it would stop; it's using too much that isn't him to hold the edges of him together. And there are edges, he feels them grinding. The sound it makes inside his skull is trees creaking, 'scrapers swaying in the wind, a vivid memory of his bones cracking as Pill worked him over.

"You should have stayed asleep."

Shock recognizes that voice. Bear. He can't stand to move his head by lifting it. He rolls it instead, using his whole body as a lever. The movement causes brilliant sparks of light to shoot across his vision. Pain or damage? No way to tell. Bear is gazing at him. Soft eyes. It has such soft eyes.

The gold of it shines too bright in the bland whiteness of the room; it hurts to look at. Or is that the damage too? He thinks he's really very much in trouble. Beyond Zen even.

"You're part of the prison. Do you make her sleep?" His voice is raspy. Dry. He needs water. Sleep. He needs to sleep so bad. Needs a Polar Bear of his own.

"Don't sleep again. You may die. They hit you too hard. Or rather she did, through them. Over-excitement. She's damaged you badly. It made her angry enough that I managed to wrestle back control. It won't be for long though. Can you get up?"

"I wouldn't want to try."

Bear makes a face. An actual face. A cross between a frown and a grimace. What is it? It's an avi but it's not. Shock can only vocalize as an avi because he has the right vocal chords for speech and because avis are essentially life, though a very specific kind. If Bear could learn to talk somehow it would maybe growl, or vocalize the way bears do. Not form words. And there's no distortion from teeth or jaw shape. It's perfect. Then again, it's likely Breaker's work. If anyone could imagine a bear avi with speech into being, it'd be him.

"Breaker, he made you?"

The bear tilts its head. "He did not make me, he adapted me. I was a sacrifice."

"A sacrifice?"

"To the world." Polar Bear's head falls forward, listening to its belly. "She's waking. Hoard your resources, Haunt. Don't let her out."

Easier said than done. He wants to say it but Polar Bear already has its eyes closed, and Zen's are opening, bright and hard. She peers down at him and makes a chuffing noise, much like a bear would. If he could laugh without puking, he'd laugh out a lung.

"I made a mess," she says, but she's not talking to him. She's barely even seeing him. "Never to mind. Everything I need is intact."

Blinding pressure hits his drive and the unfamiliar swell of a mind, steeped in bitter lemon taste he recalls with a pang of terror. Such *strength* she has, to leave this taste in Slip. He has no enthusiasm for seeing her up close and personal but cannot help peek as she squeezes way in. Traumatic memory recalls Queens doing this, so many vast minds inside his, looking for footholds to try and drag him out of himself, to scour him out so they could fill him with themselves. Zen's not doing that. She's after switching Emblem off again. Fuck knows what she plans to do to Shock then.

Probably erase him.

Dimly, he registers blood beginning to pour from his nose, but he's not afraid any more; he wants to laugh again. Lying here, broken and bleeding, her presence rolling in his drive like sickness, he wishes he had the energy to mock her for this misjudgement. For her pure arrogance. Emblem's *everywhere*. Can't switch Emblem off now; there's nothing left in it vulnerable to switching off. Same for him pretty much. Why the hell does she imagine he's still alive with this fucking catastrophic head wound?

If she wants to control Emblem, she'll have to become them both. Fight for control. And she'll be fighting forever. Control is not something he's willing to hand over under any circumstances. Five weeks ago, he made a decision that changed his whole existence, and now his actual humanity. He doesn't regret that decision. All he regrets is that he didn't fully embrace it sooner.

What is human after all but the capacity to make choices?

Too far behind. They're too fucking far behind. Shock's in serious trouble, his signal intermittent enough to tell them he's badly hurt, and they're too far behind. That's all Amiga can focus on as they speed away from Hong Kong Hub on a stolen shuttle; not the hell she raised getting them out of there, the sheer *amount* of dead bodies she left in her wake, or the fleet of shuttles that pours out after them, sirens blaring.

"Fuck!" Deuce whips them into heavy cloud, but they've been seen.

Hong Kong is inside Earth's atmosphere at this hour, charting a course over the ocean set to take it close to the Gung. Not near enough to see, but near enough for the convenience of easier imports and exports. Shock's far off planet by now, and headed for another hub. They need to get moving, to follow his path. Fast enough to send them all tumbling, Deuce aims the shuttle up and they burst out into space. The sound of the sirens cuts off as they pop through. Only the lights can be seen, pulsing away like dying stars. Floating to the window, Amiga watches them burst through one by one.

"Buckle in," Deuce tells her. "We have to break the speed limit to get outside their jurisdiction."

Hubs have jurisdiction zones. Outside those, they can contact other hubs to intercept, but most don't. InterHub and Planetary systems of law are generally incompatible, each hub having its own legal system and bureaucracy. Extraditions are costly, often fraught. Most hubs prefer to hope anyone fleeing their jurisdiction will end up offending on the Gung. Offenders with outstanding InterHub warrants end up on the severe, almost uninhabitable Yellowstone Burr—a mountainous drift of continent deep in the Pacific used as a sort of penal colony.

Beyond the reach of Hong Kong, Deuce strikes out in Shock's current direction. At this point he's still moving. It's when he stops she'll worry. That promise she made to Mollie keeps coming back like bad rice. Killing Zen. How can she do that? *Can* she do that? Mollie's sick. She's a Zero. Zen is controlling the Zeros. She's something else. Worse. Something it might not be possible to kill. What if there's no way to stop this?

Even so, she has to try. The possibility of Shock being under Zen's influence makes her want to smash things. That bitch has no right to him. But his shuttle is so far ahead, and things have already happened to him that Amiga has no control over. It's like Pill, knowing she was twenty minutes away and how much damage torture can do in twenty minutes. Hell, some damage you need less than a minute for. Whatever they find, she'll have to judge it on sight and hope that killing Zen won't mean killing Shock.

The trail of broken signal leads them a couple of hours east, where several Trans-American Hubs make their orbits. Giving herself the biggest forehead slap in the history of slapped foreheads, Amiga calls it there and then. Gotta be New York. Plain sight. The Lakatos family made their home there. Sure enough, that's where his signal leads: the Peace Tower. Despite being built for the Lakatos family, it's essentially a public building and full to the brim with New Yorkers and tourists. Amiga swears a streak of Javanese her mother and aunties would have screamed about, their hands fluttering.

New York's docking system, as befits a Trans-American hub, is payment based for non-residents—Deuce does some wizardry that will keep feeding the glitchy, crappy payment system ghost-flim until they need to fly out. Leaving a couple of volunteers behind to rescue the injured Hornets on the shuttle Zen's Zeros stole, the rest of them waste no more time, grabbing any weapons they have left and racing out of the bays, intent on getting Shock back.

NYC Hub has no caterbike hire system; it has a cranky mono and an even crankier subway, neither of which is particularly safe. They head straight for the underground link from the docking station. The lights down here are dirty yellow and gangs of muggers work the lines in shifts. Most people are used to either packing heat or carrying nothing of value, though some carry a dummy wallet with minimal flim and low-cred chips in for fear of being killed. Better, they think, to lose some money than lose their life.

The Hornets take seats and pay no attention to the muggers on shift, who give them a wide berth. Perks of being pretty much head to toe in dried blood. No one wants to tango.

Running up filthy stairs to daylight, Amiga looks left, in the direction of Shock's signal. The Lakatos family's contribution to the Hub's skyline, the Peace Tower, is pure-white glass in silver-grey steel. Ugly and somehow tacky despite the flowing lines and whimsical design, but the locals love it for the art galleries and museums, the indoor botanical gardens and, most impressive of all, the oceanarium on the ground floors. You can't enter the building without passing through the oceanarium, surrounded on all sides by creatures from the oceans of the Gung—it's like Slip IRL, a multifarious collection of remarkable sea life, both tiny and vast. They even have a blue whale. Passing through today, Amiga doesn't see it, but there is a flash of sea turtles, some so tiny they can only be infants, and a shoal of tuna, bright silver as they flow past.

Amiga thinks of them in gold and misses the avis so acutely her chest burns. Somehow she imagined they'd appear at some point, because she knows Vivid won't let them down. But maybe it's not that simple. And that burns too. Brighter. Fiercer. That's a burn right down to the bone, blackening to char.

The oceanarium covers four floors; it's full of tunnels and walkways, restaurants, and even a hotel where you can sleep surrounded by sea creatures. On the third floor Shock's signal changes, stuttering dangerously and they race for the fourth-floor shoots. Amiga can't calm her heart. She's never felt stressed going in to conflict; there's no point, but this is different. This is Shock. The thought of losing it, of losing *him*, makes her want to tear down this whole fucking tower.

Deuce slips his hand into hers, his palm warm. "It'll be okay."

"And if it's not?"

"We'll make it okay. He won't just let her kill him, you know that, right?"

She knows. Doesn't help worth a damn. Funny that. Funny too that Deuce has no problems with how she is with Shock. Trust him of all people to grok what it is they mean to each other and be cool with the fact it's not anything he could be, not anything she *needs* him to be.

Shock's signal drags them past the public floors to the Lakatos family home on the upper levels, a ridiculous twelve floors for what she thought was two people, and now likely only the one, unless there are other Lakatoses she hasn't heard of. The doors, naturally, are locked. Auto-locks. Bio-print. Zen must have forced her prints through Zero flesh to get them in.

"Fucking *hell*!" Deuce does something she's never seen him do. He loses his cool. Slams a boot just beneath the lock, sending the doors crashing open. He blinks surprise. "Manual jacking," he says, slightly breathless. "Who knew?"

The ground floor is grand. Deserted. Designed to look like the entry hall of a Georgian mansion, with a great double sweeping staircase. Amiga looks at the landing. He's up there. Somewhere.

"Oh fuck me." Ravi. Too quiet. She looks where he is and sees the blood. Lots of blood.

She hits the stairs at a dead sprint, the Hornets at her back. Blood like breadcrumbs brings them to the mid-level. Six. A level all in white, visually bewildering. Chasing blood, Amiga runs down long corridors contorted to a maze, her hand trailing the walls—white-silk cool under her fingertips. Room by room, corridor by corridor, she pares it down. Measures time in breath and the flex of muscles, the susurration of her heels on thick carpet, until she finds herself at a threshold to an empty room so drenched in white her eyes struggle to see anything at all, the walls and floor melting together.

Blinking, she struggles to focus. Sees everything all at once. The Zeros at the walls. The ruin of them. The way some are slumped bundles of limbs with hands like bent branches. Shock on the floor in a heap. Too limp. Too small. His head rests in a circle of red-drenched carpet. Then finally, the sphere, painted in dull red hieroglyphs. The golden Polar Bear with the woman in its belly.

Rage hits so hard, she loses the ability to breathe.

Look at Shock. Look at what that *bitch* has done to him.

Without thinking, barely even feeling, she lifts her gun

and empties the clip into the glass, hearing it shatter from what seems like an implausible distance. Why wasn't it bulletproof? Some part of her expected it would be, expected that it *should* be, or what the hell were Josef and Breaker *doing*? Part of her didn't care either way. Most of her maybe. That part was hoping the bullets would smash through and *devastate* the flesh inside. She wanted to see that bitch bleeding.

There is blood, for sure, but Amiga gets only a second to admire her handiwork before the bear bounds out, a surge of gold and fury, and slams into her, throwing her across the room and against the wall.

"What did you do!" it roars in her face, huge paws pinning her down. What? Its claws are drawing blood. And it's speaking. *Speaking*. "You don't let her out!"

Amiga scrabbles at the paws on her body. "She's wounded. I hit her. Maybe she's dead."

The bear snaps at her face, huge jaws inches from her flesh. "If I'm not dead, she's not. Fool. You should have saved a bullet."

Through the gold body of the bear, Amiga watches as Zenada, her face a study in disbelief, steps out to the carpet, one leg after the other, jerking like some awful stop-motion puppet. She touches the wounds on her torso. Licks the blood off her fingers and *laughs*. Oh fuck. Oh holy fuck. That's a monster. It's not the blood licking or even the laughter. It's the emptiness in the eyes. The *chasms*.

"I'm sorry," Amiga mutters, to herself, to the bear, to Shock most of all. "I'm sorry."

Zen staggers over to Shock, marionette-staccato. Bends down to stare at him. Her fingers pincer his chin, yanking his face up. Zenada leans in close, teetering. Places her other hand behind his head, getting herself covered in his blood.

"Open wide," she says to him, her voice dry as dust, and rams her fingers through the fracture in his skull into the back of his head.

life's a circus, pal

Space being at a premium on Shanghai Hub as much as it is on any hub, the Jīn yún mǎxì is housed in a garden tower, one of several built to emulate a feeling of spaciousness. Old Shanghai, and those who deify it, refuses to acknowledge these additions, but the citizens of Shanghai spend much of their free time wandering the gardens and balconies, enjoying the entertainments and restaurants—watching the stars from the crown viewing platforms.

Contained on the mid levels, their circus is set into one of the parks, a permanent red-and-white striped triple-point big top surrounded by stalls and amusements with the circus folks' homes scattered at the rear; a profusion of tents, caravans and tiny huts with wide wooden porches. Getting back there is easy. Getting any one of the performers to stop and talk with strangers? Boss-level hard. They're eyed up as if they're trouble walking, which isn't far from the truth.

It's noisy too. Not any old noise. Fundamentally the kind of noise that cracks your brain open like a coconut and pours inside until it fills you up, breathing it in and breathing it out, holding it in your cells, knowing that if you live tomorrow and the day after, and the day after that, this noise will haunt your ears, hang in your mind, thundering there amongst the internal motions of heart and lungs and refuse to be ignored any more than it is now.

Making their way back out to the stalls and amusements, they try sweet-talking them as they play. The response is glacial and KJ, quick to boredom, wanders off. An hour later, when the rest of them have given up trying to make circus folk talk about anything except how many darts they want to buy or what sauce they want on their pancake, he returns with a group of three performers in skin-tight leotards, all talking at once. Trust KJ to find the people here most like him—he thinks she doesn't know that he used to dance. Probably forgets that every time he gets drunk he tells her all about it, sobbing into her shoulder, breaking her heart over and over with how broken his is. How much he misses what could have been.

"These are my friends," he says as they get close, and she genuinely doesn't know if he's talking about the Hornets or the performers, but suspects it may encompass all of them. "We're all on the same wavelength here."

The smallest one, a minute woman with brown hair scraped into a high pony and braided, leans her head on KJ's shoulder and smiles. "I'm Marnie," she points to the others. "This is Case, my hub, and Bell, as in the type that rings. KJ here says you need to speak to the bosses. We'll get you access."

Walking with performers warms the entire place to them, the atmosphere relaxing considerably. They even garner a few smiles on the way back to the rear. The change makes Vivid feel a stupid need to warn them, because she can see these are good people, of course they are. Anyone who simply accepts avatars as family is all right in her books.

"We're not asking something small here. Or safe."

"Yeah," Case says. "It's cool. KJ was real with us. Look, we want our avis back. We could pay the tariffs for performances, sure, but for real they're friends and we don't want to be part of treating them like fucking slaves. We put in a complaint to Tsai Holdings and it literally went nowhere. I mean, these guys aren't interested. They're a big deal in Shanghai, they probably think they can do what they want, and frankly no one's arguing."

"We have an interest in arguing," Vivid responds firmly.

The look she gets speaks volumes. "So do we."

The circus bosses are a middle-aged couple called Manny and Seb. Seb's the money man and Manny's the big personality who leads as ringmaster for every performance. They already have stream images of the main Tsai Holdings building up when they arrive, trying to work out the best ways to approach. They know who the Hornets are from streams coming out of Paris Hub—according to Manny, it's the only reason they agreed to meet them. After their complaint was ignored, they realized the only way to get their avis back would be to take them, and they figured that was a pipe dream. Until now.

There are no architectural blueprints of Tsai Holdings available in J-Net when KJ and Sandro go to look, so Manny hooks them up with a jacker friend of his, name of Simone. She has some fairly complex self-built scanning apparatus. Handheld. With Manny tagging along, they take it to the rooftop they were staked out on overnight and scan the main Tsai Holdings tower. On the screen, in ghostly white, all the sub-routes in the building appear; the air con, service corridors and shoots.

"Well would you look at that," Manny says. "Beautiful."

They plan their incursion for two in the A.M., to give them time to scan for security patterns and shifts, see exactly how many of Tsai Holdings staff remain until late. Ahead of attack time, the contortionists and acrobats will go through the air con with KJ and Sandro, to get into sec rooms and disrupt systems. Then the Hornets and Manny, who's an ex-strong man and stunt performer, will take everyone else in from the front.

In anticipation of their part, Sandro and KJ suit up in borrowed acrobat costumes, skin-tight and colourful. Marnie runs her hand across KJ's torso, the mangled flesh visible in the tight fabric.

"What happened to you?" she asks, horrified.

KJ is Viv's favourite person for many reasons; he might be jumpy and often melodramatic, and he may hide his damage, the mental as well as the physical, but he's not ashamed about who he is or how he got here. He smiles. Shows her the remains of his ear.

"I said no, and these are prices I paid."

"Worth it?" She looks worried, probably thinking about what her circus is about to do.

"Of course," he says. "If I could go back, I'd say it louder. More often. I'd shout it in their faces. Saying no lost me some of my gorgeous looks, but it gave me more to love about myself than I'd ever had before. It also gave me a family. Pretty fair trade-off to be honest."

Tsai Holdings' air-con ducts are concealed within the architecture of the building on every level. They have a modern aeration system, the kind hub Corps and landlords have used to minimize issues with hub airflow. Instead of sucking in air to cool the building, they have open airways designed to allow air to move freely through the floors, cooling as it goes.

Watching through her goggles as the advance team heads in, Vivid finds herself crossing her fingers. The way in for them relies on distraction; a team of tumblers keeping the attention of the bottom-floor security and staff as the others pry off a vent cover and slide in one by one. Sandro opted to go last, worried he wouldn't fit. He does, though he looks uncomfortable going in feet first, his face all screwed up with concentration.

Luck, she sends to them all.

You too, KJ sends back.

They've given the advance team an hour to get ahead before they move in. Vivid counts the seconds between one and two A.M., leaving her IM wide open just in case, all set to go in guns blazing and rescue the hell out of the advance team if need be. At ten to the hour, KJ sends word they're in the sec rooms. He says Sandro doesn't like the look of the cycling speeds on the systems, wants them to move early. Just in case.

The only approach to Tsai Holdings' open-plan reception hall is brightly lit, so they're going in as a roaming entertainment group, all of the Hornets dressed in performance gear of one kind or another. Vivid has spangled stunt clothes on, black leather with glitter. It's too tight, rubs at her thighs, but she's enjoying the sheer gonzo daftness of how they get into the building too much to care, laughing as she gets her weapon out and firing before anyone can ask what the hell they're doing here. It's glorious. Brings sharp, aching memories back of the old days, of crazy shit they'd do to make ends meet. The sheer joy of invention and desperation colliding.

By the time building security pick their jaws up from the carpet and get their act together to fight back, they've managed to race to the seventh floor, scattering bullets like glitter. And that's where security keeps them, cut off from the exits and crouched for piecemeal protection behind the thin partition walls. Snatching swift glances to gauge positions, Vivid fires off shots with a gun borrowed from a circus sharpshooter. Chunks of carpet explode around her, stinging as they strike her bare face. Sharp splinters of plastic partition embed themselves into the meat of her back and buttocks, little niggles of pain.

She waits for something to give, not knowing what it'll be.

When the break moment arrives it's backwards, paradoxical, outside of any expectation she had of miracles turning the tide in their favour. Tsai Holdings blacks out. Lights gone. Systems down. The clicking sound of doors unlocking all around them. A wholesale destruction of Tsai's systems.

What's happening? she yells to anyone listening. Gets so many replies she has to douse them all and focus in on KJ. Ask again.

He's laughing so hard he can barely talk. *Literally we were trying to jack in and one of the performers comes over and pours an entire litre bottle of green tea over the innards of the system desk. It pretty much exploded in our faces. I think I singed my eyebrows off.*

She wants to ask how, to question, to get a grip on what the fuck just happened, but there's no time. The lights flicker on, illuminating frozen guards, guns temporarily lowered, waiting for instructions they'll never get. Their comms have gone dark. Vivid looks over at Manny's strong folk and stunt performers. Finds them up and moving in neat lines, blasting away at security who, left to their own devices, abandon all delicacy, shooting to kill or cripple. It's fair enough, their jobs are on the line, all they can do to keep them is annihilate the people who've managed to get past them and into their building. And this is where the strong folk come in most useful, picking up whole, heavy table units to fling at the guards.

The tables slam through bodies, cracking limbs, pulverizing faces to red ruin and dark bruises. And they take down dozens. More effective than bullets. Than knives. An exercise in brutal efficiency. In this way, they barge up the tower, one floor at a time. Shit. Of all the stories Vivid might live to tell, this is the one no one will believe. She barely believes it: the day we jacked and overran a Corp with circus performers and iced tea sounds no less than ludicrous. Nonetheless, here she is, strong folk on the left, stunt performers on the right—acrobats in the fucking air ducts.

Ludicrous.

They sweep the corridors thoroughly as they go, tying any remaining staff into their chairs. Trying to leave as few dead bodies in the wreckage of the offices as possible. The aim here is not to kill, it's to get to the labs, find the system the disconnection was distributed through and try to reverse it.

Get the avis *out*.

The labs take up the whole centre of their floor, a secured, multi-faceted set of units with a single corridor running the whole way around. Every code-locked entry on that corridor is barred by teams of guards in protective gear. Nothing like a welcoming party. This close to the labs, to possibly saving their avis, no one is about to quit. Backing out to the level below, they grab up some of the heavy tables as shields and go back, splitting to two groups, one going left, the other right. Tables at the forefront then, they plough the way. The corridor isn't wide enough for security to evade the battering rams; they end up squashed, trapped, locked in. It's like shooting fish in barrels.

When the corridor is clear, the guards removed to the floor below, they focus attention on the labs. Inside, the few workers who stayed late have dropped everything to stare out of the reinforced windows. None of them looks much motivated to open the doors, and in the sec room, KJ and Sandro confirm their worst-case scenario: lab security is not only separate, it's controlled from within.

What do we do?

Marnie thinks she's small enough to get in through the air con. They have a smaller system for the labs. Bit cramped, but doable.

What then? She's not a J-Hack.

No, but she used to be a pickpocket.

You're kidding.

Nope. How about you get some distraction on?

Get your arse here and help then.

It takes less than fifteen minutes for KJ, Sandro and the circus acrobats to get to lab level, Marnie making her way down through the air con from the roof. She keeps in contact via IM right to the moment she gets to the exit duct. All exit ducts open from both sides, with clips. She keeps them informed by IM as she works carefully to unclip the grate without making a sound. Then she's in, light-footed and on the hunt for a likely target.

Considering the lab workers aren't expecting one of their attackers to be inside, she finds one with unsurprising ease. All the violence they've wreaked getting up here, and the best moments are these: iced tea on a circuit board and the slender fingers of an acrobat plucking a keycard so swift and silent she might as well be the wind. If they don't rename the circus after this, Vivid will eat her fucking nipple tape.

Once in, the labs are easy to control. Lab workers aren't up for a fight; they just want to go home. All except one who didn't even seem to notice the ruckus. He's absorbed in his work in the main lab, carefully labelling vials and stashing them in a fridge. Vivid places a hand on his shoulder. He reacts as if she's shot him, the vials he was putting away scattering the floor. They bounce and skitter, hitting her legs.

She reaches out to him.

"Hey. *Hey*. It's okay."

He blinks up at her through expensive glasses, and it hits her: Exec Pharm. These guys are the geniuses. She side-eyes the floor, the vials. What's in them? Is he the cage culprit?

"That what I think it is?" She demands. "Disconnect?" She looks for a name tag. Anything. He's not rocking any form of ID. He's so secret he's not official. Fuck. "And who are you?"

Startled green eyes rake across her face, looking for hell alone knows what. "Keel," he says, throwing the word out. "Who are you? Why are you here? Does Evelyn know?"

"Hell no, hon. Did you create the drug to cage the avis?"

He looks distracted again. "Of course. No one wants them."

"Who the hell told you that?"

"Who would need to? It's obvious."

She grabs his chin, forcing his face up. "Beg to differ. Everyone here in this damn room apart from you wants their avi back. No cages. No tariffs. No taking the piss. They're private property. If you didn't buy them from us you had no right to them."

He frowns. "They were property of Fulcrum."

"Fulcrum fell, shug. Did you not see the fucking streams?" KJ interrupts from somewhere behind, riding his bitchiness hard. Vivid would cheer, but she's too busy sitting shotgun on the selfsame derision.

She rolls her eyes at Keel's look of confusion. How can anyone not get this? "Seeing as that clearly flew over your head," she says, trying to be calm and failing like Keel's grasp on basic reasoning. "Fulcrum falling means we own our avis by default. Give them the fuck back."

Keel sighs. Frustration. Irritation. His gaze drops to the ground, to the vials. He picks one up. "If it was this," he says. "If it was administered to the flesh, then maybe I could reverse it. But I digitized it. I turned it into code. I can't just undo that. It would take as long to figure out how to undo it as it did to do it."

Vivid's heart plummets to the fucking floor. "That's not possible."

"Nonetheless it's true. Now if you'll excuse me."

He goes to leave, but she grabs his arm. "Oh no you don't. I know the Pharm who made the original. We're going to go and find her, and then you're going to help her fix this."

Keel blinks. "But I don't want to."

"Well I didn't want to have my avi ripped from my fucking head," she snarls in his face. "But we don't always get what we fucking well want, do we? Life's a circus, pal." She turns to Sandro then. "You know what to do. This bitch took fucking liberties. I say we take some back. I say we plunder the shit out this Corp and raze it to the ground. Show her what happens when you take shit without asking."

"J-Hack revenge. Cold. Real cold. I love it. Shall we make a few choice donations in her name?"

"Oh let's. And before you burn her files, make sure you remove this fucker's files to take to Volk. If anyone can jack a drug locking a few billion cages, it'll be her."

Sandro and KJ working together take roughly ninety minutes to pulverize Tsai Holdings' systems, releasing incriminating evidence of dodgy deals, stealing Keel's notes, and doing creative, thoughtful acts of kindness with all of its money, including some accounts Evelyn Tsai probably thought she'd managed to keep secret.

Job done, they leave the Corp virtually smoking in their wake and drop the circus folk home, swapping hugs and taking their stream deets to keep in touch because friends who bring down Corps together stay together.

They might never meet again, but they'll talk, always. And the second Volk knows how to crack the cages open, these good folk will have their avis back first. That's an easy promise to make, because without these good folk, they'd still be sat on a 'scraper-top, waiting for a window that might never come.

Turning back to Earth after leaving Shanghai is weird. Homeward bound, ocean bound; for the *Resurrection*, for Volk, Vivid thinks back to when she wondered if they'd get through this alive. Well, they're alive. Most of them anyway. Is that a victory? Considering the cages remain locked and may do so for weeks longer, she can't call it with any kind of accuracy. But it feels good to have acted. Feels good to have left Tsai Holdings crushed.

The only thing she wishes for as they descend through space, back toward the pale curve of Earth's atmosphere, is to be a fly on the wall, watching Evelyn fucking Tsai wake up to find her empire in ruins.

in a new york minute...

Gunshots. The smash of glass, falling all around him. The roar of fury, and then gold smearing his vision as Bear leaps over his head. What the hell has Amiga done? Shock can't process it. It's not like her to react. She responds. She thinks. Has she lost her damn *mind*? Where are the others? Deuce would have stopped this. Reaching out for them, he finds them mere seconds behind. Seconds too late.

Then Zenada steps down from her prison, and shoves her fingers into his head.

It's a strange sensation. All pressure, probably too much pain to process. If he were any more human or less Emblem, he'd pass out. He can hear her in there as well as feel her, digging in. Hunting. Until her fingertips touch his drive and she launches in like a rocket, all sharp edges, strength and that oh-so-familiar bitter lemon taste, the one that accosted him briefly in Slip mere days ago, but so much stronger. Screaming danger, and hell yeah she's all danger. All power. But this bitch, she's as dangerous outside Slip as inside. Way more dangerous than him.

Shock shivers violently. Her fingers are hot and cold in his head, his mind. His body, suddenly too acutely aware of everything, ripples with pain like heat and heat like pain, indistinguishable, consuming every thought but one: is she trying to unplug him now? Hasn't she guessed there's no way to now? He thought she was smarter than that. She's wasting so much time doing pointless shit. Maybe she just wants to hurt him.

"Get the *fuck* away from him!"

An Amiga-sized projectile slams into Zenada, tearing her fingers from his head; they leave icy trails of agony on the way out. The Hornets rush past, grabbing Zen's arms to hold her back. He tries to talk, but his voice won't work. He needs to tell them—she only looks like she's restrained but bits of her are still inside him, fighting for precedence, that bitter lemon taste soaking his drive, and he knows she's waiting. Only waiting. They need to get away. They need to run.

Ravi drops down beside him, his knees by Shock's shoulder, those gentle hands of his moving aside Shock's hair. He hisses. Breathes, "Jeez, Shock. Shit."

He tries to talk again, but the connections between brain and mouth are cycling too hard. His mind is a spinning top filled with the whir and hum of system failure. Bloodied arms curl around him then. Warmth beside his ear. The soft trickle of tears falling into his hair, down his neck. Amiga. Her whole body hunched over his. She needs to *move*. He has to make her listen. He can't fail her too. He needs to *talk*.

He tries to IM, finds that he has no voice there, has to swallow several times to find his voice IRL, and even then it's so hard. Every word feels like a battle, but he's determined to win. "Get out of here, Tanaka."

Still crying, she touches his face. "Gold eyes in blue. Oh fuck, Shock. *Baegchi* Pao. *Machi naega neol eul tteonal su-issneun geos cheoreom.*"

He blinks away tears. Hers, not his, blurring in his eyes. "You speak Korean?"

She laughs, hugging him closer. "That's what you get from this? Shit. *Shit*, Shock."

"Please go," he says, lifting a cement-heavy hand to touch hers. The effort sends shivers of exhaustion through his whole body. He's disappearing back into unconsciousness. Disassembling. "Be safe."

"It is safe. We have her," she says, rocking him a little. "We could go. We could just go."

Zenada laughs. "He's not safe," she says, not bothering to struggle against the Hornets holding her back. "Neither are you."

Amiga twitches. Then Ravi collapses, just missing Shock's head. Amiga topples backwards, pulling Shock with her. The Hornets holding Zen slump to the floor. He can't tell if they're breathing, he's sinking back to unconsciousness by degrees and he can't stop. If he had a voice left he'd scream, but it's all gone and he's crying now. Weak body. Weak mind. If he was stronger, smarter, less selfish, this wouldn't have happened.

He's learnt nothing.

Zenada's delicate hands frame his face. She leans in close, wordless, her head tipped to one side as she watches him sink backward from his eyes. He can see it reflected in hers, the gradual fading of gold to blue, and then all he sees is darkness blossoming inside of him. She follows it in, trying to wrestle him away from Emblem, to separate them out like wheat and chaff.

Finally, in frustration, she tries to overwrite a tiny portion of him, no more than a handful of neurones, and it works after a fashion. That part of him is threefold: Emblem, Shock and *her.* He wants to scrape her off like fungus, like a scab. Pushing hard, Zen tries for more. A cluster. A whole section. It hurts so fucking much. Too much.

Shock can't conceive how there's enough of him to register this level of pain, a bright-red light smouldering inside the remaining shreds of him, turning him to smoke and embers. Small pieces of him flaring and simmering heat like teeth. A jaw yawned wide and full of razors. A pink throat, ribbed and gleaming.

Shark.

Not pain but Shark, the essence of it, that untamed conflagration its loss left behind, thrashing away inside of him. Red, red rage and heat and fury. He could laugh if there were voice or mouth or will to laugh with. Better late than never, but it's too late. Surely. Still he welcomes it, teeth, red, rage and all, sinking into it, allowing it to curl around him, warm as Amiga's arms, strong and reassuring even as he wishes some of Puss were here too, even if it were only the weight of her gaze, settling his heart.

And rage speaks for him, through him, without need for thought. Lashing out, it latches into the drives around him: Hornets and Zeros and patrons in the bars and museums and restaurants, families in the oceanarium. Given no time for relief that his friends are okay, he connects through them all, networking them together as Zen hits her stride and speeds up, swirling into him, bringing all she is. Worse than the Kraken. Than Queens. It's like harbouring disease, the black rot of necrosis.

A bit like dying.

He felt Shark dying like it was his own death, and that loss is on replay in some deeply buried corner of his brain, a rat on a wheel, paws agile and agitated, burning from too much movement and desperate to stop. Is that grief? Never being able to forget the moment of loss, the savage snap of life as it leaves?

As it happens, the difference between not dead and dead is only a single breath, a moment of absolute stillness that becomes gaping emptiness, because what was there can never be replaced. Death is erasure. Excision. Once you've been close enough to it to fully understand that, you can never forget it. Never pretend that life has no full stop moment, that it might roll on forever if you just look at it sideways and ignore the darkness waiting on the horizon.

And maybe *that* is grief. A loss of innocence.

Disappearing into her, under her, his sensation of himself thins, leeches to a membrane of self laid too deep to have any effect on his body, his mind. He understands then what it will be like to have her driving him, and wants instead to find that memory of Shark's death—recreate it as his own. Will himself out of existence.

He'll be saving more than his autonomy; he'll save the minds the Shark part of himself has connected together. Fucking stupid. Once she's done swallowing him, she'll move into them. And through them. She's a tsunami in human form. A sickness. Viral and vile. That's what she was doing with the Zeros, what she intended to do with Mollie and Maggie—he sees it all clear, her thoughts as his own, the offhand appropriation of life nothing to her.

Mere convenience.

Whatever the Shark part of him wants to do, it's too dangerous, risks too many. If it doesn't work, they'll all be gone. They don't have an Emblem to protect them. He'll be engulfed by her, alive and suffering, alive and knowing they're all her puppets. He tries to stop his Shark self, but like it was in the hangar, it's listening to nothing but rage. Lashing back, it pours all that power, all that concentrated force from a thousand drives and more into turning the tide. Into writing Shock over Zenada.

She snarls. Fights back in the same way she's being fought, reaching out for minds, screaming frustration when the only ones she can reach are the infected. Her answer is to pour energy into the virads, force them to evolve, to spread faster, further, taking as many minds as she can, so many innocent lives swallowed all at once he screams somewhere deep inside to see it.

The reversal process stops. Turns back in her favour. She rams her fingers deep into his head and twists. Punishment.

His head flares pain and light. Red rage.

Into the red and the bright flare of light comes gold. He opens his eyes. Sees Polar Bear towering over her, huge. Two metres of furious ursus risen up to crash down with its jaws around her neck, teeth breaking flesh, drawing blood. It pulls and her fingers pop out of his head with a sucking crack. Those golden eyes fixate on him.

Carry on. Write her over. Quickly.

Unable to respond except by complying, Shock casts out as far as he can, connecting to more drives until he feels strong enough to fight back. It takes a *lot*. Thousands more. Block after block of New York Hub connected to his drive. When Shock's gathered enough to be able to fight her, Zen resists for endless seconds, clawing at Polar Bear, her fingers sending gold sparks to hit the carpet and fade, until, abruptly, the tide begins to turn. Bit by bit, then in a rush like breaking out of deep waters.

And that's when the battle stops. Freeze-frame. No more loss and gain. Just him and the red heat of Shark's rage seething over her, taking back everything she overwrote and turning the tables. It happens fast. Much faster than it was to him. She's not inside him and then she is. Part of him. A scrap of Zen in every cell, like a memory. He can access everything she is, and she can do nothing. She *is* nothing, her body limp in Polar Bear's jaws.

He feels Polar Bear too. She's light. Gold and pure. Effortless grace. Sizzling with knowledge like electricity. And every part of her, every atom-small snippet of code forming the immense bulk of her being, is imbued with *self*. Having no physical distinction, no definite body/mind synthesis, the one being the cup of the other, she's all self, no barriers, no safeties, no protections and her vulnerability is *startling*, appalling.

The way it's been exploited even more so.

Untold swathes of damage rupture her, fissures and schisms and splinters raw as wounds in flesh. She's a mass of untended agonies. Raw and bleeding, running on pure emotion, all of it *hurting, raging, howling*. He recognizes this. Felt it every day, waiting on life to gift him Sendai somehow—the desperate harrowing of *need*.

Breaker did this? He understands the imperative, but abhors it. Nothing this beautiful should suffer as she's suffered.

Polar Bear lies down next to him on the carpet, her head rested on his torso. He's exhausted too. Every last cell. He doesn't think he'll ever not be this exhausted. It feels like there's no way to come back from this. Inside him, Zen's aware of having lost. Her rage is a poison, a pathogen in his body. She is. She slides under the surface of him, seeking cracks. Cringes away as he looks into her.

With Zenada all through him, Shock sees her memories as clearly as his own. She wasn't always like this. Younger. Far more innocent. *Soft*. Polar Bear was her first avatar, her given avatar. Her softness is what was once Zen's. The Queen is what Zen became after Kamilla pushed her to create and took all she made, giving her no recognition. Controlling her every move and thought. She made Zen feel worthless. Then furious. It was the fury that changed her. The injustice.

But it's how you respond that defines you, and Zen

chose the worst possible response—she became the worst version of herself. Combined herself with bio-ware and embraced the lack of emotion, the loss of conscience, riding minds like cattle. Using them. Playing with lives. Playing god with the Queen, who she created to expand herself. With them at large, Slip became dangerous. Deadly. Her family were left with no choice but to contain her.

They stole my freedom. Her voice is tiny, a wisp.

After what you became? They did what they had to.

And so would I. So will I. You realize this is the worst you can do to me. I'm here for good. Don't think I'll accept it. I'll seep into you and one day, you'll wake up inside me. *I'll use your mind to tear the last of the world apart.*

He thinks of the mountains of Shandong, the trees and towers of Sendai. The glistening roll of the ocean under sunlight. Under moonlight. The extraordinary beauty in the juxtaposition of steel and stars against the night sky. The *impertinence* of it, the astounding contrast, fighting with and acquiescing to, how the fight becomes surrender sometimes and therefore unbearably beautiful.

I can't let you do that, he says, and believes it more than he's ever believed anything.

She laughs. *And how will you stop me? You can't. You're a ruin. Your drive is damaged. A large portion of your brain. You do realize that even Emblem's hard work may not have rescued all your faculties?*

He does realize. But she's wrong. He heard what Bear said to Amiga when she shot the glass orb trying to kill Zen. Sees the truth of it from here on the inside. The infinite connections between Bear and Zen, a fragile cat's cradle entwining them. In making Bear a prison, Breaker tied her to Zen impossibly, intimately, made them a self-sustaining circuit. Interdependent. Did he know you could kill one by killing the other? Probably not. Breaker wasn't a killer. But Shock is. Zen underestimates him. She has no idea what he's willing to do.

He lifts his hand, placing it on Polar Bear's head. There's this awful, wrenching shift and he's surrounded by gold, by *Bear.* Her belly is indescribably warm. It tingles. Ripples over his skin like electricity. To kill her, he has to dismantle her chain by chain. It'll be arduous. Painful. May kill him as well as her considering how melded they are. The only things he'd wish for are to know the Hornets and Amiga are okay and see Puss one last time so he can tell her why they might have to die.

He misses her. He doesn't want her to think he died for nothing.

Deep breaths, he says to Polar Bear. He's offered no choice to her, but he feels her acceptance of it, and that's enough to ease him.

You breathe for both of us, she says. *I'll do my job and keep her locked up.*

Reaching into the gold all around him, he begins to pluck Bear apart at the seams, unspooling tiny portions of her, pieces that briefly flare before they fade. She's like stardust in his hands, she shimmers as she dies. Somewhere inside of him, feeling herself disintegrate, Zenada starts to scream, to struggle. It's awful. A full body shudder too deep to ignore. Willing himself to endure it, Shock carries on pulling Bear apart.

He thinks at first that he's okay, that he'll be okay, or as much as he can be given the huge damage to his skull, his drive. Then parts of him begin to flicker, sputtering like lights in rain. And one by one, they go out.

the shape of things to come

Evelyn Tsai wakes to a world changed. A world without Tsai Holdings. Her world in ruins. Thanks to her preference for solitude, no one is there to see her less-than-controlled response, the scream she lets out, the items from her dressing table flung across the room and shattering on the far wall. All her work, from desperate beginnings clawing her way to the heights of success. Gone.

The streams are full of it. Tsai Holdings was burnt to embers sometime last night. Not physically. Digitally. But not before the release of any incriminating information about the Corp, all her underhand dealings, her criminal ties. The truth of her wealth and acquisitions laid bare. She can never show her face in polite society again. And Keel is gone, taken with Disconnect no doubt.

Fucking Hornets.

She wants their heads. She wants to see them destroyed slowly, with painful precision. To administer such destruction herself. But all she had is gone. Her reputation, the most important mask she held, ripped away before the whole of Shanghai Hub. No one of any worth will deal with Evelyn Tsai again. She's already seen interviews with at least ten of her most respected patrons and investors severing all ties.

She's done. Finished. The best she can do for herself now is to gather her dignity and leave. Go somewhere she can safely plot the ruination of her new enemies. Throwing clothes and beloved belongings into her cases, Evelyn begins the long process of accessing the first of her secret stashes, the accounts she's filled with flim over the years.

It's empty.

In place of the tens of thousands she'd accrued are digital receipts—proof that the funds therein have been distributed to the charities of her choosing. Evelyn has never and would never choose charity. Abandoning her cases, Evelyn accesses other accounts. All equally raided, bearing identical receipts. This is what finds her screaming again. Why her belongings, even the most beloved, hit the wall. Evelyn has been played. Bested. Outmanoeuvred. But worst of all, she has been laughed at. No one, but no one, has had the guts to make a joke of Evelyn Tsai for decades. Those who know the woman behind the mask wouldn't dare and those who believe the mask wouldn't dream of it.

Yet the Hornets have. Comprehensively.

She only realizes the full extent of their mockery when, twenty minutes after accessing her account, Shanghai's security forces smash into her apartment and arrest her. They tagged them. The bastards tagged her accounts.

They knew she'd try and use the flim to run.

Faced with a squad of security, Evelyn abandons all pretence. Abandons any control.

Grabbing a shard of broken glass from the carpet, she launches herself at them, screeching and slashing at their eyes, at any vulnerable flesh she can find. Fighting with all her might right up until the moment she's slammed face down on the floor and restrained, heavy bodies sat on her legs and her back. They grind down until her spine creaks, until her bones begin to ache.

"I've been here before," she snarls at them, her voice muffled by carpet. "I rose up and built an empire. I can do it again. And all of you, all of you will pay."

One of the guards has the temerity to laugh. She crouches down and whispers into Evelyn's ear, "I liked having an avatar. So did my friends here. I wonder if you can tell me who's going to pay? I wonder if you can tell me who's *not* going to make it all the way to the Security HQ?"

As she's lifted, Evelyn starts screaming again, calling for help.

Usually restrained, obsessed with propriety, every last occupant of her exclusive tower comes out to watch her pass. To applaud. She hisses at them. Spits at their feet. In her last moments alive, Evelyn Tsai abandons all semblance of civility and curses them with every word she ever learnt in Pínkùn Dìqū—in her last moments she is more herself than she's been in decades.

* * *

Groggy consciousness creeps across Amiga's mind, brings her out in tiny revolutions from darkness to the dazzling white walls of Zen's prison room. Zen. *Shock*. Amiga sits up, groaning, her body is sluggish. EMP. Must have been. She's seen people get hit with handheld EMPs, the meshes Sec Forces have on the Gung. Ain't pretty and, yeah, she sure as hell feels *ugly*. Worst hangover ever combined with a head cold.

Turning to look for Shock, seeing the state he's in, is like being tazed to wakefulness. She's up and around immediately. Has him in her arms. Somehow, she feels him in her drive, connected to her, and he's disappearing. Dying. Why? Why is he dying? Gold scraps float around her. Around the room. She blinks, confused. Realizes a second later that there's the bottom part of a belly. Legs. Bear paws behind and in front of her.

He's dismantling Bear. Killing Zen. And because she's inside him, it's killing him too.

How the *hell*? Emblem's taken him over, with him in her drive she can feel the strangeness of him, the presence of Emblem a complex pattern that only becomes more confusing the harder she tries to understand it. Beneath that, the remains of Zen, still somehow fighting, still somehow screaming. Amiga knows she'll carry on until the last chain of Bear fades into white carpet.

Shock shouldn't be dying though. The wound on his head is fucking terrible, yes. Deep and dire. But Amiga's seen him in worse shape. She's seen him cut up like an apple pie casing, gaping to yellow fat, the shining coil of intestines visible through gaps in his abdomen. He survived that. He hung on. Shark and Puss wouldn't let him die.

"Oh shit."

That's the difference. Shark is gone, and Puss is locked away. She's probably going crazy. If she could get to him…

"Deuce!"

Reaching out with her foot, Amiga boots her unconscious boyfriend in the back. Once. Twice. Until he's groaning and shoving her foot away.

"Geddoff."

"Wake *up* then!"

He cranks his head up an inch or two, cracks those black eyes open just enough to glare at her. "What the *hell*, Amiga?"

"Shock is *dying*."

Deuce springs up like she did. Faster. He gapes at her. "He's in my drive."

"Yes. Do you *see*? We have to get Puss out. She can keep him alive."

He reaches out to touch her cheek, wiping away tears she had no idea were there. "How, Amiga? She's caged. He can only access her through his drive, and he'd have to pay. Shock can't pay, he's out."

She growls at him, furious that he's not *thinking*. "Deuce, we're fucking connected. This is the moment I tell you I fucking *know* you're a higher percentage than you admit. You're leet. Are you trying to tell me you can't jack his drive? Are you going to lie to me now?"

He sits back on his heels, his face paling. "Right. You guessed. Okay." His jaw works a little. "It's not why you think."

She grabs his wrist. "I actually don't give a shit why it is, Deuce. All I want is that you jack his drive right the fuck now and help me get Puss to him!"

Bless his moral ass, he doesn't argue, just leaps in. Says as he does, "We'll need a lot of flim. She can't just pop out and then pop in again. The tariff for long-term connect is steep, Amiga."

After outing his deception over his percents, Amiga feels comfortable outing her own tiny little secret. "And I have a stash that's pretty deep. You get into his drive, throw me his account deets and I'll load him with enough flim to keep her out for a year."

Deuce huffs out a laugh. "Dark horse. Your only stash?"

"Yes."

He looks up, his gaze frank. "You'd give it all to him? All your security?"

"In a heartbeat."

The beautiful smile he seems to save only for her flashes across his face. "There's that heart," he says. "Don't hide it again. I like seeing it on your sleeve."

Without warning, he pulls her into the Byzantine convolutions of Shock's drive, from whispers of connections to shouts; so much of Emblem in it she takes a moment to recognize Shock in the swirling patterns, the vast turning of complex puzzles.

Quite the key, Deuce says. *Lucky I like puzzles.*

He works fast, deep in concentration. Frowning. Only when he begins to smile does she start breathing properly again. As she does, the swirling patterns change direction. They pulse and contract, coalescing for a moment into a vast ball of patterns moving in different directions. The ball slows, clicks around a few times, and stops.

When the layers move again they shuffle themselves to something less confusing, a glorious multifaceted mandala. Through them, she can see the tariff app glowing. It says "select".

Can I?

Yeah, he says. *Go right ahead.*

The total for twelve months, for immersion jobs, is an eye-watering sum. It's not all she has, but most. She doesn't care; Shock needs Puss to live, and she needs Shock to live. So here it goes, the one thing she hasn't done since it all went down five weeks ago, checking in to the account she made last year when she started to genuinely plan escaping from Twist. Theoretically. Every job she did, she threw a percent of flim in. The amount would support the Hornets for at least six months.

It would give her a means to run if need be. But she doesn't need one any more.

The moment she presses the payment button, Puss bursts out beside her, an explosion of gold tentacles and grief.

Can you keep him alive?

Only by staying with him. Puss swivels an eye in her direction. *How long do I have?*

Rather than replying, Amiga simply shows her. The

squeeze of tentacles around her midriff is unexpected. Makes her breath hitch. A moment later it loosens. Falls away. Puss sinks deeper into Shock, half her gold disappearing into his flesh. When she comes out, she seems frantic. Inconsolable. The essence of her churns in Amiga's drive. So strange to feel this deeply with an avatar not her own.

What is it?

I can't hold him. I haven't got enough to shore him up. He isn't finished. If she's not all gone…

Amiga and Deuce exchange a heavy glance. Asking and responding. It's weird to know somehow who sees what she wants without having to tease it out of her, or ask. All he needs is to look and he understands what she's thinking. And the best bit? The motherfucking jackpot? He's in sync. Absolute accord. Neither of them is willing to let Shock die. Neither will suffer Zenada to live, especially not in the shell of Shock's body.

What do you need? he says to Puss. *Us? Our avis? Would they help?*

Avis. I need avis. Energy.

"How much of that stash do you have left?"

"Enough. How do we do everyone at once?"

Deuce indicates Puss. "She can help me. Like she helps Shock."

"But she's not your avi."

He smiles. "Shock's in our drives. At the moment, she's just enough of my avi for it to work. Right?" He turns to Puss.

Right.

Then let's do this.

Puss's tentacle going into Deuce's drive is surreal. Gold flares in his eyes, a state so similar to Shock Slipping IRL that it stuns Amiga to witness it. Holy shit, her boy is passing strange. Puss narrows her pupils at him. Speculative.

He's bigger in here than I thought, she says.

Yeah, he's been hiding his light.

Interesting.

Isn't it?

The first avi they go for is Leopard Seal. Talk about going for the slay. Her heart's on the floor, bruised and battered, but it's so fucking good. Different. Less somehow thanks to the way Disconnect still holds them apart. But still good. Leopard Seal comes to float beside her, tucked up to her side, to watch Deuce and Puss work as if they've cooperated in this way forever, moving drive to drive, jacking and paying, letting the avis loose one by one.

This sudden temporary waiver of avi prison terms wakes all but the most damaged of the Hornets, and Ravi's no sooner awake than scrambling over to Shock to work on his head. His hands are trembling. She thinks he's suffering the effects of the EMP, until she sees the tears in his eyes.

"He's such a mess, Amiga." He wipes his eyes. "I'm not sure I can fix it. Too much damage."

"Don't let me down, Rav. Try."

The nod she receives is more of a spasm. She trusts though, despite his uncertainty. Ravi's better than he knows. He's saved Shock once; she believes absolutely that he can do it again. Even if only some of Shock is left, he'll save it. And some is better than none.

Finally drained to near enough nil, the amount Amiga had left bought one hundred and fifty avatars for ten minutes and ten avis for five. And Deuce being Deuce he gets his avi last, when there's barely enough left to pay for it. Puss makes the most of every second she's gifted. Gathering the avis, she creates, with their help, a glistening sheet of what looks like avi-stuff, molecule fine. Sinking it down into Shock, she weaves it with painstaking care, creating a barrier of sorts, a separation—something to stop him from disappearing. It's so tightly woven only a very few minute scraps of him manage to escape through.

Polar Bear only has paws left at this point. Incongruously fluffy.

Watching them disentangle and fade away, Amiga suffers a pang, too similar to grief to call anything else. That's the last of Bear. Something so beautiful, gone forever. It's unjust. Shouldn't have to happen. Because of that, she forces herself to witness until the last tips of claws fade into embers and dissipate. The avis have long since begun to unwind back to the cages at this point.

Amiga wants to reach out and hold them here, just in case. But there's no more flim. No more time. Finally, Leopard Seal starts to unwind. She moves to brush past Amiga's cheek as she goes. One last warm tickle of whiskers.

He's still there, she says. *And so am I. We'll wait. It's…*

And then she's gone, the emptiness too much. Numb

to her core, Amiga sits and watches Shock's chest rise and fall. There's enough of him to breathe. To pull air into his lungs. Is there enough of her to do that? There'll be sirens soon. Guns. Always more guns. She has to breathe enough to help get them all out of here.

And where will they go?

At the moment, all she can think is that there's no going home. Home isn't there any more. As long as they're in the crosshairs, they can never have a home. If she had the energy she'd sink into bitterness again, railing at the unfairness of it all, but honestly, all she wants to do right now is get her family to safety.

deuces are wild

Getting back to the shuttle activates old-school Hornet skills Deuce thought he'd never need again. Funny how life takes such trouble to roll you backwards, remind you who you were. How it grabs at your coat tails and tries to yank you down. Hold you there. Make you act your worst self. He does what he's always done at these times, gives life a middle finger and does whatever it takes to do what needs doing without ever compromising his personal code.

It's a hell of a tough call to sneak back through a hub where your face is on a million streams, and several outstanding warrants for destruction of public property, disruption of public life, terrorist activity and murder are riding your back. Especially when many of your number are wounded. But they do it. All together. All safe. Although there's really no *safe* here any more, and they're all wrecked in one way or another.

Heading straight for the cockpit, trying not to look at Tracker because he'll want to fucking punch something,

Deuce fires up the shuttle, wondering where on Earth or hubs that he can take them. Where they might hide long enough to heal.

The Hornets are his life's work. His family. He has no idea how to deal with this situation. What to do. It's not a state Deuce is familiar with. He was born capable. Trained from birth by his father to adapt to every situation life might throw at him. Hiro was afraid of how high Deuce's percents were. He was afraid Corps might warp him. Use him. That's not what Hiro wanted for his son.

To Hiro, what mattered was not status or wealth, or power, what mattered was how you make it through a day, the small things, the worthy things. Who you matter to. Who matters to you. His code is Deuce's code. And Camille, Deuce's mother, who's made it her life's work to build things that help people, is his biggest inspiration. He's never once managed to disappoint them. Not even when he Failed. But he thinks he might now. Look at this mess. Look at this awful mess.

He's not capable of fixing it.

So many Hornets are down for the count. So many people infected with the virads. Zen took out thousands when she let loose. He felt it through Shock, can still feel it—the resonance of virad chatter roiling in thousands of minds. Zenada's connection to them is gone, but all that's changed is the frequency of their confusion. Without order, they are unravelling to chaos, and taking the minds they fill with them. They're another thing he can't fix. Mollie, Maggie and EVaC too. There's so much fallout. So much devastation.

It's making him re-evaluate his beliefs. His convictions.

Making him wonder if his code can stretch to accommodate new ways of thinking. Of acting.

The fear he held on to after Fulcrum, the insanity of living with an eye over their shoulders, ready to scram at a moment's notice, that's never going to change now. Running never helped. Nothing seems to help. Frying pan to house on fire to volcano to the heart of the fucking sun. Only so much you can do, only so far you can go, always running. Jacking like crazy to try and keep a shield over the heads of the people you love. Always worried it will fall apart and they'll be seen. And what of the avatars and their safety? What if they free them?

Guaranteeing them a world with no threat of cages can't be done. Not with the world as it is.

There'll always be another Evelyn Tsai. The inevitability of it happening again and again. People scared and reacting. The cruelty of those reactions. The consequences. What avis might become if pushed too hard, hurt too much, and what that might mean for their human counterparts. It's not their place to police the world. Not his place. But what about protecting it? Surely that's acceptable.

Reaching out, he nudges Puss.

Can we talk?

You want to rewrite the world, don't you?

How does she do that? Does she do that with Shock? *I've had a minor epiphany. Or a breakdown. I dunno what the fuck it is. I only know I can't tolerate this any more. Not for my family, not for anything that matters.*

Shock calls me his conscience. Do you want me to be yours?

To his surprise, he doesn't. *I want you to be my gestalt. Like you were earlier.*

And if I disagree?

Then we'll run. Hide. Forever if need be. It'll be harder, they have all our faces now, but we can do it. We'll have to. Need is a great driver.

How will you live?

He laughs. What a question. *Are you kidding? We're Hornets. We've worked from nothing before. We can do it again.*

Her gaze is so heavy he can feel it rested on the back of his head. *Ask the others. If they say yes, then we'll do it. I won't act without their agreement.*

Neither will I.

Opening his IM out to embrace the minds on the shuttle, Deuce lays it all out there. What he wants to do. The moral implications of it. Why he's even *thinking* like this, let alone willing to act upon it.

Deuce is a math whiz, but no way he can figure the odds on what way the dice will fall from here. What's more of a surprise? Their agreement? Or the vehemence with which it's given? But then the Hornets have lost so many friends, taken so many hits and kept standing for what's right, nonetheless. They're tired of unwarranted blame. Uncalled-for hatred. They're all burdened with a weariness of being targeted for nothing. Ravi pretty much sums it up.

"Fix the fucking world," he says. "Make it a lie. We'll bear it with you, no questions asked. We're fucking *family*. All in, all the time. And god*damnit* are we fucking done with being pissed on. And I know you, *we* know you. No way you'll do anything more than need be. It's not in you."

"Is it in you to do *enough*?" Amiga. Giving him a frank sort of appraisal he's not experienced from her before. He's being re-assessed. If he had any, he'd pay good flim to hear her conclusions.

"What do you think?"

Her eyes spark a little, fire and ice, heart and viscera. "Yeah," she says. "I think you might just pull it off. But not alone, leet or not."

"I have Puss," he says. "I won't be doing it alone."

Puss, in fact, does pretty much all the grunt work. By necessity more than anything else, her not being his avi but only faintly linked to him through Shock. Throwing him into full submersion, she hovers him near the surface of Slip, that illusion of the breach between air and water, floating in rippling fingers of sunlight.

It's an eye-opener to see how Shock might see. And absolutely astounding how much Slip has grown. How much it's changed even since the avatars were caged.

Between vast new worlds, the roll of hills, the sleek rise of towers and muddled mass of towns and cities cast in gold, masses roam, slow-moving as cattle: some of the masses float, others crawl the bottom, slide between the info-shoots. Aimless at first glance, it takes moments to see the patterns in them, to sense the purpose within the masses. The slow thought unlike anything he's encountered before.

He thinks they might be some attempt at new avis. Reaching out to them, amazed by how far he can go with

Puss guiding him, he brushes the surface of one as it floats past. Has to check twice to be sure of what he's seeing, what he's *experiencing*. No way.

These masses are Slip. Slip moving. Slip thinking. Slip learning.

How the fuck?

Puss shrugs. *How does anything happen? By chance, by accident, by design perhaps. It must have begun with all this change. Look at how much they've done. Taken an ocean and made it into a universe. I suspect the impact will resonate for decades. We haven't yet begun to see what might become of it all.*

Stretching a little, she opens to Slip, letting it flow through her into him. All of Slip resounds with change. Water becoming architecture, becoming worlds. This place belongs to everyone now, but it also belongs to itself, and there's no way people aren't going to notice. Doubtless they're already looking at those masses and wondering.

It hits like lightning: whatever he puts in place for the Hornets, the avatars, needs to expand to cover Slip. And the Zeros. The virads. He should have a closer look at them too. Zen forced them to life. Evolved them to infect thousands more. Without her to drive them, they've lost all direction. They're sinking into a form of dementia, and taking those they've infected with them.

The sickness, Puss says softly. *It can't go on.*

I know. I don't know what to do.

You have to decide if virads are allowed to think. To be what she made them. They're only scraps of viral code. You could shut them down. It wouldn't matter in the scheme of things.

Her saying it kind of makes it matter, which was maybe the point, her being a conscience of sorts and all. He's not one bit fooled by her apparent nonchalance.

So let's do it. Can we do it here?

The Zeros? No. We'll have to start with the source. The patient zero of the virad infection as it were. I believe Maggie and Mollie have him in their care.

Okay. So we'll do this, then we'll go to the Gung.

She extends a tentacle to him. *What shall we make them believe?*

Deuce squares his shoulders, feeling the heavy press of water, the heat of false sunlight, the weight of real responsibility.

The impossible, he replies.

zero sum game

Serene under a canopy of stars, the tensions bubbling under the surface only a few days before smoothed to tranquillity by night and maybe Deuce's work in Slip, the Gung is strange tonight. Or maybe she's strange. Changed. She doesn't feel the same, like some part of her has skipped a beat and gone out of sync with what it was before.

Amiga's a different tune. One she doesn't know the words to yet.

Everything surprises her. Most of all Deuce. His courage. The sheer amount he took on in the name of protecting his family, protecting more than that. The Hornets have kept the knowledge of those changes as a pact of sorts. They'll be the ones to remember, because it's their doing, their wrong to make a right. So here she is, seeing the new laid over the old like illusion and knowing it's real.

Today the world knows that Tsai Holdings and Fulcrum were criminal Corps brought to justice after brief, fierce wars by the Sec forces of the Gung and Shanghai Hub. They know that their avatars have been out forever and will be restored to them soon, that Slip is coming to life in more ways than one and, like avatars being alive, this is just the way things are. Normality. Not everyone will like this, but they will have no power to change it. Most of all, most profoundly of all, when the Gung wakes in a few short hours, it will be to a life without Psych Evals. No more Pass or Fail. No more choice as strait jacket. Only the future, reeling out, open to any possibility.

The thought of it is giddy. Electric. From the lowest of office fauna to the highest Exec, it's all up for grabs.

Sat in the back of a rickety truck, holding Shock steady again and feeling déjà vu like fuck knows what, Amiga drinks in the sight of 'scrapers, of narrow roads, the grime and rubble of the Gung and allows herself to hope for its future as they travel back to the warehouse holding the Zeros. It's some stupid hour of the morning, but this is all they have left to do and they need to get it done, to fix the hell Zenada created, mainly because Deuce wrote it right and they need to bring reality in line with that. Exhausted beyond anything she's ever felt before, Amiga promises herself a respite for at least three weeks once they're done with this. She can't promise longer than that. Too much inaction is her kryptonite.

When they arrive, dawn still a few hours distant, she leaves Shock under the watchful eye of Ravi and goes into the warehouse with Deuce—Puss wrapped around his torso. Weird to see her there. Almost disconcerting in fact.

Inside, one of the few people left not yet sick leads them to see Maggie and Mollie. Amiga drops boneless into a chair at the sight of their pale, thin bodies. Maggie's on her side, facing Mollie, who's been draped into bed beside her, her wires dangling around them, limp and somehow too dull. Her light isn't meant to be dimmed. She's the neon angel, she should be blinding. Greasy with sweat, their skin is riddled with veins torqued to letters. No longer zees, which is a small mercy. These new symbols make Amiga's eyes swim with strain, like they're working too hard to make sense of a riddle. She smooths a hand over Maggie's brow, trying to ignore how unsteady she is.

"Can we fix this?"

Deuce lets out a breath he seems to have been holding forever. "I hope so. You felt what Zenada did to them?"

"Yeah." She shudders. Full on goose over the grave shit. Zenada was something else. Secretly Amiga's banking on this narrow connection to Shock disappearing real soon, much as she loves the skinny bastard. The echoes of Zen in his memories are giving her major nausea issues. "Rather forget it if you don't mind."

"I'm going somewhere with this, Amiga. That was all her work. So was her name on Zero bodies. But this?" He looks down at the obscure patterns on Maggie's body. "I think this is all them, attempting to communicate."

"It's a virus. That's all."

"No. She messed with them; they changed. They woke up, like Slip has. Then she took them over. Puppet viruses. The kind of thing she was doing with the Queen if you've been paying attention to those memories of hers still whacking around in Shock's head."

She goes to laugh but the funny in the situation eludes her. Hijacking bodies. Hijacking newly sentient viruses to hijack bodies. That's a horror right there. The violation of her friends, of anyone infected by Zen's last stand, has her jonesing to turn back the clock to the moment she jumped Zen and take a few seconds to stamp all over her fucking face. Stamp it to unrecognizable mush.

Might have prevented Shock from needing to throw his life into the abyss.

"So can you fix them without making it worse?"

"Maybe."

"Maybe? It's a fucking virus and it's killing them. If you can't put a full stop on that shit, then the choice is not difficult. If I had to choose between them and some stupid self-aware advertising code, I'd pick my friends. Every. Damn. Time."

Deuce closes those poker chips of his for a second, and damn it if it doesn't feel like he's shutting her out. She is not disappointing the fucker. No way. Not in hell. This is nothing to disappoint about. It's not kittens, or children, it's nothing but the kind of shit she used to have to flush out of her drive if it happened to hit her unawares during Slipping.

"Well my vote is a no," she says, as if her opinion weren't obvious.

"Noted," he growls and promptly pisses off with a guy called Eddie, to go hunt out the first Zero infected, apparently kept somewhere in the main floor of tanks. Maggie would know exactly where, but Maggie's here. Mollie's here. Both silent. Still. Too sick for her to bear.

She holds Maggie's hand, and then reaches across to grasp Mollie's as she waits for him to come back, wanting to hang on to them. To let them be aware she's here. That they're not alone. It takes a long arse time, or else she's so fucking tired that minutes have stretched to hours in her perception. Whatever it is, Deuce looks wiped when he walks back in. Wiped and weary in ways he's never looked before. He doesn't look sad, though. That's a positive, right?

"Spit it out. Did you do it?"

"We gave them a voice," he says, and his voice is blurry with exhaustion. Almost non-existent.

"I don't understand."

Puss speaks then, watching her from his torso. She looks tired too. Fuzzy. *We gave them one voice to speak for them all. A tutor. A source.*

Will it cure everyone?

Look.

Amiga looks down at Maggie, at Mollie. Their skin is marginally less pale. And perhaps, unless she's mistaking hopeful imagination for the real world, they're breathing easier too. This relief is different, almost dizzying. She feels as fuzzy as Puss looks, as Deuce sounds.

How long before she's well, before the rest are? Will *they all be? Even the ones like Tracker?*

The Hornets will be fine, Amiga, so will the people Zenada hurt. But it will take a while. Virads are hard to herd—it took most of our time and energy to make them understand, but they're making their way to the host now, to learn language.

Once they've all gone, the sickness will run its course. I suspect only the sickest and weakest of the Zeros will struggle to become fully well.

You think some will die?

Yes.

Which means you didn't make the host the original infected Zero.

No. We didn't.

Amiga goes to ask who they picked, but then she catches a glint in Deuce's eyes. Guilt. Hold the hell on. "You did *not*. Not EVaC. No way."

Deuce bites his lip. It'd be adorable if she didn't want to punch it. "What do you want me to say, Amiga? It's done."

"And what about EVaC?" This isn't really a betrayal, not of her, but it feels like one. She feels utterly betrayed.

"He gave permission."

"Are you sure? What if it was the virads talking? What if he stays sick?"

Not that she wants to be questioning him, but how can she not? Her vote was a no, and it's EVaC he's risking here, because it *is* a risk. Virads are two things: viral adverts, and unusual life. Dangerous life. What if they decide they'd like a body to use like Zenada did? She thinks she might be furious with him. Feels like she needs to have been there, seen for herself. Because what if he's wrong? What then?

Understanding her as he always does, Deuce crouches down by the bed and takes her hands. "He won't stay sick. They want to help him. To have him help them. And I promise you I would not have done this if I doubted, even for a *second*, that EVaC was making his own choice, that he could handle this, that we could trust the virads to simply learn and not use him. Do you trust that, at least, Amiga Tanaka? Do you trust me?"

Oh. Wow. Talk about a slap around the proverbial. Talk about a question designed to kick her out of her stupid self. Theoretically, she could lie to herself right now, and to him. She's done it before. But she lost him then, long enough to wound them both, and getting him back was—to her mind—pure serendipity, AKA nothing she's willing to chance again. Besides, she's not really afraid of this truth any more. Not all truth hurts. Not all truths are difficult to face.

Squeezing his hands between her own. Hanging on. Letting him feel the strength of her conviction, Amiga flips a hard middle finger at her need to control shit and allows him to catch her for once. Completely.

"With my life," she says. "I trust you with my fucking life. So I guess I can trust you with his."

Leaving Mollie and Maggie and the rest of the Zeros behind in Eddie's care, they take EVaC and head out to the shuttle. Next stop, a rendezvous with the rest of the Hornets. Time to sleep, eat, share stories. Time to begin again, without the targets on their backs. With one hand on EVaC, just to know he's there, Amiga holds Shock in her lap, Puss wrapped around the both of them like seaweed; watches out of the window as Deuce flies them away from the Gung.

The sight of her home city from a height is one she'll never get over. Huddled alone in a patch of ocean, mountains to its rear, and all but dwarfed by the vast ranges of 'scrapers upon its back, the Gung is disordered, ragged, brooding. Crowded and too loud, too jumbled, all cheek to jowl and teeming with people, an ant farm on overload, groaning at the seams. It lacks elegance. Charm. Dignity. And somehow all of that combined makes her hungry for the sight of it, happy to drink it in through her pores. Even though she may never go back.

As they move away, climbing to higher altitudes, clouds reel out beneath in a layer so thick they look more physical than water vapour has any right to be. Ruffled landscapes of creamy white and jewel-like greys, eerily still—the soft haze of thin cloud moving above them the only clue that they're not what they seem. The first time Amiga saw clouds like that, she wanted to run on them. She's never been as foolish since.

The world has stolen her whimsy.

The shuttle moves lower, into the cloud bank, transforming it to a mist of white. Breaking through to bright sunlight bouncing off ocean so still it appears frozen in place. Not a land ship in sight. Not a peak of broken continent. From the left, moving parallel to them, the flukes and flumes of a pod of whales appears, giant shapes gliding serene and steady beneath calm waters so clear she can see the scars on their bodies, the gentle sway of their tail fins propelling them through the water. She catches her breath. Takes a snapshot of the moment to store in her drive.

Swooping in from the West, they hit the outskirts of the Russian Straits, a series of ribbon-like estuaries between the jutting hulks of what was Russia, the Siberian ranges. Amiga leans forward, her nose pressed against the glass, watching as a small group of land ships navigates one of the larger estuaries of the straits, the metal in their structures glinting, mirroring the sunlight bouncing off their wake. Not such a rare sight this, they're probably hunting for communities to pillage, other ships to steal. But from here they look innocent. Beautiful.

They're so bright they make her blink, colourful cities on mobile scraps of land ploughing bright-blue sea between the livid green of the cliffs surrounding them, that verdant growth all but swallowing the broken remains of buildings. The cliffs are steep in this section of the Straits and only birds live here, thousands of white specks, roosting and diving, billowing in raucous clouds.

On other journeys, flying through different Straits, Amiga's seen communities clinging to the mountainsides. Marvelled at their tenacity. It's a narrow life, and dangerous, with land ship pirates on the ocean and wild animals grown resilient and fearless. She shudders at the thought of being prey. At her core, Amiga is a predator. She couldn't accept any other reality, and she made her peace with that now. Fully. No pain, no shame. No confusion.

Which makes the reality she's heading toward one she can fully align with.

Out on the ocean, on the land ship *Resurrection City* with her team and the Pharm Exec who created the cages version of Disconnect, Vivid's waiting for them to join her. She sent word via IM not long after Deuce fixed the world, when hiding wasn't really necessary any more. Amazing how things work. They'd have had a place to go even if they'd voted not to do it. But none of them regret it. How can they? It's not just their lives they were protecting. Not just their lives they were saving.

Amazing too how much Amiga, a creature of cities right down to her core, is looking forward to being on a land ship in the middle of the fucking ocean. But this land ship, she's not just any old land ship. She's a warship that fights on the right side. A salvage ship. A community. A motherfucking pirate ship. After all they've done together, after everything they've been through, despite all her rebellion, her deep-seated need to act on her own, Amiga's proud to call herself a J-Hack. The collective noun for a bunch of J-Hacks just happens to be "pirates".

Where better then for them to end up, than on a pirate ship?

the view from here

The ocean is a multi-layered illusion, deep and delirious, mimicking the sky from blue surface to space-dark deeps, revealing all its secrets in shimmering lines. The peaks and troughs. The valleys and flats. All filled with the flit of fish, their specs flashing beside them, and the leviathan weight of giants, some gentle, some terrible.

Above it, over it, draped like a veil, glistening and silent, lies the greater ocean. The Slip. Today it is all but entirely changed except for the still-startling lack of the vast majority of golden avatars who used to swim and hover from bottomless deeps to sun-speared heights. Volk and Deuce are working on breaking them out, with Keel's very reluctant help, but it's taking time.

Everything is changed. Undone and remade.

Watching it all, Shock experiences himself profoundly: a multi-layered illusion.

He blinks the Slip away, choosing to see only ocean and sky—blue into blue into grey horizon and bulbous cloud. The world is real. He has to remember. The world is all too real. But it can't be trusted. It can be rewritten so easily. Recently, the Hornets voted to rewrite it. Deuce went into Slip with Puss and set the world to rights in so many ways. They did it for him. For the avatars Volk's working hard to save. For the parts of Slip that somehow woke up. For the virads Zen forced to evolve.

He'll never forget waking to that. They wrote him in on the changes so he wouldn't be confused, never dreaming that he might be bemused. Blindsided. Surprised by what they would do for him. Unexpectedly touched. He doesn't feel worthy of their regard. Of their sacrifice. Of Amiga's. Not just because it was his fault Zenada managed to do so very much damage, but also because his life is entirely contingent upon the presence of Puss.

Without the constant press of her presence, whether in Slip or IRL, he wouldn't be awake. Wouldn't be aware. Wouldn't be functional. Emblem did all it could to save him, but the damage caused by Zenada's attack, by his destruction of her, has taken a terrible toll. He's a mishmash of Emblem, Shock and, worst of all, Zen memories. Waking nightmares. Hallucinations. Things he'd give anything to scrub from his mind.

As for his body… Parts of him are paralysed. They only work because of Emblem. He can't actually feel them. His mind is oh-so-slightly tattered. He forgets things. Loses focus and drifts away, unravelling. But here he is nonetheless. Awake. Alive. Present. And as long as Puss is here, he will be too. He's not afraid of that changing. If they can't jack the cages, Volk and Deuce will re-jig the system to take ghost flim. One way or another, they're getting the avis out.

One way or another, he'll always have Puss.

Beneath him, the *Resurrection* ploughs into a wave, sending up a seventy-metre spew of foamy seawater. Shock struggles up out of the way, yelling, as it splashes down soaking him from head to toe, a dousing of water so cold, the parts of his skin that have feeling shrink and ache. Gasping water from his mouth, he plucks his wet shirt from his chest. Begins the long climb back up to the surface of *Resurrection* on unsteady legs, trusting Emblem to keep his footing on slippery wooden walkways and ladders. He has to trust Emblem. He can't do it himself.

Back up near the surface, the noise of *Resurrection* begins to drown out the crash of waves against her massive sides. Shock immediately feels himself cringing, wanting to retreat back down to the quiet of the sides, broken only by the shouts of the wheelmen and the raucous screech of sea birds, the slap and roar of waves.

They've been part of *Resurrection*'s crew for nineteen days. This is a generous ship, and a friendly one, and he is grateful, but he wishes he had something to do apart from attempt to hide in his room—impossible with the Hornets, Volk, and Petrie, the ship's bosun, determined to keep an eye on him—or skulk about on the sides and risk a drenching. Truth is though, he's not well enough. He will be. One day. Maybe. Until then, he'll endure their concern, the boredom, because he's here and he genuinely did not expect to be.

Cassius, the Captain of the *Res*, gave them a large complex amidships to share. Plenty of room. Plenty of rooms. Many of them, unfortunately, communal, which is totally a *Res* thing and so anathema to Shock's being he wouldn't endure it if it weren't the Hornets and the folk of the *Res*, all of whom are family. Family he *wants*, even if he has to hide from them most of a day just to stay sane.

To his relief, the Hornets are all out working as usual, including Gail and EVaC, both recovered, the latter just a little weird, but then he's also a colony of virads, learning to talk, most of it passing strange and incomprehensible still. The Hornets enjoy being pirates, especially Amiga, who *is* in today. On Ravi's orders. Supposed to be resting in fact. Instead, she's dangling from an ankle brace in the middle of their communal lounge area, swinging to and fro and looking furious in a nest of windblown hair.

"Hey," he says as he walks in.

Amiga waves. "Close the door would you? Fucking KJ came in for a bevvy and left it open. I've been waiting ages for someone to come and fucking close it for me."

Hard to shut a door without showing a hugely perceptive Cleaner how hard he finds it to do stuff. It leaves him irritated, as well as desperate to get warm. "You couldn't get down and close it yourself?"

She looks at him like he's gone off the wrong side of crazy. "You shitting me? You have any idea of the gymnastics it takes to get into these things alone?" She waggles a foot, jingling the buckles on the brace cuffs.

"Why exactly are you upside down?" he asks, because

that's the dumbest thing he's ever seen apart from himself about twenty minutes ago. "Have you been there all morning? Not sure that's advisable with your damn ribs needing to heal."

Amiga bends round and lifts the edge of her t-shirt from around her middle, revealing skin marred by a torque of angry red surrounded by the dullest of bruises, tinges of yellow and green spread out in a stain. The bruising, and the cracked ribs beneath, are a recent addition from jaunting off to do stupid shit with Petrie every time the *Res* hits a shard range or encounters a hostile ship.

"It's not hurting at all," she says. "I can't be bothered to keep resting. Besides, I believe this is something of a pot and kettle moment. I don't see you following anyone's damned advice either. Why *are* you wet, by the way?" She raises a brow, the single eye he can see through the mess of her hair glinting sardonically.

He looks down at his feet, purposefully avoiding that aggravating eye. Snaps, "The cross ploughed up a wave."

"On the sides again!" Amiga applauds. "Bravo, dumbass. Maybe I should tell Ravi about this? You know how he feels about you getting that head wound near salt water until he's happy it's all peachy keen and good to go."

"If you rat me out, I'm telling Ravi *and* Deuce about you jaunting off with Petrie tomorrow," he counters.

Amiga folds her arms. She looks dangerous. This is not unusual. "*Maybe* we should agree to keep each other's secrets hanging over each other's heads in perpetuity."

"Maybe we should."

She points over to the large open doors at the end of the lounge opening on to their deck, which currently holds two or three lines of laundry blowing in the breeze.

"Towel over there, *baegchi* Pao."

He tries not to crack a smile, but he loves it when she busts out the Korean. "Thanks but no, *seong-gasin*, Tanaka, I'm not going to dry off, I'm going to shower and change."

"Wimp."

"Next time we're on the walkway, I'm pushing you overboard."

She offers him a needling smirk he wants to rip off her face and stamp on. "*Geojismal jaeng-i*. You don't fool me. I see you, paralysis and all. You'd only drown your idiot self."

The eyes on her. Clinical. Fucking scalpels. Why did he think she wouldn't see? Why did he imagine she'd treat him any differently? She's Amiga after all. "Fuck you."

"Ugh. For real. Go get dry so I can vomit over that image in private."

Flipping her an embarrassingly unsteady bird, thank you very much hands, you bastards, he walks away, forcing his persistent fucking grin down like bad medicine. Whatever goes wrong in the world, whatever goes wrong inside of him, it would appear there are things he can count on. Absolutes. Irrevocable truths that can't be rewritten by anyone.

He'll hold on to them. Hard. They'll be the lock holding him together, the key to everything he is and wants to be. The reason why, when it comes down to it, *if* it comes down to it, he'll place himself on the front line without thinking and risk everything he is to protect them. Again. Always. Without hesitation. No matter how little of him is left in the end.

Even if it's nothing.

acknowledgments

For yanking me back when I went waaay off piste and making me write the book this deserved to be (and for general freaking awesomeness), my editors: Cath, who made like superwoman and had a baby halfway through. And Cat, who swooped in heroically and knocked editing my word spew right out of the park. Literally the best.

To my agent Jen, for oh… just about ever'thang. You rock.

Hugest of hollers to Anne Mhairi and Colin, the best sounding walls and pep talkers in the Wild West. You guys helped me stay sane. Cannot thank you enough.

And finally, the spawn, again… my Musketeers, my posse, my merry pranksters. We can totally go on holiday now. Promise.

about the author

Ren Warom lives in the West Midlands with her three children, innumerable cats, a very friendly corn snake, and far, far too many books. She haunts Twitter as @RenWarom, and can be found on her YouTube channel, talking about mental health issues and, of course, books.